"When I want a powerful read full of emotion and angst, my go-to author is Kellie Coates Gilbert. *A Reason to Stay* delivers on all counts. I cheered, I cried, I fell in love. An excellent read."

—**Deeanne Gist**, bestselling author of *Tiffany Girl*

"Once again Gilbert's seasoned pen paints a heart-tugging, emotional landscape as unpredictable and stunning as a Texas spring. Kellie gathers the broken shards of a woman's life and with masterful precision pieces together a poignant and victorious story of committed love."

—**Lynne Gentry**, author of The Carthage Chronicles

"A fast-paced, emotionally poignant read. With a strong premise, clever characterization, and a heroine you'll root for until the very last page, Gilbert is sure to win the hearts of her readers with *A Reason to Stay*."

—**Nicole Deese**, bestselling author of the Letting Go series and *A Cliché Christmas*

"A deeply honest portrayal of one woman's battle for her life and marriage. *A Reason to Stay* is an absolute must-read for anyone who has ever doubted the power of love. Kellie Coates Gilbert has given readers another unforgettable story."

—**Tina Ann Forkner**, author of *Waking Up Joy*

Books by Kellie Coates Gilbert

Texas Gold Collection

A Woman of Fortune

Where Rivers Part

A Reason to Stay

★ TEXAS GOLD COLLECTION ★

A REASON TO STAY

A TEXAS GOLD NOVEL

KELLIE COATES GILBERT

Revell
a division of Baker Publishing Group
Grand Rapids, Michigan

Published by Revell
a division of Baker Publishing Group
P.O. Box 6287, Grand Rapids, MI 49516-6287
www.revellbooks.com

Printed in the United States of America

Library of Congress Cataloging-in-Publication Data
Gilbert, Kellie Coates.
A reason to stay : a Texas gold novel / Kellie Coates Gilbert.
pages ; cm. — (Texas gold collection)
ISBN 978-0-8007-2274-6 (pbk.)
I. Title.
PS3607.I42323R43 2015
813′.6—dc23 2015020131

This book is a work of fiction. Names, characters, and incidents are the product of the author's imagination or are used fictitiously. Any resemblance to actual events or persons, living or dead, is coincidental.

Published in association with MacGregor Literary Agency.

15 16 17 18 19 20 21 7 6 5 4 3 2 1

To my little Peanut and Gumdrop.
Grammy loves you.

1

There's no need to fix something that isn't broken.

At least that was what Faith Marin's mother always said. And goodness knows, her mother was *never* wrong.

Unfortunately, the station's executive news director had expressed the exact opposite sentiment in his office yesterday. "Okay, listen. I'm not saying what we're doing isn't working. I'm only suggesting we might have to consider changing things up a bit. No one else is going to keep Faith Marin's star shining. You have to do that for yourself. Right now, your Q score remains high, but you and I both know this is a nearsighted business. Viewers are fickle, which is why we spend an inordinate amount of time and money keeping the *Faith on Air* brand fresh and relevant." Clark Ravino pointed at the stack of Nielsens on the corner of his desk. "And sometimes a bit of recalibration is in order."

"Are you saying the show's brand needs recalibrating? Or mine?" He'd been getting a lot of pushback on her series after folding to her campaign for the station to take a risk on quality programming, instead of the popular morn-porn shown on nearly every other station in their market area. Personally, if she had to see Miley Cyrus gyrating half naked one more time, she would be sick to her stomach.

The devilishly handsome man sitting across from her slowly placed his starched shirtsleeves on top of the desk and steepled his fingers. "To be honest, the answer is both."

"Oh, c'mon, Clark. Are we really going to be another butterfly station, never landing long on anything serious, instead fluttering on to the next pretty flower that smells good? And then the next?" She'd had this argument with Clark on numerous occasions. "Look, whoever is coming up with this nonsense is simply not giving women enough credit. Our viewers are smarter than that."

He gave her a patient smile. "You're missing the point."

She scowled. "We went over all this last month. You agreed the show was getting too fluffy, that we needed to incorporate stories that significantly contribute to women's lives."

He tapped on the stack again. "The demos are telling us otherwise. The Most Valuable Viewer age is getting younger every day. I don't need to tell you the station's news shows subsidize the entire rest of the day's programming. Even a tiny drop in household rankings is material when it comes to advertising dollars." He pointed to the ceiling. "You can argue all you want, but that's what matters upstairs."

From across Clark's desk, Faith squared her shoulders and looked her producer directly in the eye. "So the line you fed me months ago over dinner at Brennan's was bunk? You said if I agreed to stay on the morning desk, you'd help make *Faith on Air* Houston's premier morning show, that you'd let me do the kinds of stories that would position me to move on to a national market."

Clark held up his palms. "I know what I promised. I think what we have here is simply a perception problem. If we let our ratings slip, so does your viability in the top three DMAs. You think the honchos in New York, LA, or Chicago aren't interested in market percentages?"

He stood, came from around his desk, and placed his hand

on her shoulder, but not before letting his fingers casually brush against her neck. "I'm on your side, remember?"

Faith had played that entire conversation over and over in her mind, losing valuable sleep last night. And it showed in her reflection in the station's makeup mirror this morning.

"Girl, there ain't enough concealer to hide those dark circles under your eyes."

"I know, Shanika." She sighed. "Just do your best."

Trying to hide her exhaustion, she glanced past the cameras at the countdown clock and thought about all the sacrifices she'd made.

A shrill alarm clock had pulled her from a warm bed at two in the morning far too many times to count since she'd moved into the anchor chair at KIAM-TV. While the rest of Houston slept, she'd pulled on her favorite nylon hoodie and yoga pants, grabbed a mega mug of coffee, and made the lonely drive to the station, singing to the radio to warm up her voice.

Her daily bedtime was no later than seven in the evening, which wreaked havoc on her social life. Her only friends were business associates. She'd left steaming turkey and dressing on her plate to cover a Thanksgiving Day explosion in the Channelview shipyards that left dozens fatally wounded. The receptionist at her dentist's office teased that they always wrote her appointments in pencil, knowing how often she failed to show for her scheduled cleanings in order to report on some tragic fire, a sensational murder, or a high-profile arrest. General assignment reporters covered the day-to-day remotes, but big stories warranting breaking news status often required lead anchors to do live broadcasts from the scene.

She'd sacrificed much—success had come with a price. She recognized that now.

Sure, her job was glamorous in many respects. Certainly she'd attained celebrity status and was recognized wherever she went. The heels of her Jimmy Choo stilettos were finally parked on the higher rungs of the ladder. But one misstep and her professional life would follow her dismal personal failures.

Now, more than ever, she couldn't afford to let that happen. This career was all she had left.

If she worked hard enough, stood up for what she knew was right, the tough choices she'd had to make would pay off. At least that was what she told herself when her exhausted head hit the pillow at night—in the bed where she now slept alone.

At the close of the first segment, Faith forced a smile at the camera. "The Houston Humane Society warns that all dogs found on the street without proper tagging and licensing are subject to confiscation. We'll be right back after this commercial break."

In this morning's broadcast, they'd led with a story about a cruise ship stranded a hundred miles off port with mechanical issues, a charity event at the Golf Club of Houston, and a projected rise in house prices reported by the Houston Association of Realtors. Traffic was tied up in the southbound lanes of the Southwest Freeway, a result of a semitruck that illegally changed lanes and crashed into a Toyota pickup. Remarkably, there were no fatalities to report. And Doppler radar was picking up a system approaching in the Gulf, causing the meteorologist to predict rain by Sunday.

Then her Humane Society piece.

After they returned from the commercial break, the producers aired a human interest segment, a story about the unveiling of a wax figure of Katy Perry at Madame Tussauds in London.

Mike Jarrett, her coanchor, gave the camera a wide smile. "Now, that sounds like something worth seeing."

"Sure does, Mike. I'm sure all our viewers traveling to London will want to pen that one in on their travel itineraries." Faith smiled even wider, hoping her sarcasm hadn't come across in her voice.

She was minutes from signing off the broadcast when Clark entered the studio, followed by a young woman in a stylish short hairstyle and an outfit not unlike those Faith often saw on the

Pinterest boards she studied at night, trying to stay on top of what women found fashionable. She thought of changing her own hair to something similar—a pixie-cut style recently made popular by Jennifer Lawrence. Of course, before she shortened her hair, she'd have to get the blessing of some focus group.

The cameraman gave the signal it was time to wrap up.

Mike leaned slightly forward. "And that's our broadcast this Thursday morning. I hope you'll tune in again at midday for KIAM-TV News at Noon."

Faith straightened her scripts and gave the audience a final smile, showing off her expensive veneers. "And thank you, Houston, for letting KIAM-TV be your eye on the news."

The music cued and the station's logo, an eye with their call letters, flashed across the monitors. Lucas Cunningham, the technical operations manager, stepped forward with a clipboard in his hand. "Good show, everyone."

Faith stood and took a deep breath. Out of the corner of her eye she caught Clark and the woman moving in her direction.

"Faith, I'd like you to meet Lynna Scowcroft. She's going to be spending some time with you over the next couple of weeks."

She extended her hand and gave the perky young woman a weak smile, knowing Clark's careful wording was code for: *This gal, who barely looks past nineteen years of age, is the media consultant du jour who will be evaluating your every move and then reporting on ways we can make your life miserable.*

"Hello, it's nice to meet you," Faith said politely before turning to Clark, giving him a look that left no doubt how she felt about her new shadow. If Lynna Scowcroft noticed, she didn't let on. Instead she pulled her buzzing iPhone from her bag and brought it to her ear while mouthing that she was sorry, she needed to take the call. She stepped back out of the bright lights and into a dimly lit corner of the studio for privacy.

Clark grinned. "Hold back your enthusiasm," he teased.

Faith shrugged and lowered her voice. "You couldn't find a grown-up to rake me over the image promotion coals?"

"You got the memo. We're working to attract a younger audience willing to spend recklessly on consumer goods they don't need." His slightly bantering tone did nothing to defuse the reality of his statement. They both knew the station was strongly beginning to favor pop culture news. The difference between them was that as executive producer of the news division, Clark Ravino was determined to disregard his personal feelings in order to embrace what was on the horizon. Faith wouldn't give in that easily.

Under the heat of the lights, he unbuttoned the cuffs on his shirt and rolled up the sleeves. "A call came in to the assignment desk while you were on air. Senator Libby Heekin Rohny has scheduled a press conference out at the Johnson Space Center. Rumor has it she's going to announce some very unpopular budget cuts. I want you to cover the story."

Faith's eyes lit up. They both knew he'd just thrown her a bone—a story with national importance. If she played this one right, she'd corner the senator and urge her to come on *Faith on Air* for an extended (and exclusive) interview. A coup for sure, and the kind of airtime that would build her portfolio. "Thanks, Clark. I owe you."

He gave her shoulder a squeeze. "*De nada, chica*. But you'd better get a move on. You have a little over two hours." He leaned his head in the direction of Lynna Scowcroft, who had just put away her phone. "Take her with. And be good," he added.

"Tell Tinker Bell to get a move on then." Her mouth formed a wicked grin. "And about that perception thing you mentioned earlier—I'm not fresh off the playground. Faith Marin has busted her bunnies for years and she *is* good." She winked in his direction and motioned for the consultant to follow.

Like a pro, Faith squared her shoulders and headed for the door, determined to face whatever was ahead.

2

From the expensive Santoni loafers and the rich leather Michael Kors tote slung over the woman's shoulder, Faith figured Lynna Scowcroft's career choice must be lucrative. That, or she had a rich daddy subsidizing her expensive tastes. Either way, chalk up one more reason she distrusted the size 2 jackhammer who would spend the next days pounding her image into something young viewers would find palatable.

As they made their way across the parking lot, she pointed to her designated spot. "We'll take my car."

Lynna glanced around. "Where are the news trucks?"

Faith clicked the doors unlocked. Had this one even been on a remote before? Everyone in the business knew the equipment guys always tried to arrive early to set up. "The crew left twenty minutes ago."

Lynna nodded and pulled her buzzing phone from her bag. Inside the car, she again apologized while her thumbs worked the face, tapping out a message. "Sorry, lots going on back in my office."

Faith pulled from the station's parking lot and headed for the on-ramp to the Southwest Freeway. "Where is that? The office, I mean," she asked with an edge in her voice, knowing how often media consultants worked incognito. At least this girl wasn't trying to hide under the guise of being an intern, unlike the last one.

Lynna brushed her fingers through the side of her cropped hair. "Look, we're on the same team, metaphorically speaking of course."

"Of course." Faith merged into traffic and accelerated.

"So let's, like, try to dispel any tension that might exist. We both know what my job is here. I'm a senior branding consultant from Preston Media Group. We're located in the San Fernando Valley but have offices in New York and Chicago." She flipped the visor down and checked her face. A face that barely wore—or needed—makeup.

Faith took a deep breath. Preston Media Group. Those folks upstairs had hired the big guns. She glanced across the seat and tried to sound friendly. "And you?"

"I live in LA." Lynna snapped the visor closed and leaned back in her seat. "Our company philosophy is different from most, but fairly simple, really. We assess everything from a completely customer-obsessed brand persuasion mind-set."

Faith found herself gripping the steering wheel a little tighter. "Oh?"

Lynna riffled through her bag and pulled out a pack of gum. "Yeah, we try to look at things without wearing rose-colored glasses." She offered the pack up to Faith.

"No thanks." What did she mean, *rose-colored glasses*?

As if Lynna could read her thoughts, she unwrapped a stick of gum and explained. "A news station's personnel, owners, and particularly on-air talent can be too close to the situation to dispassionately evaluate the connection programming is making with consumers. I applaud KIAM-TV's recognition of this fact, and for taking proactive measures to retain a competitive edge." She slid the gum into her mouth and continued while chewing. "Preston Media Group will provide unbiased, good honest feedback and guide you back to soaring consumer confidence."

"Back? I wasn't aware we'd gone off course." The savior-like attitude of this marketing twit was beginning to grind on her nerves. "I'm unsure what reports you've been given, but KIAM-TV morning news and my show *Faith on Air* both rank high in year-over-year growth in viewers."

"Don't get defensive. I agree, but both shows were down several percentage points during last quarter's sweeps. I'm here to help you freshen up appeal to those consumers who are drifting over to online venues to get their hard news. If we want people to tune in to a live broadcast, we have to offer fare not otherwise available. In order to retain your credibility with this new generation of viewers, I'm going to show you ways to deepen your emotional connection on air, and how to make programming more appealing. Especially to my generation."

Faith internally grunted. There couldn't be more than a few years between them—okay, maybe, but not that many.

She merged into the exit lane heading to the Sam Houston Tollway. "I don't think we're as broken as you're projecting," she tried to argue, even though at times she worried the producers overteased a segment. "Fast-food hamburgers are appealing, especially to the younger crowd. But eat too much and your body will pay the consequences. Likewise, we need to care about what we feed our viewers."

Lynna laughed. "You've just likened your programming to broccoli. That alone makes my case."

Faith adjusted the air-conditioning, realizing this argument couldn't be won. No doubt this California girl's mind-set was aligned with her job security. She had to make the case for the need to revamp everything, or she'd be unable to afford her *emotional connection* to those expensive wardrobe accessories.

They rode in silence past a freeway sign announcing the exit to I-45 was less than a mile ahead. When she could stand it no longer, she turned to Lynna. She didn't want to sound insecure, but something she'd heard plagued her. "When you mentioned the emotional connection thing earlier, you—did you mean the station, or—"

Lynna's iPhone buzzed from inside her bag—again. This time she muted it. "Look, in large measure, you are the face of the station. Sure, you have a male cohost on the morning news and other anchors, but viewers in those daytime slots are primarily women. Women who do most of the purchasing for their households. Like it or not, these key viewers assess everything about you—what you wear, your hairstyle, even whether or not you wear too much lip gloss."

Instinctively, Faith knew that. She'd learned to build a pretty façade, no matter the turmoil in her private life. It was how the game was played, in life and certainly on television.

The consultant tossed her phone back in her bag. "For years, Katie Couric carried *The Today Show*. ABC's Diane Sawyer tested far more credible when it came to intellect and serious reporting, but she and Charlie Gibson sank under the weight of Matt and Katie, especially after Katie tragically lost her husband. Every woman in America tuned in to follow the grieving young widow."

Faith maneuvered south onto the freeway. "So, I just need to tragically lose my husband then?" she asked, not bothering to hide her sarcasm.

Death they'd get behind. She doubted very much viewers would embrace the fact her marriage was circling the porcelain and about to be flushed.

"Uh, yeah. About that husband—we'll need to talk."

Faith scowled as she drove in the direction of the Johnson Space Center. "Talk? What do you mean?"

Lynna Scowcroft gave her a disingenuous smile. Insincere people only smile with their mouths, not their eyes. "We'll have to carefully manage any divorce."

Faith's head whipped around. "How did you know—?"

"It's my job to know everything about you."

An angry tremor ran down Faith's spine as she considered the implication. What else did Lynna Scowcroft and her Preston Media Group know? Had they learned about her mother, and her brother? Her family situation was not pretty. And her crippled marriage was definitely off-limits.

The consultant must have understood she'd hit a nerve. She busied herself on her iPad for the remainder of the drive.

Faith took the exit to NASA Parkway, and when the bright blue space center sign came into view, she pulled behind a line of cars, determined she was never going to discuss her personal life with this stranger.

Maybe her marriage couldn't be resurrected. But that was no one else's business. When—*if*—she filed for divorce, she'd deal with the hit her career would take then.

Sure, things didn't look good right now. They'd both made mistakes, but she wasn't quite ready to seal the fate of her relationship with Geary. Even if at the moment it looked like she might not have any other option.

Using her Bluetooth, she called ahead to the crew. "Where are we at?"

Production engineer Scott Bingham's voice came through. "Drive past the visitor's center and take a left on Saturn. We've set up in front of the Johnson Space Center sign at the entrance. You'll have to proceed through the security kiosk, and the guard will immediately direct you into the lot adjacent to the Rocket Park building."

"Got it."

Minutes later, Faith stood in front of a small crowd to record her intro. Lynna Scowcroft stood nearby studying the process and making notes on her iPad.

Faith cleared her throat and watched for Scott's signal.

"Empty restaurants, a struggling floral shop, and a transition center packed daily with job seekers are among the lingering effects of the loss of thousands of aerospace jobs over this past year. While the area's economy is benefiting from a surge in the oil, gas, and chemical industries, the impact of the job cuts associated with the end of the space shuttle program clearly remains evident."

She stopped, finished her count, and gave Scott a nod. He raised his forearm and sliced the air, signaling to the cameraman to stop filming. By this time, Senator Libby Heekin Rohny had climbed from her town car and her handlers were miking her. After testing the sound system, a woman in black slacks and a light blue sweater positioned the senator in front of the sign.

In addition to several other news crews, a crowd of about fifty people gathered to listen to Senator Rohny's announcement, including a little boy holding on to the hand of his mother. Despite the urgency of the moment, Faith dug for one of the KIAM-TV Junior Anchor stickers she always carried in her pocket. "Do you mind?" she asked the mother.

The woman smiled. "Not at all."

Faith bent and secured the emblem on his Thomas the Train T-shirt. He beamed in response. "Fank you."

She gave the little guy a final grin, then scurried into place. Against the heat of the late-morning sun, she secured her earpiece and adjusted the volume on her battery pack. "Testing . . . one, two."

"You're clear," she heard Scott report back.

Lynna stepped next to her. "Nice move."

She turned to the consultant. "What?"

"The sticker. That was a nice gesture."

Faith gave her a distracted nod and directed her attention to the senator, waiting for her to begin.

"Good morning, everyone. Thank you so much for being here."

Senator Libby Heekin Rohny was an attractive woman Faith

guessed to be in her early sixties. A staunch conservative, Rohny was in her third term as US senator from Texas after easily challenging the sitting liberal incumbent in a landslide election.

Rohny served on the United States Senate Committee on Finance and held an influential seat on the appropriations committee that set the funding levels for NASA. While the senator enjoyed immense popularity among Houstonians, she definitely had vocal detractors who claimed she'd not done enough to maintain funding for the JSC, which had put many out of jobs and hurt the local economy. No doubt she was here to soften the blow of what was rumored to be on the horizon.

"At its peak in 1966, NASA funding amounted to 4.4 percent of the entire federal budget. In 2012, that decreased to 0.48 percent. And now in 2014, despite my personal efforts, we're bracing for another proposed $200 million cut. As you can imagine, ensuring NASA and in particular the Johnson Space Center budgets are protected is a demanding job in a fiscal environment where space exploration is seen as a nonessential and the competition for funding is fierce."

Faith jotted several notes on a pad of paper, planning how best to approach the senator for an exclusive interview. Despite what people like Lynna Scowcroft claimed, her *Faith on Air* viewers were intelligent, thoughtful women who cared about politics and how these decisions affected their lives.

POP! POP!

Lynna grabbed Faith's arm, her eyes wide. "What was that?"

A scream interrupted the senator's speech. Faith felt more than saw people start running.

POP! POP! POP!

Her heart froze in terror. A shooter!

Instinctively, she dropped her notepad and ran. Where, she wasn't sure. She only knew she had to get away.

More screams. Chaos.

Her way was blocked. Someone nearby shouted, "He's got a gun!"

In horror, she watched a man wearing a khaki-green jacket step out of the crowd armed with what looked like a semiautomatic rifle. He aimed at the senator and shot a round of bullets.

The woman crumpled.

More shots and several of the senator's team went down as well.

Out of nowhere, she heard Scott Bingham's voice in her earpiece. "Faith, get down!" Dazed, she looked in the direction of the news truck and saw him running toward her. The motion caused her to stumble and she fell, twisting her ankle in the heels she wore. Pain shot through her leg.

A voice near her begged, "Please—no—please no."

Terrified, Faith dared a look in that direction. The man with the gun stood over the mother she'd seen earlier. The frantic woman was on the ground huddled on top of her son, trying to protect the little boy.

Despite her pleas, the man shot anyway.

Faith squeezed her eyes shut against the nightmare happening around her. Suddenly, an image formed in her mind—that of her estranged husband. Who would tell Geary if . . .

She dropped to the ground and went to cover her head, but not before two booted feet moved within her view. Her heart pounded. She glanced up to find the gun pointed in her direction. She heard another loud scream.

She couldn't help it. She wet herself.

POP! POP!

A body crumpled to the ground next to her.

Faith held her breath and watched as dark red blood pooled beneath Lynna Scowcroft's short blonde hair. Lifeless eyes stared back at her.

She struggled to breathe—to comprehend it all.

Strangely, her senses went on high alert. The smell of freshly mown grass, the warm air, the droning sound of a plane overhead all sharpened in her mind.

She felt a figure blocking the sun. Heard a loud click.

And she knew then . . . she was next.

3

Thick black receded, leaving behind a foggy gravy of muted charcoal pierced with shards of light.

Faith shifted her chin uncomfortably, wincing at the thunder in her head. She was soaked in sweat, helpless.

A siren wailed, the amplified sound so near she might reach out and touch it—if her hands weren't made of stone.

"Faith—honey, you back with us? Don't leave us now."

A needle of light scraped across her blurred line of vision.

Why couldn't she breathe? What was that weight on her chest? Each heartbeat exploded inside her rib cage.

Where was she?

Panicked, she tried to bolt. Restraints thwarted the attempt.

She tried again.

"Whoa, honey."

She felt a hand on her shoulder—heard a woman's voice. "Shhh . . . calm down. You're going to be all right."

A man's voice shouted, "Get the ketamine from the RSI kit—*stat*."

Her vision turned red—the top of her skull seemed on fire.

She moaned.

In the background, yet another voice. "We're en route with a twenty-eight-year-old victim from the shooting at JSC. Patient has sustained gunshot fragments to the abdomen and a perforating injury to the upper left quadrant of the cranium with resulting TBI. BP is one eighty over ninety, pulse fifty. Respirations ten and irregular. Open head wound with profuse bleeding—"

"Honey, stay with us now. C'mon, look at me."

Faith tried to turn toward the voice. The sirens screamed in protest.

Was the man talking about her? Was she dying?

An image of Geary formed in her terrified mind, followed by a rush of regret. Tears welled.

She wouldn't get to say goodbye.

"Okay, sweet thing—hold on, here we go."

A sharp prick pierced her arm. The air instantly grew heavier, darkened—she thought of Geary, how they'd met—until the commotion was sweetly snuffed by a thick dreamy blanket of black.

As the news van pulled to a stop in the parking lot, Faith nervously glanced back at the producer's notes in her hand.

On the northern outskirts of Houston, Lake Conroe was home to some of the biggest largemouth bass in the nation, or so the notes claimed. Once a year, the small bedroom community of Conroe ballooned to accommodate fifty skilled bass fishermen and a mass of spectators for the Toyota Texas Bass Championship, a three-day event filled with competition, headliner entertainment, and a party like none other.

"Hurry, let's go!" Chuck Howell hollered as they both climbed from the van. Her cameraman hoisted the equipment bag onto his shoulder and maneuvered across the lot tangled with boat trailers. He waved for Faith to follow, which she tried but found difficult to do in her Cole Haan platform pumps she'd bought special for the occasion, spending nearly her entire monthly grocery budget. Her first official camera appearance at KIAM-TV, and she needed to look great.

Covering the story this year was Faith Bierman's first solo foray into field reporting. Fresh on the job and loaded with a can-do attitude, she scrambled toward the docks in the early morning hour, ready to show the world her rising star was about to shoot into news broadcasting space and make its mark.

Traffic had been a bear, even at dawn, with people gathering to watch the big launch from Waterpoint Marina, an area filled with restaurants and tourist shops. Past the slips, boats were already lining up.

They had less than fifteen minutes to set up in order to shoot footage of the anglers taking off. In minutes, contestants in shiny bass boats with brand names like Skeeter or Tritan would scream across the lake into their prime fishing spots, trying to beat out dozens of others with the same idea in mind.

Chuck paused and turned back in her direction. "Are you coming?"

She nodded and scrambled to keep up, well aware her auburn curls were beginning to droop in the humidity.

At the entrance, they flashed their media badges at the officials taking tickets and hurried past brand-new pickup trucks to be awarded as prizes to tournament winners along with huge amounts of cash. Until she'd studied up on the bass tournament circuit, she had no idea how lucrative the profession could be for the lucky ones who pulled monster lunkers from the depths of the murky water.

She'd also studied big mouth bass habitats and lures and water temps, all in hopes of being ready to ace her interviews today. A bass tournament might not be equal with, say, an exclusive with the mayor of Houston revealing the first glimpse of a new tax measure, but she was determined to bloom where planted. Today she was planted at Lake Conroe and fully intended to burst onto the television scene and make a good impression.

That attitude was what spawned her next idea.

"Hey, Chuck." She watched the cameraman bend down to unzip

the oversized black bag of equipment. "Let's move a little closer to the action."

He didn't bother to look up. "What action?"

"C'mon—follow me." Without waiting, she pushed her way forward through a small group of onlookers, past the media center, where she recognized a reporter from their competitor station drinking coffee from a Styrofoam cup. Ignoring the way he stared, she headed for the docks. Without stopping to engage the tournament official standing guard at the launch area, she simply flashed her badge. The generously built man, with eyes that reminded her of raisins in dough that had risen around them, pulled his cap from his balding head and swiped his forearm across his brow before holding up his palm. "Whoa, where y'all heading, little lady?"

She ignored his grating salutation and mustered a calculated smile, not needing to check her watch to know she had very little time left. "Any way I can film my report from over there?" She pointed to a boat tethered a short distance from where they stood.

He looked in that direction. "Uh, I'm not supposed to allow anyone to interfere with the launch. We're asking everyone to—"

"Ah, c'mon," she pleaded in her sweetest voice, well aware his raisin eyes were now pointed in the direction of her legs. "Cut a girl a break, huh? I promise we'll stay right there and not go any closer." She lifted her brows. "Please?"

He smiled back and slowly nodded. "Oh, all right. But stay where I can see you and don't get too close." He nodded in the direction of the big tent that served as tournament headquarters. "Or I'll take some heat."

She thanked him profusely and breezed past with Chuck now following close behind.

"Why are we filming from clear down here?" he asked as he set down the equipment bag.

Faith sighed, knowing it was those attitudes that differentiated future Emmy Award–winning journalists from the small town variety who never progressed into major markets. "Because this will work much better, you'll see," she assured him. "Just set up so you can capture a clear shot."

In yesterday's production meeting, she hadn't gotten far with the assignment editor when she'd argued for live coverage. But as she suspected, a bass tournament, even one with national fame among fishing enthusiasts, didn't warrant a lead. Even so, she intended to deliver a compelling stand-up.

She climbed onto the boat and headed for the bow.

Chuck glanced at her with raised eyebrows. "Faith, are you kidding? Do you even know who owns that boat?"

She shook her head. "No, I don't know and I'm not kidding. And I'll want wide shots of the lake in the background of the boats as they launch, then zoom in for a tight shot when I start talking about what's at stake here for today's challengers."

"But you can't even see the leaderboard from here," he argued.

"We'll get that shot later. I want to humanize the story first, start with a little background and get the viewers invested before we move to tournament positions."

Chuck looked at her like she'd lost her mind.

Never mind his small thinking. Going with the flow was no way to stand out in this business.

Moisture formed on the back of her neck. Hopefully, they could wrap this footage before the sun rudely peeked its irascible head over the horizon, making the heavy air even more miserable.

Out of the corner of her eye, she noticed a boat with a red sparkly finish slowly making its way to the adjacent dock. Inside, a man with dark hair seemed to be eyeing her and the situation. As the boat crept closer, she could see the guy was affiliated with the tournament in some manner, based on the bright yellow plastic vest he wore with the word VOLUNTEER emblazoned across the chest.

She held her breath, hoping for the best. They wouldn't have time to set up again somewhere else and get as good a shot.

Chuck likely thought the same. "Oh, here we go."

The man in the boat gave them a polite nod, and she bobbed her chin in acknowledgment before quickly turning back to Chuck and his camera.

The motor shut down as she began her mike check. "Uh, excuse me, miss?" the guy said, threatening to interrupt her plans.

She pointed to the camera. "Sorry, I'm about to go live."

"But you might not want to stand there when—"

She cupped her ear with her free hand, feigning not to have heard him. They had a show to do, and she couldn't risk him telling them to move along. Not now. The better way was to just go for it and pay the consequences later.

Suddenly, a boat engine started from several yards down shore. Then another. Before the entire line of boats followed suit, completely drowning out her voice, she gave a quick nod to Chuck. He positioned the camera on his shoulder and held up three fingers, doing a silent countdown. She pasted on a wide smile.

"Good morning, everyone. We're broadcasting at this early hour here in Texas from the shores of Lake Conroe, where in just moments some of the best bass fishermen in our nation will launch across this lake in hopes of landing bass that will win hundreds of thousands in prizes and the distinction of being named the Toyota Texas Bass first-place champion."

She let the moment wash over her, basking in the thrill of being in front of the camera. She had trained for this. Broadcast journalism was her destiny—her ticket to having her life matter. She felt it inside her soul.

Taking a deep breath, she told viewers what to expect on the final day of the Texas Bass Classic. Fifteen anglers remained. Each would spend the next hours on the lake trying to pull in an accumulated weight that would put them at the top of the leaderboard at the end of the day. Fans were already gathering along the shoreline and on the decks of nearby restaurants, hoping for a record-breaking performance from their personal favorite.

She shifted slightly closer to the camera to create a sense of urgency, as she'd been trained. "In moments, officials will give the signal and these boats positioned along the shoreline will launch three at a time."

Chuck turned the camera to catch a shot of the launch.

As if on cue, idling engines roared to life. The first three boats in the lineup inched forward. Applause drifted from across the inlet where a crowd of onlookers gathered on a deck outside Wolfies, a popular local restaurant.

At the signal, the low-profiled boats heavily festooned with sponsorship decals simultaneously screamed into action, speeding across the lake and leaving enormous plumes of water jetting from the rear motors. Three more bass boats immediately followed. Then another group.

Out of the corner of her eye, she saw the man in the yellow jacket edge his boat closer. He watched her now from only a yard or so away. Continuing to ignore him, she recorded her voice-over, using enough volume to be heard over the distant engines. "And there they go, folks," she said with bright enthusiasm. "The final day of the Texas Bass Classic has officially begun."

The boat she stood on wiggled slightly, causing her feet to become unsteady in her heels. Suddenly, the wake from the launched boats landed against the side of the boat she stood on, knocking her off-kilter. She scrambled a bit, tried to catch her equilibrium.

Oh no! she thought, feeling her body shift recklessly. She moved her left foot to catch herself. Then her right.

Too late.

A second and much more forceful wake hit. This time the increased impact caused the boat to pitch in a way she didn't expect.

Frantic to catch her balance, she reached for something to hang on to, her eyes wide. She heard Chuck curse. At the same time he jumped back onto the dock, her fingers loosened and she dropped the microphone.

Her ankle gave way, her pretty pump slipped from her foot.

"H-help!" she screamed.

She tumbled, barely having time to hold her breath as she listed over the side, arms flailing.

Splash!

She squeezed her eyes tightly shut just before hitting the water's surface. Sound muffled and she sank into the depths of the murky green lake, her arms wildly pummeling against the water.

Suddenly, arms folded around her back and she felt their strength pull her in an upward motion through the water. Seconds later, her head broke the surface. She sputtered, choked.

"Are you all right?" Chuck grabbed her arm and pulled her back onto the deck of the boat, next to where her notes and microphone lay abandoned.

Faith rubbed at her eyes. After barely daring to open them, she grabbed at a piece of something slimy clinging to her face. She yanked the offending plant off her cheek and coughed.

A spindly stick of a man with teeth too big for his face rushed up the dock. "Hey, that's my boat!"

Chuck held up his hand. "Sorry, dude. We're sorry."

"Is the lady okay?" the owner asked, frowning.

Chuck stood. "Yeah, she's fine. Just wet."

She wiped her face again, already feeling the heat of humiliation warming her cheeks. What had she been thinking? She'd let her zeal for a good shot unknowingly place her in a vulnerable situation that led straight to catastrophe. Now what was she going to do?

Chuck helped her rescuer into the boat then. The dark-haired volunteer, the one she'd purposely ignored, perched himself next to her. He was drenched, his legs dangling off the bow of the flat bass boat. Tiny pieces of green plant particles clung to his yellow vest. He gave her a sideways look, and Faith couldn't help but notice his blue-jean eyes lined with thick dark lashes.

"Uh, thank you," she murmured, grateful the embarrassing incident hadn't been broadcast on a live shot. It was bad enough the small crowd watching from the shore had seen.

Hopefully, Chuck could edit the footage and save the broadcast. Unfortunately, they'd have to wrap the footage with what they had. And she'd missed having him shoot a great close-up of her closing out the segment.

Her hands brushed dripping auburn hair from her wet shoulders. She'd also have to see to it the cuts didn't show up on some blooper reel at a future office party. As it was, she'd have to bribe Chuck not to make her the laughingstock at the studio for weeks to come.

The guy who'd pulled her from the water studied her, his dark blue eyes narrowing as he sized her up.

"What?" she said, her tone a bit more curt than intended.

He held up his palms. "Hey, sorry."

Immediately, she felt like a heel. She shook her head. "No, I'm sorry. It's just that, well—"

"Do you always do that?" he interrupted with an annoying grin.

"I beg your pardon?" He was teasing her, and she didn't like it. Not bothering to hide the fact, she tucked her bare foot beneath her and scanned the boat for her missing shoe. "Do you mean staying focused, because a good reporter—"

"Uh-huh." His eyes twinkled and he grinned even wider. "I meant ignoring someone's warning."

He was *laughing* at her.

She grabbed her shoe and slipped it on her foot. "Look, thank you and all—but we're busy here." She retrieved the microphone she'd dropped.

He lifted his chin and looked toward the sky, still grinning.

She scrambled to her feet. "Yeah, so I guess all this is pretty funny."

Only feet away, Chuck watched them with apparent amusement as he apologized again to the owner of the boat and promised him they'd be moving along. Even her cameraman was grinning now.

Faith wrung out her dripping hair. "Glad everyone is so easily entertained, but we still have work to do."

"Hey, I don't mean to state the obvious here." Chuck shook his head as he wound a thick black cord. "But you can't go back on air like that. You'll need to find a shower or something."

Faith gave him a tight-lipped nod. "There's got to be a motel close," she ventured, already planning to keep the expenditure off her expense report. Why risk inquiry and further embarrassment? Instead she'd take it out of her personal budget—cut back on her trips to Starbucks this month.

Her smug rescuer ran his fingers through his wet dark hair and stood. "Hate to tell you this," he warned, following her off the boat. "But you aren't going to find an open motel room between here and the Woodlands, not during the Texas Bass Championship."

Drat! She hadn't thought of the mob of people in town for the event. Faith looked to Chuck as if expecting him to come up with another plan. He remained quiet, obviously not having one.

The guy from the boat jumped onto the dock and extended his hand. "My name is Geary—Geary Marin. Look, I live just over there." He pointed to a condominium complex on the point across the inlet. "You're welcome to use my place."

She dared a closer look, noticed his ratty cowboy boots, wet and crisscrossed with scratches. He wore faded jeans, a belt with some type of fish on it, and a light blue shirt. He bent and retrieved a Bassmaster baseball cap from off the dock, where he must have dropped it before making his water rescue. His rolled shirtsleeves revealed forearms deeply tanned and muscled.

Cute, but definitely redneck.

She wondered what he did for a living—when he wasn't playing volunteer.

She squared her shoulders and shook her head. "No—I'm not sure that's a good idea."

He shrugged. "Suit yourself." He turned and headed for his red boat tethered to the dock. "Take care," he said as he moved on.

She realized then that she didn't have a better choice. Or any other choice, for that matter. Where else would she be able to clean up?

In a moment of panic, she reached in his direction. "Wait!"

Geary turned.

"Look, I guess my options are fairly slim here." Faith glanced at Chuck. "You're coming with, right?"

Chuck nodded, clearly amused at the situation. "We'd better get a move on if you still want to try for interviews with some of the wives."

She nodded. "We'll have to stop at a drugstore for a hair dryer."

Geary Marin slipped his cap in place. "Not a good idea if you're in a hurry." He cocked his head in the direction of the highway, now clogged with traffic. "Why don't you let me take you over to my place in the boat?" He raised an eyebrow. "That is, if you are up for taking some advice."

She ignored his loaded remark and simply repeated herself. "I need a hair dryer."

"You can use mine," he offered.

Okay, she was already uneasy going to this stranger's house. Using the guy's personal toiletry items was going well beyond her comfort level.

"We don't really have a choice, Faith." Chuck was already heaving his black bag into Geary's boat. He turned and tossed his keys to her. "What are you waiting for? Get your other suit out of the news van and let's go."

4

From inside Geary Marin's boat, Faith watched the marina fade from sight as wind whipped her hair. She turned and nestled deeper in the seat, her hand clutching the handle on the side as they raced across the water at a speed that made her a bit nervous.

As if reading her mind, he shouted over top of the engine, "You okay?"

She nodded and held on tighter as the boat hit rough water, hating that her only choice had been to accept his invitation. He was nice to offer and all, but she didn't really have time for this little detour. The sooner she could get showered and back to business, the better.

In what seemed like no time, they neared the shoreline and he slowed, easing the boat to the dock. The condominium complex was not so unlike her own, except for the expansive lawn between the buildings and the lake, and all the pretty landscaped beds filled with sego palms and hibiscus. Her own building near downtown Houston was surrounded by cement parking lot and sadly lacked any foliage.

Faith wasn't sure what a fishing enthusiast's place would look like, but when he opened the door, there were no muddy fishing boots near the entrance, no lures or empty frozen dinner trays stacked on the counter as she expected.

The modest living area was neat and orderly, everything in its place, like something out of a magazine. Modern even, with walls painted the lightest shade of gray, the sofa slipcovered in a textured chevron print in a darker shade. The lamp shades were definitely Pottery Barn.

Frankly, his decorating taste surpassed her own, even if she picked up all the clothes off the floor of her tiny apartment.

"Can I get you something to drink?" their host asked.

Chuck dropped his camera bag on the floor. "Sure. A beer, if you've got it."

"Sorry. I have sweet tea or lemonade."

Chuck shrugged. "Lemonade, I guess."

Faith shook her head. "I just need a shower, thanks." She needed to hurry and get cleaned up and out of here. Even now, she should be shooting crowd reaction to the tournament.

Noticing several other networks setting up in the parking lot as they'd started across the lake annoyed her to no end. She'd been benched by her own stupidity. The only thing she could do now was hurry and get back to the action.

Geary smiled. "Shower is in this direction." He led her down a hallway lined with doorways and framed photos. He stopped at his linen closet and pulled out a few extra towels.

"Are these your bass?" she asked, pointing to a couple of shots with him holding sizeable fish in front of him.

"Yeah," he said, grinning. "Those were all caught here at the lake. Snagged that fifteen-pounder about twenty yards off the dock out back."

Another showed him on a stage accepting a large trophy. "So, you fish these tournaments too?"

"Yup," he said as he handed off the towels.

"But not this one?"

He shook his head. "Not this one. I didn't have enough points this year to qualify." He led her to a bathroom located at the end of the hall. "This is the guest bath. There's shampoo over there." He pulled out a drawer next to the sink. "And here's a hair dryer."

She extended her appreciation, glad he wasn't expecting her to use his personal shower and hair dryer. Something about that seemed just too—well, too intimate.

"Okay, well, I'll just leave you to your business." He smiled and backed out the doorway, shutting the door behind him.

She turned and glanced at herself in the mirror. What a wreck! Thank goodness he'd offered her his place to clean up. Otherwise, she wasn't sure what she would've done.

She hung her change of clothes on the door hook.

If pressed, she'd have to admit he wasn't hard to look at. Under different circumstances she might even find him attractive, although she'd never really gone for outdoor types.

Faith dumped the damp blouse on the floor and unzipped her skirt.

She'd not gone for anyone, really. There had been a couple of guys in college she was mildly interested in, but she'd needed to focus and not get bogged down with romantic complications.

It was cliché perhaps to blame her parents for her attitude toward men, but watching their relationship had definitely colored her own view about such things and influenced nearly every decision she made, particularly the ones about love, marriage, and the way she had chosen to live her life.

Her earliest memories included waking to shouting and her mother's accusations about her father sneaking home in the predawn hours, followed by slamming doors and the sound of glass breaking.

If she ever married, she'd choose a stable, trustworthy man who would be dedicated to her and supportive of her career. And they would never ever fight like that.

In the shower, she mentally revised her rundown sheet to include this unexpected alteration in the schedule. She'd still like to get crowd reaction shots, but her main interest was in the wives. If she teased the story and built up what was at stake for the challengers through the eyes of their spouses, she might expand the viewing audience and create more appeal. Research showed viewers would be more affected when a news story created an emotional connection, and she intended to take full advantage of every tool at her disposal.

Finished, she stepped from the shower and wrapped herself in one of Geary's thick bath towels. High quality, like the kind found in expensive hotels. Surprising for a guy who fished bass tournaments.

She hurried her makeup, wanting to get back across the lake as soon as possible. When she emerged from down the hallway a half hour later, she unfortunately learned Geary had made sandwiches and a fresh fruit salad, expecting them to stay for lunch.

"It's nearly time to eat and the restaurants will be packed," he explained as he carried a tray to the small dining table.

Chuck was already moving toward a chair. While she was in a hurry, she had to admit she was pretty hungry. Reluctantly, she gave in and smiled. "Thank you. But you didn't have to go to all this trouble."

"No trouble," he assured her as he pulled out a chair.

She thanked him and moved into the seat. "The entrants are scheduled to come in at four o'clock," she warned. "Chuck, I don't want to run into any problems with timing."

Chuck grabbed his iPhone to check a text. "No worries. We'll have plenty of time to push film back to the station for the evening broadcast." He checked his watch. "And we can still squeeze in your special interest segments before the anglers return for the weigh-ins."

Relieved, she pointed to a framed photo perched on the counter and attempted small talk. "Your family?"

Geary turned back to the counter for the salad. "Yeah, that's us. A crazy bunch, for sure." He held up a pitcher. "Tea, or lemonade?"

"Tea's fine, thanks." She placed a napkin on her lap. "So do they all live around here? Your family?"

"We have aunts, uncles, and cousins scattered all over Texas, but my immediate family members all live here in Conroe."

Chuck finished his text and slid his smartphone back in his jeans pocket. "Must be nice at holidays." He grabbed a sandwich from the platter.

Geary set the pitcher on the counter, then slid into his place at the table. "Uh, do either of you mind if I say the blessing?"

Chuck dropped his sandwich on the paper plate in front of him. "Sorry, no. Sure, go ahead."

Faith lowered her head, thinking that answered a lot.

First, their host rescued her from the drink, then extended hospitality even when her earlier tone had been brisk. She thought about the photos down the hall, the one of him in his graduation gown flanked by a man and woman, likely his parents. There was a photo of a younger gal with a resemblance to him taken in front of what looked like a church. His sister, maybe? She was very pregnant and her face beaming. There were shots of him playing baseball, several of him fishing, and one of him with his arms wrapped around the feeble shoulders of an elderly man.

None of him with a girlfriend or wife.

He finished the blessing, then offered up the bowl of fruit salad. "So, I take it this is the first bass tournament for both of you?"

Chuck didn't look compelled to answer anytime soon, given his mouth was full of turkey sandwich. So she responded.

"Yes," she admitted, taking the bowl from Geary's hand. "But I knew this shoot was coming up, and I did my research."

He moved a sandwich from the platter onto his plate. "What kind of research?"

She explained how she'd spent hours on the internet, studying how the tournament was composed of winners from six divisions, combining the top PAA anglers from the FLW Tour, Bassmaster Elite Series, and PAA Bass Pro Shops Tournament Series. She'd memorized the tournament rules and learned not only the professional but the personal histories of the fifty competing anglers, including their wives' names and where they grew up.

"Really? All that?" he teased her with a slight grin.

She let herself smile back, pondering his laid-back style, his precise housekeeping skills, and the fact he kept enough groceries in his refrigerator to host an impromptu luncheon.

She had to admit she was also slightly enamored with the fact that he didn't seem put off by her frank style and driven nature. A lot of men were.

That, and the few men she'd encountered drank too much and had octopus hands. Seems they believed if they bought her dinner, she needed to pay them back in some physical manner. Same as those older men who had taught her journalism classes, who intimated her affections would be well awarded with recommendation letters.

Yes, she wanted to climb the corporate news ladder, but not that way.

She ate her sandwich while Geary and Chuck talked about how the high temps might affect the depths the bass anglers would have to go to snag a winner.

Chuck shook his head. "I really admire you, man. Not many have one of those on their shelves." He pointed to a trophy.

"Did I miss something here?" she said, dabbing at the corners of her mouth with her napkin.

Chuck reached for his lemonade glass. "Are you kidding, Faith? Don't you know about Geary Marin?"

She shook her head, hating that Chuck knew something she didn't. She looked across the table at their host. "So, who *are* you?" she asked.

Chuck set his glass down. He grinned and exchanged glances with Geary. "This guy was last year's second-place winner."

Oh, great! She'd researched the most minute details and knew the first ten-pounder caught in B.A.S.S. competition history was snagged on February 8, 1973, by J. D. Skinner on the St. Johns River, but somehow she'd climbed in a shower belonging to a runner-up in the main hoo-ha and missed it. And he was now sitting across the table from her—grinning.

Again.

If falling in the drink hadn't impressed him, she'd certainly just sealed the deal by touting herself as being in the know while completely missing the fact that he was a major contender in the bass fishing world.

Stalling, she took a long sip of her tea.

Finally, she looked him in the eyes (those really nice eyes) and made things even worse. "So, why didn't you qualify this year?"

He gently pushed his plate back. "I had something important that demanded my attention."

"More critical than the possibility of winning over a hundred thousand dollars?"

He nodded. "I bowed out this spring in order to take care of my grandpa."

She blinked, understanding creeping into her thick head. She dared to open her big mouth again. "Your grandpa?"

Geary stood and gathered the empty plates. "Yeah, he suffered pancreatic cancer last year. Terminal." Sadness instantly shadowed his features. "Family matters to me, and sometimes everything else has to go on hold. It was a privilege to care for him clear till the end."

Faith melted like a candle to a flame. This was the second time she'd acted like a heel, and instead of leveraging his position and taking advantage, he extended a pleasant and polite attitude, even so far as being nice back to her.

Chuck coughed uncomfortably. "Sorry, man. That's rough."

"Yes, me too—I'm so sorry," she said in earnest, recalling the photo in the hallway. "You must have loved him."

"Yes, I did." Geary tossed the used paper plates in the trash. "He was a very special man."

She scrambled to help clear the table.

He held up his palm, seeming to ignore the fact she'd struck out three times on the impression meter. "Nah, leave it for later. Let's get y'all back to that tournament."

He delivered them across the lake and to the main dock in record time, bypassing the masses of crowds that had now gathered and packed all the roadways and parking lots.

Geary then offered to make introductions to several of the tournament officials standing in the holding area by the stage, which gave her ample opportunity to secure exclusive interview footage.

"Why are you being so nice to me?" she asked when she'd finished. She unclipped her lavalier mike. "Especially after—uh, this morning."

"Because I'm hoping you'll stay for the fireworks show tonight."

Those gorgeous eyes seemed to twinkle, and one thing became immediately clear. After he'd been so charming, she couldn't possibly say no.

5

The low hum of medical equipment and muted voices pierced Faith's consciousness, pulling her back from inside her head. She tried to think, to clarify the sounds floating around her.

Her mouth, her throat—so parched the skin inside seemed to stick together. She needed a drink of water.

Through the tiniest slits, she realized the room was dark. She struggled to lift her weighted eyelids a bit more, but the effort was too much.

It hurt to breathe. She hurt all over.

Where was she?

Her mind tried to think. Tried to remember.

"Don't worry, honey. You're all right."

She attempted to turn toward the voice, but her head felt like a block of cement. Her vision blurred and she felt confused. She opened her mouth—her dry mouth—to speak. But no sound came out.

"Here, baby, this will help." A stranger—a woman—leaned over the bed. "Just sleep now. Everything's all right."

Immediately, every muscle relaxed. Her eyes closed, and she let the gentle voice soothe her mind.

Slowly, she slid back into total darkness.

★

Faith knew her heart was headed for trouble.

In a totally uncharacteristic move, she skipped racing back to the station after the final shoot. Instead she parked herself inside the news van and worked with Chuck to edit the package, electronically filing it with their producer in time for the ten o'clock broadcast.

"Well, as they say, that's a wrap." Chuck slipped his monitor closed and slid his computer into a black leather backpack. "You used great storytelling in that block."

The compliment made her beam. He could be throwing her a bone after the lake incident, but not likely. In her short time at the station, she'd learned Chuck was one of their best cameramen and didn't have much to prove, a guy who didn't frost any cupcakes.

"Thanks, Chuck. Your edits made me look better than I had a right to today," she conceded. "I appreciate it."

He winked. "Your secret's safe with me."

Chuck tossed her a set of keys, then migrated in the direction of the media tent to take advantage of free food and drink with a girl he'd met earlier that afternoon.

Faith hung back to change clothes in the back of the van. Every instruction manual she'd studied clearly stated that a good reporter always carried multiple outfits, extra batteries, and a flexible attitude.

Geary showed up just as she was locking up the van.

"Hey," he said as he approached.

She adjusted her belt. "Do you think the van will be secure here? I mean, there's a lot of expensive equipment inside."

Geary pulled his phone from his back jeans pocket. "Don't worry. Got this covered."

She watched him dial. "Who are you calling?" she mouthed.

He winked and held up his forefinger. "Hey, Jake. There's a KIAM-TV news van parked over here in the lot next to the boat slips. Can you keep an eye on it?" He listened to the voice on the other end, then nodded. "Yeah, thanks."

He slipped his phone into his jeans pocket. "Okay. All good to go. My buddy at the PD will make sure the van and your equipment are still here when you get back." He reached for her elbow.

She placed the strap of her purse on her shoulder and walked alongside him as they moved across the parking lot toward the main stage area. "Do you always do that?"

"What?"

"Do you always play the hero and sweep in and save the day?"

Geary chuckled. "Sure. I just leave my cape in my tackle box."

They neared the food tents located in the same direction as the main stage where Montgomery Gentry served as the headline entertainment, thrilling the crowds who'd assembled in Conroe for the Super Bowl of bass fishing.

"You hungry?" Geary asked, pulling his wallet out.

"Starved," she admitted. It'd been hours since they'd eaten the sandwiches at his place.

Up ahead, a long semi rigged with a black-and-white-striped awning and a massive grill displayed a sign boasting they served the world's best mesquite-smoked brisket. "This okay?" he asked.

The air was filled with that wonderful barbecue smell. "You bet. Smells delicious!"

They purchased homemade root beer from the Wild West Soda Saloon vendor next door and made their way to an empty table.

"Oh my, this is so good," she said, trying not to gorge on the tender smoky-flavored beef covered in tangy sauce, very aware what the calories were doing to her slim size 6 figure. She didn't want to end up looking like the crackly blonde passing by their table with her ample midriff poking over the top of too-tight jeans.

He noticed too. "Quite the crowd, huh?"

She caught a glimpse of a man in shorts and white tube socks and a cap that said *Shut Up and Fish*. He lugged a loaded cooler while his wife carried folding chairs and led a string of kids behind.

Out here, camouflage-print shirts seemed to be the fashion

statement for men, while an overabundance of chunky turquoise jewelry and tattoos adorned many of the women. At the final weigh-in, the announcer had held up a prize-winning fish, calling the eleven-pounder "as freaking amazing as all these hot Texas women."

To say this was not exactly her crowd would be an understatement.

Geary wiped his mouth with his napkin. "I enjoyed watching you today. You have a way of drawing people out and getting them to tell you interesting stories." He studied her, a look of admiration in his eyes. "Seriously, how'd you get those wives to talk to you like that?"

She smiled and savored the compliment. "Secret's out. I got passed over when they were handing out hero capes, but I do have a pair of Wonder Woman wristbands back in the van."

He chuckled at that, his eyes twinkling—those seriously deep blue eyes.

He was a good head taller than she, solid-looking with broad shoulders and muscular arms deeply tanned. Short dark hair hung careless around his angular face shadowed with stubble. The look *GQ* models worked hard to attain, he managed with ease.

His cheeks dimpled when he smiled, which he did a lot. Nothing seemed to ruffle the man.

And he was easy to talk to.

He asked about her job—his sincere interest punctured her wall of reservation and caused her to spill.

"I love everything about television reporting," she told him. "Especially learning about breaking news before anyone else." She recounted an occasion when former president George H. W. Bush was hospitalized for shortness of breath. "It was just before Christmas, and I was sent out with a field team to cover the story. We were the first to arrive on the scene. This might surprise you, but since I was fairly new I hung back a bit."

"That is surprising," he teased.

"Well, my lack of confidence paid off. After letting the others go ahead, I rounded a corner and found myself face-to-face with Barbara, his wife."

Geary leaned forward, looking genuinely interested. "No kidding?"

Faith sipped her root beer. "Nope. For real. She even had on her signature pearls." She fingered the straw. "I told her I was so sorry to hear about her husband. The best part? A CNN crew arrived on the scene a few seconds later with cameras flashing. Guess who ended up on national television the next day?"

He smiled widely, sharing in her enthusiasm. "That's what our family calls a God-thing."

She tilted her head slightly. "What about you?"

He grinned. "Me? Oh, nothing as interesting as all that." He leaned back and let his gaze fall over the crowd. "I tend to gravitate toward the simple things in life." He looked back at her then, and bless his heart—he looked nervous.

"Like bass fishing?" she urged, suddenly wanting to learn more about this man sitting across from her.

"Yeah, but not all this, really. I mean, sure, tournament wins pay the bills, but the real thrill of bass fishing is when you're out on the lake all alone, pulling into your special spot just as the sun breaks over the horizon. You cut the motor and grab your pole—the one you rigged up the night before with a crankbait you just know is going to hit."

She watched his eyes fill with the same excitement she had felt earlier knowing that camera was about to go live.

When they'd finished eating, he gathered their empty plates and cups and carried them to a nearby trash receptacle. When he returned to the table he held out his hand. "Dance?"

Startled, she glanced around. "Me? Uh, I don't—"

Geary grabbed her hand. "Oh, c'mon. Let loose a bit."

Her heart pounded from nerves as she let him drag her toward a crowd of line dancers shuffling to a rousing rendition of "God Bless Texas." The only other time she'd danced was in a college exercise class, but in what seemed like no time she was sliding in step and clapping with the rest of them. And it was fun!

The next song started, and she laughed as he grabbed her waist and swung her around. By the third song, she felt winded and her hair hung at her shoulders, damp from the humid night air. She didn't even care, she was enjoying herself so much. She rarely let loose, and especially not among a crazy crowd like this.

Geary Marin was extremely fun. She had to give him that.

He grinned. "You're killing me! I need something to drink."

"I'm killing you? Who asked who to dance, I want to know?"

He swiped his damp forehead with his forearm before leading her to the edge of the dancing mob where an ingenious entrepreneur sold ice-cold water from a vendor cart.

They quickly polished off a couple of bottles, then melded back into the crowd just as the band announced their final song of the evening. The notes of a slower ballad rang out, and Geary's hand went to the small of her back. "One more?" he asked.

She nodded and placed her right hand in his and leaned her head against his shoulder, savoring the feel of his quiet strength.

Geary rested his head against hers and sang along to the chorus: "'But I know I'm a lucky man—God's given me a pretty fair hand.'"

Deep down she suspected the lyrics were his own life motto. Rarely had she encountered someone so authentic, so genuine. So sure of himself.

She envied all that.

Later, when they sat at the back of his boat anchored in a nearby slip to watch the fireworks, she realized that he was getting to her. That hollow spot inside her was filled with something pleasant, and she liked how it felt—liked him.

Despite how the morning had started out, she'd laughed today, which was good. When had she last laughed?

After years spent studying night and day, she'd graduated at the top of her journalism class with a diploma and summa cum laude designation in hand. She'd spent the following months stalking the KIAM producers, showing up where she knew the station manager and his management staff ate lunch every day, soon landing an interview, then acing her audition.

Since then, there'd been no play for her, no downtime. Not if she wanted to position herself for quick promotion. She had an eye on a prize, and wouldn't leave the so-called carnival until she held the overstuffed bear in her arms—or in her case, an anchor slot.

And that was just the beginning. She intended to work hard and make her life matter. She believed in herself, and no amount of criticism from those who thought her too focused could convince her otherwise.

But tonight—well, she was off the map, off the grid, behaving like someone she didn't recognize. On this particularly unexpected evening she let herself enjoy another side to life.

"You warm enough?" he asked, casually placing his arm on her seat back as if to ward off a chill.

Faith nodded and looked up into the now blackened sky as the first rocket launched upward. The corners of her mouth turned up. They both knew the air had to still be at least ninety degrees.

Overhead, the nightscape popped and crackled as the black sky above burst into a brilliant shower of red and blue lights.

As focused as Faith was on the beauty of the fireworks, she was even more aware of Geary's thumb as it lightly brushed her upper arm, up and down in tiny strokes—a small but intimate gesture that set her senses on high alert. It was a powerful, heady feeling that made her feel warm and tingly inside, and—well, safe.

In her estimation, men were a lot like dogs. Some were scraggly puppies, ones who constantly needed their ears scratched, impulsive, who took more than they gave. German shepherds asserted dominance and wanted women at their beck and call, always meeting their needs without question. Occasionally, if you were really unlucky, you'd run into a jealous pit bull who wouldn't think twice about lifting his leg to mark his territory.

Faith gave Geary a sidelong look, sizing him up.

No doubt about it. This one was a golden retriever. Sweet-natured and trustworthy. The kind of dog she'd pick for herself at the pet store.

Not for the first time today, she felt her reservations melting, folding into the comfort of his presence more easily than she would have expected with someone she'd only just met.

"Isn't the sky beautiful?" she asked drowsily, lulled by the gentle rocking of the boat. In the distance, she could hear cicadas singing their strange song from the trees lining the shoreline.

Geary agreed. "Don't know when I've seen a fireworks show like this one." He leaned closer. "I'm thinking maybe it's a signal I ought to make a pass at you."

She couldn't help it. She laughed out loud. "I might not stop you."

A low rumble drew their attention away from the moment. Within seconds, the first flash of lightning streaked across the sky. An audible moan drifted from the nearby crowds. And from Geary.

"Ah, no," he said, obviously upset at the development.

Anyone living in southern Texas was used to sudden and unexpected storms triggered by hot gulf air converging with cooler air fronts coming in from New Mexico. Still, no one wanted this evening to end prematurely. Her especially.

Geary scanned the sky with a deep frown on his face. "This doesn't look good," he said as the wind picked up. "We'd best get ready to go. Looks like we're about to get caught in a storm."

She nodded and moved to gather her bag.

Without further warning, the sky opened up and it poured. Big drops of water coming at a surprising rate threatened to drench everything.

From across the way, an announcer's voice broadcasted over the loudspeaker, advising the conclusion of the fireworks show. Sadly, they'd have to skip the grand finale. The announcer had just finished his remarks when a bolt hit too close for comfort and all the stage lights went dark.

Geary grabbed a light rain jacket from a compartment in the side of the boat and draped it over her head in a near futile attempt to keep her from another good soaking. "C'mon—we'd best get off this lake."

Like hundreds of others scattering across the parking lots to their vehicles, Geary and Faith darted to the news van. They reached their destination just as the rain stopped as suddenly as it had started.

Geary laughed and shook the raincoat, sending water flying. "Uh, sorry," he said with a sheepish grin. "So much for playing the hero."

She smiled back at him, sorry for the evening to end. His hair was dripping wet, sending a stream of water down his forehead and across his cheek. Before he could rub it away, she reached and lightly diverted the rogue moisture from his face. "Guess there's just no staying dry here in Conroe," she teased.

His hand caught hers before she had time to pull it back. He held it there for a couple of brief seconds. "Can I—I mean, I'd like to see you again."

Faith let a timid smile form. "I'd like that too."

"Hey, guys." Chuck came jogging up to the van, soaked as well. "Great night, huh? Too bad the rain ended everything early." He glanced between the two of them. "Oh, sorry. I—I can come back if you want."

Both of them shook their heads. "No, that's not necessary," she told him, aware Geary's deep blue eyes remained focused on her face. She broke eye contact long enough to retrieve a business card from her purse and handed it to him before saying good night.

"I had a great time tonight," she said.

He lifted her card. "I'll call you."

Later when she'd arrived home, she'd no more than unlocked her front door when her cell phone buzzed, alerting she'd received a message.

She pulled the phone from her bag and glanced at the screen. Her face immediately broke into a wide grin.

You've snagged this fisherman's heart. Is tomorrow night too soon to see each other again?

6

Faith whistled as she scooped her morning yogurt and fruit into her blender, happier than she'd been in months. She found herself smiling while driving to work, even when a small accident backed up traffic on the West Loop, nearly making her late for the morning rundown meeting.

While she wrote copy for the feature on the rise in storage and moving theft, her eyes kept drifting to the wall clock. Distracted, she found herself mentally rehearsing last evening in her mind and counting the hours until she'd meet Geary for dinner tonight, behavior reminiscent of her college friends and totally out of character for her.

What had gotten into her?

Even Chuck mentioned the change in her demeanor. "You're looking happy this morning," he said in a low voice as he grabbed a cup of coffee in the lunchroom. "Seems you've *fallen* for someone?" He winked, obviously taken with his own sense of humor.

Normally, she'd have rolled her eyes and brushed off his sappy pun. She'd have told him she was too busy for joking around. Instead she stirred the sweetener into her own coffee and grinned back at him in silence.

She even whistled on her way back to the orange room to check on the Twitter hashtags used for her segment.

This type of distraction was not what she needed right now. She didn't have time to focus on anything except becoming an on-air talent as quickly as possible. Yet here she sat—thinking about a guy who had barely left her mind in the last twenty-four hours.

"Hey, Faith."

She turned her head in the direction of the voice. Cathy Buster, an associate producer, barreled toward her.

"Grab your stuff and c'mon!"

Faith slipped her iPad into her bag, grabbed her lavalier, and followed. "What's going on?"

Cathy answered over her shoulder. "The assignment desk just caught a police scanner reporting a jumper on the Fred Hartman Bridge."

The news of a potential suicide immediately amputated Faith's good mood.

She tossed her half-drunk Styrofoam cup of coffee in a nearby trash receptacle and followed Cathy through the newsroom and down the short hall leading to the back parking lot. "You want me to go out on the field report? Alone?" The minute the words left her mouth, she wished she could gobble them back. "I mean, I—I'm on it."

Cathy waved her over to where the news helicopter was waiting on the helipad. The engine started and the blades overhead slowly turned. "Jack and Ned are already out on that day care fire over on Alabama. I just sent Cara out to cover a robbery. Busy news day. You're all I've got." Cathy ducked her head and ran toward the door of the helicopter. She yelled over top of the whopping rotors, "Just stand there and report what you see." Her hands thrust a lavalier mike into Faith's hands. "Listen for my cues and follow. Got it?"

Faith placed her hand on the door frame, hesitated. "But what about a camera crew?" she shouted over the noise.

"I'll have them right behind you. Now go!"

Faith nodded. She stepped on the flat step mounted above the landing skid and climbed inside, then positioned herself in the passenger seat, sliding her safety earmuffs in place while Cathy fastened her harness. She felt more than heard the belt click into place.

Cathy gave her a thumbs-up and stepped back out of the way. Seconds later, the door slammed closed. The pilot adjusted some dials on a small panel in front of him, then turned and gave her a smile.

The aircraft lifted straight up into the air, sending her heart pounding. She'd never ridden in a helicopter. Directly in front of her, the windscreen extended down and merged into the chin bubble at her legs (that was what she'd learned it was called in her broadcast reporting class), giving her an incredible view of the city beneath, and her stomach a weird sensation.

They flew east over the West Loop Freeway, and minutes later the Reliant Center and Astrodome came into view. Tiny cars pin-dotted the parking lots surrounding the large sports complex.

Her earpiece crackled. "Faith, Cathy here. What's your ETA?"

She looked to the pilot and pointed to her watch. "How long?" she mouthed.

He held up all ten fingers, then gave her a thumbs-down sign.

"Looks like just under ten," she reported back into her lavalier.

When the San Jacinto Bay showed up on the far horizon, Faith took a deep breath. She exhaled slowly.

This was it. Never would a rookie get this kind of a chance again. At least not for a while. For some reason, she'd gotten a lucky break, if you could call it that. But she couldn't make another miscalculation like her lake snafu. She'd have to muster all her training and keep her wits. She'd need focus.

They landed directly on the Fred Hartman Bridge, on top of a strip of highway just past the police blockade. Faith quickly assessed the situation from inside the helicopter.

From the looks of things, law enforcement had not had the area secured long. There was no sign of other news trucks or reporters yet on the scene. KIAM-TV could scoop the story, if she hurried.

She exited the helicopter and ran toward the tangle of police cars with their lights flashing. "Cathy, I'm the only one. We're it."

"Excellent!" The associate producer's voice was filled with cautious excitement. "Now, get up there and position close. We've got a news truck and videographers en route. They'll be there in minutes. In the meantime, use your cell phone and capture what you can and shoot it back to me in an email. I'll throw up whatever you capture, but I want to be first."

"A—a selfie?"

"You can do this," Cathy assured her. "And Faith?"

"Uh-huh?"

"We have word the jumper is Oliver Hildebrand's eighteen-year-old kid."

Faith's heart lurched. That news definitely raised the stakes.

Hildebrand Enterprises, known for its luxury hotels located across America, had been making headlines over the past five years or so by expanding into Dubai, Bali, Singapore, and most recently Jamaica, where Oliver Hildebrand acquired and developed a twenty-three-acre tract of land bordering the famed Negril seven-mile, white-sand beachfront.

"I don't have to tell you what's at stake here," Cathy's voice warned through Faith's earpiece.

The thought of not having a camera crew to back her up niggled in her mind as the helicopter's engine shut down and the door released. Faith scrambled out and rushed forward in the direction of the flashing lights. She took full advantage of the early chaos at the scene and flashed her media badge. In a stroke of luck, no one really paid attention and she was able to pass freely onto the bridge and make her way forward, closing the gap between her and the Hildebrand kid.

She could see him now, up ahead.

The young man, who didn't even look fifteen, had climbed on the other side of the railing and was hanging there, his sandy-blond hair blowing slightly in the breeze. Two older men in dark blue Windbreaker jackets with official-looking emblems emblazoned on the shoulders stood nearby, talking to him.

Without giving prior thought, Faith walked directly up to the scene. She gulped and flashed her badge, despite the fact no one seemed to be paying attention, then quickly slapped it back in her jacket pocket. "What have we got?"

She half expected to be ordered away from the scene, but surprisingly one of the men glanced at her. "You the lady from Suicide Prevention?"

Surprised at his assumption, she shook her head, half wishing she was. Before she could clarify further that she was with KIAM-TV, the teen shifted closer to the edge.

She held her breath. Her gut squeezed.

The man quickly waved her closer. "The kid's name is Brandon Hildebrand."

Taking the officer's cue, she stepped forward, dangerously close to the edge herself. "Hey, I'm Faith," she said, her voice wavering.

The kid shook his head. "No! Don't come any closer."

The outburst caused her to take a step back. She held up her hand. "I'm not here to talk you out of anything."

Both the men turned their heads in her direction, frowning.

She nodded, assuring them she wasn't nuts. They didn't know, but she was no novice at talking a person off the so-called ledge. "I'm with KIAM-TV. I'm a reporter." She held her breath, half scared he'd jump, despite her appearance of bravado. "Your name is Brandon?"

The kid nodded, his eyes shadowed with despair. "Yeah, so?"

Overhead, she could hear approaching helicopters. No doubt other news crews were arriving on the scene. She could sense more than see the crowd building at the police barricade. She'd lucked out and been given extraordinary access, perhaps because she'd been mistaken by some as being affiliated with Suicide Prevention. Didn't matter. Cathy would say she'd been given a lucky break and tell her to run with it. And she would—later.

Right now there was a young kid who might end his life with one slip of his fingers from the rail. A quick image of his family formed in her mind, of the despair she knew they'd feel if that happened.

She made determined eye contact. "So, I was thinking you might want to tell your story before . . ." She let her words drift off, not wanting to acknowledge his intentions or encourage him in any manner. At that moment, she'd give anything to reach out and take his arm and pull him to safety.

"What's your story, Brandon? What do you want people to know?" She looked at him more intensely, aware the network's cameraman now stood only yards away with his lens pointed in their direction. "You have time. Tell us."

He dropped his head. She could see him take a deep breath. In a voice almost inaudible, he responded, "I'm so tired."

She inched closer, aware the officers were watching. One looked to even be praying. "What's making you so tired, Brandon?"

He raised his head slowly. "Ever feel like no matter what you do, it's just never enough?"

She gave him a weak smile. "Yeah, I know that feeling far too well." And she did. No one knew the performance trap more, the need to show the world your value. "I get tired too sometimes."

She saw it then. That tiny glimmer in his eyes that said she'd made a connection. Even if only a small one.

"Sometimes the pressure to do everything people want you to do, and do it well, gets to be a real pain. Worse? Sometimes that pressure is from inside. Yeah, I know exactly where you're coming from."

A flash of anger crossed his features. "Do you know what it's like to be me? To be the Hildebrands' kid? To constantly be told that it'll all be yours someday and you need to step up and get ready? Study harder. Work more. Go to the right schools. Hang with the right people. I'm sick of it. All of it." He turned then and looked down at the water.

Faith could hear the officers gasp. Her heart pounded inside her chest. "So, when it's all yours you can set up a trust and give it all away. You can make a difference. More, you can shed the responsibility if you want, and walk away. Have any kind of life you want." She dared to approach. "Brandon, no one gets to tell you what life you will live. No matter who your family is or what expectations are forced upon you because of their actions—you alone get to choose your own destiny."

Hadn't she done that very thing? Hadn't she made a decision to distance herself from her own beginning and leave all that garbage behind?

"*You* get to choose, Brandon," Faith repeated. "No one else. You."

His eyes pooled with tears. She could tell he wanted to believe her.

A boat circled below. Perhaps the Coast Guard or police. A voice blared from a loudspeaker. "Brandon. This is your father. Don't do it, son. Please, don't."

The kid looked at her then. Faith reached out her hand. "You can stop all of it without this—and rest. It's your life. No one else's."

Brandon Hildebrand shifted his body.

Faith scrunched her eyes closed. If he let go, she couldn't bear to know.

She heard a scuffle and forced herself to look.

His arms were clutching the railing. The two officers scrambled forward and grabbed him. As they quickly hauled him over the railing, a faint cheer rang out from the crowd that had gathered in the distance.

Only then did Faith let out the breath she hadn't realized she'd been holding.

Minutes later, she handed off her cell phone to the crew. While they did their technical magic to download the footage she'd recorded, she let herself bask in the fact the kid was now safe.

A reporter from a competitor station thrust a microphone in her direction. "How does it feel to be a hero?"

Over the course of the next hours, she told the story over and over, each time recounting how she'd carefully constructed a connection with the potential jumper, how she'd communicated with him on an emotional level and ultimately saved his life. What she didn't reveal is just how scared she'd been inside, knowing from experience how things could've taken a nasty turn and ended much differently.

Back at the station, champagne was uncorked and the entire news team broke into applause. In a fortunate twist of events, Faith found herself smack-dab in the middle of the spotlight, and she wasn't going to lie—it felt good.

KIAM-TV had scooped the story, and word was coming into the station that everyone in Houston was talking about the young field reporter who had saved the day—literally. They'd cluster this report for days, milk every opportunity. She almost felt sorry for their competitor stations that would be forced to endure their rankings sliding into the toilet, while KIAM-TV ratings soared. This was the human interest story of the summer, and viewers would tune in to hear every detail.

Later that evening, the station's general manager ordered in dinner, catered by the swanky restaurant Que Huong, known for their Blue Nile cuisine. "Nothing too good for this occasion," he bragged after promising Faith that she would be going places at the station, and very soon. No doubt he knew she was probably already getting messages from other GMs, offering the moon if she'd move and let her rising star shine over at their stations.

Wait—her phone.

She quickly wiped her mouth with a napkin, then turned to the video engineer she'd passed her phone to earlier. "Do you have my cell?"

"Oh yeah—sorry!" He set his champagne flute on the desk and headed for the control room. Seconds later, he returned with her phone in hand.

She was laughing at one of their technical coordinators mimicking their competitor station. Like the cantankerous junkyard dealer on the syndicated television show *Sanford and Son*, he simulated a heart attack, accentuated by clutching his chest and crying out, "Oh, this is the big one, Elizabeth! Our ratings are plummeting and I'm coming to join you, honey!"

Still giggling, she took the cell phone from the video engineer and thanked him, then pressed the button on top to turn the unit back on.

Immediately, messages appeared, alerting she'd missed dozens of voice calls and texts. Her fingers scrolled briefly through the alerts. Suddenly, she stopped at a series of texts.

Hey, I'm here.

Don't know what happened. Tried to call you. I'll wait a little while longer. Call me.

Then finally . . .

Well, I'm heading home. Catch you later.

Oh no! She'd completely forgotten her date with Geary Marin.

Faith quickly made her way out of the newsroom and away from the big celebration. She could have at least texted her new friend that she'd been held up. Maybe not before the scene at the bridge. But certainly she should have made time after.

What he must think of her now!

Her thumb pressed the callback button.

At the same time, she mentally formulated an explanation she hoped Geary would understand.

7

Faith nervously tapped her thumb against the steering wheel as she exited off I-10 and merged onto the North Freeway. As she entered the outskirts of the Woodlands, her mind sifted through a dozen things she needed to say to her new blue-eyed friend when she saw him. None she hadn't expressed at least once over the past forty-eight hours, either verbally or by text.

She needed Geary to understand how neglecting to call him when her plans had changed could happen, to forgive her thoughtless oversight. Caught up in the aftermath of the big scoop, she'd completely pushed everything else from her mind.

"Hey, don't worry about it, Faith. I totally get it," he'd assured her on the phone. "Look, I'll let you make it up to me. My family is having their annual crawfish feed out at their place this weekend. Why don't you join us?"

The idea of a crawfish anything didn't really tickle her toes. And meeting his family felt—well, entirely too early. I mean, they hadn't even had a real date yet. But what could she do after leaving him hanging, wondering why she hadn't shown up? Turn him down?

For a quick second she considered talking him into a nice quiet dinner downtown instead—maybe at The Lake House on the south shore of Kinder. In the end, she simply swallowed her reservations and accepted his invitation.

The road leading to the address Geary provided was off Highway 105, several miles west of the marina in Conroe where they became acquainted. He'd offered to meet her at Sam's Boat House and guide her out to his parents' house, but she'd quickly assured him that wasn't necessary. Her GPS would get her there.

Now she was having second thoughts about that decision.

She glanced at the screen on her phone. Lake Pine Road was just ahead. According to Geary's directions, the turnoff to his family's house would be on the right, four miles from the highway.

From Lake Pine Road, she wheeled onto an unmarked paved road lined by a white farmhouse-style fence, a lovely lane shaded by loblolly pines and red oaks that extended about a half mile before finally opening into a large area filled with vehicles.

She wedged her car into a space between a small red SUV and a Dodge pickup with massive wheel wells. Upon climbing out, she could hear music coming from the back of the house. A song by the Dixie Chicks, she thought.

This was no small party she'd agreed to attend.

She glanced down at her wedge sandals, a little splurge to go with her tangerine-colored tunic and white capris. She wasn't entirely sure she'd dressed appropriately for a crawfish feed, but she looked cute. That was what mattered.

The house was two stories, the lower made of brick and the upper of white clapboard with black shutters and dormers. The front wraparound porch was lined with neatly trimmed low hedges and sported several rocking chairs, the kind she'd often seen for sale at Cracker Barrel restaurants. On either side of a red door, pots filled with pretty pink vinca and multi-hued purslane gave the house a welcoming feeling.

More cars were pulling in now. She crossed to the winding sidewalk that led to the front porch, taking in the rural feel of the place.

Before she had a chance to knock, the red door swung open and Geary stepped out. "There you are," he said over the commotion inside. Dressed in jeans and a blue polo that matched the shade of his eyes, he leaned in and gently brushed her cheek with a kiss, then guided her into a large yet unassuming foyer. "Glad you could come," he said, smiling generously in her direction.

In the large open living area, sofas with crocheted afghans folded over the backs and upholstered recliners with terry washcloths placed to protect the arms were scattered across oak floors. Small pockets of people stood chatting around colonial-style coffee tables filled with bowls of cheese puffs, pretzels, and chips.

Her eyes were immediately drawn outside the windows, to an expansive lawn filled with pop-up awnings and more people in lawn chairs. "Wow, this is some party."

He grinned. "Yeah, Mom knows how to throw a shindig. Everybody looks forward to her annual crawfish boil."

Faith followed Geary to the door leading to the back deck. "Well," she admitted, "this is my first."

He stopped and turned to face her. "Ha, a crawdad newbie? Well, you're in for a treat." His blue eyes twinkled. He grabbed her hand and pulled her across the deck.

"Hey, everybody," he shouted across the crowd. "This is my friend Faith. Y'all might've seen her earlier in the week on the news. That big story about the kid on the bridge."

A buxom woman with dark auburn hair and wearing red canvas shoes and jeans slid a glass pitcher of sweet tea onto a long table covered in brown paper. She quickly wiped her hands on her apron and rushed over, arms extended.

"So, you're Faith." The woman hugged her. "I'm Geary's mother. Welcome to our little party." She waved over a man standing with a hose in his hand, running water into a huge white cooler. He passed off the hose to a guy standing next to him.

After wiping his hands on his camouflage printed apron, he

extended his palm for a handshake. "Welcome to the annual Marin Family Crawfish Feed. We're all so happy you agreed to join us."

Geary's father eerily resembled the actor Craig T. Nelson. He even raised his eyebrows slightly when talking. "I'm Geary's dad."

Faith took his hand. "So nice to meet you, Mr. Marin."

"Nope. Not Mr. Marin—I go by Dad, Grandpa, honey, or Wendell. Take your pick." He placed his arm around Geary's mother. "And this here is Veta, my pretty bride."

Beaming, Geary's mother gave his shoulder a playful slap. "Oh, you! You'd best get over and get some more pots going." She turned to Faith. "And he's right, no one calls us Mr. and Mrs. around here."

Mrs. Marin—er, Veta—took Faith's arm and guided her across the lawn, with Geary following close behind. "Dilly!" She waved over a pretty young woman with long red hair. "Dilly, this is Geary's new friend. We watched Faith on television earlier this week, remember?"

The woman hoisted a toddler onto her hip. "You bet I remember. Hi—I'm Geary's sister."

"Younger by twenty-four months," his mom added. "And this one"—she chucked the little boy's chin—"this is Sam."

The tiny brown-haired guy plugged his mouth with his thumb and nestled against his mother's chest, looking back at Faith with reservation. "He's shy," Dilly explained, then pointed across the lawn to two slightly older children, a boy and a girl. One was chasing the other, holding what must be a crawdad. "Those are the twins, Gunner and Gabby—short for Gabrielle. They just turned five last week."

A short guy stepped up next to Dilly. "Hey there. I'm Bobby Lee." He shook Faith's hand. "I'm the ringleader of the Sitterle family circus." His dark brown hair had that uncombed look and he sported some serious stubble. He wore an AmWest Drilling T-shirt, jeans, and flip-flops—one with the toe piece taped. "Nice to meet you," he said, his warm smile overriding the impression his appearance made.

For the next half hour, Geary introduced her to guests. Often his mother would be within earshot and add, "She's the news reporter girl he's seeing. You know, the one I told you about."

There were nods then, and murmurs of admiration for how she'd handled the bridge incident. "You saved that Hildebrand kid, you know," one woman claimed. "We were all praying as we watched on television."

The proud smile on Geary's face made her feel warm inside, especially after that initial reporting fiasco he'd seen on the boat. She *had* done a good job on the bridge piece. The public had noticed and her journalistic career would benefit.

Geary took her elbow. "C'mon. Let's go supervise Dad. He's about ready to add the crawfish to the pots."

She'd never eaten a crawfish before, which would surprise some, given she'd been born and raised about an hour or so from the Louisiana border.

She remembered her father bringing a small sack of the crustaceans home once, but her mother squelched the idea. "We don't eat those nasty things," she said, sliding the bag from the counter.

At the time, she'd thought her mother's attitude harsh. Especially given the deflated look on her father's face as he watched his wife toss the bag in the garbage. But now, looking down into a large white cooler teeming with a mass of hard-shelled bodies clicking against one another as they tried to escape by climbing the sides, she wasn't so sure her own attitude didn't line up with her mother's.

"What's the matter?" Geary teased.

She scrunched her nose and lowered her voice. "Uh . . . they're kind of creepy, don't you think?"

"Nonsense!" His dad gave her a hearty pat on the back. "Follow me," he said, unaware he'd given her a start. He led her to where five massive stainless steel pots were steaming over open-flame cookers. He lifted the lid of the first pot and invited her to check out the contents. Inside, corn, red potatoes, and onions simmered in a broth. "Now, that is good eating about to happen."

"Wow." She pasted on an enthusiastic smile she hoped looked authentic.

"Stand back, now." Wendell picked up a bucket and scooped the live crawfish out from the cooler and slid them into the boiling mixture.

She couldn't help but squeeze her eyes shut.

Geary chuckled. "What's the matter? You a bit squeamish?"

"A little," she admitted. She smiled back at his dad and tried to avert further critique. "Is that garlic I smell?"

"Sure is. And lemons too." Wendell tossed in some cut-up sausages and whole mushrooms, then slid the lids on tight. "And there's a secret in there too."

"Dad," Geary scolded.

Veta marched up and playfully slapped her husband with a tea towel. "Oh, cut it out, Wendell." She leaned over to Faith. "That man used to tell all the kids he spit in the pots for special flavor."

Faith swallowed, hoping that whole thing was indeed a joke.

Suddenly, she was bumped from behind. A set of little arms wrapped around her legs. Just as quickly, they let go. "Hey, Papa! Did you spit in the pot?"

"Yeah," a similar voice said. "Did you put in the secret ingredient?"

"Okay, you two." Geary moved the twins back. But not before the little girl who had grabbed Faith's legs left a mark on her white capris—something red and sticky.

Geary's mom frowned. "Oh, honey. I'm so sorry. Let me get something for that."

Later, when everyone gathered and the pots of food were poured out on the brown butcher paper covering the tables, Faith made sure she and Geary were not at the same table as his niece and nephew. Admittedly, she didn't know much about kids, and they were cute and all, but those two were like noisy motorboats constantly idling on high.

Before eating, Wendell blessed the food. Shortly after, she learned Geary's dad was pastor of Lake Pine Community Church, a small congregation of people who met in a building located just miles away. She remembered passing the church property, a building that looked like a warehouse of sorts, with an inviting entry and a steeple and cross on top.

She wasn't sure what to think about all that. Sure, she believed in God and everything, but the whole religious thing wasn't exactly big in her family while she was growing up. When she most needed them, the miracles she'd read about never came, leaving her to wonder if God just wasn't that into her.

Regardless, the miracle she most needed at this particular moment was to not embarrass herself entirely while learning to eat these things.

She leaned over to Geary and whispered, "Where's the plates?"

He grinned. "No plates. Just scoop some from the pile in front of you and eat right off the paper."

She slowly nodded. "Oh—okay."

Geary scooped a crawfish from the pile. The little freshwater crustacean resembled a miniature lobster. "Here, like this."

She watched, aware people all around were taking in the scene. As a crawfish newbie, no doubt she was the source of afternoon entertainment.

Geary's sister stood and leaned over the table. She picked through the mound of food and took one of the larger crawfish off the pile. "If you find one and the tail isn't curled, toss it. That means the crawfish was dead when cooked, and you won't want to eat that one."

Faith nodded weakly and thanked her for the warning, then turned her full attention back to Geary.

"Grab between the thorax and the head, pinch and twist. Peel the first layer of the shell back. See?" He proudly showed off a piece of white meat sticking out from the shell.

Wendell tucked a paper towel in his shirt like a bib. "Ignore that yellow stuff inside. Just stick the thing in your mouth and go for it."

Faith felt her stomach go queasy. Wanting to make a good impression, she took the offered crawfish from Geary. She swallowed her nerves—and her reservations—and tentatively pinched and twisted as she was shown. Then she drew the tiny shelled piece to her mouth.

"Now squeeze the tail and suck," Geary told her.

She followed his instruction and the dab of meat launched into her mouth. She closed her eyes and chewed.

The flavor was unfamiliar at best, and a little bit sweet. She couldn't say she disliked the delicacy. She might even learn to love—well, like—the fare that was so embraced in the southern states. And by the people around this table.

She remembered her father, rest his soul, and how he'd been robbed of this eating adventure.

Here's to you, Dad, she thought, and reached for another crawfish.

Faith ate crawfish, red potatoes, corn, and sausage—all spiced with Cajun seasoning—until she thought her stomach would pop. So when Veta Marin set an enormous bowl of peach cobbler with a scoop of Blue Bell vanilla bean ice cream mounded on top in front of her, she tried to decline.

"No peach cobbler? Oh, c'mon." His mom held out a spoon, her eyes hopeful.

Faith let out an overstuffed sigh, knowing there was little way to politely decline. She smiled and took the spoon his mother held out.

As soon as she'd taken a big bite, Geary's mother wiped her hands together and stepped away in satisfaction. Geary leaned over and placed his hand on Faith's arm. "Don't feel bad. She gets all of us like that."

Across the table, Wendell grinned and nodded in agreement. "No one can say no to my wife, especially when she's armed with her famous peach cobbler."

When the crowd at the tables dissipated and Faith noticed her hosts were beginning to clean up, she rose from the table and offered to help. Veta waved her off. "No ma'am, you're our guest." She grabbed her son's arm. "But you, son, are not."

Geary's head bent back and he laughed. "Sure thing, Mom." He turned to Faith. "I'll only be a minute."

Across the lawn, Gabby chased Gunner with the hose. "I'm telling," the little boy hollered at his laughing tormenter.

"So, *you're* Geary's new friend."

Faith turned, sizing up the woman before her. "Yes—uh, I suppose," she responded carefully. The size 4 wore tight jeans and a carelessly low-cut peasant blouse, her shoulder-length hair dark. The color of coffee, without cream and sugar—dark and intense.

The same could be said for the gal's expression. She arched her finely tweezed brows. "Are you enjoying the Marins' little party?"

"I am." Faith's gaze darted around the lawn, looking for any sign of Geary.

"He's helping his mama with the dishes." The woman pursed her garnet lips and extended a hand, showing off manicured nails to match. "I'm Stacy Brien."

Faith shook the young woman's hand.

Bobby Lee stepped forward and joined them, rubbing at his eyes with the heels of his hands. "Man, there's something blooming out here that's really getting to me."

Stacy smirked. "Bobby Lee."

"Stacy." Bobby Lee dropped his hands. "Hey, did you know somebody nicked your car door out in the parking lot?"

Immediate alarm spread across the gal's overly made-up features. "My Jag?"

He cocked his head. "Is your Jag silver?"

Stacy let out an expletive. "Rednecks. They never learn to park right." Without bothering to say goodbye, she turned her well-shaped torso and faded into the crowd.

"Wow." Faith couldn't think of anything else to say. Well, that wasn't necessarily the truth. She could think of a lot to say, none of the pondered phrases necessarily polite.

"Be careful of that one," Bobby Lee warned.

Faith frowned, even though relief flooded her. Bobby Lee had just confirmed he felt similar distrust for the woman she'd only barely met. "What's her deal? I mean, if you don't mind me asking?"

Bobby Lee's face took on a conspiratorial expression. He leaned forward. "She views you as, uh, the competition."

"For Geary?" She stared at him, the thought incredulous. "Did he? I mean, were they—?"

Bobby Lee shook his head. "Naw, Stacy Brien ain't Geary's type."

His statement was both a relief and a little bit disconcerting. Why would the Marins invite someone like her to their party?

As if reading her mind, Bobby Lee pulled a toothpick from his T-shirt pocket and scraped at his bottom front teeth. "Her family owns one of those big places on the lake. They go to Lake Pine Community."

"Ah, I see." But she didn't. Not really.

"Generous contributors, I suspect." He flicked the toothpick on the grass. "Wendell and Veta aren't like that. They just love on people, you know? But they've been around the block a time or two. They snub Stacy in any way, and the evil one will make good use of that."

Faith suddenly wanted nothing more than to find Geary. Bobby Lee seemed to sense that too. "C'mon, follow me," he said and led her inside to the kitchen.

Geary was at the sink wiping a pot with a tea towel, his back facing the doorway. His niece was parked on the counter next to him, her legs swinging. The little girl wiped at her forehead with her arm. "That lady is so pretty."

Geary set the pot down, unaware Faith stood within hearing distance. "Who's so pretty?"

"That lady you brung."

"Brought," he corrected. "And I think so too."

Bobby Lee patted Faith's shoulder and walked away, leaving her to eavesdrop.

Geary wiped the counter down. "I'm pretty sure Faith is pretty on the inside too."

The little girl stopped swinging her legs. Her voice grew serious. "I bet you she's a princess, Uncle Geary."

"Yeah?" he asked, egging her on. "You think I have any chance of being her Prince Charming?"

"What if she doesn't want a prince?" she challenged.

Faith brought her hand to her mouth, stifling a chuckle.

Geary placed his hands on each of his niece's knees and looked her in the eyes. "Oh, but every girl deserves to be cherished." He tweaked her nose.

He noticed Faith then, standing in the doorway. Their eyes met and he grinned. "Sometimes even smart, hardworking, and amazing girls like Faith want to feel special."

8

Within weeks of her report from the bridge, Faith was promoted to weekend anchor. She celebrated the boost to her career by inviting Geary to dinner. This time, her treat.

Typically, reservations at the popular Sky Bar Steak and Sushi needed to be made days ahead, but in a stroke of major good luck, there'd been a cancellation minutes before Faith called.

She couldn't wait to introduce Geary to her favorite restaurant on Galveston Island, a short forty-five minutes from downtown Houston where Faith often spent days off wandering Old Galveston Square, the Strand District, or sometimes the lobby of the historic Hotel Galvez, the grand dame of all island hotels.

It was there her dad took her to the gift shop as a child and bought her a necklace with an anchor charm. Last year she'd scraped some money together and had the anchor plated in gold and placed on a gold chain. Perhaps in some weird way, he'd unknowingly sensed who she was destined to become.

Geary rubbed at his chin. "Sorry, I'm not sure I can stomach raw fish."

Faith looked across the table and grinned. "Oh, c'mon, Geary. A little sashimi isn't going to kill you! Besides, I watched defenseless live crawfish get dumped into boiling water, and then I learned to squeeze their heads off and eat their insides. So buck up, Prince Charming."

He shook his head. "Huh-uh. Nope. Mr. Charming likes his fish baked, boiled, or breaded and fried crisp, with lots of tartar sauce."

She tapped the edge of his plate with her chopsticks. "Fine. You can eat your sirloin," she said. "But first, at least try one of my California rolls. Nothing raw inside."

He still appeared skeptical. "Okay, but just for you." Having already given up on chopsticks, he stabbed the piece of sushi roll with a fork and examined it carefully before dipping the rice and cooked crab rolled with nori into a bowl of wasabi and soy sauce.

He popped the roll into his mouth and chewed, barely able to disguise his hesitancy. The way he grimaced before swallowing made her laugh again.

Geary Marin had many qualities she adored. First, there were those eyes. Stark blue and bottomless, complex even from across a room. He stood taller than most men she'd dated and wore his thick dark hair in a casual short cut. Not like the carefully tended styles most of the male anchors wore down at the station.

She loved the way his broad shoulders looked in a white button-down rolled up at the sleeves and that he wore plain old Wranglers. His hands were large and slightly calloused and he walked with determination, like a man who didn't have a thing to prove to anybody. Never had she met anyone more genuine, more warm-spirited and open.

A strange thing happened to her when she was with Geary Marin. She forgot to be self-conscious and nervous, and she found herself laughing breezily, countering his light banter with clever, witty comebacks so atypical for her.

They could talk for hours on the phone, sometimes into the wee hours of the morning—even when she had to be at the station early.

She loved how his face lit up when he saw her. Loved how he intertwined his fingers with hers when they walked.

Faith hated to admit it, but she'd secretly enjoyed the envy in Stacy Brien's eyes that day on the Marins' lawn. No doubt Geary Marin was a catch, and she'd been the lucky one to lure him in.

Using her chopsticks, she reached for some seaweed salad. "Tell me more about your fishing."

"What do you want to know?"

"Obviously, you must be pretty good to make a living at something so competitive," she prompted.

"Yeah, I've got to admit fishing is a pretty good gig. The tournaments can get intense, and sometimes the monetary benefit gets a bit spotty. But there's nothing like being on the lake with a rod in your hand as the sun breaks over the horizon."

She thought about his nice place. "But you must do well at it."

His sizzling steak got delivered to the table then. She waited until the server was gone before using her chopsticks to lift a piece of calamari from her plate.

Her hand paused midair. "So how do you do it? What's the secret to snagging the big one?" She popped the calamari into her mouth and chewed, waiting for him to answer.

He leaned back in his chair. "Ha, that's the big question. A question with a lot of answers, depending on who it is you're talking to. Bass are ambush predators. On bright-bluebird sunny days the fish hold tight to cover, stumps, shady areas, and ditches. The strike zone gets smaller because they won't chase. When clouds, wind, and low light strike, the zone expands. Bass are intelligent fish—and extremely difficult to catch, really. Rarely happens by accident."

"If catching bass is so hard, why do you love it so?"

"For me, it's the lack of proven method that intrigues me the most. I can find a spot where I know the habitat is there under the surface, I can select the perfect lure, the right test line on the best rod, and use the finest reel—still, nothing guarantees success." He took a sip of his water, watching her. "Maybe that's it—the thing that draws me to fishing for the big ones."

"What's that?" she asked.

"I can use my best equipment and skill, but most times success comes from outside myself. The sport is definitely a solo act, yet it's as if I'm partnering with some unseen hand—maybe God, I don't know. Makes the big catch all the sweeter when it happens."

She didn't quite understand his logic but nodded just the same. He reached across the table and covered her free hand with his own. "So why the news?"

"Huh? Oh, I've wanted to be a journalist since as long as I can remember. On Sunday nights growing up, I'd wrap up in a blanket on the sofa to watch *Lois & Clark: The New Adventures of Superman*. I loved watching Teri Hatcher portray Lois Lane, the feisty, shiny-haired news reporter who was always seeking the truth. No doubt, I knew that was exactly what I wanted to do. In high school, I mustered the guts to send an email to the editor of Baytown's local newspaper. I told her I wanted to be a journalist and that I'd do anything to work for her newspaper, even cleaning the floors, making coffee, or doing filing. A few days later, she called me and said she needed someone to do write-ups on the local high school football games. I was elated. As far as I was concerned, it was my big break! I knew nothing about the game. But I learned. And somehow I eked out an article each week, with play-by-plays of the game."

She noticed how intently he watched her, and continued. "When I began attending the University of Houston, I was a writer for the student newspaper, the *Daily Cougar*. One day the director took me aside and told me I'd be perfect for KUH-TV—the first public television station in the United States, owned by the University of Houston System. I was all ears. Of course, I wanted to be considered for their relief anchor. The day of the audition, I walked around campus like a pack mule because I didn't have time to go back to my dorm before tryouts. I strapped on an extra backpack stuffed with makeup, hairspray, and a curling iron, I carried a pressed button-down shirt on the hanger from class to class, and I scooped my hair into a claw clip on top of my head so I'd have some volume in my hair by the end of the day. I don't remember the audition. But I got the gig!"

Geary laughed with her while cutting his steak. "Then what?"

"Well, during my senior year I interned, which gave me the opportunity to shadow some of Houston's local news anchors, hanging on every word they uttered about their craft and watching them scribble on page after page of yellow notebook paper while out on field reports. I spent my days and nights basically following reporters around and sitting in the back of their live trucks when they'd jet off to stories. And as a college female with my career aspirations, that was the score of a lifetime." She paused and a smile nipped at the corner of her mouth. "As far as I'm concerned, I'm still living the dream."

After dinner, she and Geary stepped outside the restaurant just in time to witness the sun's final show before it dropped from the horizon. The sight caused them both to stop and take in the kaleidoscope of color the sinking sun cast across the Gulf.

Geary squeezed her hand. "Do you need to get home early?"

She shook her head. "Not necessarily. What do you have in mind?"

"C'mon, let's go get some coffee," he said, pulling her toward the crowd of tourists wandering the sidewalk.

At nearby Catalina's coffeehouse, they found a quiet corner and nestled into two overstuffed chairs. He had dark roast, she had tea with a touch of coconut milk. Though still stuffed from dinner, they shared one of the largest cream puffs she'd ever seen.

"My mom makes these." He took a bite that left a touch of powdered sugar clinging to the corners of his mouth.

"She makes cream puffs? Like from scratch?" Her mother could barely pour dry cereal out of a box.

Geary nodded. "And homemade maple bars and glazed donuts."

"Goodness, that's . . . *domestic.*" She dabbed her mouth with a napkin. "Once, my mom decided to cook an elaborate jambalaya dish after she'd watched Emeril's cooking show on television." The minute she mentioned the fact, she wished she hadn't let her guard down.

"Yeah?" he said, reaching for his coffee mug.

Faith looked down at her lap, silently scolding herself. She tried to whisk away stray powdered sugar that had landed on her black slacks. The effort left a gray spot she covered with her napkin.

"Tell me about it," he urged. He took a long sip of his coffee and watched her over the rim of his mug, seeming to sense her sudden discomfort.

Despite his inviting tone, she wasn't ready to fully give in to her blunder.

His eyes grew soft and thoughtful as she considered how to respond. Finally, she took a deep breath and proceeded with a sanitized version.

Her mother had tuned the radio to a jazz station and went to work in their kitchen, carefully measuring the ingredients. Earlier in the afternoon, after that cooking show had aired, she'd grabbed her wallet and raced to H-E-B, yelling over her shoulder for Faith to watch her little brother. That she'd be right back.

She returned two hours later with bags filled with the needed ingredients, including a five-pound bag of onions, dozens of bell peppers and tomatoes, and a large box of Minute Rice. "She made enough jambalaya to feed seven families," Faith remarked, trying to make her voice light.

She didn't tell him her mom had substituted plain hot dogs for andouille sausage and used canned shrimp ("It's absolutely ridiculous what that fancy sausage and shrimp cost!" her mom complained), or how she'd accidently gotten mixed up and purchased a little can of cinnamon instead of paprika, but shrugged at the discovery and decided to use it anyway.

When a bowl was placed in front of her, Faith complained the food tasted *icky*.

Her mother screamed in response, "There are kids in Africa who don't even have food!" She grabbed Faith's plate and scraped it in the sink, then whirled and pointed her glossy red nail back at the table. "Now, you get yourself to bed. We'll see if little Miss High and Mighty appreciates her food a little better by breakfast time."

Sitting next to her at the table, her younger brother, Teddy, grew wide-eyed and quickly shoveled the nasty stuff into his mouth. "I like mine just fine, Mom," he said, his cheeks bloated with the food. "It's good."

Later, he admitted he had to gag the horrible mixture down, but Teddy Jr. would do nearly anything to please their mother.

But there was no need to tell all that.

Gripping her teacup, she let her gaze rest on the soggy leaves floating at the bottom. "My dad used to claim my mother always did everything in bright Technicolor, even back when the world was broadcast in black-and-white."

Geary set his coffee mug down. He reached across the table and took her free hand in his own, his fingers gently stroking hers. "So where are they? Your family."

She struggled to find the right words. "My father died when I was young."

Geary's expression turned concerned. "I'm so sorry."

She shrugged. "Eh, that was a long time ago. You move on—you have to."

"And the rest of your family?" He stirred creamer into his coffee and waited.

Faith swallowed, aware these questions would eventually come. "Well, my mom died too. A couple of years back." Before he could express condolences, she hurried on. "And my brother lives somewhere here in Houston. He's a bit of a loner. I don't see him often."

That was an understatement. She hadn't seen her younger

brother in over two years, not since days after her mother died. She didn't know where he was—or even if he was alive.

Geary Marin was fortunate. He was raised in a loving and fairly stable family. Not so for her. The Biermans had been anything but steady.

"Tell me more about *your* family," she urged, changing the subject.

Geary was lost in thought for a moment. Finally, as if sensing she wasn't going to say anything more, he drew his hand back. "Well, as you know, my dad's a pastor. He and my mom have been married nearly thirty-five years."

"Wow," she said, not bothering to hide her surprise. "Thirty-five years is a long time. What does your mom do? For work, I mean."

He folded his napkin. "She's a pastor's wife. That can be a full-time job. And she had me and my sister to raise."

Faith looked across the table, wondering if he knew how lucky he was. "Sounds wonderful."

"Yeah, I've got a great family," he easily conceded. Again, his eyes turned thoughtful, and with a flicker of hesitation he circled the discussion back around. "What did your dad do for a living?"

Without intention, Faith held her breath. If she was her mother, this was where she'd claim her father owned a large recreational vehicle distributorship, when in reality he'd managed an RV lot in Baytown owned by some guy who'd made his real money in oil. She'd describe their tiny house located in a subdivision backing up to a smelly marsh in Baytown as a comfortable ranch with a water view.

But Faith had already determined long ago she never wanted to be like her mother.

She stared down, fingered her spoon, and let the truth spill. "He was a blue-collar worker of sorts, managed an RV dealership. My folks didn't last as long as yours. Their marriage, I mean." Taking a deep breath, she decided to come clean. At least in part.

"Seems my father had a love for bourbon—and other women, or at least that's what my mom claimed. They were in the middle of a nasty divorce when he died in a car accident, inebriated and with a twenty-three-year-old blonde in the car. I was nine."

In the few times Faith had ventured to tell her dark family secret, this is where the person would look at her in pity.

Geary didn't.

Instead he simply nodded and gazed across the table at her with incredible tenderness, a look that held no judgment. A look that wrapped her emotions around him even more. "That's rough," he acknowledged. He leaned forward, placing his forearms on the table. "Any other siblings?"

"No, only Teddy Jr. Four years younger." She just wasn't ready to tell him the rest.

"Your mom ever remarry?"

"No, she saw a few men over the years. Some got serious. But—" She hesitated. "But nothing worked out."

Thankfully, the young woman from behind the counter approached their table, interrupting the conversation before he could make further inquiry into things she'd just as soon not talk about.

"You want some refills?" the woman asked.

Geary held his hand over his mug. "None for me, thanks."

She shook her head. "No, thank you. It's getting pretty late."

She was relieved when Geary picked up on her cue and glanced at his watch. "Well, hey. I know you probably need to get up early. But I'd like to show you something before I take you home."

Minutes later, he drove them the short distance to Seawall Boulevard and into a parking lot still heavily dotted with parked cars.

She looked across at the popular tourist destination, Pleasure Pier. "Uh, I don't do Ferris wheels. Or roller coasters."

He grinned. "No rides." His hand slipped into hers. "C'mon, I want to show you something."

"Where are we going?"

They crossed the street. Instead of heading for the bright lights and tangled crowds, he led her to the sandy waterfront. "Follow me."

Her curiosity was piqued now. "Geary Marin, you're crazy. Where are we heading?"

Abruptly, he stopped and bent over. In the light cast from the line of streetlights, he untied his tennis shoes and fastened the laces together, then flung the tethered shoes around his neck. "Here, give me yours."

"My shoes?"

"Yeah, give me your shoes." He held out his hand, waiting for her to comply.

She scowled and did as he asked. After passing off her sandals, she ventured to ask again, "What are you up to?"

"Come with me." He grinned and pulled her along. The tide was out, leaving a shoreline of wet sand, the cool feel against her bare feet a huge contrast to the dry sand still warm from the day's sun.

Geary ducked around the underpinnings of the pier and dodged a massive piling. Faith followed close behind, wrinkling her nose at the pungent tar aroma painted on the pylons in order to protect the wood from decaying under the salty water.

Above her head in the shadows, several birds cooed to signal that the human presence had interrupted their nighttime sanctuary. She could only hope one of them wouldn't reciprocate by dropping a surprise onto her hair.

"Okay, here." Geary stopped, breathless, a wide grin on his face.

She frowned. "We're where? Under the pier?"

He chuckled and pointed. "Look."

Her gaze followed his finger. It was hard to see in the dim shadows. She stepped a little to the left, allowing light to illuminate where he pointed.

One of the larger pylons had been wrapped with fencing, the kind made of thin galvanized wire welded together to make chicken wire. On the fencing were hundreds of padlocks. The locks were of all sizes, in many colors. Some had writing on them, which were actually inscriptions—many faded by the water, but a lot of them still discernable.

She leaned closer to take it all in. "Wow. What is this?"

He folded his arms, looking pleased that she was intrigued. "There is a bridge in Paris, France, known as the Love Lock Bridge. That's not the real name, but that's what all the locals know it by, and the tourists who encounter the phenomenon in their travels. I saw it when spending a few days in Paris with some buddies on a layover from a mission trip to Romania the summer after our junior year in high school."

She looked at him, puzzled. "I'm not sure I get it."

"Lovers worldwide leave a token of their commitment to one another by attaching a padlock onto the fence lining the bridge, and then throwing away the key into the water below. The idea quickly caught on and these types of love lock fences started popping up all over." He stepped closer and fingered a couple of the locks attached. "When we got back, me and my friends decided to start one here."

She raised her eyebrows. "You did this?"

He grinned. "Well, yeah—a long time ago. We put the fence up and a bunch of friends from high school attached the first locks. Not all of them represent romantic situations." He pointed to one up at the top. "That one's mine. I put it there as a sign of my commitment to Christ and my desire to be a good person."

For some reason, the notion struck her funny. She let out a slight chuckle. "You must have been pretty gung ho fresh off that mission trip."

He laughed. "Yeah, I suppose I was."

"What about all these other locks? I mean, there are so many of them."

She could see Geary's deep blue eyes twinkle, even in the dusk. "I know. Pretty amazing, huh?"

He dug into his jeans pocket and pulled out a small padlock and a black Sharpie pen.

"What—what's that?"

He pulled the cap off the pen and wedged it in his teeth, then drew a heart on the face of the lock. Inside he wrote:

G + F = Forever

The gesture immediately pricked at a deep place in her heart. A bit overwhelmed by the unexpected emotion, she tried to make light of the moment. "I love it, but the inscription is a little junior high, don't you think?" Still, she couldn't help but smile widely. Especially when she thought of how he'd brought along these items with every intention of bringing her down here tonight.

He didn't respond immediately. Instead he pulled a tiny bottle of epoxy from his jeans pocket and painted over the inscription to preserve what he'd written. Then he reached high and found a vacant space on the wire fence. She watched as he attached the lock. When he'd finished, he turned and offered her the key.

"Throw it," he said.

She gave him a puzzled look, her heart pounding.

"Throw it," he repeated. "No matter what is ahead, you have my heart and friendship, Faith Bierman."

With shaking fingers, she slid the miniature key from his palm.

What are you doing? she asked herself.

But despite her reservations, she wanted desperately to give him her heart as well. So she closed her fingers around that little piece of metal, brought her fist to her lips, and kissed it for good luck.

Faith turned and looked into those deep blue eyes. Eyes that held such tenderness and sensitivity. Geary Marin represented a stability she longed for. He was a Prince Charming in every manner.

And she deserved that. Didn't she?

Convinced she did, she took a couple of tentative steps in the direction of the water and held her breath.

Then with wild abandon, she flung her arm and let go.

9

Dark. Stillness.

In the distance, voices from above the waterline invaded, breaking into her deeply immersed twilight. Light broke through in similar manner. Images slowly formed, warbled by water.

"Faith. Faith, can you hear us?"

She should move to the surface. She wanted to.

Lift your arms. Paddle your legs.

Both remained heavily weighted in place.

She tried to lift her eyelids. They fluttered yet seemed glued shut by something unknown.

"Faith, if you hear my voice, lift your fingers."

Her fingers. She let her muffled mind imagine an arm, her arm. The length of it. At the end, her fingers.

She scowled. Concentrated.

Why was all this so hard?

"That's it. That's the way." The voice sounded enthused. "Now the other."

Her mind searched for the other arm. Confused.

Her arm. Yes, the other one. She could find—wait, where?

Panic bloomed.

She needed air. Needed the surface. Needed to get out.

With all the strength she could muster, she fought to break free of the water.

She needed out.

She felt herself lift. Closer. Near the voices.

The voices clarified . . . slightly.

"That's it. There she is. I think she's joining us now."

More commotion. More light. More voices.

She broke through the surface then. Much-needed air flooded her nostrils. Warmth covered her skin. Her muscles, still tense from the strain, could finally relax.

"Faith? Faith, you with us?"

Open your eyes.

She couldn't.

Breathe in. Breathe out . . . Again.

The pain hit.

Crushing in its strength. Blinding in intensity.

Her eyes flew open.

Medical professionals swarmed. They checked machines. They checked her vitals, her pupils.

She groaned when the tiny penlight slashed across her line of vision.

"I think she's awake. She's awake, isn't she?" A vaguely familiar figure rifled his fingers through his dark hair.

A man with gray hair and white at the temples patted her hand. "Yes, good. I think Sleeping Beauty is back with us. At least for now." He leaned over the bed. "Faith, look at me. I'm Dr. Wimberly. Are you in any pain?"

Faith blinked several times. The motion brought a wave of nausea. The ache in her head pounded.

She lifted her chin slowly, then lowered it again, trying to say yes.

"Okay, Faith. We'll give you something to take the edge off. But we want you nice and awake now."

There were more of them now gathering in the room. More activity.

She tried to open her mouth. So dry.

A buxom woman with red hair, wearing a uniform tunic printed in little monkeys, swabbed her mouth with a large Q-tip-looking thing. The cotton was wet and tasted like mint.

"Let's raise her up a bit." Dr. Wimberly motioned to the nurse, who sprang into motion.

Faith heard the grinding sound of a motor and felt her upper torso lift slightly. The room tilted out of focus for the briefest seconds, then clarified with a dull ache that pounded in her head with every heartbeat.

She swallowed against a throat that felt like the skin inside had been rubbed off with sandpaper. "Thirsty," she mouthed.

Dr. Wimberly grinned. "That's a good sign. Let's get her a few cc's of water. Not much. She's still vulnerable to swelling."

While several technicians examined surrounding machines, the nurse placed a straw inside her lips.

Faith sucked, letting the water flow into her parched mouth and throat. She sucked again, much harder this time. And again.

"Whoa, not too much, sweetie," the nurse said and pulled the straw back.

Faith cleared her throat. "Where—" Her voice sounded tinny. She tried again. "Where am I?"

Dr. Wimberly gave her a broad smile. "You're at Memorial Hermann, Faith."

"Hos—pital?" she asked, trying to take in the information. "Was I—an accident?"

The doctor nodded. "Yes. Of sorts."

She closed her eyes, trying to recall.

An accident?

"Faith, we're going to check a few things. Just relax."

Exhausted, she closed her eyes while the medical professionals poked and prodded.

"Faith, do you feel that?"

She let her eyes drift back open, wondering what they meant.

"How about this?"

"Ouch!"

"Okay, that's good." Dr. Wimberly patted her right shoulder, then turned to the others in the crowded room.

While they were talking, she reached forward. The movement took great effort, but she needed to—

Dr. Wimberly turned. His eyes showed concern, then grew soft. "Faith, you have a head injury. We operated on you four days ago." His hand stroked his neatly trimmed white goatee. "Do you remember?"

Frightened and a bit confused, she tried to shake her head. She remembered nothing.

He pulled a chair to the bed and sat. "Faith, I know you're scared. But you are going to be all right. You've been here at Memorial Hermann for four days. You have a brain injury resulting from a trauma that required surgery. Currently, you still have a lot of swelling and fluid buildup, which is likely the medical impetus for the lack of feeling and impairment. But rest assured we have every reason to hope all that will resolve, given time."

She listened wide-eyed to the information. While she understood the words and even the meaning to some small extent, she still couldn't comprehend how she got here. Exhaustion seemed to weigh down her ability to think, and try as she might to focus, her mind seemed to have a life of its own. Despite wanting otherwise, she didn't know how to formulate the myriad of questions pummeling her intuition. There was more, she knew. Additional information not provided.

"I want—when?" Her words faltered, betraying her intentions.

The doctor pushed his chair back and stood. "You're going to be with us awhile, but I promise everyone here is committed to getting you better and back home as quickly as possible."

He turned and walked out of view.

"Why is her skin so yellowed?"

Faith tried to place the familiar voice as the discussion continued from across the room, but her muddled brain wouldn't cooperate.

Finally, the familiar voice faltered. "So what are we looking at, Dr. Wimberly?"

"I'm not going to sugarcoat the situation. The trauma she suffered from the bullet is severe. Her long-term prognosis is hopeful. We are wise to acknowledge miracles."

The bullet?

Even in its broken state, Faith's mind raced. Snippets of images formed.

The blue sky.

People running.

A little boy in a Thomas the Train T-shirt.

"Noooo!" The word broke through her trembling lips without forethought. Tears flooded her eyes and she flailed her right arm wildly. "No!"

Immediately, her bedside was crowded with people in white coats. The woman in the monkey fabric grasped her forearm, pinning it to the bed. "Dr. Wimberly," she hollered with alarm.

"Okay, I entertained the possibility this might be too much too fast. Let's give her some relief." He shouted instructions and the people around her bed went to work. Dr. Wimberly leaned over her and gently said, "Faith. It's going to be all right. You have nothing to fear. We're here to take care of you." He nodded to the nurse who busied herself at Faith's arm. "Time to go night-night."

Her thoughts grew fuzzy, like cream gravy poured over a lump of mashed potatoes.

Then something amazing happened.

The man she'd seen earlier stood near, worry rusting the shine in his eyes.

"Is she—?" He wedged in closer, alarm apparent. "Faith?"

Their eyes connected for the briefest of seconds before fog rolled in and she sank back into the depths of the water.

His hand brushed the side of her face. "I'm here, baby. I'm not leaving you."

She listened to his voice while descending deeper and deeper—her mind locked on those intrepid blue eyes.

10

Faith had never considered herself the kind of woman who yearned for a knight in shining armor to ride into her life on a white horse.

She had her career. And that was certainly going well.

In just under a year, she'd gone from weekend anchor to also filling in on the morning show—*twice*. Her career at the station barreled along ahead of schedule and hinted at a bright future. Certainly, that alone was enough.

But there was something about Geary Marin that caused her to rethink everything—and especially her commitment to a solitary lifestyle.

Whenever a love song played on the radio, she'd taken to turning up the volume instead of switching to a news channel.

After running out of her favorite cologne, she used one of those paper samples tucked inside a magazine. When Geary told her she smelled nice, she frantically scanned the cosmetic counters of three stores until she found the brand and bought a large (and expensive) bottle.

She carried her phone into the bathroom so she could jump out of the shower if he called.

And every night, she drifted to sleep thinking about the times they'd kissed—the way his lips felt against her own, soft at first and then more intense, the way his touch created a gentle need inside her soul.

So when Geary prodded her to go fishing with him and she reeled in her line to find a diamond ring secured at the end, she couldn't help but give in to Prince Charming and his promise to make her life a fairy tale.

Not wanting to wait, they scanned their busy calendars and found an open weekend in April. Geary's schedule allowed for a few weeks between tournaments. And the weather would be perfect, not too hot.

Both she and Geary agreed a small ceremony would be appropriate. She wanted an intimate gathering of family and friends held at one of the many elegant waterfront venues on Lake Conroe. Geary quickly reminded her how hurt his mom and dad would be if they didn't hold the ceremony at Lake Pine Community.

"I don't know, Geary. I don't want our special day to revolve around the church." She didn't confide her real worry. People from the station would be there. Important people who had the power to shape her career. Wendell and Veta could come on a little bit strong. She didn't want a church service disguised as a wedding shoved down people's throats. She'd once attended a ceremony where the pastor officiating touted Scripture for over a half hour before ever turning attention to the couple and their vows.

"My family loves you, Faith. They're all thrilled we're getting married. They just want to share the day with the church family as well."

He was probably right. The Marins had been nothing but gracious and welcoming. Still, she remained adamant she wanted a simple ceremony—something tasteful. She'd compromise to some extent, but she wanted the affair to center around the joining of their lives, not to be a reason for another sermon.

This was her wedding day. And she told Geary so. "There's no question your dad will conduct the ceremony, but just tell him to make sure and tone it down. Okay?"

Geary frowned. "Well, sure. I understand what I think you're saying, but this is my family we're talking about. You have nothing to worry about. And it just wouldn't be right not holding our wedding at Lake Pine."

She wasn't so sure the church members wouldn't push things over the top, but she hated seeing the concern on his face. "Look, you're right. Of course we should get married in your dad's church."

When she folded, he looked relieved. "We'll hold the reception where you like," he offered.

The compromise was one she could accept. No doubt this would be the first of many future times they'd have to meet somewhere in the middle, both giving up a little in order to preserve unity in their relationship. At least that was what many marriage experts touted on the morning news shows. That, and the stack of marriage books on her bedside table with titles like *You Can Be Right (or You Can Be Married)* and *The Seven Principles for Making Marriage Work*.

Her only example, her parents' relationship, wasn't exactly marital bliss. In fact, the verbal assaults they hurled at each other on a regular basis could better be described as a marital war zone.

Her mother in particular sliced her father with emotional bayonets and threw histrionic verbal assaults like bombs. Theirs was a war to win and their tactics lethal, neither willing to make a truce, even when their hellish aggression left her and Teddy Jr. bloodied roadside victims.

She wasn't about to repeat that pillage. If she had to compromise here and there, so be it.

In the end, she was rewarded for making the compromise.

When Oliver Hildebrand got wind she was getting married, he showed up at the station, wanting to personally extend an offer to pay for the entire wedding affair. "And I'm sending you and your guy on a two-week honeymoon. You'll stay in our grandest honeymoon suite at St. Viceroy Negril. My gift," he said.

She'd argued, of course. The sentiment, while appreciated, was entirely too much.

He insisted, and in the end she finally accepted his generous offer.

She couldn't wait to break the news to Geary. They were to spend the evening with his parents out to dinner, with the intention of discussing wedding plans.

She wrapped up at the news desk early and filed the proposed copy for her weekend segment on the opening of a new pet shelter. After leaving the station, she headed out of the city and made the forty-minute drive north.

At Geary's place, she learned they'd be meeting his folks at Wheelers, a little mom-and-pop-type place on the outskirts of town. His dad's favorite, Geary told her.

"I'm starved," Wendell announced as they moved inside the restaurant.

A waitress led them to a table topped with a green-checkered wax cloth and bottles of Heinz ketchup and Tabasco. Geary pulled out one of the mismatched chairs and she took a seat.

"Y'all want menus? Or our buffet?"

Wendell's eyebrows lifted. "What y'all serving tonight, Agnes?"

She pulled the pencil from behind her ear and placed the tip on a tablet she retrieved from her shirt pocket. "Meat loaf and chicken spaghetti."

Geary's dad gave their waitress a wide smile. "We'll all have the buffet," he replied without checking with any of the rest of them.

The waitress slid her tablet back in place. "Alrighty. Plates are over there. Help yourself. Drinks come with—Dr Pepper or sweet tea. Your choice."

Geary must've noted her sour expression. "You want me to get you a plate?"

She shook her head. "No, that's okay."

They stood and moved to take their place in a line of people. Wendell winked at Geary. "This is going to be good. Ben Wheeler makes the best chicken spaghetti." He turned to Veta. "No offense, dear."

When they returned to the table and started eating, Faith decided it was time to tell them the good news. She cleared her throat of the rubbery green beans she'd just sampled. "Uh, I have some great news."

Wendell looked up from his bowl of iceberg lettuce blanketed in thick Thousand Island dressing. "Yeah? What's that?"

She placed her fork on a folded paper napkin. "Well, you remember last year about the same time I met Geary, I was called to the field and reported from the Fred Hartman Bridge."

Veta nodded. "Oh yes. You talked that young man out of jumping. On live television." She nudged her husband. "We still have people in our congregation who mention that. We're so proud of you, honey."

"You did a fine job that day," Wendell added.

She smiled. "Well, when the boy's father, Oliver Hildebrand, heard of our pending nuptials, he offered to pay for our entire wedding." She turned to Geary. "He said the sky is the limit. And he's giving us a complimentary two-week honeymoon at St. Viceroy Negril, his resort in Jamaica. Airfare included."

She paused to let the news sink in. This was like a thousand Christmas presents all rolled into one big package, and she watched Geary's face closely for his reaction.

He rubbed the back of his neck. "Jamaica?"

She brushed past his lack of enthusiasm and clasped her hands. "Yes, in a beautiful honeymoon suite overlooking a bay of turquoise saltwater." She looked over at Veta. "With palm trees and white sand, dolphins, and frozen drinks with little umbrellas!" Faith could barely contain her excitement as she went on. "He offered to pay for a fancy reception and catered sit-down dinner. I thought the clubhouse at the Bentwater Country Club would be perfect."

Veta looked across the table at her son. "But what about the big dinner the Women's Auxiliary had planned?"

Geary shifted uncomfortably. "Uh, about that . . ."

Faith lifted her eyebrows as understanding dawned, squelching her delight. "You haven't told them about our compromise? About what we decided?"

"Told us what?" his mother queried. Her expression looked none too delighted as well.

Wendell quietly laid his fork across his still full plate. "Honey, let's go get some of that lemon meringue pie I'm so fond of."

Veta lifted her chin, thought a minute, then nodded. "Did you see if they have some chocolate cream?"

"I think they do. And if not, Ben usually has cherry pie. You like that."

Geary's parents left the table, leaving their son to face her not-so-hidden ire.

"Okay, what's going on?" she demanded. "You haven't told your parents about what we talked over and decided? That we'll marry at Lake Pine but the reception won't be at the church?"

He rubbed at his stubbled chin. "No. No, I told them we wouldn't be at the church. But I didn't think you meant the women couldn't provide the meal, even if we hold the reception off-site."

She closed her eyes in frustration, trying to collect herself before responding. Finally, she looked back at him. "So let me understand this correctly. We're going to have an elegant sit-down dinner in a country club overlooking the lake and serve—what? Green Jell-O salad and—" She pointed to her plate, her voice rising. "Chicken spaghetti?"

"Faith, don't be mad—"

"Are you kidding me?" She forced her voice lower and urged him to understand. "Listen, Geary, I make my living on television in front of thousands of viewers. My image matters."

His jaw sharpened. "You make us all out to be rednecks."

"I didn't say that. What I meant was—"

He dropped his fork to the table. "Okay, I'm listening."

"Last week, your brother-in-law let loose and passed gas." She paused for emphasis. "At the dinner table."

"Well, yeah—that. But—"

"And he grinned at his children and said, 'Boy, now, that's gonna itch when it dries.'"

He nodded then. "Look, babe, I know my family can be a handful. But they mean well. And they love us and only want to help." Geary reached for her hand. "Please, Faith. Try to understand the position I'm in. Surely we can find a way to—"

Wendell and Veta showed back up at the table then, their hands loaded with plates filled with enormous slices of pie.

Wendell's eyes narrowed. "Everything okay?"

Veta assessed the situation as well. "Look," she said. "Wendell and I think we've come up with a perfect solution. One that will work for everyone. Let's move the wedding ceremony up and hold it at eleven in the morning." She slid back into her chair. Wendell also sat. "We'll let the ladies put on their luncheon immediately after, in the church basement."

Veta glanced at Wendell and he encouraged her on with a nod. "Then that evening we'll have the grand reception you'd hoped for, dear. An affair done up right with all your friends from the studio. The Marin family cleans up pretty well. You'll see. We'll have that party and do it up big, all paid for by that wealthy fan of yours." Geary's mother looked across the table and gave them a hopeful smile.

Faith took a deep breath. Slowly, she nodded. "Yes, okay. That'll work."

Under the table, Geary pulled her hand into his own. "Yeah, that's a great solution."

Veta beamed. "Then we're all set. Now all I have left to know is your wedding colors."

"My colors?" Faith asked.

Her future mother-in-law picked up her fork and scooped a large piece of chocolate pie, leaving it suspended in the air. "Uh-huh. I'm making the deviled eggs for the luncheon and I want to dye the yolk filling to match."

11

On the morning of her wedding, Faith panicked.

Not just a little, but one of those full-blown panic attacks where your heart pounds, sweat sprouts across your forehead, and you can't catch your breath.

What was she thinking?

Faith sat alone in a tiny room in the church, temporarily designated the "bride's room." Her reflection in the mirror confirmed that even the limited amount of time she'd spent shopping for a wedding dress had paid off. The gown, a simple A-line cut in ivory lace with crystal appliqué over a satin sash and an empire waist, created the perfect effect. She wore her hair knotted at the nape of her neck, with an ornament that matched the appliqué. The ivory pearls at her neckline had been her mother's, the only thing she had left of the woman who had raised her.

For years now, she'd successfully deflected questions about her family, or lack of, but regardless, she couldn't look in the mirror on the morning of this special day without a lump in her throat. While she'd never exactly envisioned her mother by her side on her wedding day, and an accident had robbed her of a father who would walk her down the aisle, she'd also never contemplated spending the morning of what was supposed to be the happiest day of her life feeling this . . . *alone*.

Not to say she actually was alone. Geary's family offered more than ample help with nearly every decision, leaving her feeling a bit cloistered in that regard.

After they'd all ironed out the venue predicament, Geary's mom and sister continued to weigh in on every decision. Dilly leaned toward chocolate wedding cake. Veta said white cake looked prettier when cut. Dilly thought they should include satin ribbons on the pew decorations. Veta agreed.

"We could use the bows left over from the Torgeson ceremony, if we steam them. They're in a box in the church attic. Bobby Lee could carry them down," Dilly offered. "The color of the ribbon is really close."

Dilly also brought an entire scrapbook over to dinner after church one evening filled with wedding magazine photos she'd cut and pasted inside. Veta and Dilly both had very definite ideas on dresses. Dilly liked large-hooped Scarlett O'Hara–style gowns. The flouncier, the better.

Veta liked long trains. "Nothing prettier in wedding portraits," she pointed out. "What do you think, Faith?"

"Oh, yes. Those are, uh, nice," she agreed, while trying to figure out how to extricate herself from these unpalatable options without hurting anyone's feelings.

Veta asked to do the flowers and had her heart set on brightly colored gerbera daisies. "Maybe you can place a bright pink one with some baby's breath in your hair." She turned to her daughter. "You know, like your friend Betsy did in her hair. That was so pretty."

Their chatter buzzed in the air, like bees too busy to land.

Finally, Faith spoke up, interrupting the planning. "I was thinking more in the line of white hydrangeas and ivory tea roses."

The two women glanced at each other. Dilly cringed. "No color?"

Veta looked confused. She shrugged. "Well, of course, dear. If that's what you want, we'll certainly make that happen."

Twice, Faith had to go to Geary quietly and ask him to intercept and tone down their "help."

She wasn't the kind to get all overworked about these kinds of things. She simply wanted a quiet, elegant affair fitting of the love she and Geary felt for one another and the commitment they were entering into.

Period—end of story.

The final straw was when they all showed up one evening over at Geary's place, when she'd wanted to have a quiet dinner with her fiancé, a task that seemed nearly impossible as of late.

Both of them had been so busy. The news director had pulled her in to help with a broadcast series on the abysmal literacy rates in Houston. Of the most populous cities in the United States, Houston was recently ranked #60, with #75 being the least literate.

Likewise, after the extended break to care for his grandfather, Geary found himself needing to pack his schedule with smaller tournaments he might have passed over just a year earlier. The divisional qualifying process remained a mystery to her, but she knew he had a lot of work to do to rebuild his standing.

After weeks of this, they'd made plans to meet up at his condo to spend some much needed time together and to finalize a few wedding plans. She'd stopped for takeout, Asian dim sum, making sure to include the steamed dumplings she thought he might like.

But when she pulled into the crowded parking lot outside his condo, the second row of vehicles included his dad's Chevy pickup, his mom's little blue Toyota, and her future brother- and sister-in-law's new Buick Enclave, a purchase right in line with Bobby Lee's propensity toward impulse buying.

She had a complete meltdown that night. In retrospect, she should have seen it coming—her inability to cope. Their constant suggestions, opinions, and ideas made her feel like they were blasting right over top of her life.

She'd survived her own destructive family—barely.

In the years that followed, she'd suffered lonely holidays and birthdays, graduation ceremonies with no one there to applaud. Hard as it was, she'd adjusted.

She was one to go with the flow in most things. But there was no easy way to conform to the Marin bunch.

First, Veta was already in Geary's kitchen, dishing up her homemade tuna casserole, a sticky concoction Faith had already had to gag down twice before. She hated canned tuna—actually, any canned fish or meat, including those little Vienna sausages that smelled the same as an open can of dog food. Not surprisingly, those were Wendell's favorite snack. He ate them while watching television, even if others sitting next to him on the sofa had to enjoy the aroma.

Then, she'd only just stepped inside the door of Geary's condo and been smothered with hugs and kisses, when little five-year-old Gabby came marching down the hallway singing "Onward, Christian Soldiers" at the top of her lungs, wearing Faith's Stuart Weitzmans, the bridal pumps that cost her over five hundred dollars. She'd accidently left them the other day after showing them to Geary.

"Gabby, get my shoes off your feet!"

Faith knew she sounded sharp but couldn't seem to help it. One more wobbly stomp and the delicate heels would snap.

Even Geary looked taken aback by the way she barked at his niece.

Dilly immediately defended her daughter, whose eyes were already puddling. "Hey, don't yell. She doesn't mean anything by playing in your shoes."

Faith knew they all thought she was overreacting. She should apologize, she supposed. But she was bone-tired and disappointed she couldn't have even one stinking night alone with her fiancé before the wedding.

And she wanted cashew chicken. And steamed dumplings!

She took a deep breath, trying to collect herself. "Look . . ." She glanced around the room, hoping his family might understand.

Someone did immediately clue in to her emotional state. The little curly-haired darling scrunched her face and made everything worse. "You're mean!" She sobbed like Faith had just run over her pet kitten.

Her twin brother, Gunner, joined the fray from behind a chair where no one else could see. He scrunched his eyes tightly closed and stuck his tongue out at her.

Faith's palms clenched in frustration.

"Hey now, there's no need for all this drama," Wendell said, intercepting the emotional volleyball game being played out in Geary's living room, with most of the action spiked in her direction. "Let's all take a deep breath and calm down." He looked at her when he said this.

On the converse, her future mother-in-law didn't look at her at all. Instead Veta bent and smoothed her granddaughter's hair off her tear-moistened cheeks. "There, there—no more tears. That's enough. There, now."

Faith looked at Geary. His hand rifled through his thick, dark hair. "Anyone want sweet tea?" he asked before he quickly turned to the refrigerator and buried his head—in more ways than one.

She'd had enough.

"Will you all excuse me, please?" She swallowed hard to fight the tears that threatened to expose her sudden feeling of vulnerability.

In the bathroom, she closed and locked the door against voices coming from the other end of the hall. Everyone was no doubt talking about her, about how she didn't fit in.

And she didn't. Not really.

That was what she tried to explain to Geary when he came for her.

She heard a light rap on the bathroom door. “Faith? Honey, let me in.”

From her perch on the toilet seat, she sniffled and rubbed her wrist against her nose. “I’ll be out. Just a minute.”

She grabbed the toilet paper roll and wadded some, pressing it against her nose. She blew.

“Faith, c’mon. Open the door, please.”

She sniffed. “I will. Just give me a minute.”

She stood and moved to the sink, where she ran cold water into a washcloth and held it for several seconds against her puffy eyelids, aware Geary stood outside the door waiting.

Finally, she took a deep breath and unlocked the door, then slowly pulled it open.

He gathered her in his arms and lightly kissed the top of her head. “They’re gone.”

She leaned back and glanced over his shoulder to confirm the truth of his statement. Down the hallway, a quiet living room.

She buried her head against his chest. Her eyes burned again, simmering with emotion. “I’m sorry, Geary. I don’t know what got into me. I just—”

“No. I’m sorry. My family can be pretty intense sometimes.” His thumb lightly rubbed the side of her face. “I should’ve stepped in, and didn’t. Forgive me?”

His apology was sincere, his regret apparent. Unfortunately, it changed nothing about how low she felt about her own behavior. She’d acted ugly in front of people who had done nothing but open their homes and heart to her.

Sure, they had annoying ways. Certainly, those children needed some—uh, guidance. But she hated that she’d caved in to her emotions, let them whisk her into a situation where she felt out of control.

She hated how her voice had sounded dangerously close to her own mother's when she was angry.

Faith felt weary, like her bones might crumple and she'd fold to the floor if he wasn't holding her. "Geary, I—"

As if sensing the sick feeling working its way through her gut, he stroked the back of her head and whispered, "Don't worry. This whole wedding thing is a lot of pressure. They understand."

She nodded, wondering what he must think of her now. "It's just—I'm not sure how to deal with your family," she tried to explain. "Most of the time, I don't feel like I fit in." Silently, she added to herself, *Or maybe I don't want to*.

"There's no question I love my family," he said. "But they're the crankbait. You and me? We're the rod and reel." He looked at her with a funny grin, clearly hoping she'd appreciate his stab at lightening the moment with some fishing humor.

She couldn't help herself. She laughed and patted his chest. "Don't quit your day job, mister. You'll never make it as a comedian."

Later, between bites of pork dumplings, Geary sat cross-legged on the floor with her and told how after she left the room, his dad had quickly sent everyone packing. Wendell lingered for a few minutes.

"Dad told me there was something very important he wanted to share with me." Geary gave her a sheepish smile. He reached across and took her hand. "Among other things, he said I am your protector. You need to be able to count on me to be there, no matter what." He leaned forward and cupped her chin. "I want you to know, Faith. I'm not a perfect man. But with everything in me, I want to be that for you."

Now, here in the bride's room, Faith let those words seep into her soul again, let his assurance lift her panic.

Outside the church window, a yellow-breasted warbler caught her attention from a nearby crepe myrtle, the bird's feathers out of place among the mass of white blooms.

She fastened her veil in place, then turned and faced the mirror, admiring the stunning reflection of a bride about to join her groom at the altar.

I'm counting on that.

Then she took a deep breath and headed out the door.

12

The private plane banked sharply to the right, allowing a perfect view from the porthole window. Below, clumps of palms lined a white-sand beach that stretched for miles. Sailboats dotted the bay, with water so intensely blue Faith's eyes nearly ached from the beauty.

"Oh, Geary!" She pulled at his sleeve. "Have you ever seen anything so stunning?"

He peeked out the window over her shoulder. "This is going to be an amazing two weeks."

Unlike commercial resort destinations, Hildebrand's boutique getaway equaled a one-of-a-kind sanctuary for the rich and famous, the fortunate ones who could afford to go anywhere they desired. The sort of guests who only stayed at the most exclusive, most luxurious destinations.

Faith nearly had to pinch herself. *This* was where she and Geary would spend their honeymoon. For the next two weeks, they would escape the pressures of their ordinary lives and focus on each other—all against a backdrop of lush Caribbean beauty.

Massive white stone and wrought iron formed the entry into St. Viceroy Negril. Their driver showed credentials to the security personnel and then steered them down a winding paved road lined with banana palms and hibiscus bushes filled with deep red, orange, and yellow blooms. As far as the eye could see, blue pools lined with rock and waterfalls stretched to pockets of tall palms swaying in the gentle breeze. In the distance, the white-sand shoreline buffeted by the bay created a postcard view.

From the backseat of the town car, Faith nestled her head against Geary's shoulder, trying to take it all in.

He whistled. "Boy, that Hildebrand guy sure knows how to land one."

She agreed, not with the fishing analogy necessarily, but she couldn't even imagine owning all this. She fingered her new husband's chin. "For the next two weeks, St. Viceroy Negril is ours to enjoy. I plan to savor every second."

Their suite consisted of seven rooms, all beautifully appointed and decorated in white and creams with hints of light aqua and sea-foam green in the pillow prints and wall art. The building front facing the beach was an open lanai leading to a private zero-clearance pool.

The attendant handed Geary the room keys. "You need anything, mon, just ring the concierge desk. Every want will be immediately furnished."

While Geary thanked him and handed the uniformed gentleman a generous tip, Faith checked out the complimentary tray of fruit and champagne on a bamboo table next to a window overlooking an expansive green lawn, manicured and bordered with coral-colored plumeria.

She should be exhausted. They'd danced until the wee hours of the morning at their reception, and then they rose early to catch their flight. All that should have depleted her energy level. But at this moment, her mind was running on a high level of excitement.

She raced from room to room, taking it all in.

"Honey, come quick!" She summoned him to the main bathroom. "Look at this."

He rushed to join her. Together they marveled over the glass floor that exposed a stunning view of the underwater depths below, complete with tropical fish and shells. "Amazing," he agreed.

Despite all her pre-wedding angst, their special day had come together without a hitch. Well, except for one of the twins spilling red punch down the table at the church luncheon. Thankfully, Geary had quietly suggested the evening party might not be a place for young ones.

The ceremony itself was perfect. Not too long, and focused on the commitment they were making to one another. Before their vows, her new father-in-law referenced a beautiful passage in Ecclesiastes about a three-part cord and urged them to intertwine their lives with God at the center, making their union stronger.

His words were just right.

The only thing missing—her own family. She'd fielded a few questions by simply stating that her mother and father had died and her brother did not live near and had been unable to attend.

Dilly hadn't been so easily convinced. "That's just strange that your brother wouldn't be here on your wedding day."

Yes, there'd been a few minor issues. Still, the day she'd married Geary Marin would go down as the single best day of her entire life.

Now they had a honeymoon and years ahead to enjoy.

Their first dinner in Jamaica was served on a white linen-covered table positioned out on the beach surrounded by tiki torches. Seven long courses, the first a coconut lemongrass soup. Next they were served roasted figs wrapped in bacon with a brown sugar glaze. The salad came next—hearts of palm placed over a bed of arugula drizzled with balsamic vinegar and sprinkled with finely diced hazelnuts.

The main course was lobster—the biggest she'd ever seen. Both the claws and the back tails extended over the edges of the platters the waiter mistakenly called plates. Little cups of butter sat warming over tea candles with live flames.

"I'd like to propose a toast," Geary said, holding a glass of a frozen fruity concoction decorated with a spear of fresh pineapple and a tiny umbrella. "To the most beautiful bride ever."

"Oh, I bet you say that to all the women you marry," she teased, clinking her glass with his.

They passed on the dessert, little chocolate cakes formed in the shape of volcanoes with molten cherry chocolate sauce oozing from the top. Instead they slipped off their sandals and headed for a walk down the beach, hand in hand. Just like in so many movies she'd seen, the moonlight glistened across the softly rolling waves landing on the sand. The warm water pushed up the shore by some invisible hand until it broke across their bare toes.

"Thank you," Geary said as he slipped his arm around her bare arm and pulled her close.

She leaned into the capacious comfort of his broad shoulder. "For what?"

"What I'm about to say is going to sound sappy," he warned.

"Yeah?"

He gave her a slight squeeze and stopped walking, turning her so they stood face-to-face. "Thank you for agreeing to spend the rest of your life with me." He brushed a strand of her hair back. "And for making me the happiest man alive."

His finger touched her mouth, her bottom lip.

She pressed into him, felt the warmth of his body through the linen of his shirt. Geary Marin was a good man, not filled with pretense but solidly authentic. And trustworthy.

He'd vowed to be her protector, her Prince Charming.

She turned her face into his hand and pressed a kiss against his slightly calloused palm.

And she believed him.

"Faith." He said her name, sweet and heady, desperate with need. Even in the moonlight, she could see his eyes were deeply shadowed with longing.

He scooped her up into his arms, leaving her legs dangling above the sand.

In response, she wrapped one arm around his neck and leaned against his shoulder. Her free hand tightened on his shirt, clinging to the strength of his embrace. This man was now her husband, her solid rock against shifting sand.

Overhead, a bright moon illuminated the night sky. Pieces of light whispered through the palm fronds, casting a hopeful glow across their path.

"I love you, Geary." Her lips barely moved as she whispered her declaration. Goodness, did this man know how solidly her heart was wrapped around his?

His arms tightened around her, pulled her closer. "I love you too."

Then, as if they were in some romantic movie playing out on the big screen, he carried her back in the direction of their luxury suite . . . and the night both of them had been waiting for.

13

Faith opened her eyes to walls the color of water, not the bright turquoise of the bay outside their honeymoon suite, but the muted hospital gray of the shadowed cove where they'd snorkeled—where she'd seen a turtle with black eyes watching from the crest of a rock peeking above the surface.

The sounds differed as well.

No gentle trade wind blowing through palm fronds. No chorus of tree frogs pulsing in the distance. No waves splashing onto the sand in rhythm. Not even the faint chords of reggae music drifting from a distant poolside club.

Instead a ventilator's asthmatic rhythm interrupted the silence of the dimmed hospital room.

A man in a tweed jacket, with a stethoscope hanging from his neck, leaned across the bed.

"Faith, I'm Dr. Wimberly. I'm your doctor and you are at Memorial Hermann. You have a trach tube down your throat, but we're going to remove that now. Then you'll be able to talk. Do you understand?"

She blinked several times. And nodded ever so slightly, her head feeling bulky and unwieldy—a bit like a basketball seven times bigger than the normal ones you'd see during a Houston Rockets game.

Her doctor smiled. "There, yes, that's good."

They removed the tube, one she was told had been placed when early signs of pneumonia developed. The removal process made her gag and left her throat feeling like she'd swallowed glass shards.

Afterward, she tried to speak, but her voice wouldn't cooperate. Nothing she told her body to do seemed to be effective.

Frustrated, she tried again. This time a low-volume squeak passed through her vocal cords and out her lips.

A nurse, a black woman with a kind smile, lifted a straw to her mouth. "Can you take a sip, baby?"

From Dr. Wimberly, she learned she'd been in a coma, one he'd induced temporarily by using pentobarbital, a drug that allowed her injured brain to rest while it healed.

Funny, she could vaguely remember this doctor, but not clearly. She couldn't clearly form any memory, really, her mind foggy and hungover like a college student who had drunk far too much tequila the night before. But then, if what Dr. Wimberly told her was true, she'd been asleep.

Hadn't she? And . . . why?

She reached for the doctor's arm, finding her left hand unmovable. She could see the length of it on the bed, resting against her leg as if the appendage belonged to someone else. But she knew this was her arm.

She quickly diverted her gaze to the other side. Her other arm.

Yes, she felt that one.

Relieved, she lifted her right hand. Reached for the doctor again.

He took her hand in his own. "I know you must be confused—maybe even a little frightened. But you are getting the best care we have to offer, and I promise you are past the worst dangers."

She swallowed against the raw in her throat. "Where—where am I?" She barely recognized her own voice.

He gave her a patient smile. "You are in the intensive care unit at Memorial Hermann Hospital. You've suffered a head injury, and then a bit of a setback with some unexpected swelling, but you are well on your way to getting well. Your long-term prognosis is good."

Her eyes widened. She tried to assimilate what he was saying.

"Faith, do you know where you are?"

She scowled. What kind of game was this guy playing? Hadn't he just told her? "I'm at the hos—the hospital."

Dr. Wimberly nodded. "Yes—yes, you are at the hospital. Good."

She tried to moisten her lips with a tongue that still felt paper-dry. "Why? What—what happened?"

"I'm afraid you suffered a pretty severe trauma that fractured your skull and sent bone fragments into the upper right surface of your brain, the cortex that manages your motor association and coordination of physical action on your left side."

She drew a sharp breath. "My—my brain?"

The doctor patted her arm. "I lead a medical team of some of the best and brightest professionals available in the country. Within hours, we placed you in a temporary induced coma, which limited the electrical activity in your brain, allowing the tissue to heal. Upon arrival, you were able to breathe on your own, but we placed a ventilator to prevent windpipe infection and pneumonia. As hoped, you've made significant progress."

Standing behind Dr. Wimberly, a younger guy in hospital garb made notes on an electronic tablet.

Faith glanced back at Dr. Wimberly. "When?"

"You've been with us four weeks."

Four weeks? She'd been in a hospital four weeks?

She clutched at his arm. "Why?" The single word came out crackly and weak.

Dr. Wimberly squeezed her hand, a failed attempt at reassurance. "Can you tell us what you remember?"

Her head hurt. She pulled her hand back from his and reached up to it. Her fingers landed on what felt like gauze fabric and metal.

Metal?

Her lungs did another sharp intake of air. She tried to sit.

"No, don't try to sit up. I'll answer your questions. Just lie back and—that's it." Dr. Wimberly stroked her forearm. "Faith, your injuries required surgery. We removed a portion of your skull, and what you are feeling is an orbital helmet. We'll reinsert that piece of skull very soon, possibly in the next day or two. I'm happy to report that the risk of brain tissue swelling is no longer a threat." He gave her a gentle smile. "Do you understand?"

She nodded, feeling the weight of the helmet. Her hand lifted and she touched the protective gear again. "I was shot."

The statement seemed to surprise everyone standing at her bedside, including her. "I was shot," she repeated, outwardly showing nothing of what now cracked inside her.

"Yes—yes, you were."

Faith squeezed her eyes shut and concentrated. Tried to remember more. But couldn't. Her mind wouldn't conjure any sequence of events. Only that a gun had been pointed—fired.

And her head had exploded.

The next time she woke, little had changed.

The room appeared exactly the same. With no windows, there was no way to estimate whether it was day or night. Not that it mattered. Time seemed of little value inside this place—this place of quiet noise, antiseptic smells, and equipment monitoring every bodily function.

She had a PEG tube in her abdomen providing nourishment. Tomorrow the dieticians would introduce a liquid diet. If it was tolerated, the tube would be removed and she'd progress to tasteless soft foods, and eventually solids.

Bags hanging from the bed railing collected and measured urine output and other bodily excretions. Monitors surrounded her bed, measuring every breath, every heartbeat, the pressure of her blood flow, and a multitude of other things not fully known to her.

Faith lost track of the faceless medical personnel rotating in and out of her room, all dressed in hospital smocks and drawstring trousers, all poking, touching, and telling her not to worry—she was doing just fine.

She wasn't doing fine.

She hadn't been out of the coma but a few hours, and she was already tired of lying still. The helmet was foreign and cumbersome and uncomfortable.

Her right side ached with stiffness.

Her left arm felt nothing. Several times her brain commanded and the body part would not respond—a petulant child who would not bend to the will of its mother.

Her senses tensed and wrestled each other for attention. Mixed with crude and unprocessed thoughts, emotions foreign to Faith clogged her ability to survive a building level of dull-edged fear.

Moving her right hand to her mouth, she rubbed the pads of her fingers against her lips—something she did when she was confused and worried. Her eyes filled with tears, a silent clarion of the despair she felt building inside.

Her mind remained muddled. Dizziness enveloped her even as she contemplated—or at least tried to place her circumstances in some sort of context.

She'd been shot?

Her mind trudged through that barest of memory, trying to capture the snippet of images flashing in her head. Or was that flash—

Involuntarily, her entire body shuddered, at least the part she could feel. Why couldn't she wrestle her panic-flooded mind into submission, gather illusive thoughts into some semblance of understanding?

The bilious taste of fear rose again. No doubt a certain reality couldn't be argued.

She was broken, inside and out—and terrified.

"Faith?" A petite woman in scrubs moved into the room, a clipboard tucked under her arm. "Are you up for a visitor?"

"A visitor?" She quickly wiped at her eyes with her only working hand. "Who is it?"

"The man who has barely left your side," the woman reported.

She saw his face then, in the doorway.

Prince Charming.

14

The pilot maneuvered the Citation Bravo down the tarmac and taxied to a private hangar east of the main terminal. Faith and Geary collected their luggage, then made their way to the parking area.

"I can't believe two weeks went by so quickly," she lamented as she climbed inside Geary's pickup truck.

Geary sighed and started the engine. "Yup. Back to the real world."

The real world with rising temperatures and humidity, clogged freeways and iPhones buzzing with social media alerts. Her email inbox held hundreds of unopened messages. She groaned and started sifting through until one particular email caught her attention.

She frowned. "Oh, honey—I hate to ask, but it looks like I need to stop by the station before we head, uh, home." She felt funny calling his place her home. Especially since she hadn't yet completely moved her stuff in.

Geary changed lanes. "Now? We just barely got back." He reached across the seat and lightly drifted his fingers up her arm in a suggestive manner.

She apologized, hoping he'd understand. "I promise, just a quick stop. Apparently, we have a new executive news director—a guy named Clark Ravino. They're having a quick meet and greet at four." She looked up from her phone and turned to her husband. "I can't miss that."

Geary nodded. "Yeah, sure. I mean, that's going to put us in five o'clock traffic, but I agree. That's pretty important."

She was glad he understood. As much as she'd adored their time sequestered away on a remote white beach, a tiny bit of her felt anxious knowing she wasn't at the station keeping up with everything. News was a highly competitive sport, and she had to guard the goal line closely so someone didn't sneak one past her.

All she had to do was sneeze and five other wannabe anchors would be hoping she was out of commission so they could slide into her weekend slot. Especially DeeAnne Roberts, a spray-tanned gym bunny who lived on gossip and raw celery sticks.

"I'll wait here," Geary said from inside the truck. He turned up the radio.

"Okay, I won't be long. I promise." She closed the door and hurried to the front lobby.

The receptionist looked up from behind the counter. "Well, hey—look who's back! You look great, Faith. White sand and sun agree with you."

"Thanks, we had a marvelous time." She glanced at the clock on the wall above the bank of television screens. "Do you know where everyone is meeting?"

The receptionist buzzed her through the door so she wouldn't have to use her security card. "Everyone's gathered in the area back by the orange room. You'll have to hurry."

She gave the gal a grateful nod and scurried in that direction, rounding the corner and joining the group just as the station manager, Mark Grubie, started speaking. When he noticed her, he smiled. "Welcome back, Faith. I trust you had a nice vacation."

Everyone turned.

She held up a hand. "Yes, wonderful time. But glad to be back." It wouldn't hurt to remind everyone she had her priorities straight.

"Well, look—I know everyone is on a tight schedule and we have the five o'clock looming, so let's get on with this. You can read his full bio in the email I sent out, but I wanted to take a few minutes to introduce Clark Ravino and let him say a few words."

Mark patted the shoulder of the man standing next to him, a guy who was tall and incredibly handsome in a Cary Grant kind of way. His black hair had grayed at the temples. When he smiled, the corners of his eyes broke into a set of creases that suggested he did that often—smiled, that is. Unlike the rolled-up sleeves on Mark's shirt, Clark Ravino's crisp white shirt was impeccably pressed, and the cuffs were fastened at his wrists with gold links.

In one word, she'd describe their recently hired news producer as *class*. Pure class.

He rubbed at his chin and smiled. "Thank you. I'm glad to be here. As you might have heard, I came from Portland, Oregon—a smaller and much cooler market." He grinned even wider. "I'm talking temperature."

The crowd laughed.

"But I'm here to make each of you a promise. More than the temperature is going to heat up over the next months here in Houston. I'm thrilled to be producing in one of the top ten markets and at an O&O station—not that I minded an affiliate-run outfit, but the independence at an owner-operated station provides ample opportunity for us to position ourselves for mighty achievements." Like a politician, he championed his cause. "Building on the tremendous strengths of this news organization, I intend to take this station straight to the top!" He leaned slightly forward. "And not only is this station going to soar to the top in the rankings, but those of you willing to help in the process will become our rising stars as well."

Clark Ravino looked directly at her. She noticed, and so did others.

His cheeks dimpled as he smiled, giving him a handsome boyish charm. "Oh, and we'll be working to rebrand the station. A new promo and tagline will debut soon. So, like they say in the business, stay tuned."

Applause broke out in the room, some clapping with more enthusiasm than others. The station manager patted Clark on the back. "Let me tell you, everyone, this man had multiple stations vying for him to join their teams. KIAM-TV is very fortunate to have landed someone with his vision, his skill. Now, let's get back to work and show Clark he made the right decision."

A couple of people lingered after the meeting broke up. DeeAnne Roberts leaned over to her. "Sounds to me like our new station motto should be 'Change You Can Believe In.' Word on the street is Mr. Hotshot News Director plans on some major staffing moves, including canning Barbara."

Faith turned from watching co-workers who had wandered up front to shake hands with the news director. "What? How do you know that?"

"This is a newsroom. I have sources." Her co-worker sauntered back to her desk with a knowing grin on her face.

Barbara Dover Nelson was a television icon. As one of the first women to break into television broadcasting in a significant way, she often claimed she'd been poured in with the foundation. Now in her late sixties, she was still at it. Still striving for the interviews, the exclusives, the field reporting that had made her welcome in people's homes night after night.

Kicking her to the curb after all these years didn't seem fair somehow.

On the other hand, Barbara's exit from the picture opened up a very desirable slot in the lineup of on-air talent. With any luck at all, Faith could land in the much-coveted morning anchor chair.

The idea was a long shot, but strangely she couldn't help but hear her mother's voice. *Things work out best for those who make the best of how things work out.*

Suddenly, she was acutely aware of a man standing beside her. Startled, she looked up to see Clark Ravino. He smiled and extended his hand. "Hi. I've been anxious to meet you, Faith—uh—"

"Marin. Faith Marin," she said, finishing his sentence with her new name that sounded foreign even to her own ears.

"Ah yes. And you are just back from your honeymoon."

Despite her pounding heart, she forced an air of confidence. "Yes. Jamaica. We had a wonderful time."

He placed his manicured hand on her shoulder. "Look, I was terribly impressed with that piece you did from the bridge. Few in this business are gifted with your natural inclination and way of connecting with both the subject and the audience."

"Thank you," Faith managed to utter. She smiled and grasped her new boss's outstretched hand, amazed at the notion her career seemed to have moved into the fast lane by driving sideways.

Clark Ravino granted her another wide smile, staring at her with eyes the color of liquid copper. "I hope you have a few minutes. I'd like to talk to you about a story package I have in mind to kick-start our new approach."

Her hand involuntarily went to her chest. "Why, sure. Of course."

Fifty minutes later, she scrambled across the parking lot and opened Geary's pickup door. The movement and sound pulled his attention from his iPhone. "For Pete's sake, Faith, what took you so long?"

"I know, I'm sorry," she explained while climbing in. "But you won't believe what—"

"Now we're late."

She looked across the seat and frowned. "Late for what?"

He shook his head and started the engine.

"Hey, are you mad?"

He put the truck in gear and glanced into the rearview mirror before backing out of their parking spot. "No, not mad. Just—"

She raised her eyebrows. "Just what? I know that took a lot longer than I expected. But there's a good reason."

Geary took a deep breath. "It's just that they're all waiting."

"Who's waiting?"

He pulled onto the highway and merged into traffic. "My family."

She nestled her purse in her lap and held up her open palms. "Wait—apparently I'm missing something here."

"It was supposed to be a surprise. My family and some of the folks from the church are putting on a pounding for us."

"A what?"

"A pounding. You know, what a bunch of people do for a couple returning from their honeymoon?" Seeing the blank look on her face, he continued. "A pounding. I can't believe you've never heard of the southern housewarming tradition. The church throws one for every newlywed couple when they return from their honeymoon."

"Tonight?"

"Well, yeah. We're returning home from our honeymoon tonight. That's how all this is done."

He looked at her like she was crazy. But he was the crazy one to think she'd be happy to hear she had to go home to a houseful of people. "Oh, Geary. Not tonight. I mean, goodness, I'm so tired."

Seeing the deflated and confused look on her new husband's face, she quickly added, "Unless, of course, you want to."

Geary braked for a line of cars ahead. "Well, it wouldn't be so late, except we had to spend nearly two hours at the station."

"Ouch."

"I—I didn't mean it to sound like that." He ran a hand through his hair. "Well, maybe I did. But I'm sorry." He glanced across the seat at her. "Look, regardless, it's too late to do anything about it now. My mom and family are all there with people from the church waiting for us."

She quickly nodded. Her mother would've torn into her dad, battled until she won. But Faith wouldn't do that.

She extended her hand and lightly brushed her fingers through the hair at his temple. "Hey, you're right. Let's make the best of things. What's a little gathering going to hurt, huh?" She smiled, hopeful her small offering would quickly douse the heat before any argument flared.

He nodded and reached for her hand, bringing her palm to his mouth where he placed a series of kisses. "I love you, babe."

"I love you too. Now, both hands on the wheel, mister."

They arrived home and his parents greeted them at the open door. Veta gave her and Geary big hugs and Wendell waved them inside. "So, son—did you learn to do the hula?"

Geary laughed. "Wrong island, Dad."

Wendell looked confused. His wife gave him a playful slap. "You're thinking Hawaii, you old silly. The kids went to Jamaica."

As predicted, the house was filled with people. Faith recognized the children's ministry director and her husband, the worship leader—she thought his name was Ed. Craig and Cynthia Meyers, Amy Elliott, Adele Beers, the Nystroms, the Lippincotts—all brought sacks of flour and sugar, canned and dry goods meant to fill the pantry like they believed she cooked.

As if reading her mind, Veta slid a large album from the counter and presented it to her. "This is a custom among Marin women—a scrapbook filled with my recipes, and recipes from my own mother and Wendell's mother. And a few from our grandmothers."

Dilly, who had just arrived with little Sam on her hip and the twins following close behind, pointed at the book. "You gotta try the catfish fry from my grandma Marin. Oh, and Mama's peach cobbler recipe is to die for. And it's easy too." She glanced around. "Where's Bobby Lee? He said he'd be here."

Wendell bent and took little Sam from his mother. "He was here. I think he said he was making a run for ice. Isn't that right, Veta?"

"What?" Geary's mother paused unpacking grocery sacks.

"I said, didn't Bobby Lee say he was going to get ice?"

Veta rolled her eyes. "No, you old silly. He went to get rice. I sent him out for some because no one here brought any."

Unsure what to do with the heavy compilation of family recipes, she handed the weighty book off to Geary. "Look, honey. Wasn't that nice?" She pasted on a smile, hoping her good effort would stay in place until after everybody went home. Which hopefully wasn't far off.

There was no place left to sit in the crowded condo, so she moved into the kitchen currently occupied by three women trying to talk over the noise the twins were now making.

"Dear, where do you want to keep your raisins and walnuts?" A woman with full cheeks, someone she failed to recognize, stood with a bright red and yellow box in her hands, waiting for her to answer.

"Uh, I'm not really sure."

Another turned from an open cupboard. "Where would I find your Tupperware lids, honey?"

Before she could tell them she had no idea, Dilly moved into the kitchen and joined them. She stood at the sink, opened the cupboard to the right, pulled out a plastic tumbler with a Taco Bell logo, and turned on the water. "Sooo . . . how was it?"

"It?" Faith repeated.

Dilly filled her tumbler. "You know . . . the big night." Her sister-in-law winked and moved the tumbler to her mouth, eyeing her from over thc top while she drank.

The woman with the package of raisins in her hands grinned and focused her attention in their direction as if wanting to hear her answer as well.

Faith held up a finger. "Uh, could y'all excuse me a minute?"

Holding her breath, she darted through the crowded living room and made her way down the hall, toward their bedroom. She needed a couple of minutes alone to collect herself.

Geary caught up with her before she made it to the door. "Honey, you okay?"

She held up her hand. "I'm—uh, I'm just fine." She hated hearing the edge in her voice. "I just need a few minutes. I'll be right back."

He looked confused. "Uh—okay."

Relieved for a brief respite, she shut the door and leaned against it. She closed her eyes, trying desperately to find a calming point.

Deep inside, she knew his family and friends were trying to be nice. Still, those were her cupboards—well, Geary's cupboards, but hers too now. She wanted to be the one to organize them. She couldn't remember the last time she'd cooked with raisins or walnuts—not that she cooked a bunch. She was more the takeout type.

Perhaps her inability to cope with the unexpected interruption could simply be attributed to being overly stressed after learning the station had staffed the news director position with someone new. Clark Ravino seemed to have singled her out by inviting her in on a series of stories he planned on Houston's most affluent neighborhood and its residents. But she still had a lot of work ahead to cement his favor.

Success in the cutthroat news business required acumen and savvy. There were no pause buttons, only reject knobs, and she'd have to play hard and fast to stay ahead. Ask Barbara Dover Nelson.

She glanced at the suitcases stacked over by the bed, wishing she could open and unpack. She couldn't. Not yet, not until this pounding thing was over.

The room was just as they'd left it, the bed made up with a downy duvet comforter. Geary's place was already tastefully decorated. Together they'd elected to leave everything the same, that is, except the bedroom. The one room they wanted to create together.

In the weeks before the wedding, they'd made a trip to the Woodlands Mall, ending up at Pottery Barn, one of her favorite stores. She wasn't much of a shopper, but the items in that store made her drool.

Upon the advice of the in-store decorating consultant, they went with off-white walls painted Heron Plume and a king-sized upholstered headboard. At first Geary had preferred a more nautical theme, but he'd easily given in to the beautiful duvet comforter in oyster with a muted paisley print in shades of beige and ice-blue, hoping to please his soon-to-be wife.

She smiled, remembering the way he looked over at her while they were putting the sheets on the bed for the first time.

All right. She could do this.

She went into her bathroom to freshen up a bit and reached for the cabinet door, where she knew Geary kept his aspirin. Strangely, the door was slightly ajar.

Scowling, she opened it. Inside, what looked like a brand-new tube of toothpaste lay on the bottom shelf. The lid was screwed on funny and was caked in fresh toothpaste. Not something Geary would normally do. He was far too neat.

She lifted the sticky tube from the shelf, noticing that the paste oozing from the lid was fresh.

By instinct, Faith unscrewed the cap and brought it to her nose. She wasn't sure what was inside—but it definitely wasn't toothpaste.

She tossed the tube on the counter, whirled around, and marched through the bedroom, out the door, and down the hallway lined with Geary's family pictures. The crowd had not thinned. If anything, the small living space was teeming with more people.

Including Stacy Brien, whose mouth drew into a slow smile when she saw the look on Faith's face.

Geary was next to the sofa, talking to his dad and Harry Olson, an elder at Lake Pine.

She weaved her way through several small pockets of people until she got close to her husband. "Uh, excuse me," she said. "Geary, could I see you for a minute?"

He looked at her, puzzled. "Sure. What's up, babe?"

"Alone?"

As soon as they were out of earshot, Faith explained the reason for her ire. "Someone has been in our bathroom."

"Yeah, there's quite a crowd. I'm sure—"

She shook her head. "No, I'm not talking using our bathroom. I mean someone has been in our bathroom, rummaging through the cabinet." She motioned for him to follow.

In the bathroom, she held up the toothpaste tube. "Smell this."

He took it from her hand. "Smell it?"

"Yes, smell it. That is not toothpaste."

He nodded slowly. And smiled.

"What's so funny?"

He hesitated. "Well, sometimes a pounding includes—uh, a few pranks."

"Pranks? What kind of pranks?" She didn't know why he'd find that the least bit amusing. She didn't relish the idea of anyone helping themselves to her private things, especially to pull a prank. Then it dawned on her. "Bobby Lee?"

"That'd be my guess," Geary admitted.

She grabbed the tube from his hand and slammed it into the trash. "You have got to be kidding me!"

"Now, Faith. Calm down."

"You're telling me to calm down? When Bobby Lee has been pawing through my bathroom? What, has he been in my drawers? Did he go through my nightgowns too?" she demanded.

Geary sifted his fingers through his dark hair. "No, it's not like that."

She pointed back at the tube in the trash. "Please—please tell me what it's like then?"

He pulled his cell phone from his back jeans pocket. "Look, I'll call him. See what else he did."

Immediately, she felt like a heel. Geary couldn't control what his wacky brother-in-law did. Obviously, he felt bad. Her fit sounded far too much like her mother. She wanted to take back her reaction, sand it down a bit, polish her words, and place them back in his hands. She couldn't, so instead she shrugged. "Look, I'm sorry. Obviously, I overreacted a bit." Faith let herself smile then, ever so slightly. "Could be worse, I guess."

Geary immediately pulled her into an embrace and kissed the top of her head. "Yeah, Bobby Lee could've been your rescuer when you toppled off that boat." He made the remark in that way he had, often finding the humor in a situation. "I love you. Now, come back out to the party. Everybody is asking where you are."

She nestled into the warmth of his neck. "I love you too."

Anyone looking at this relationship from the outside might wonder about her attraction to a man so clearly her opposite. In fact, in the early months of their dating, that very question had sometimes plagued her.

Finally, she'd discovered her answer after stumbling across footage of the infamous Bette Davis telling Barbara Walters in an interview, "I was always competent, earned my own way, and nobody would have thought I needed someone to watch over me. Sadly, I never did find that person."

Luckily, Faith had.

Geary placed his hands on her shoulders. "You good?"

"Yes," she assured her husband. "I'm good."

She sent Geary back out to their guests, then turned to the mirror to freshen up, as had been her original intention.

Goodness, she was going to have to learn to lighten up a bit. Not only was she letting circumstances dictate her emotions, but this constant scowling was creating creases between her eyes, and the camera had a way of picking up and amplifying those things.

Before she rejoined the party, she needed to relieve herself of the large glass of tea she'd drunk earlier. She sat, marveling that she could still make out her father-in-law's voice through two closed doors.

Suddenly, the backs of her pant legs were wet—soaked, actually.

After letting out a yelp, she jumped up and turned. "What in the world—?" she murmured out loud.

Then she saw it—the plastic wrap taped under the toilet seat.

15

High television ratings are not always achieved with stories about convicted murderers or candidates running for an elected office. In fact, more often, viewers are fascinated by celebrity and will sit glued to any program that highlights the personal side of the stars they see every day in their favorite sitcoms and on the big screen.

Clark Ravino looked at Faith from across his desk. "People would be surprised to know how many extremely wealthy people, including celebrities, live here in Houston, and in particular the River Oaks area." He leaned back in his black leather chair, tapping his pencil to his cheek. "I want to tap into this. But I think it's a good idea if we backdoor this one."

DeeAnne Roberts, who wanted desperately to make it to the anchor desk, opened her notebook and took a pen from behind her ear. "What do you mean?"

After the big introduction meeting and her private chat with Clark, Faith believed she'd been singled out for a plum assignment. In the short weeks that followed, she'd realized their new producer had pulled a classic management tool, pooling his best talent and setting them out on the same task—which created a competition of sorts. A competition she intended to win.

She rubbed her lips with the pads of her fingers, thinking for a few seconds before she popped forward in her chair. "You don't want the story about *who* or *where*, but about the *how*?"

He pointed his finger at her. "Exactly! But I don't want this one written on the nose."

She pulled in a deep breath, satisfied she'd pinpointed what he was looking for so quickly. Even better, he'd noticed.

"Let's give our viewers a taste of what it's like to be that wealthy. We'll showcase the schools and parks, the grand homes. Give our viewers an inside peek into how the rich and influential in this city really live. Not what publicists want portrayed, but what it's actually like to live that opulent lifestyle."

Faith thought about the oil barons, the real estate moguls, even the minister who had made millions in book sales. She needed a special angle, that special exclusive piece of information that Barbara Walters calls the "get."

She glanced at the uneasy expressions on the faces of her co-workers, the assignment no doubt catching them all off guard.

Living with a volatile mother had taught her to think fast on her feet. While pulling together a killer exposé on the wealthy might not exactly be a piece of cake, the idea didn't leave her anxious. Just the opposite.

A challenge of this nature magnified the very reasons she'd gone into the news business. Her keen perception of people and situations, combined with her drive and a decent amount of luck, could become the very catalyst for boosting her career into orbit.

She said as much to Geary as she plated the salads she'd picked up at Trader Joe's on her way home. "No doubt this report is going to take some real work on my part, but Clark and I think a lot alike, and I'll have a real opportunity to show him what I'm capable of." She moved to the table and set the plates down on the pretty new placemats she'd received as a shower gift. "I need to prove myself. The earlier the better."

Geary looked at the plate with a puzzled expression.

She slid into her chair, unfolded her linen napkin, and laid it in her lap. "What's wrong?"

"Well . . ." He lifted his brows. "Uh—is this all?"

She reached for the pepper mill, another gift. "What do you mean?"

"Are we having any meat?"

She laughed off his comment. "There's plenty of protein in the feta and chickpeas, which also provide a healthy dose of potassium, vitamin B6, and iron." She wasn't exactly a health food nut, but she needed to stay trim for the camera.

Her husband nodded a little reluctantly and grabbed his fork.

"Anyway, like I was saying, I'm pretty sure anyone else contributing to this package would bring nothing more than tabloid gossip to the table. On the other hand, I plan to find that hidden nugget of information that matters. News means nothing unless told from the perspective of why it matters to the viewers."

Geary nodded and speared a chickpea. "What do you call these?"

"Chickpeas—legumes sometimes also called garbanzo beans."

His face grew more puzzled. "And the white stuff?"

"Oh, for goodness' sake. That's feta cheese." She scooted her chair back and stood. "Look, your mom left another of her casseroles in the fridge last night. I think it has some meat in it."

His expression brightened. "Yeah, that'd be great. I mean, I'll eat this too, of course."

Not about to let his annoying eating habits pirate her enthusiasm, she kept talking while rifling through the packed refrigerator for her mother-in-law's Tupperware container. "I can do some preliminary research in the evenings this week. I'm probably going to have to work through the weekend. Maybe spend some time in town." That was a term she'd picked up since moving to Geary's condo on Lake Conroe. "Maybe Oliver Hildebrand would be willing to make some introductions or get me invited to a social event where I could scope out things from the inside."

"You're going to miss church?"

She set the casserole on the counter and kicked the refrigerator door closed with her foot a little harder than she'd intended. "Well, yes, that's very possible. This story is really important."

"Oh, yeah—I know. It's just that the children's department is putting on some show for the congregation about Joseph and his brothers, and the twins are some kind of animals. I think Dilly was counting on us being there."

"Well, we'll see," she said, not wanting to commit.

Geary brought the subject up again as they were getting ready for bed. "Hey, you think you could show me how to use that fancy camera of yours?"

His eyes followed her fingers as she unbuttoned her top. She turned her back to undo her bra, still a bit shy about undressing in front of him. "Yeah, sure. Why?"

"I'd like to get some shots of Gabby and Gunner on Sunday."

Feeling like a heel for not giving in to going to church, she drew her nightgown over her head and tied the sash. She turned back to the bed as he opened the duvet cover and climbed in, his eyes extending a silent invitation to join him.

"Hey, you're not supposed to sleep on those," she told him, chastising his disregard for the pillows she'd carefully selected to match their duvet.

"On what?"

"The Euro squares, and all those shams. They're for decoration." She moved to the beautiful wooden trunk at the end of the bed and opened the lid. She pulled out pillows covered in white cases. "These are what we sleep on." She walked to his side of the bed and handed one to him.

"Oh," he said in a teasing tone. "What was I thinking?"

His eyes lingered on the sheer fabric of her nightgown for a moment, then he reached out and pulled her down. His cocky smile lasted only briefly before his mouth met hers, playfully at first, then he kissed her deeper, his longing apparent.

She loved the solid feel of his arms around her, couldn't help her heart from speeding as he flipped her and they sank against the downy duvet.

"I love you," he said in a throaty voice.

"I love you too." She closed her eyes and gave in to the feel of his lips against her neck, her bare shoulders. His fingers slipped beneath the straps of her gown and slid the silky fabric down.

In his arms she felt safe and loved—cherished.

He kissed her again, and she responded in kind, giving herself to Geary with surprising abandon.

In the minutes that followed, their bodies and souls became one.

Afterward, in the darkness, she rested in bed, still so as not to disturb her slumbering husband. Outside the window, a sliver of moon reflected over the lake, causing the water to shine.

Tears sprang unexpectedly.

For years, she'd wondered if she'd be lucky enough to find a man worth loving, someone who would share a life far different from what she'd seen growing up.

She'd once asked her mother if she loved her father. "Well, of course I love your father. He's my husband," had been her reply.

How many times had she watched her mother at the table, chain-smoking and waiting for her father to walk through the door?

When he did, smelling of cheap cigars and drugstore perfume, Faith knew what would follow—a war mounted of words and accusations that would eventually topple their family. No one could launch more deadly missiles than her mother. They viciously loved—and along with their marriage, both parents had imploded.

She had vowed to never let any man ruin her.

In Geary Marin, she'd found someone who would safely hold

her heart. Despite their differences, and she was learning there were many, she still knew she could trust him never to stomp on what really mattered.

With the back of her hand, she brushed away the moisture from her cheeks, evidence of her deepest fears. Looking through the window out over the water, she silently whispered a simple prayer. Perhaps her first.

Please, Lord, don't ever let what we have slip away.

16

On Saturday morning, she rose to find Geary lounging on the sofa eating a bowl of Fruit Loops and glued to a Road Runner cartoon on television.

"What are you—ten?" she teased as she headed for the coffeepot.

Her husband grinned. "I like how no matter how his plans backfire, Wile E. Coyote always gets back up and tries again."

She poured coffee into her travel mug and fastened the top. "Yeah, but he's always trying to take out the Road Runner. I mean, what did the bird ever do to him?"

"I never said he had a good plan. Only that he never quits." Geary lifted his bowl and drained the milk. "You going somewhere?"

Faith rolled her eyes. She marched over and took the empty bowl from his hands and placed it on the counter. "Uh, you're cute, but cute does *not* excuse bad manners. And yes, I told you I planned to go to River Oaks today for research." She grabbed her purse off the back of the barstool. "And about the twins' program at church tomorrow. No promises, but I'll try."

"You sure? 'Cause that'd be great." He pulled her into an embrace, nearly spilling her coffee despite the lid. "Got time for me to adequately thank you?"

She wiggled free. "Don't push your luck. Not all of us have your schedule." Smiling, she headed for the door.

See? She was good at this marriage thing. All it took was some compromise.

The clock on her car dashboard read nearly eleven o'clock by the time she exited the 610 to Westheimer Road. Armed with an iPad loaded with electronic files of information she'd researched, she turned north on River Oaks Boulevard, at LaMar High School. To her left was a church elegantly made of light gray stone. On the right was a shopping center, like any small strip mall you'd find in neighborhoods across the metro area.

Only this wasn't any neighborhood—this was River Oaks, the most affluent neighborhood in Houston.

It didn't take long before the scenery abruptly changed. A single lane turned into a boulevard with lush grass medians and stone monuments, marking the entry to an enclave of stately homes that were partially tucked out of view behind gated fences, pines, oak trees, and meticulously manicured hedges.

Some of the homes, she'd learned, were over twenty thousand square feet with multiple pools and garages that could shelter a dozen vehicles. Most included separate residence quarters for household staff, nannies, and gardeners who worked full-time for the wealthy families fortunate to live there. Many of the estates had been passed down several generations, but a good portion were purchased in recent years by businessmen who had admirably hit it big in oil or real estate—or both.

There were, of course, the occasional women who had built a name for themselves—many of them colorful characters. Take, for example, one of the most well-known and highly regarded residents, Lynn Wyatt, who made the social columns on a regular basis for hosting outrageous parties attended by worldwide celebrities. Years back, she'd hosted a dinner party for Princess Grace with Mick Jagger attending.

In her research, Faith stumbled on an article that said when Houston's former first lady, Elyse Lanier, moved into her peach-colored mansion bordering the country club, she removed the fence. When a friend warned that people dining at the club could now see into her backyard, she replied, "Exactly."

No doubt, ingredients for tabloid-type exposés highlighting celebrity and the lifestyles of the rich and famous were plentiful. But as a serious news reporter, Faith had to ask herself why any of that mattered to her viewers.

When she stumbled on the answer to that question, she'd have her story.

After taking a quick preliminary driving tour through the streets of River Oaks and snapping a few photos for future reference, she decided to head to a spa she'd seen online last night, located not far from that church she'd seen earlier. She passed DeeAnne Roberts on the way. Faith couldn't help but smile to herself, knowing her competition wouldn't recognize her in Geary's pickup.

While her fellow reporter would likely seek exclusive interviews with the famed residents, Faith would go for an entirely different approach.

She hated to waste the pedicure she'd just paid for less than a week ago, but a reporter had to do what a reporter had to do.

Door bells tinkled as she opened a heavy wooden door flanked by terra-cotta pots filled with bright red geraniums and blue lobelia. A tall girl with long blonde hair looked up from the sleek counter. "Hi, welcome to Jacques Bonheur. Can I help you?"

"I'd like a pedicure, please."

A sympathetic expression crossed the girl's magazine-quality face. "I'm so sorry. We are booked weeks out," she said in a voice slightly tinged with a foreign flair—one Faith suspected might be fake. The girl lifted a pen to a large appointment book. "Can I schedule something for you?"

Faith sighed. She should've expected this.

She gave the size 2 darling her own brilliant smile and dug into her bag and retrieved her wallet. She plucked five twenties from the bill compartment and placed them on top of the appointment book. "I'm afraid my schedule won't allow for a future appointment."

The girl's brows knit, then she looked up again. Recognition dawned.

Before the tony receptionist could speak, Faith leaned across the counter and placed two more twenties on the counter. "I'm Faith Marin of KIAM-TV, and I'm going to be broadcasting later today and *really* need that pedicure."

The girl quickly nodded. "Oh, I so understand. Let me see what I can do." She directed Faith to a sugar-pink divan with stainless steel accents, positioned against a window overlooking a beautifully manicured planting area leading to the parking lot. "Wait here. I'll be right back."

The girl returned quickly, sporting a broad smile. "We're in luck. One of our technicians will work to fit you in. Can I get you a glass of wine or some sparkling water while you wait?"

"The water would be great." Faith picked up a magazine, hoping she didn't have to sit long before being called back.

The receptionist returned with a stemmed glass of water, garnished with a sprig of mint. "You're that gal who talked the Hildebrand kid off the bridge."

Faith nodded, never sure how to respond when someone posed in a statement what probably should've been a question. "Uh, yes. That was my story. Now I anchor the weekend broadcasts."

The front door opened and three women entered with identical airbrushed complexions—Botoxed, microdermed, and chemically peeled unnaturally smooth.

The receptionist quickly turned in their direction. "Hi, ladies. We're ready for you."

Upon returning from taking the beautiful trio back, the girl slipped a card into Faith's hand. "I'm really interested in the news business and would love to talk to you about what it takes to break in."

Faith nodded and tucked the card in her purse before responding. "Sure. You can call me anytime." While she wasn't necessarily dying to open the proverbial career door for a young and stunningly beautiful wannabe, the contact might prove valuable at some point. Good reporters worked to build a large and varied network of story sources.

With a conspiratorial wink at her new friend, she added, "Hey, I'm just curious. Who were those women?"

The girl grew reluctant. "Uh . . . those women?"

"I'd be happy to arrange a private tour of the station," Faith quickly offered, causing any reservation the girl had about sharing customer information to suddenly vanish.

The receptionist responded by revealing their names. "The women come in quite often, always together," she said while checking the computer screen. "I don't think they live here in the Oaks." She typed something and then lifted her head. "Ah yes. They reside about sixteen blocks away." The pretty blonde receptionist lowered her voice. "If you want to know the truth, I highly suspect they're hunters."

"Hunters?"

"Yeah, you know—women who are looking to marry wealth."

A picture of the ill-fated Anna Nicole Smith formed in Faith's mind, and how the buxom blonde who'd looked so dumb had outsmarted many by marrying oil-soaked billionaire J. Howard Marshall, a former resident of River Oaks. The marriage lasted only fourteen months before Marshall passed at the age of ninety, leaving his twenty-six-year-old widow dripping in wealth, even though the funds were tied up in protracted probate litigation.

Maybe there was something here.

Minutes later, Faith sat in a plush leather recliner with her feet immersed in warm water that smelled slightly of jasmine. She was tempted to close her eyes and lean back against the massaging rollers. Instead she focused on the conversation of the three women located only feet away.

Faith started making mental notes.

She listened carefully. In very little time, she realized she had it. Her story.

Across from her were three career gold diggers, but it was Faith Marin who had just struck the real gold.

17

Faith slipped into the program on Sunday morning twenty minutes late. She hurried into Lake Pine Community Church and was quickly redirected to the older section of the small complex, which was connected to the worship center by a breezeway where the children's performance platform was erected at one end, with rows of aluminum folding chairs filling the remainder of the large room.

The Marin family sat in the front left row, an alarming discovery given it required her to march up the entire center aisle, alerting everyone in attendance that she was not on time.

Any effort to reduce the distraction her entrance caused was nullified given the need to murmur "excuse me" repeatedly as she brushed against the knees of Penny Baker and her daughter-in-law and past Dr. and Mrs. Brock before finally reaching her empty seat beside her husband.

"Hey, where've you been?" Geary whispered.

"Sorry, time got away from me," she whispered back, hoping he'd understand. He'd wanted her to go to church with him, but she'd begged off, needing extra sleep from working all night at the dining table. She'd promised to meet him for the twins' program, not expecting to get caught up again when she'd peeked at her project this morning. Before she knew it, her coffee had grown cold and she'd cut the time so close she had to skip a shower. Instead she simply pulled her hair back into a ponytail and put on a dab of mascara, glossed her lips, and raced out the door.

Her mother-in-law, obviously overhearing their exchange, patted her knee. "Don't worry about it, dear. Glad you're here now."

Perhaps it was the lack of sleep, but the comment only served to magnify her guilt. In the dim light of the room, she worried her nail between her teeth. Could she help it if juggling all this was getting to be a little bit too much? The pressure to bring in a story that was fresh and interesting, that would help her stand out, was immense. On top of that, fitting into the Marin family was a bit like walking a muddy field in heels.

Instinctively, she knew they all thought she had her priorities wrong. But none of the Marins really understood the demands of her job, one that sometimes required everything in order to succeed.

Geary fished for a living. Sure, she knew his profession carried a certain amount of stress, but nothing like what she experienced. His schedule was much more flexible.

Besides, it was her job at the station that provided their health insurance, retirement benefits, and a steady paycheck. Geary and his family should understand when she often had to make her career top priority.

Up on stage, a group of toddlers finished singing "Jesus Loves Me." Well, at least they stood up there while the teacher sang. One little guy, Faith guessed him to be about three, picked at his nose, stopping only to wave at his parents while exiting the stage.

The pianist immediately switched to a lively tune while a group of high school kids set up a canvas backdrop hand-painted with a tent and palm trees. Another couple of kids hoisted in buckets and poured sand at the base of the scene.

With the stage set complete, a Sunday school teacher led about a dozen children, all kindergarten age, up the steps and centered them in position. All wore sandals and were dressed in long tunics with colorful sashes, except for the two on the end—Gabby and Gunner.

The Sitterle kids wore white T-shirts and sweatpants covered in large white cotton balls with matching hats that sported ears. Apparently, Geary's niece and nephew were sheep.

Down the aisle several seats, Dilly beamed. Bobby Lee elbowed Wendell with pride.

Faith had to admit, her husband's niece and nephew were pretty cute up there.

She slipped her hand into Geary's and gave a squeeze, a signal that she wanted a truce, even if war had never been officially declared.

As if reading her mind, he squeezed her hand back.

Veta leaned in her direction. "Those costumes were a real pain to make," she whispered.

Faith listened to the story of Joseph and his brothers, of how they sold him into slavery as a result of their jealousy. Years later, God would turn what they intended for evil into good, ultimately setting up a situation for Joseph to bless the very ones who'd hurt him most.

She'd heard that story a number of times and wondered if Joseph felt bitterness in those years when he'd been exiled at the hands of his family—the ones who were supposed to love and care for him but didn't.

She wondered if he felt like God had abandoned him.

Her own mother had done her best, she supposed. Perhaps she'd tried to love well, and couldn't. Wasn't that the whole gist of the Bible story? What good would it do to harbor ill will for all the ways her mother's love fell short, when all that would do was sap her energy and keep her from becoming all she could be?

Even so, her mother had definitely fallen short of winning any parenting awards.

One Easter, her mom made a big deal of going to church. She bought brand-new outfits at Sears—a little pinstriped suit for Teddy Jr. complete with a tiny blue tie, and for Faith a light yellow dress with white polka dots and a wide satin sash that tied at the back. "Now, don't get your clothes dirty," she warned as they shuffled into the car.

Unfortunately, Faith got a bloody nose on the way home from church. "No!" her mother screamed when she saw the dark red splatters on the front of the dress.

Ignoring her bloody nose, Faith's mother tore the dress from her back as soon as they reached the front door, then ran to the kitchen sink with it, dousing the fabric with dish soap and running cold water over the stained portion. Her mother scrubbed harder and harder, murmuring under her breath.

A few days later, Faith accompanied her mom back to the Sears store. Handing a receipt to the clerk, her mother smiled and said, "I'd like to return this dress. I'm afraid it didn't quite fit my little girl."

The woman behind the cash register scowled. "Store policy is not to accept returns on purchases that have been worn. I'm sorry." She tried to hand the dress back.

Faith's mother refused to accept the garment. Instead she shook her head. "What do you mean you won't take the dress back?"

"The dress has been worn," the clerk repeated.

This seemed to push her mom over the edge. She screamed in protest, "What kind of fool are you? Do you know who my husband is? Are you aware I am a loyal customer who has shopped this store for years?" She pointed her polished red nail at the distressed young woman. "You'll take that dress back or I'll never bring my business to this store again. Do you hear me? Never!"

A small crowd gathered, some pointing and whispering. Faith recognized a little girl from school. The commotion seemed to scare her and she hid behind her own mother's legs.

Geary leaned over and startled her back to the present. "Are you okay?" he whispered.

"Huh?" Faith let the bad memory slip from her mind. "Yeah, sure."

Up on the stage, the teacher bent down on one knee and addressed the kids in the program. "Can anyone tell me what the moral of this story is? What are we supposed to do when our brothers or sisters do something that makes us mad?"

Gunner glanced sideways at his sister. "Smack 'em," he loudly announced without giving his answer a second thought.

His quick response garnered a laugh from the audience, despite the misdirected nature.

Gabby, on the other hand, didn't find her brother's remark so funny. She scowled and paid him back with a shove. Before Gunner had a chance for retribution, both Dilly and Bobby Lee darted onto the stage, taking hold of their little darlings. They marched them off the stage while the Sunday school teacher, who now looked a bit harried, quickly closed out the program and thanked everyone for coming.

When the lights came up, Veta shook her head. "Dilly and Bobby Lee sure have their hands full with those two."

Wendell agreed. "Nothing a little party on the backside wouldn't cure."

"Now, honey, we raised our family. You let them raise theirs."

He folded his arm around his wife's shoulders. "Yes, dear." He winked at Faith. "But I think a refresher sermon on training up your children might be appropriate for next Sunday."

As they parted in the parking lot, Wendell waved and shouted in their direction, "See you at the bowling alley."

Faith looked at Geary as they neared his pickup. "The bowling alley?"

"Yeah," he answered as he took out his keys. "Mom promised the kids we'd all go to Gutter Busters after the program. And I think Dilly said she had some big news she wanted to share."

She looked at him like he was crazy. "But, honey, you know I'm on air tonight. I need to spend this afternoon working on my story."

"All day?"

"I told you that. I want to have my idea ready to pitch to Clark tomorrow. At least in skeleton form."

Geary opened his door. "But what do I tell my family?"

Really? Was he going to pull that on her again? Make her feel guilty? Especially after she just gave up her entire morning to watch his niece and nephew in a church program?

"Fine! I'll go." She stomped to the passenger door and yanked it open. "You'll have to bring me back for my car."

"Are you going to be unreasonable about all this?"

"Unreasonable? My job can't always take a backseat to your family plans." She turned on the radio, dialing into her favorite classic channel.

Geary scowled as he pulled out of their parking spot. "Jobs come and go. But family is what is really important, don't you think?"

His comment made her blood instantly run thicker, warmer. "What does that mean?"

"It doesn't *mean* anything, only that—"

She raised her eyebrows. "Sounds like you're accusing me of not having my priorities straight."

Couldn't he recall all the concessions she'd been making lately? Seems the compromises were getting pretty one-sided. She didn't see him making a lot of adjustments in their married life.

"Don't put words in my mouth, Faith. You're overthinking things again. That's not what I meant." He pasted on an exaggerated smile and waved at the Hendersons as he nosed his pickup forward.

"Well, what did you mean?" she challenged.

"I mean, we don't want to start this marriage with all the emphasis being shifted from what's really important. That's all."

He leaned over and changed the channel to a country western station. "Sundays are supposed to be a day of rest, a time to focus on family."

Oh, he didn't really just change her channel! She glared at him and reached for the radio dial.

He looked across the seat at her. "Oh, now that's a bit childish, don't you think?"

Shaking inside, she held up her hand. "Look, I'm not doing this." True—she could verbally spar with him, try to make him see what a jerk he was being. But what was the point? She certainly wasn't about to turn into her mother here in the church parking lot. "Fine. Have it your way."

Geary rubbed at his chin. "Okay, listen, I'm not trying to start a fight here. I just wanted to make sure—"

In exasperation, she glared back at him. "Please don't push your luck. I gave in and said I'd go already."

His jaw locked. "Fine."

"Fine," she repeated.

They rode to the bowling alley in silence, a silence that marched across the sunbaked asphalt with them and through the front door.

Inside, Gutter Busters was like any bowling alley, with bright flashing lights, far too much noise, and the smell of fried food mingled with the slight aroma of lane oil.

Just her idea of a great way to spend a Sunday afternoon when she had work stacked up. Especially when she and Geary had let themselves grow sour with one another.

At the rear of the building, the owners maintained a full-service Chinese restaurant with paper lanterns hanging over booths with red leather bench seats. A large wall menu announced that they offered kung pao chicken, chow mein, spring rolls, and fried rice, in addition to four kinds of pizza and hand-scooped milk shakes in thirteen flavors.

Geary joined his dad up at the counter. He and Wendell sparred about who would pay. Wendell won.

Without saying anything, Geary put his hand on Faith's back and guided her to their assigned lanes. "You need my help?" he asked.

"Nope. I got it."

His mother watched, looking first at him, then back at her. "Everything okay?" she asked.

Faith forced a bright smile. "Yeah, sure. I haven't been bowling for years. I just hope I can keep up with all of you."

Veta was too polite to press the matter. Instead she patted Faith on the back. "Well, c'mon. Let's show these men how it's done."

The Marin family found ways to be enthusiastic about almost everything, but never more than bracing for some good old-fashioned competition.

Wendell quickly split them into two teams—Geary, his mother, and Bobby Lee on one team, Wendell, Faith, and Dilly on the other.

Geary placed his ball on the return. "Hey, Dill. You up for this?"

"Goodness, yes. I'm not sitting anything out," Dilly replied. She lifted little Sam into one of the hard plastic seats on the other side of the ball return.

Faith gave Geary's nephew a little smile. He stared back, his thumb tucked deep inside his mouth.

Bobby Lee stepped forward. "Before this competition begins, Dilly and I have news." He placed his hands on his wife's belly. "The Sitterle family just learned we're having another baby."

Dilly giggled. "Yup, we prayed for the Lord to rain down blessings and he forgot to turn off the faucet."

Veta's hands went to her mouth. "Oh my goodness. That's wonderful." She rushed to her daughter and drew her into a tight hug.

Wendell patted Bobby Lee on the back. "Well, God said to be fruitful and multiply. Congratulations!" He turned to Geary. "Better take lessons, son."

Faith cringed. Sure, she wanted children when the timing was right, but certainly she didn't want Geary's family weighing in on their personal decisions.

Dilly said she was about two months along, and that she wasn't even getting sick this time.

Faith gave her sister-in-law a hug. "I'm so happy for all of you," she said, while trying not to think about how Dilly and Bobby Lee barely controlled the offspring they already had.

As if on cue, the twins tore across the badly stained industrial carpet toward the arcade room—that is, until Bobby Lee hollered and told them to get back. Without acknowledging their father's instruction, they diverted and chased each other, running in front of the neighboring teams.

Dilly marched in that direction. "Gabby! Gunner! Get over here," she shouted.

The twins ignored her as well and raced over to the vending machines near the back wall. "Dad, can we have a quarter?" they shouted over their shoulders while pounding the glass.

Faith looked over at Geary. Normally, their eyes would connect in solidarity, exchanging a silent understanding that they would raise their own children differently when the time came.

Geary wasn't paying attention. He grabbed his rental shoes and bent to put them on.

She picked up her own rental shoes, set her resolve, and sat in a seat opposite him. She removed her leather flats and shoved on the ugly brown lace-up rentals, wondering how many pairs of sweating feet had been inside. She pulled the laces tight and tied them, then stood, primed for a face-off.

Bobby Lee frowned. "Well, look who's here." He pointed toward the door.

Her eyes followed where he directed. Walking toward them was Stacy Brien. Her dark hair was pulled up and carelessly clipped at the top of her head, showing off large gold earrings dangling from her ears. The image gave off the exotic look of a gypsy.

The vixen waved.

Great. That's all I need this afternoon on top of everything else.

Bobby Lee wiggled his fingers in a wave at Stacy, then turned back toward Faith, his eyes flashing yellow lights of caution.

Wendell clapped his hands together. "Well, look who's here. You up for some bowling, Stacy? You're welcome to join us."

She smiled and shook her head. "No thanks, just heard y'all were over here and thought I'd come watch for a bit before my massage appointment."

Wendell nodded. "Ah—well, okay then." To everyone else he said, "Okay, Marins, y'all ready for this?" He moved to the ball rack and tried several out, finally settling on a dark navy ball with tiny white specks.

Veta set up the electronic score sheet, seeming to punch buttons randomly. She hollered back over her shoulder, "We're the Lane Changers. What's your team name going to be?"

Dilly pulled her long red hair back and secured it with a rubber band. "Uh, we'll be the King Pins."

Bobby Lee pointed at his wife's stomach. "More like the Diaper Pins."

She playfully slapped his arm. "People don't even use those anymore, silly."

Stacy slid into a seat not far from Geary. He nodded hello and she gave him a brilliant smile, which irked Faith to no end.

Bobby Lee sidled in next to the vixen and pulled off his boots. "Whew," he said, waving one near her. "Dilly, I think you'd better buy some more of that foot powder."

Stacy didn't hide the fact she was repulsed by the smell. She darted up and moved over behind Wendell and Veta.

Bobby Lee winked at Faith.

Wendell seemed to second-guess his initial choice of bowling ball and eyed another on the rack. Dilly sidled up next to him and bumped her dad's shoulder with hers. "C'mon, Dad. The ball doesn't matter. It's all in the follow-through." She showed him by example, though her practice swing seemed a bit off-kilter.

"The mighty King Pins will whoop on the Lane Changers any day of the week, and twice on Sunday," she bragged. "Oh, well, will you look at that? It's Sunday," she said loud enough for the entire bowling alley crowd to hear.

Bobby Lee grinned. "That so?"

Dilly nodded. "Yup, you just wait and see." Her head turned. "Gabby! Gunner! Stay close now."

Bobby Lee waved his children back. "Do what your mama says or there will be consequences."

Faith let out a heavy sigh. Critical work hours were ticking away, and she was stuck in a bowling alley of all places, with misbehaving children wreaking havoc on her mental state. And a dark-haired diva who set Faith's nerves on edge every time she came near.

Still, she'd agreed to sing along, no matter how off-key the situation. Now she just needed to make the best of it.

Dilly was up first. Her sister-in-law positioned her ball against the top of her stomach, then took several quick steps toward the foul line and swung through, releasing the ball down the lane. She scowled after discovering she'd only knocked down five pins.

Her second try resulted in a disappointing gutter ball.

Little Sam popped the thumb from his mouth and clapped his chubby hands together.

Dilly returned to her seat and kissed the top of his head. "Thank you, baby."

Geary looked back at his sister and gloated. "Ah, too bad. Guess it's my turn now." He stood and retrieved his ball from the return. Acting like a pro or something, he waved first one open palm then the other over the air jet.

Faith rolled her eyes.

"Watch and see how it's done," he said to no one in particular. Stacy mouthed "good luck" in his direction and flashed him another brilliant smile.

Dilly scooped up Sam from the adjoining seat and handed the toddler off to her family's friend. "Stacy, do you mind? I swear, I seem to have to go to the bathroom every ten minutes."

Stacy opened her mouth to protest, but Dilly scurried away.

Geary lined up with confidence.

"Careful," Wendell warned his son with a wide smile. "Pride goes before a fall." He stood with his hands on his hips and watched as Geary made his approach and drove his ball down the lane.

In a near perfect arc, the black bowling ball made its way down the right side, very near the gutter, then turned at the last minute to knock down all the pins.

Geary pumped the air with his fist. "Strike!"

"Very good, son. Very good," his mother commended.

Stacy clapped. Little Sam mimicked her and pressed his pudgy palms together several times.

Faith sighed. Obviously, Geary was not new to this bowling business—a game she'd only occasionally tried, each time playing badly.

Veta turned. "Faith, dear. You're up next."

She stood. She needed to save face and not make a fool of herself. Stepping forward, she tried to ignore the pressure and mentally conjured the little she remembered about how to line up and just where to aim the ball.

"You got this?" Wendell asked, hopeful.

Faith nodded. "Yup, I got this." Her words sounded far more confident than she felt. Still, she drew a deep breath, suddenly hearing her mother's voice in her head. *Fake it until you make it.*

She stepped onto the wooden platform and positioned herself at the foul line. All she had to do was aim her ball at the center arrow painted on the lane several feet ahead of her. She might not make a strike like Geary. But she wouldn't completely humiliate herself.

She squared her shoulders. From behind, Geary was no doubt watching her every move. As was Stacy. Even though it was a long shot, she wanted to score a strike and wipe off the smug smile she imagined on that woman's face.

With artificial confidence, she took one step and pulled the ball back. Her feet moved through the rest of the approach and she followed through, letting the ball make its way down the alley.

She held her breath, watching as the ball slowly rolled forward, a little too much to the right, she was afraid. Then, in a stroke of pure luck, pins flew.

"Attagirl." Wendell watched from the sideline. "A baby split."

A what?

She looked over at her father-in-law, trying to hide her confusion.

"You can pick up the two and the seven. You can do it," he assured her.

She nodded and retrieved her ball from the return, passing right in front of Geary on the way. Not daring to look at her husband, she mimicked drying her palms on the air jet.

Just fake it, she reminded herself.

Her second try wasn't as big of a success. She only took down the seven pin.

"Ah, better luck next time," she heard Geary say, in the same syrupy manner one might use to give condolences to a child whose pet frog had died.

She didn't need any superfluous sympathy, thank you very much.

She parked her bottom in the hard orange chair, then yanked her iPhone from her bag and scanned some of the articles she'd bookmarked.

Little Gabby planted herself next to Faith. "Are you all mad again?"

Dilly quickly waved over her daughter. "C'mon over here and

let me do something with that hair." She licked her fingers and settled some wild blonde tresses behind the little girl's ear.

Gabby wiggled away and went back to chasing her brother around the seating area, accidently bumping against Faith as she ran by.

Frustrated, Faith slipped her phone back in her purse. Her sister-in-law stood and rubbed at her back. "I think I'm the one needing that massage."

"Yes, and on that note I'd better get going." Apparently, Stacy had quickly tired of sitting on the sidelines, in more ways than one.

Everyone bid her goodbye, then focused back on the competition.

While Geary leaned over his mother, explaining again how the automatic scoring worked, Faith folded her arms tightly against her chest and waited for her next turn.

"Hey, are you guys hungry?" Bobby Lee plopped down several white cardboard containers on a nearby table. "Anybody up for some spring rolls or crab Rangoon?"

Gabby and Gunner slammed up against the table, out of breath. "I'm hungry," Gunner said, brushing sweaty hair off his forehead with his arm.

Gabby leaned over with her arms on the table. "Me too. I'm starving, Daddy."

Faith's own growling stomach suggested she was hungry as well.

"Okay. Now, stand back," Bobby Lee instructed. He motioned little Sam over and opened the tops of the steaming containers. Before he doled out food, he handed the twins and Sam fortune cookies, reversing the common "dinner first" mantra.

Her brother-in-law saw her watching and tossed her a fortune cookie. "Here, catch."

She ripped off the clear cellophane and broke the crisp cookie in two, shoving a piece inside her mouth. The fortune inside read, *He who climbs fastest doesn't always climb higher.*

She groaned and crumpled the piece of paper, no longer hungry. Even the fortune cookie was laying guilt on her.

Wendell stood behind his wife, looking up at the scoreboard. He rubbed his wife's shoulders—even though she was the competition.

Maybe she'd gone a bit overboard with her reaction. Truth was, she really could hang out with Geary and his family for another couple of hours and still make the broadcast. She'd just hoped to squeeze in more research before tomorrow. And Geary's attitude had rubbed her wrong, the way he didn't understand her priorities.

Of course, she didn't initially embrace his either.

If she let this battle escalate, would she really win? Her parents' relationship was a clear answer to that question.

Still, it wasn't easy when what she wanted to do and what she *should* do were in conflict.

Bobby Lee stepped up and aligned his shot. He pulled back his arm and let his ball go, sending it speeding down the lane and knocking down the entire ten pins. A strike!

Her brother-in-law celebrated with an embarrassing amount of gusto. First he squatted and waddled along the foul line, screeching like some waterfowl in mating season. Then he stood and grabbed his mother-in-law's arm, pulling her out of her seat. He twirled her around. "So how does it feel to be a winner, Queen Lane Changer?"

Veta laughed. "Good. Feels really good."

Faith couldn't help but smile. No doubt Geary's family was a bit offbeat—even annoying at times. But they were also kind and generous and devoted to one another.

Hadn't both Dilly and Bobby Lee had her back when it came to Stacy Brien?

Geary patted his brother-in-law on the back. "Nice one, Bobby Lee."

In the end, the Lane Changers won, leaving the King Pins licking their wounds.

Wendell didn't bother to hide the fact he hated losing. Frowning, he scooped a fortune cookie from the table and broke it open. He popped some of the hard cookie in his mouth, then read the fortune. "Now I'm warned this will not be my lucky day?" he complained, raising the piece of paper in the air. "Ah, what does some cookie maker know? Every day with this pretty lady is my lucky day." He took Veta into his arms and dipped her, ending with a Rhett Butler/Scarlett O'Hara kiss that made even Faith blush. He puffed his chest. "That's how that's done, boys."

Geary laughed and eased his feet out of the rental shoes. "You know what they say—those who can't bowl, kiss."

Dilly joined them with little Sam on her hip. "Oh really? Who says that?"

Their eyes met then, Faith's and Geary's. His gaze lingered.

She swallowed the lump building in her throat—and her pride. With a timid smile, she mouthed, "Congratulations."

He rewarded her feeble conciliatory gesture with a smile of his own, the same one she'd seen on their honeymoon when she'd suggested they might go for a hike on the island, take in the scenery.

"The only scenery I care to enjoy is right here," Geary had teased while pulling the coverlet up over their bare shoulders for the third morning in a row.

She'd easily agreed. As much as she loved the idea of exploring nature, the contours of his muscled forearms were far more intriguing, the hard ripples of his chest more entertaining.

Faith loved the way his lips nibbled at her shoulders, loved feeling the coarseness of his stubble against her neck as he found his way to her earlobe. She loved the weight of his body as he shifted, his breath ragged. The way his eyes found her own, communicating utter desire, as he abandoned himself to her—and she to him.

In those moments, she'd never felt more vulnerable.

Until now.

Geary reached out his hand and she let him pull her up to him.

His fingertips went to her cheek. "Hey, babe. Let's get you home now."

She buried her head in his chest. "I love you," she whispered.

Suddenly, a child screamed.

The commotion pulled their attention to the back of the lanes, where the sound had originated from behind the pins.

Dilly thrust Sam at Faith. "Oh my lands, take him!"

Frantic, her sister-in-law scrambled over a small pile of discarded rental shoes and tore down one of the lanes, with Bobby Lee and Wendell close behind.

"What in the world?" Geary left her holding his nephew and bolted that same direction.

Gabby's head popped up from behind the pins, from the darkened space where mechanical pinsetters scooped and reset everything back in place. "Gunner's stuck," the wide-eyed little girl reported just as screams filled the air again.

Veta's hands flew to her mouth. "Oh Lord, help," she muttered.

The entire bowling alley went into shutdown mode, including the obnoxious music piped in overhead. An Asian man's voice came over the loudspeaker. "Attention, bowlers—please stand by. We have a—well, a situation we hope to resolve very, very quickly."

Emergency workers arrived, blowing through the bowling alley carrying black medic bags. Minutes later, they'd extricated Gunner and carried the frightened little boy out on a stretcher board.

Dilly jogged alongside. "Mommy's here, baby. Everything's going to be all right."

The entire Marin family followed, shaken but thankful the unfortunate event had resulted in minimal injury—a broken arm. Apparently, his arm had gotten caught in the automated equipment.

A harried-looking owner also walked them outside. He wrung his hands. "If there's anything we can do . . ."

Wendell squeezed his shoulder. "Thank you, Mr. Heng. This was not the fault of your establishment. Those kids should never have been playing back there. I'm sorry for the disruption to your business."

Mr. Heng bobbed his head. "Ah, thank you. You will not sue then?"

Wendell extended his hand. "Absolutely not. Of course not."

Worry slipped from the owner's face. He and Wendell shook hands, then everyone headed to their individual cars.

Faith buckled her seat belt. "Is Gunner going to be okay?"

Geary nodded. "Yeah, but he'll need a cast. It shook Dilly up pretty good, though. Bobby Lee too."

She leaned her head against the seat back. "Well, all's well that ends well, I guess. Maybe in the future, they'll watch those kids a bit closer."

Her husband's face closed in. "It was an accident, Faith."

"Well, I know. I only meant—" She stopped mid-sentence and quickly doused her words so as not to let any smoldering tension flare. "I'm just glad he's going to be fine," she offered, surprised their interaction had so easily turned fractious again. This was something new, this relational obstacle course.

"Me too," he confessed. One of his hands went to his cheek and he started rubbing. "I've got to tell you, seeing my nephew caught in that machine scared me. His little arm was pretty mangled."

She looked across at her husband, sensed a fracture in his normally calm exterior. Perhaps that was why he was so testy.

Those kids were unruly terrors, in her opinion. But she knew Geary adored Dilly and Bobby Lee's children. They were cute, especially little Sam, but goodness knows they needed some discipline.

Geary's hand went for the radio knob. "Do you mind?"

"No, no—go ahead."

She reached across the seat and lightly brushed his arm, hoping the gesture might abate his tension. He responded by taking her hand and tucking it inside his.

They rode like that for several blocks, content to sit in silence until they hit a red light. When the signal changed, Geary drove forward instead of turning on the road leading back to the church, where her car was still parked.

She looked over. "Geary, where are you going?"

"To the hospital," he said, anxiously drumming the steering wheel with his thumb. "There's a chance—however small—Gunner might need surgery. An orthopedist can only rule the possibility out after an MRI, to see the extent of the tissue damage."

She pulled her hand from his grip. "But I've got to go home, get dressed, and head for the station, or I'll be late for the broadcast."

His fingers tightened on the wheel. "Can't you call in? I mean, this is pretty important."

"Geary, I'm the weekend anchor. I can't just call in. Especially two and a half hours before broadcast."

"All right." Without signaling, he veered off into a CVS Pharmacy parking lot and whipped around and headed back in the opposite direction.

"Oh my goodness, are you mad at me? This is my job." Her anger flared, still braided with her desire for him to understand.

His foot pressed the accelerator and they sped up. "I think we already had this conversation today."

"This—is—my—job," she repeated. "Why are you being such a jerk?"

He turned to her. "Because this is family, and family always comes first. Is this how it's going to be when we have kids? Are you going to rush off to work, no matter what their needs?"

She fisted her hands, pressing her nails into her skin so hard it hurt. "Are you going to dock your bass boat and get a real job? One with a guaranteed income and benefits, 401(k)s and bonuses, so I can stay home with our kids when they get runny noses?"

Her words hung in the air for several seconds, and she found herself wishing she could gather and stuff the truth of them back in hiding. But it was too late.

Her thoughtlessness exploded like shrapnel.

She reached for his arm. “Geary, I—”

Instinctively, he pulled away from her. She knew then that more than just her temper had blown up.

The tears came, and the guilt. She wanted desperately to move the needle back to before those dreadful words left her lips. But deep down, she realized there would be no taking back what she’d said.

Especially when she saw the hurt on her husband’s face.

18

Geary stood at the doorway of her hospital room, familiar . . . and hesitant.

He wore jeans and a white button-down shirt. His dark hair short with tiny curls at the neckline. In many ways, he looked very much like he had that first day at the lake. Except for his eyes. His blue eyes were hollow, puddled with worry.

"Faith?" The way he said her name invited a visceral reaction in every cell of her body, at least those she could feel. It was as if the proteins and nucleic acids within their membranes had a memory of their own. She found this strangely comforting, given the unreliability of her own mind.

"Can I come in?"

She couldn't help it—her eyes welled with tears.

He rushed to her side. "I'm here. Faith, I'm right here."

He stroked her left arm. She couldn't feel his touch.

The bandages—the helmet. She must look awful. Despite wanting to hide from his seeing her like this, she clung to his arm with her right hand, afraid to let him go.

"I—was—shot." Tears streamed down her face as she forced the words through her lips.

His own eyes filled. "I know, babe." His words were ragged and brimming with grief. He blinked several times. "But the doctors say you're going to survive. The roughest part is behind us."

The word *us* did not pass her notice.

Her fingers dug into his flesh. "What—happened?"

Geary's forehead wrinkled. He squinted, examining her face, her words.

"Shot. What—happened?" she repeated.

He quickly nodded. "Yes, you were shot. What do you remember about that day?" His question mimicked her doctor's earlier approach.

She closed her eyes. Took a deep breath.

A few details began to form. The blue sky. Lots of people. A little boy.

Her eyes flew open in panic. Even the slight recollection punched at her gut. She inhaled, the frantic effort jagged and sharp.

His hand tightened on her arm, as if he were trying to hold on for the both of them. "Don't—don't think about any of that now. There's time for all that later." His fingers went to her cheek. "You're going to make it through this," he managed, his voice strangled. "And I'm going to help you."

There was a rap at the open doorway and Dr. Wimberly walked in. "I'm glad you're both here."

Geary stood and shook hands with the doctor, a familiarity between the two men apparent.

Her medical team had no doubt looked to Geary to make critical decisions on her behalf while she was in the coma. He was, after all, still legally her husband.

Dr. Wimberly pulled up a chair and sat. He motioned for Geary to do the same before reaching for Faith's hand. "How are you feeling?"

Before she could answer, Geary spoke up. "A few memories are coming back."

Dr. Wimberly slowly nodded. "Ah . . ." A look passed between him and her husband. "Yes, I would expect that. I think we'll find

Faith's cognitive recovery will accelerate rapidly over the next few days." To her, he said, "Faith, I think you are at a point where I can explain in a little more detail your injuries and our treatment plan from here. First, are you hurting?"

"No." She pushed the single word out against the raw thickness in her throat.

Dr. Wimberly nodded. "The irritation from that tube will subside rather quickly," he assured her. "Your recovery has been quite remarkable. Much better than we'd hoped, even."

She learned emergency personnel had rushed her to Memorial Hermann after the shooting. Miraculously, a sniper's shot had knocked off his aim. The bullet that would have been fatal instead grazed the top of her head.

"You have a brain injury resulting from a trauma that required surgery. We performed what's called a craniectomy, where we removed the fragments of bone and relieved the intracranial pressure by not replacing the bone flap immediately. Currently, you still have minor swelling and fluid buildup, which is likely the medical impetus for the lack of feeling and impairment. We have every reason to hope that will resolve, given time."

Geary's blue eyes turned hopeful. "Does that mean the issues with Faith's left side might improve?"

Dr. Wimberly nodded. "We hope for that resolution, yes. Of course, brain injuries are a bit finicky. There is no way to fully predict the course of recovery, or the extent."

She nodded, trying to absorb the information. She'd been shot and had been in the hospital for weeks with Dr. Wimberly and his team of neurosurgeons fighting to keep her alive.

The knowledge was too much to fully comprehend. Exhausted, she focused her thoughts on Dr. Wimberly and made every effort to listen as he explained what was ahead.

"In terms of treatment, our next step, now that we have the swelling under control, is to secure the bone flap back in place."

Geary cleared his throat. "And when will you do that?"

"I've scheduled the procedure for first thing in the morning."

"Tomorrow?" The faint alarm in Geary's voice matched her own reaction.

"The risk is minimal," the doctor quickly assured them. "The upside is we'll be able to remove the helmet at that point, and Faith will be a lot more comfortable." He stood, talking to Geary more than her. "As soon as we're medically able, we'll move her over to TIRR Memorial, the rehab center of our medical system. I'll continue to follow her there, but another team of professionals will guide the second phase of her recovery."

Geary stood as well and followed Dr. Wimberly to the door.

"She no doubt has a long road ahead, given the extent of her injuries. Still, your wife's prognosis could have been far more grim." The doctor stopped and placed his hand on Geary's shoulder. "Her recovery so far has been nothing short of a miracle."

"Believe me," Geary said, "masses of people have been praying. Faith is alive." His voice choked with emotion. "I'm incredibly grateful."

Dr. Wimberly gave Geary a quick pat, then continued down the hall, leaving Geary standing with his back to her, rubbing at the base of his neck.

He returned to her bedside, swiping at his eyes with the back of his hand. He looked wrecked. The past weeks had definitely taken a toll.

In her weakened state, she still recalled the hurt between them—before. How she'd wounded his spirit.

Yet he was here.

With her good hand, she picked at the blanket. "Tell me—more."

He'd learned of the shooting when his mother frantically called after seeing the story break on the news. He'd rushed home from Arkansas in the middle of a tournament, leaving his boat docked at Lake Ouachita and booking a charter flight out of Little Rock.

When he finally made it to the hospital, she was already in surgery. "I was afraid I'd never see you again," he confessed, emotion clouding his expression.

Wendell and Veta organized a round-the-clock prayer vigil. Their care to rally such support was remarkable, given the disintegration of her relationship with their son.

"On the fourth day, doctors adjusted your level of sedation so they could draw you out of the medically induced coma to do some testing. We were all thrilled when you responded to questions and were able to follow Dr. Wimberly's instructions to raise your fingers on your right hand—a great sign." Geary wove his fingers through her own and squeezed.

The part of her brain that processed instructions was not fully damaged, even though a bullet had traveled the full length of the surface of her left hemisphere at a thousand feet per second. All things considered, she was phenomenally lucky. The bullet had not sliced a major vein or artery in her brain.

Had the bullet passed through the area any deeper, it is unlikely she would have survived. There would have been too much damage.

As it was, her ability to follow a command meant the centers in her brain were intact and communicating with each other, a positive sign.

No doubt, in those early hours Geary had been terrified she might not recover. And helpless at the thought there was nothing he could do to make her well.

If there was anything she'd learned being his wife—Geary Marin really wanted nothing more than to be her Prince Charming.

She didn't deserve his devotion.

In the predawn hours of the following morning, two women entered her room dressed in blue scrubs and caps. One held a clipboard and moved to the monitors near her bed, looking over the top of her reading glasses at the graphs and numbers displayed.

"Looks like you had a rough night," she noted.

How could the nurse come to that conclusion from simply viewing data? Did those machines record what it felt like to wake in a fog, to be told life had been forever altered? Did those little flashes and beeps, the machines and bags of body fluids hanging from her bed, so easily decipher this terror?

In less than an hour she would undergo a surgical procedure where a piece of her skull stored in specialized refrigeration would be replaced with tiny plates and screws. The whole idea sounded like something out of a science fiction novel.

Yes—she'd had a very bad night.

The nurse with the clipboard left and a white-coated attendant swooped into her room, carrying a large white cover. "Here," he said. "This will keep you warm until we get you down to the surgery unit."

After giving Faith something to take the edge off her building anxiety, the nurse leaned across and patted her good shoulder. "Are we ready?"

She closed her eyes and nodded, suddenly feeling very alone.

"Okay, Faith. This young man is going to take you on down to surgery. We'll see you when you get back on the floor."

She heard a loud click and the bed began to move.

Despite the slight sedation she'd been given earlier, she pushed her right hand against the white sheet tucked around her body. Her eyes searched frantically back and forth. "Wait!" she managed to say through the fog of sedation.

The white-coated attendant pushing the metal gurney paused. "What's that?" he said.

She heard pounding footsteps—growing closer.

"Faith—Faith, I'm here!"

The helmet kept her from turning her head. Geary rushed up alongside. He pulled the sheet down and grabbed her hand. "Sorry, babe. Traffic." He tried to catch his breath. "I'm here now."

His presence calmed her, made her feel safe somehow. Geary walked alongside the gurney, holding her hand.

Seconds later, they were outside the surgical suite. "I'm afraid this is where you have to say goodbye," the attendant told Geary, who nodded.

Her husband brought her hand to his lips. "You're going to be all right," he promised, almost more to convince himself than her.

Suddenly, she could barely keep her eyes open. Despite earlier reservations, she looked at him in desperation. "Don't—leave—me."

"I won't. I promise. I won't leave you."

Minutes later, she lifted her heavy lids to see a man in matching blue cap and scrubs. He smiled. "Faith, it's Dr. Wimberly. I'm going to take good care of you." He nodded at the anesthesiologist, who administered something into her PIC line. Dr. Wimberly's face softened. "Time to go night-night."

Before the thick darkness completely swept her away, she saw Geary's face in her mind. As unconsciousness closed in, her thoughts strangely sharpened.

A television guest had once explained how when a bear is caught in the wild, by instinct it will chew off its own appendage in order to be free, even if it means limping for the rest of its life.

Facing unmet expectations, she and Geary had peeled the skin off their relationship one tiny slice at a time, until they were bare and their souls exposed, their marriage crippled.

Even so, their hearts were still attached as securely as the lock still in place under that pier.

And she knew one more thing.

If she could turn the clock back, she'd change everything.

19

In the weeks following the incident at the bowling alley, a lot about her marriage began to dawn on Faith.

The realization her husband failed to understand her job and what would be required to succeed was sobering, to say the least. Worse, he questioned her priorities and commitment to family.

Yes, family was important.

While she was very fond of the close-knit Marins, she'd only meant to convey that she simply couldn't afford to place her career on hold every time one of them sneezed. When the time came for her and Geary to have their own children, and that was still years down the road, she'd shift her world to accommodate their newly created family unit. Surely Geary had to know that. Until then, her work was important and there would be times the station must come first.

Even more sobering was acknowledging how she felt about *his* career choice. She wanted to be supportive of his fishing, but truthfully she wasn't all that enamored with the idea their financial security rested in large measure on whether or not the bass were biting on crankbait or woolly buggers, or that the season, time of day, and weather could determine the size of his paycheck.

While she would never admit it out loud, Prince Charming would look far better sitting behind a desk wearing a suit and tie.

Oh yes, she knew how that sounded. At best, she'd been disingenuous. At worst, she was a complete imposter, hiding her true feelings from even herself. But when placed in hot water, feelings come to a boiling point, and he and his family had turned up the heat too far that day. Without meaning to, she'd ended up spouting her true sensibilities.

But she'd never meant to hurt him.

Now she slipped in the back door of the station, hours earlier than her typical Monday mornings.

If her meeting with Clark Ravino went well, everything could change for them financially. But after last night's broadcast she'd seen DeeAnne Roberts exiting Clark's office buttoning her blouse.

If their newly hired news director was one of *those*—the ones who required favors to be considered for promotion—she was sunk before she ever pitched her idea.

Newsroom politics could be grueling, and never more than when a new person with power was dropped into the mix and everyone at the station scrambled to gain position.

There was a much-talked-about anecdote of a crime reporter in California who tried to impress his new station owners by paying desperate street kids to commit crimes, allowing him to scoop every other reporter in his market.

Faith was not willing to employ any outrageous tactics. She'd simply be the smartest, most hardworking anchor and would deliver top-rate stories that would attract viewers.

She kept those ideals foremost in her mind as she rapped on Clark's door frame.

He looked up. "Hey, Faith. Come on in."

Over the next hour, the station's news director sat across from her with his elbows on the desk, listening with rapt attention as she explained how she'd driven out to River Oaks and the idea she'd stumbled on. "This story has everything, Clark. Highlighting an issue about young women and what they believe about the need for a good education, and how that plays into getting ahead in life, will not only prick society's sensibilities but will also resonate with those watching for the human interest appeal. I mean, if the attitude I intend to expose gains traction among young women, we might as well go back to the sixties."

He stood and came around the desk. "I absolutely agree. You've hit the jackpot. Something told me I could count on you, Faith. You've got what it takes to go far. Not only the drive but an intuition few exhibit in this business."

Faith couldn't wait to share her ecstatic news. In fact, something this big deserved a celebration. She could use this opportunity to mend things with Geary, maybe dial back the chill that had descended over their relationship.

Normally, she'd prefer to commemorate an achievement by going out to dinner at an exclusive restaurant. Instead she'd cook. He'd like that.

On the way home, she stopped at H-E-B and picked up steaks. Even though the price was exorbitant, she splurged and bought top sirloin. She also picked out two large Idaho baking potatoes and wheeled the grocery cart to the dairy aisle for real butter and sour cream.

Geary said he loved his mother's home cooking. Well, she'd blow him away tonight. And she'd dress really cute, maybe wear that pink blouse he liked.

Before heading for the checkout she even splurged on a bottle of Napa Valley cabernet. They only had wine on select occasions, but tonight was special. This proved she'd been right to make her work a priority for now.

Geary constantly talked about what might be possible for him on the bass champ circuit. Likewise, this opportunity would open doors for her, providing potential to move up—maybe even to weeknight anchor. Beyond that, she could go national. If Katie Couric started at a local station and made it to the top, why couldn't she?

She arrived home before Geary. After unpacking the groceries, Faith marinated the steaks using a recipe she found on the Food Channel website. She scrubbed the potatoes and wrapped them in aluminum foil, then tried her best to duplicate a salad she'd found on Pinterest, one with arugula lettuce topped with chèvre and blackberries. She'd decided to skip trying to make the dressing and had bought a bottle of vinaigrette that cost nearly six dollars.

For dessert, she spooned store-bought panna cotta into little bowls and drizzled honey over top. Smiling, she scooped a sample into her mouth with her finger, then garnished the desserts with mint and placed them in the refrigerator.

The clock on the dining room wall showed nearly five o'clock. She had time for a quick shower before Geary was due home.

Faith was drying off when she heard the front door close, signaling her husband had arrived. She quickly dressed, then spritzed her favorite cologne, Romance by Ralph Lauren, across her décolleté using the bottle Geary had bought for her birthday.

A thrill of anticipation fluttered through her tummy. While his mother could put a spread of food on a table that would rival Paula Deen's, she hoped to prove she could hold her own, even if on this rare occasion. Geary would be impressed.

She headed down the hallway lined with his family photos. As she passed by, it dawned on her she'd never added their wedding portrait to that wall, and she made a mental promise to remedy that.

"Hey, honey." She entered the living room and leaned to accept his kiss on her cheek. "I hope you're hungry because I cooked up a little something special."

He frowned. "Uh, didn't you get my text?"

"What text?"

"Mom fried up a big batch of catfish to take over to Dilly's.

I ate some before I came home." Seeing the look on her face, he repeated, "I sent you a text."

She turned away to hide her brittle reaction. Of course he'd eaten at his mother's.

Faith grabbed the towel and wiped her hands, then let it drop to the counter. She forced a smile. "Oh well—I guess we can eat the steak tomorrow night."

"Yeah, about that—I'm heading over to Toledo Bend in the morning. One of the finalists came down with a stomach bug, opening up a spot in the Big Bass Splash tournament. I should be home late tomorrow night."

She swallowed her growing irritation. "That's great, honey. You've been wanting to get some more points." The Bassmaster circuit qualification process was based on a cumulative score, and Geary was always looking for opportunities to advance his.

Her husband moved to the kitchen and opened the refrigerator door. "Oh, Faith. Looks like you went to a lot of effort." He reached inside and pulled a piece of white cheese off the salad. "What's this?"

She told him it was chèvre—a goat cheese with a mild, sweet flavor. He popped it in his mouth and wrinkled his nose. "From goats, huh?" He reached back in and picked nearly all the berries off the plates. "I love blackberries. Never seen them on a salad though."

He tossed the dark purple berries inside his mouth, then folded the towel she'd left crumpled on the counter and placed it neatly next to the sink.

Determined to hide her disappointment, she reached around him and put the butter and sour cream back in the refrigerator. "Well, I guess we can still eat dessert." She reached for the panna cotta. "I have news."

He pulled off his cap and placed it on a barstool, then slid into a chair at the small dining table. "You had that meeting, right?"

"Yes, with Clark Ravino, our newly hired news director." Give her husband two points for remembering. "He really liked my idea for the River Oaks story."

She placed the little dishes of panna cotta on the table.

His eyebrows lifted as he grabbed his spoon.

"Panna cotta, with honey," she said before he could ask.

Geary nodded and scooped up a bite and placed it in his mouth. "Hmm—that's interesting." He looked at her then, with those blue eyes. "Look, I'm sorry about dinner. Really, I am."

She shrugged. "No, it's fine," she said, amazed she could so easily lie after her earlier epiphany. Of course, she'd come from a family of liars.

Geary's bunch, on the other hand, gave new meaning to the word *enmeshed*. Add the church "family" to the mix, and she could easily suffocate in the crush of familial relationships.

With renewed determination, she told Geary all about how she'd pitched her idea, how Clark had reacted even better than she'd hoped. "I've really impressed him," she confided. "I mean, it really feels good to have someone of his stature recognize my journalistic abilities and give me praise."

"That's good to hear." Geary finished his dessert in four bites and placed his spoon back on the table. "By the way, I hope it doesn't wreck our budget, but I bought a case of Swamp Donkeys off Eddie Gentry."

Faith scowled. "A case of what?" She picked up their empty bowls and moved to the sink.

"Swamp Donkeys. Bass lures fashioned like a hollow-bodied frog. They stopped making them a few years ago but Eddie found some on eBay. He took pity when I begged and sold me some."

She'd hoped he would share her enthusiasm over her coup at work. Apparently, he just didn't understand what she'd accomplished and what could be ahead for them financially if this story idea panned out.

Here was where she had a choice. She could gently remind him he was being insensitive and risk the night going sour, or she could let it go. Frankly, she hated fighting and just wasn't up to another night of angry feelings.

So she forced a smile, determined to enjoy the evening and not get out of sorts.

He seemed to have the same idea as well. The enjoying part, anyway.

While she was cleaning up, he grabbed her around the waist, picked her up, and carried her to the sofa. She giggled when, like a frat boy, he tossed her into the cushions and made a production of unbuttoning his shirt.

With a wide grin, he steadied himself with one hand on the wall while the other pulled off his boots. "I'm Mr. Big-Shot News Director, and frankly, I'm really impressed with my cute reporter," he teased.

Relieved the tension between them seemed to have finally broken, she laughed. Taking his cue, she reached for him. "Take me fishing, Mr. Swamp Donkey. Take me now."

He rubbed his palms together and scurried to the window to close the drapes, then hurried back to join her on the sofa.

Geary gazed down at her, the sudden widening of his eyes adding to her anticipation. Their teasing quickly turned more serious. Suddenly, she didn't care that he'd been insensitive, or that she'd have to throw two expensive sirloins into the freezer. Weeks had passed since they'd been together, and she was hungry for her husband's affection.

He rubbed her chin with his thumb.

Faith stilled, savoring his touch. The roughness of his thumb sent tingles down her spine, all the way to her toes.

He leaned and kissed her. She felt the familiar warmth of his stomach, his muscled chest against her bare skin. Shoulders broad and firm.

"Faith," he whispered into her hair.

He wanted her, and she wanted him. She ached to tell him so.

He pressed his mouth against her lips a second time, planting a kiss brazen with possibility. His fingers traveled along her quivering chin, making a bold path lower—

Suddenly, the front door opened.

"Son?" His mother froze. "Oh my—oh dear, I'm sorry." Veta quickly turned away. She shielded her eyes with her hand while both of them scrambled to cover up.

"Mom—for goodness' sake, what do you need?"

Faith grabbed Geary's shirt he'd tossed on the arm of the sofa and covered herself. "Uh, excuse me." She jumped from the sofa and scrambled down the hall.

In the bedroom, she quickly dressed in a pair of jeans and slid a T-shirt over her head, then moved into the bathroom, where she yanked her hair into a ponytail, fastening it with a band she found in the drawer.

She did all this while rehearsing in her mind what had just happened. Had his mother really just walked in without knocking? Had her mother-in-law seen them on the sofa in a—well, in a compromising position?

The thought angered her. She liked Veta, really she did. But this was where she drew the line.

She told Geary that when he finally pushed the bedroom door open and timidly peered inside. "Faith?"

"Is your mother gone?" she asked, her tone clearly communicating she was miffed.

He dropped onto the bed, sitting next to her. "That was my fault," he said.

She whipped her head to face him. "Your fault? How was the fact that your mother barged into our house without knocking your fault?"

His head lowered. His thumbs nervously played against one other. "I—I didn't lock the front door."

She stood. "My goodness, Geary. You shouldn't have to." She marched around the room. "Your family has absolutely no boundaries. None!" Her fists clenched. "This is *my* house, and none of them seem to recognize that fact."

He looked up. "Faith, I don't think you're being entirely fair."

"Not fair? Are you kidding me?"

"What I meant is, maybe you're overreacting just a little."

She stomped her foot. "I soaked my pant legs because your brother-in-law helped himself to my bathroom and placed plastic wrap on the toilet seat."

Geary bent and picked up her bathrobe off the floor. "He meant that as a joke," he argued as he walked over and hung the garment on a hook mounted on the wall.

"Well, it wasn't funny. Not even a little."

"Look, Mom felt horrible. She didn't mean to walk in on us."

Faith drew a breath and puffed it out quickly to regain composure. "Look, I'm tired. I'm going to bed."

He brushed his hand through his hair. "I still need to pack."

Her eyes narrowed. "Well, you're going to have to do that in the morning, because I'm going to bed."

His eyes shifted into the same expression she'd seen in his truck weeks before. "Fine," he said, heading for the bedroom door.

"Fine," she popped back.

He walked out and shut the door much harder than necessary.

Alone again, Faith growled and dropped full-length onto the bed. She covered her face with her hands.

That was certainly *not* the memorable evening she'd had in mind.

20

Sweeps week inside a newsroom closely mirrored homecoming on many southern campuses. Not only was strategic planning vital to win the ratings game, but the entire news team hoped to make first string.

Head coach Clark Ravino huddled with his producers, copy writers, reporters, and anchors for weeks leading up to the critical rating period, planning the lineup that would lure viewers to tune into KIAM-TV.

Rumor had it Clark pulled an enormous compensation package when coming on board to run the news division. He had a lot to prove to the station owners and to the industry as a whole. Everyone was watching.

So when he gathered everyone in the conference room and announced her story idea would be second in the lineup, Faith could hardly believe her good fortune. Neither could DeeAnne Roberts, who accidently tipped over her Styrofoam cup of coffee when she heard.

The lead would be a special report on Houston ranking in the fasting-growing cities in America, despite declining economics.

"The recent oil surge going on in Texas is generating major job gains," Clark reported. "And Houston is at the center of that phenomenon." He rolled up the sleeves of his crisp white shirt. "We'll incorporate that data you collected," he told DeeAnne, throwing her a bone.

Faith, on the other hand, was told she'd get a dateline package that would run nearly fifteen minutes.

"The economic lead will segue beautifully into Faith's piece, which we plan to title 'Where's the Money?'" Clark leaned back in his chair at the head of the table and steepled his fingers. "We'll go with live shots on-site and integrate interview pieces with VO segments."

Faith clasped her hands on the table to keep from applauding. She was jumping inside, but on the outside she displayed the professional demeanor of a polished, career-minded news journalist.

Hiding her true feelings was becoming her art form lately, especially at home. Not wanting to escalate the building rift in her marriage, she'd gone along with Geary's act the morning following their big argument over his mother. Like her husband, she simply pretended everything was fine. What good would it do to hash over an argument? Especially when doing so might start another one.

Instead she smiled and thanked him for the cup of coffee he offered and nodded when he reminded her he wouldn't be home for dinner. "If I don't get out of Toledo Bend in plenty of time to make it all the way home, I'll text you," he said, brushing her cheek with a kiss before heading out.

Why wouldn't he just call? she wondered. Even their electronic communication seemed to be getting more distant.

Over the weeks that followed, she'd been buried with work while pulling this piece together. Geary too had been busy, traveling the circuit.

On the rare nights they were both home in the evening, they acted cordial, even pleasant. But the crisp brightness of their early relationship had dimmed.

She could scarcely admit it, but the luster had rubbed off their shiny new marriage. Without intention, they'd somehow traded a Corvette for a slightly dented Ford Taurus they now kept parked safely in the garage.

On the night her big program aired, Faith stayed at the station to watch. Those not involved in the live broadcast were gathered with her in the conference room. Catered hors d'oeuvres were spread down the table and bottles of water chilled in buckets of ice.

Large monitors covered one wall, tuned to every channel in their market.

Cathy Buster reached for a stuffed mushroom. "I hear Channel 2 is doing a story on renovation of the downtown area. With Houston set to host Super Bowl LI, officials hope to accelerate the project to have it ready by February of 2017."

Mark Grubie, their station manager, shook his head. "I agree with Clark. Faith's story is fresh and will appeal to the critical early evening viewers, mostly women in the forty-five to sixty-five age bracket."

Glass windows separated the conference room from the producer pod in the center of the newsroom, where carefully managed chaos signaled only minutes to air.

She had a sudden case of nerves.

Swallowing the bundle of anxiety growing in her throat, she dared a glance at her news director. He loosened his tie, then stood rigid, staring at the monitors with arms tightly crossed. His jaw twitched, and she knew he'd laid a lot on the line. In a few short minutes, it'd be make it or break it time—for both of them.

The familiar snappy SOT played while the station's logo circled on-screen. After the fade, the evening anchors welcomed viewers to the newscast and began the night's rundown with a cold open, followed by the leading story on economics and ending with a teaser for her piece. Then a cut to the first commercial break.

Clark rubbed his palms together. "So far, so good," he said

before picking his buzzing cell phone up off the table. "Yeah," he answered. "Yup, that's good. Uh-huh." He clicked off the phone and dropped it in his shirt pocket before reaching for the bottle of water on the table in front of him. At the same time, he gave her a wink and a quick thumbs-up.

When the broadcast resumed, the single donut she'd eaten early that morning seemed to reappear, feeling like lead in her gut. She stood and poured herself a cup of coffee before settling back into the swiveling chair to watch.

Ignoring the commotion outside the glass window and the producers who scrambled into the conference room delivering copies of the rundown, Faith forced her attention back to the monitor on the conference room wall. Her breath caught when she appeared on-screen standing at the wrought-iron gate leading into one of the extravagant properties in River Oaks.

Work hard, take risks, maybe build your own business. That's the traditional route to financial success. Of course, there's an optional path young women are taking to acquiring wealth that isn't talked about quite as much these days.

Here in the land of conspicuous consumption, marriage isn't considered a lifelong commitment; it's the ultimate accessory.

For women hoping to marry into wealth, the River Oaks area of Houston means money. Real money.

A graphic appeared on-screen showing the high number of wealthy residents.

True, it's not politically correct to go hunting for a marital meal ticket, but consider the more pragmatic bonuses of the good life. No more studying to make magna cum laude, no striving to climb the corporate ladder or scrimping and scraping to make your annual Roth IRA contribution. And no more worries about where your children will get into college, or how to pay for it.

A seven-figure donation from your beloved to the school of your choice and your kids are in the door, even if they're no smarter than grapefruit.

Sold? Many young women today are. But how realistic is it for ordinary-wage slaves, with no more ties to the jet set than a business trip to Cleveland last month, to even meet, much less marry, a billionaire?

KIAM-TV decided to find out.

Faith attempted on-screen interviews with several spouses. Mrs. Rhodes, the wife of a hedge fund manager, held up her palm to the camera and declined to comment. Same with Tippy D'Amato, the third wife of the owner of a shipping magnate.

Unfortunately, those who had already made it to Fat City refused to say how they got there.

The shot shifted to a woman's image on-screen. "I am just not telling," said one billionaire's wife over her cell phone before hanging up.

Nonetheless, we did find some who were willing to talk.

Video of the girls she'd met up with in the spa appeared—the ones who looked like beauty queens with fake tans and no inner thighs. Faith's voice-over continued.

Marrying a billionaire is not beyond a very real possibility, as long as you're willing to work hard toward your goal. In a few moments, we'll find out just how it's done from the experts.

They broke to another commercial. Clark made a decision to limit this advertising spot in order to retain viewers, a bold move nearly unheard-of in a revenue-driven enterprise like their O&O. Even more than affiliates, owner-operated stations were hypervigilant when it came to the bottom line.

The program resumed with a warm open where she captured the two highly educated girls explaining to viewers how they'd accepted very lucrative job offers but considered hunting for Mr. Richie Rich their real full-time profession.

She segued to a shot of her standing in front of the River Oaks Country Club.

Over half of the billionaires in our study met their spouses at work.

They broke to an image of Melinda Gates, who was a Microsoft manager when she met her future husband Bill at a company press event.

Get an MBA. ASAP. To worm your way into a billionaire's business, and eventually his heart, we're told you need the right career.

"Arm candy is now seen as déclassé," one of the girls noted. "These days, the more prestigious your credentials and the brainier you are, the better. You'll better your chances of marrying rich by taking an etiquette course, a wine appreciation class, study a second language, buy better running clothes, and by all means, get a personal stylist."

KIAM-TV found a woman based in Houston offering $500-an-hour private sessions on how to marry rich. She claims that in her twenty years in business, 90 percent of her clients have landed multimillionaires.

The camera cut to another shot—this time of one of the girls from the spa standing in front of that magnificent church Faith had seen on the corner of Westheimer and River Oaks Boulevard, dressed in a stunning Chagoury Couture wedding gown. The segment wrapped with the girl's voice-over.

"Some may call me a gold digger, opportunist, or whatever other negative word they can find to describe my choice, and that's fine with me. Marrying for love is admirable and brave, it's the stuff fairy tales are made of, but like I said before, life isn't all about fairy tales. While those people who married for love are arguing over rent and school fees and others are planning vacations they can barely afford to pay for, I'll be living far more than comfortably."

The shot cut to Faith. She held the microphone firmly in place and looked into the camera.

> *There you have it. For several generations, women have been striving for financial independence from men, but in this tightening economy, a growing number are leaving that philosophy behind and choosing to marry well.*
>
> *What does it matter? We'll leave that up to our viewers to decide. Back to you, Mike.*

The lights on the phone bank over on the sideboard lit up. Clark's phone buzzed and he pulled it from his pocket to his ear.

Faith leaned back in the chair and closed her eyes. She'd done it.

She opened her eyes just in time to catch Clark pumping his fist in the air. "We've hit our home run!" he shouted. "The rankings were skyrocketing the entire time we were running Faith's package."

He rushed over and wrapped his arms around her, swinging her up from the chair. "This is great!" He patted her shoulders, then stepped to the doorway and shouted out, "KIAM-TV took the five o'clock."

Noisy pandemonium broke out in the producer pit.

Mark Grubie walked over and shook her hand. "Good job," he said, grinning. "Clearly, this story resonated with the women viewers we were targeting. You have great instinct . . . and a bright future at this station."

"The idea may have been mine," she offered. "But our entire team pulled this off. Such a pleasure to work with a talented and dedicated group."

When the broadcast concluded twenty minutes later, a celebration broke out in the conference room. Someone popped a cork off a bottle of champagne. Faith could barely hear over the excited chatter.

The big party lasted over the next several hours until it was time for the ten o'clock. Because of a quick reshuffling, her piece would run again.

During the entire time Faith kept an eye on her phone, watching for a call from Geary.

A call that never came.

21

The party didn't wind down until after eleven, and still no call from Geary, who was in Emory at a small tournament on Lake Fork. *Surely he didn't forget*, Faith said to herself as she crossed the station's employee parking lot heading for her car.

"'Night, Faith. Way to kick the ratings off the roof." Chuck Howell, the cameraman who had been with her from the beginning, from that fateful broadcast at the bass championship on Lake Conroe, waved. "I can say I knew you when," he hollered into the balmy night air.

Faith waved back. "Thanks, but we still have a ways to go to get to the top, and you're coming with."

"Absolutely—you bet!"

Cicadas buzzed in a clump of trees, and in the distance she could hear a siren, likely heading to nearby Hermann Memorial.

As she reached her car, she pulled her bag from her shoulder. Before she could reach inside, her phone rang.

Thinking it must be Geary, she quickly pulled the iPhone out. Seeing a number she didn't recognize, she frowned and brought the phone to her ear. "Hello?"

No one responded. Yet something told her there was a person on the line. "Hello?" she repeated.

She heard what sounded like a sob. Alarmed, she said again, "Hello? Who is this?"

"Sis?"

Her heart stopped. "Teddy? Is this Teddy?" Her bag dropped to the ground, spilling the contents onto the pavement. "Teddy, talk to me. Is that you? Where are you?"

He sniffed. "Yeah, it's me."

Tears immediately welled in her eyes. "Oh, it's good to—I mean, it's been a long time, Teddy. Where are you?" She hadn't heard from her brother since well before she met Geary. Rarely did she allow herself to think about him, wonder about him. It was just too painful. "Teddy, are you okay?"

"Yeah, I'm good. Look, I saw you on television. That was awesome, sis. I just wanted to call and tell you that." His voice dropped to nearly a whisper. "Mom—she would've been really proud."

"Teddy, I want to see you. Where are you?" she asked again, holding her breath in fear he'd hang up. "Please, let's—I want to see you." She kicked at the pavement with her heel, listening . . . hoping. "I got married. I want you to meet him. Geary's a really great guy. You'll like him."

Even though her brother was now an adult, in her mind he remained her little brother, the kid she tried to protect—and couldn't.

Teddy laughed. "Hey, do you remember that time Mom drug us to that funeral?"

Faith squeezed her eyes shut. "Yeah, I remember."

"What was that old guy's name?"

"Leonard Walters, I think."

He chuckled. "Yeah, Leonard Walters. What a trip. Who was that guy?"

"We didn't know him," she told her brother. The cicadas' loud buzzing stopped.

"Classic. We went to a funeral of some guy we didn't even know."

He paused. "What was Mom's deal anyway? She wouldn't even let us go to Dad's funeral."

"Yeah, I remember that too." She also remembered holding tight to her little brother's hand, whispering for him to turn his head when their mother made them pass by Leonard Walters's open casket. Teddy had pulled his hand from hers and looked anyway.

Faith's phone beeped. She glanced quickly. It was Geary.

"Did we know that guy?" her brother repeated.

Faith looked up into the black sky. "No, no, we didn't know him." She wiped at her tear-filled eyes. "Teddy, are you using?"

The minute the words were out of her mouth, she was sorry she'd said them. Faith quickly said a prayer, the kind you utter in your heart without words. "Look, I'm sorry. That doesn't matter. I mean, of course it matters—you matter." She was rambling now, not making sense. "Teddy?"

"Look," he said, a sadness creeping into his voice. "I just wanted to tell you I saw the show. I'm proud of you."

"Don't go," she pleaded. "Teddy, what Mom did—it wasn't your fault."

"Love you, sis."

"No—Teddy, wait." The phone clicked and she knew he was gone.

Her lip quivered as she bent to pick up the contents of her bag. She heard the back door open. In the light, she could see Scott Bingham, the production engineer.

"Faith, you're still here?"

She quickly swiped at her eyes. "Yeah, just heading out. Good night." She unlocked her car door, then slid inside and started the engine with trembling fingers.

For a brief moment, she thought of calling Teddy back. Or even storing the unidentified number in her phone. But she knew it would be no use. She would never find him. He didn't want to be found.

He'd seen her on television. That meant he watched her.

She might not like the fact, but for now, that one-way connection would have to be enough.

She'd just pulled onto the freeway when Geary called back.

"Hey, Faith, I'm sorry. I called as soon as I got off the lake and in range. How'd the show go?"

A space inside her hollowed. He'd missed seeing her big report.

"Mom recorded your piece for me. When you didn't pick up, I called and she said everyone was so excited and proud. Their phone hadn't stopped ringing. Everyone from Lake Pine had been calling her all night." His voice took on a slight edge. "Seems we have a star in the family."

She listened, not quite sure what to do with his lack of true enthusiasm or the fact he hadn't yet seen the segment.

"They want to celebrate, take us out to dinner tomorrow night. Before I said yes, I told my folks I needed to confirm with you."

Her mouth drew into a tight smile. "Sure, that would be fine."

"I mean, you don't have to if you've got something going or anything." He sounded like a pup trying to jump into her lap after wetting the floor.

"No, I'd like to go," she assured him. "So, where are you now?"

"We didn't get off Fork until late, so I decided to stay over. It's just a little over three hours from Lake Fork to home, so I should be back by noon tomorrow."

Faith merged into the left lane in order to pass a slow-moving semi. "The tournament—did you place?"

"Second. Didn't mean a lot in terms of cash, but points are racking up."

"That's great, Geary." She wished she meant it.

Teddy's face appeared in her mind. If things had been different, he and Geary might've become buddies. There was a time when Teddy liked to fish . . . before.

"Faith . . ."

"Yeah?" She blinked away sudden tears.

"Everything okay? You sound really tired."

Faith let out a heavy sigh. The call from Teddy had drained her capacity to feel excited—even about the wild success of her broadcast. "Yeah, big night. I'm ready to crawl into bed, though."

"Yeah, me too." He paused. "Faith?"

"Uh-huh?"

"I'm really glad things went well tonight."

Later, when she unlocked the door and walked into their dark condo, she let the evening in the newsroom resonate in her heart again. What she'd pulled off with that story was quite the journalistic feat. She'd taken a fluff story and transformed it, revealing a subtle and dangerous turn in young women's minds. One that could easily catch on as young women across America bailed on the hard work necessary to be a success, instead taking an easier route to the good life.

Tonight, viewers across their market had seen a confident reporter who worked hard, knew her stuff, and presented a polished image. She'd proven with her determination she could accomplish almost anything.

After talking with Teddy on the phone, she realized something else was just as true. A fact she kept hidden, sometimes even from herself.

Yes, she was Faith Marin—a rising media star with bright years ahead. But at times, she was still that little girl at a stranger's funeral who'd let go of her baby brother's hand.

Now it seemed her marriage was slipping away as well.

22

In the long months since sweeps week and her big story, she couldn't remember a time when she'd gotten home before nine o'clock at night. While she knew her schedule was getting a bit out of hand, she reminded herself how little it mattered now that Geary had qualified for the Bassmaster Elite Series and was out on the road nearly all the time.

"If I perform well on the tournament trail, I have a real shot at the Classic," he'd told her on the phone. "But it looks like I'll have a break in the schedule and will make it home for the weekend."

She'd been in the bathtub at the time, chest-high in bubbles. "Really? Oh, Geary, that's wonderful. Let's do something fun."

The words had no more left her mouth than he popped her hopes. "About that—well, Mom and Dad want everyone over there for dinner on Friday night."

Faith immediately felt slighted. She hadn't seen him in two weeks, and he didn't seem enticed to spend their first night together alone.

She swallowed her disappointment and took a deep breath. "Uh, sure. If that's what you want."

Minutes after they hung up, her mother-in-law called to confirm.

"Oh, honey—everyone is just so anxious to see you two," Veta told Faith over the phone. "It's been weeks."

Faith tightened the belt on her robe and shook out her wet hair. "Yeah, we've been really busy. It'll be nice to get together," she said, coloring the truth a bit. Not that she didn't want to see her in-laws. It *had* been too long. She only resented that she didn't first get an evening with Geary to herself.

"Our entire Lake Pine church family watches you on television. First that bridge story, then that big exposé about those girls looking for rich husbands. You're quite the celebrity around here." Before Faith could answer, she added, "So instead of dinner out, we decided to celebrate with a potluck at our house. I hope you don't mind."

"No, that's fine. What can I bring?" No one would call her a master chef, but cooking wasn't that hard. She could contribute to the meal in some fashion, even though she wasn't sure what time she'd be able to pull away from the station.

"Oh, honey, don't you bring a thing. We've got everything covered."

Faith didn't feel right about not bringing a dish to share. So on Friday night, she stopped at H-E-B on her way home. Surely she could find something to take that would be quick to prepare. Nothing gourmet necessarily. Something the Marins would enjoy.

Inside the grocery store, a middle-aged woman with a loaded shopping cart wheeled up next to her in the baking goods aisle. "Excuse me, aren't you Faith Marin, that gal on KIAM-TV?"

She nodded and smiled. "Yes, I'm Faith." Even though she was in a hurry, she extended her hand. In this age when anyone could tweet or post their opinions on Facebook, she knew to be gracious.

"Loved that piece you did about those young women. I had no idea there were business enterprises that actually help women marry millionaires!"

She smiled. "Thank you. I'm glad you found the story interesting."

"Well, I sure did. Y'all have a great day, now." The woman wheeled off with a wide smile on her face.

Around the corner, Faith overheard the woman on her phone. "Yes, I just talked to Faith Marin. No, I'm not kidding."

She grinned and pulled out her phone and googled the Food Network website. Surely she could find something easy.

Suddenly, she remembered something her mother used to make on occasion. She scanned the shelves and threw a couple of boxes of chocolate instant pudding into her basket, then rounded the end of the aisle and headed for the frozen food section for a large frozen pie shell. In the dairy aisle, she found a container of whipped cream and nabbed a dark chocolate bar on the way through checkout.

At home, she carefully followed the foolproof instructions on the packages and made a chocolate cream pie—pretty enough to be on the cover of a magazine. Even Geary said so.

"Wow, Faith. Looking good." His fingers moved to take a scoop.

She slapped his hand away. "No, sir. Huh-uh."

He grinned and playfully kissed at her neck. A move that quickened her heart. She turned toward him and placed her hands on each side of his face, hoping for more.

Their eyes met, and he held her gaze for several seconds. Then he stepped back. "We're already late."

Seeing her hopes wither, Geary gave a wry laugh, leaned in, and quickly kissed her cheek. "But when we get home from Mom and Dad's, we might just have to revisit the issue."

His parents' house was a short twenty-minute drive. She followed him up the sidewalk and to the red door, where he reached for the doorknob.

Faith couldn't help herself. She grabbed his arm. "No, sir. Doorbell. This isn't our house."

Geary rolled his eyes and pressed the little button. Seconds later, the door opened. Wendell stood there with a confused look. "What's up with ringing the doorbell?"

Veta came out of the kitchen, wiping her hands on a towel. "Hey, you two. You're late. Wendell, take that pie from your daughter-in-law. Faith, I told you not to bring anything, honey." Veta took her by the arm and pulled her into the family room. "Look who's here, everyone."

Gina Rudd, the church secretary, placed her glass of tea on the coffee table and moved to give her a hug. "I watch you on weekends, but that big interview with those girls—I mean, wow. I just had no idea."

Veta waved over a woman standing by the counter that separated the family room from the kitchen. "You know Alma Cheesey."

Faith extended her hand to the red-haired lady with full cheeks and a round chin—the one with the box of raisins in her kitchen the night of the pounding. "Why yes, of course I remember. Nice to see you again, Mrs. Cheesey." She turned to the woman's husband. "You too, Mr. Cheesey."

Next, they were introduced to the Patricks.

"Larry and Nancy are new to the congregation," her mother-in-law told them. "They just moved here from Boise, Idaho."

Larry chuckled and wrapped his arm around his wife's waist. "Yeah, unfortunately, my Nancy didn't marry for money. She's stuck with a working bloke and I got transferred." They all laughed.

Dilly and Bobby Lee arrived then with their three little ones in tow. Gunner sported a cast on his arm decorated with zoo animals—his third since she'd known the little guy, by her count. Gabby had an identical one on her arm.

"She was a little terror until she got one too," Bobby Lee explained with his hand on Dilly's back as she lumbered across the room.

"When are you going to have that baby already?" Geary teased.

Little Sam pulled his thumb from his mouth. "Maybe tomorrow. Or maybe next week," he reported, making them all laugh.

Veta gathered everybody to the table. Before they all got seated, Wendell held up a finger. "Hold on, everyone. I'll be right back."

Gabby wiggled in her chair with excitement. "I know the surprise—"

Bobby Lee quickly clamped his hand over her mouth. "Uh, sorry," he said. He turned to his daughter. "Remember, it's a secret."

Wendell moved back into the room, his hands holding a big vase filled with a dozen crimson roses. "These are for you, Faith. This family is so proud of you, darlin'. Here's a little something to show you how much we all love you."

"Those are for me?" She admired the near perfect blooms, the velvet petals. "Thank you," she choked out over the lump in her throat. She glanced at Geary, her eyes filling with tears. She quickly swiped at her lids, uncomfortable with the public show of emotion. "I don't know what to say, really. I'm—uh, thank you."

Across the table, Gabby sat with her arms crossed and her lip jutted in a pout.

Faith gave her a little smile and waved her over. "Do you want to smell them? Come over here by me."

The little girl's eyes lit up. She looked to her mom, who nodded her approval. Gabby jumped from her seat and scrambled over next to Faith. She leaned over and took a whiff.

"Aren't they pretty?" Faith asked.

Gunner climbed down from his chair and joined them. "I wanna smell too."

When the smelling was all done, Wendell bowed his head. "Let's pray."

Dilly scooted her kids back to their designated chairs. Geary took her hand, lacing his fingers with hers.

The food was delicious. Veta's pot roast with roasted root

vegetables was possibly the best she'd ever eaten. Mrs. Cheesey had brought a broccoli salad with chunks of pineapple and raisins. Nancy Patrick had made a loaded baked potato casserole with layered cheese and sour cream. She'd also baked what she proudly told them were her mother's prize-winning rolls. She pointed to the center of the table. "There's honey butter in the blue bowl."

Not to be outdone, Dilly contributed creamed corn made from scratch and a big container of sweet Dr Pepper baked beans.

"I helped," Gabby announced, which brought murmurs of appreciation from the adults at the table.

The men loaded their plates, especially Geary. "Man, it's sure good to eat home cooking," he said, reaching for a roll.

The comment rubbed a little. She had to admit when they weren't eating in restaurants, she normally brought home takeout. But she didn't necessarily appreciate the look that Cheesey lady gave her.

She thought about her pie. Maybe she should have tried something a little more impressive. Or at least tried to make the pie dough from scratch. She thought there might be YouTube videos that would've shown her how.

In fact, maybe she could pitch a segment targeted to career women who wanted to put home-cooked meals on the table, feature women who successfully juggled those roles. Maybe she could call it . . . "Bake the World a Better Place." Yeah, that had a clever ring to it.

Dilly looked extra tired tonight, so Faith told her to sit and she helped Veta clear the dinner dishes. Veta carried out a tray of tacky decorated cupcakes she'd purchased at the church bake sale. "Eat up, I bought triple this amount," she said, explaining the youth group was raising money for summer missions.

Faith picked up her pie and paraded it to the table. "This was my mother's recipe." She wasn't entirely sure why she needed to say that. Perhaps she felt caught up in the domesticity on display at this table.

Or maybe she wanted to impress Geary, let him know that in addition to her success at work, she could keep up with the other Marin women when it came to the kitchen.

The truth of the matter was that in some way she felt like she'd been handed a script and was playing the part of the good wife. A role she didn't quite know how to play.

Nancy Patrick's eyes followed the pie onto the table. "Oh my, are those chocolate curls on top?"

Alma Cheesey grabbed her dessert fork from the table. "I've never been able to make curls that pretty. Mine always break apart."

Faith glanced at Geary to see if he'd caught the comment.

Veta lifted a serrated pie server from the table. "Who wants some?" She moved to cut the massive pie crowned with whipped cream.

Suddenly, her face drew into a frown.

Dilly looked across the table. "What's the matter, Mom?"

Veta pressed the server into the pie with a bit more force. "No worries, I've got it."

Then she started chuckling. "Now I see what the trouble is." She laughed, this time much harder.

Wendell leaned her way. "Ha, will you look at that!"

Faith pushed her chair back and stood. "What's the matter?"

Then she saw what was tickling her in-laws. While making her culinary masterpiece, she'd neglected to notice the package of pie shells contained not one but two piecrusts separated by stiff cellophane, which had melted from the heat of the oven.

In that moment, she wanted to crawl under the table and die.

And she would've too, except Dilly held up her hand and stopped the comedy show. "I hate to interrupt this fun—but my water just broke."

23

Upon learning Dilly was in labor, everyone thankfully forgot all about Faith's pie snafu and scrambled for their cars in order to form a grand parade to the hospital. "See you all there," Geary hollered as he climbed inside the truck.

"We're going too?" she asked while snapping her seat belt in place.

"Well, yeah," came his reply. "Of course we're going. We shouldn't be too late," he added. "Dilly normally has her babies pretty quickly."

Faith took a deep breath and considered her options. In her mind, the birth of a baby was meant to be a private and sweet moment between a husband and wife. Though she shouldn't be surprised that the Marins thought differently.

In Geary's family everything was meant to be shared.

They passed through the double glass doors of Conroe Regional Medical Center and headed through the three-story open atrium to the information desk. The woman behind the counter saw them approaching and pointed to the elevators. "Second floor."

Geary nodded. "Thanks, Julie."

They passed the darkened gift shop. "You know her?"

"Yeah, we went to high school together."

In the waiting room, Veta passed out little pieces of paper and pens. "Okay, everybody. Listen up. Most of you know the drill." She looked at Faith. "Except for you, dear. But you'll catch on. Now, I want everyone to guess the time, weight, and sex of the baby. Write your answers on the paper for points. Highest score is the first to hold the baby."

Gina Rudd's eyes lit up. "Is the game just for family, or do we get to play too?"

Wendell grinned and patted Mr. Cheesey on the back. "Well, I don't know why not. You're all our church family. Although you're just wasting your time. I have a special knack, you know. Won both Gabby and Sam."

Veta piped up. "And I won Gunner."

Faith looked around. "Where are Gabby, Gunner, and Sam?"

Geary placed the paper against his knee and wrote out his guesses. "They're with Dilly and Bobby Lee."

She raised her eyebrows. "In the birthing room?"

Veta smiled and passed her a pen. "It's certainly not how we did things. But they have their own ideas. We're just here to be a support." She looked at Wendell. "Aren't we, honey?"

He didn't look so convinced. "I'm pretty old-school, I guess. Don't really care for all that."

Veta leaned close to Nancy Patrick and lowered her voice. "Dilly wanted all of us in there." She pointed her thumb toward her husband. "But there was no budging Wendell on that one."

Faith felt a sudden solidarity with her father-in-law. She wasn't sure how, but she'd certainly have done her best to wiggle out of watching Dilly give birth too if she'd had to.

Veta moved about the waiting room and gathered up the contest entries.

Wendell handed his over, then popped her on the bottom. "I'm feeling pretty lucky tonight, Mama."

The first hour passed and it was time for the ten o'clock news.

Faith retrieved the television control from a nearby table. "Anybody mind if I change the channel?"

No one responded. Those seated in the stiff-backed chairs were far too busy chattering, especially the women who were trading stories about their own pregnancies.

Faith pointed the control at the television mounted on the wall and clicked. KIAM-TV's opening news credits flashed on-screen. The late-night anchors led with a story about the rising price of gasoline.

From the chairs behind her, she could hear laughter. Veta recited a story about when she was pregnant with Geary.

"Back then, we didn't have those fancy tests telling us whether we were going to have a girl or boy. Someone from the church told Wendell if we wanted to find out, all we had to do was combine equal amounts of early morning urine with liquid drain cleaner. Do you remember that, Wendell?" She laughed again. "Well, we were stupid enough to try it. Only no one told us not to put a lid on the mason jar."

Wendell interrupted. "That's right, and when Veta shook up that jar her eyes grew wide."

"And I told you the jar was turning hot."

Faith couldn't help herself. She turned to listen.

Veta's eyes sparkled with mirth. "It was. That jar heated up so fast I could barely hold on to the thing."

"So she passed it off to me," Wendell said, chuckling. "I immediately knew something was wrong and ran for the front door and gave the thing a toss." He slapped his knee. "As soon as that jar hit the ground it exploded!"

Tears were now running down Veta's face. She fanned herself with her shirt to cool down. "That's right. Boom!"

Faith stared. "The jar exploded?"

"Oh, yes. Like to done scared us both to death." Veta exchanged a knowing look with her husband.

Wendell grinned. "Moral of the story—"

"Moral of the story is don't listen to your crazy husband and his knot-headed friends."

"That friend was an engineer," Wendell reminded her.

Veta brushed him off with a wave of her hand. "That friend is a sweet soul and a fool."

Next to her, Geary chuckled. He patted Faith's leg. "I think I'm going to go down for some coffee. Anyone else want some?"

When everyone declined, he turned to her. "Sure you don't want something?"

"Nah, I'm good."

When the baby hadn't arrived by midnight, the people from church all said good night and headed home. Gina Rudd gave Veta a quick hug. "We'll be praying. You call me in the morning and let me know, okay?"

Veta promised she would.

Faith wished she could leave as well. She didn't know what Geary meant earlier when he'd said Dilly normally had her babies quickly. They'd already been here nearly four hours. In all likelihood, they would have to wait many more hours before the baby arrived.

Geary paced the floor, his third cup of coffee in hand. She motioned for him to sit. "Geary, you look pooped."

He nodded and set his Styrofoam cup on the table. "Yeah, you too. Here, I'll give you the keys and I'll catch a ride with Mom and Dad." He reached for his back pocket.

"No, that's okay. I mean, I'll stay with everybody."

Suddenly, Bobby Lee burst into the waiting room. "Girl—seven pounds three ounces!"

Geary's face brightened and he slapped his hands together. "Ha—I believe that makes me the winner." He stood and shook hands with his brother-in-law.

"When can we see them?" Veta asked.

"Follow me." Bobby Lee led them down the hall while inside Faith sighed with relief. Now it wouldn't be much longer before she could go home with Geary.

Inside Dilly's room, Faith held back and watched what could only be described as a miniature circus playing out, with Dilly the main attraction and Veta the ringmaster.

"Oh, will you just look at that," Veta exclaimed. "No red hair on that one. I think she's going to take after you, Bobby Lee."

Dilly lifted her head in her husband's direction. "You need to get that video off to your mama and dad in Tulsa."

Bobby Lee lifted the camera to Faith. "I'm not all that great at this electronic stuff. You know all about this. Maybe you can help me. Says I need to compress the file?"

He shoved the camcorder in her direction. On the little monitor she heard Dilly moan, saw her—

Faith quickly averted her eyes. "Sorry, I'm not technical either."

It was then that she noticed Bobby Lee's blue scrubs were soaking wet. She also noted the lack of a delivery bed. In fact, this birthing suite looked nothing like she'd seen on television or in the movies.

Dilly sat in what looked like an oversized recliner. She wore a loose-fitting bathrobe and held a tiny bundle.

Over in the corner of the room, Faith heard splashing.

She looked past the cluster of bodies to a small whirlpool tub used for birthing. Gabby and Gunner sat on the edge, their legs dangling and splashing in the water. "You want to come swimming, Aunt Faith?"

She quickly declined. "Uh, no, I don't think so."

Geary stepped forward. "I'm the one with the highest score." He held out his hands and his sister moved the little infant wrapped in pink into his waiting arms.

Bobby Lee beamed. "Ain't she something?"

Geary peered down. "She sure is," he said as he pulled the tiny cap from the infant's head. His fingers brushed against the baby's wispy black hair while Veta and Wendell stood close by, admiring their new granddaughter.

"You did good, sis."

Veta stepped forward. "Okay, my turn." She looked at Wendell. "And then we're all going to pray over her."

Reluctantly, Geary handed his little niece over to his mom's waiting arms. Even then, he stayed close and fussed over how beautiful he found this newborn. Clearly her husband was enamored.

His attitude didn't change, even on their way home.

"Bobby Lee said they are going to name her Violet Grace. I like that, don't you?"

"Yeah, that's pretty." Faith rubbed at her temples. "Man, I need some serious sleep." She pulled the visor mirror down and examined the dark circles under her eyes. "It's going to take some thick concealer tomorrow to hide the fact I spent a good portion of the night in a stiff hospital chair."

Geary's expression turned soft. "Did you see her little eyes?"

She closed the visor. "Yeah, pretty cute. Bobby Lee and Dilly are sure going to have their hands full now."

"And her mouth? Did you notice that perfect little mouth?"

"Mm-hmm." She leaned against the headrest and closed her eyelids.

In a surprising move, he wove his fingers through hers and drew her hand to his lips, gently kissing one of her knuckles. "Faith, I know we haven't really talked about this, but I don't like where we're at right now. You and me."

She squeezed his hand and softly said, "I don't either."

"Can we just agree to move past whatever this is?" His face was troubled as he looked across at her.

She nodded, relishing the feel of his calloused hand against her own. An unexpected but not unwelcome surge of tenderness welled inside as his hand moved to the back of her neck and his fingers played in her hair. The way he used to do, before everything turned so sour.

The ride home was strangely quiet. Neither of them seemed to know what to say next. Or maybe, like her, Geary dared not venture into dangerous waters, afraid to poke past the surface of their discussion, scared this tenuous truce might sink under even the slightest pressure to go deeper.

At home, they entered the condo and made small talk.

"What's this?" he asked, stopping in front of the counter.

She kicked off her shoes and realized how tired she really was. "That's our new Keurig coffeemaker. You remember, we saw one in the Woodlands Mall and said we might want to try one someday. So I bought one."

He nodded. "Great. That's great." He straightened the machine before turning and rifling through the stacks of bills placed next to the phone. Finally, he looked in her direction. "Well, guess we'd better get some sleep, huh?"

She agreed and followed him down the hall. "Yeah, I'm exhausted."

Outside their darkened bedroom window, moonlight hit the surface of the lake, creating a shimmer that cascaded against the barest of ripples born of a gentle breeze blowing in from the Gulf.

Faith unbuttoned her blouse. Her husband sat on the edge of the bed removing his boots.

Together they slipped beneath the comforter. Geary pulled her to him and instinctively she wrapped her arms around his broad back. He put his hands into her hair and tilted her face toward his. Looking down, he murmured, "I've missed you, Faith."

As she lay encircled in his arms, a surge of longing drew her to fasten her lips against his.

Unexpectedly, her eyes filled with tears as she clung to him, her body demanding and needy and lured by his own intensity, until finally the loneliness and ache of the last weeks subsided with their passion.

★

The following morning, Faith luxuriated in a hot shower while Geary cooked breakfast. She couldn't help but smile to herself, remembering last night. In some ways, she felt like a new bride on the morning after her wedding day.

Her spirit felt as light as the gauzy curtains on the bathroom window. It was as if heaven heard her prayers and she and Geary had been given a fresh beginning.

She headed to the kitchen, where Geary stood in front of the stove holding a spatula. "Hey, how do you work this thing?" He pointed to their new coffee machine.

She laughed and moved to show him how the little K-cups fit in the holder, how to press the lever down and start the brewing. She leaned playfully against his shoulder. "Mmm, smells good. What are you cooking?"

"Bacon and scrambled eggs. And I'm baking banana bread using those long darkened things in the fruit basket you call bananas."

"They're not all that old. Must be the humidity."

"Uh-huh. Humidity," he teased.

Faith noticed his cell phone on the counter. "Have you talked to your folks this morning? How's Dilly and the new baby?"

He turned the bacon strips. "Everyone is doing fine."

"That's great," she said, heading for some creamer in the refrigerator.

She loved this—the renewed easiness between them. She took her place at the table and watched him serve up the food.

Who would blame her for not wanting to lose him? While stubborn and opinionated, he was also deeply kind, a man of convictions, funny and attentive. Geary was one of those guys you lost your heart to, and never got it back.

He set her plate on the table. "Dilly and little Violet Grace are even going home later this afternoon."

"Isn't that soon?" She grabbed her fork.

"Mom says not. Guess there's no real reason to rack up a bunch of hospital bills when they are both healthy and ready to come home." He took his place across from her. "You know, Faith . . . I think I'm ready for one."

She looked at him. "You're ready for what?"

"A baby."

Faith slowly let her fork drop back to the table and stared in his direction. "You want a what?"

A smile played on the corners of his lips. "Oh honey, I think we should have a baby."

She leaned back, astonished. Had she heard him correctly? "Well, sure. Yeah. I want that too. Someday."

"No, I mean I want to start a family soon."

Now he had her attention. Without much thought, she blurted, "Geary, you're kidding, right? We can't possibly have a baby right now."

He looked at her, his blue eyes growing more intense. "Why not?"

"Why not? Don't be ridiculous. First off, you're busy traveling and trying to qualify for nationals. Second, my own career has just hit a trajectory. How could we fit a family into all that now? Besides, we haven't even been married a year yet, and we're hardly in a position financially to afford starting a family. There's lots of time."

Faith wasn't used to this kind of fanciful daydreaming, especially given the magnitude of this sort of decision. She was a practical girl. And Geary, though more easygoing than she and more prone to believe God could alter his carefully designed plans, was still a practical man.

"But none of us knows what tomorrow might bring—"

She held up her palm. "No—for goodness' sake, Geary. Starting a family right now is out of the question." She shook her head and gave a laugh. "I'm sorry, but no."

He didn't argue the point further. Instead he stiffened and looked across the table and out the window.

"Maybe in a year or so," she offered, trying to ease his obvious disappointment. "I mean, as soon as we—"

"I get it," he said simply.

She breathed deeply, not sure what to do with the uneasy pallor that had so quickly blanketed their relationship. He was being totally unfair to ask her to put her career aside at this critical juncture. He knew when they married how important the station was and that she planned to work hard over the next years to advance her career. How could he hold that against her now?

"C'mon. Are you mad?"

He paused as if collecting his thoughts and dusting them off before presenting them for her examination. "I wouldn't say mad."

"Well, what would you say?" Her heart pounded as she waited for his answer.

He rubbed at his chin. "I guess I'd say I just don't really get you."

So they were back to this again.

Faith raised an eyebrow and gave her husband an icy stare. "What's there not to get? I think I've been open the entire time about what is important to me. Never one time did you voice any contradiction to my career ambitions while we were dating." She pushed back the plate of eggs that were now growing cold. "I'm simply not ready to start a family. What I don't understand is why that suddenly makes me the bad guy in all this."

She could see his grip on his fork tighten.

"Faith, what I don't get is why you think some job will ever fill you up. I listen to your plans, watch your striving. In the end, do you think all that will make you happy? Didn't you express that your own family went terribly off track? Why would you want to follow in your mother's footsteps and focus on things that don't matter?"

Her fist clenched. Had he really just taken what had been so terribly hard to reveal and thrown it back in her face?

She was nothing like her mother!

And her decision to hold back and not tell him about Teddy was proving to be the right one. Why let him use that situation as more proof that he held the corner on all things family?

Somehow she'd convinced herself that despite the horror show her parents had called a marriage, she'd do better. Her marriage would be different—kinder and gentler, more respectful.

While she and Geary could never be accused of battling with the same nasty tactics Theodore and Mary Ellen Bierman employed in their short-lived union, somehow her husband seemed to expect her to be the only one doing any compromising in this relationship.

How many more times could she talk herself into swallowing her pride, stuffing her building resentment over having to look the bad guy when all she wanted was to focus on her career first? There'd be plenty of time for a family later.

She surely didn't want to mirror her parents' flawed relationship, but was the only answer to simply suck it up and move on past these incidents? Continue to butt heads at every turn?

That might have appeared reasonable in the past when she bent her will to his and opened herself to his wacko family, or let his monster niece and nephew ruin her clothes, or look the other way when his redneck brother-in-law pushed the boundaries on appropriate behavior. She'd tried to cook like his mother, be engaging like his sister.

If she didn't put a stop to all this now, she'd soon lose herself.

One morning she'd simply wake up and look in the mirror and see a reflection that was no longer her own.

Suddenly, that Prince Charming sitting across the seat from her wasn't so charming.

She could feel her own eyes darken. "I think the real problem here is you've confused me with your mother—or your sister. I'm neither."

"What's gotten into you? What does my family have to do with anything?" Geary argued. "And I resent the implication that you think I'm demanding something out of line here—or demanding anything, for that matter."

"Ha—you make your commandments known loud and clear with your silence, your judgment, your passive-aggressive comments. You fight dirty in a manner that makes you look clean. But I've got your number."

Geary stood and slammed his chair against the table. "Faith, do you even hear yourself?"

She verbally lunged at him. "The night of my big sweeps broadcast—did you even watch?"

Her comment seemed to hit him square where it hurt. "Have you torn away from that precious station long enough to go to even one tournament with me?" he countered, throwing his own verbal punch.

"That's not fair."

"Yeah? And you know I felt awful about missing your show. I even made special arrangements with Mom to record it so I could watch."

"But did you? Watch the program, I mean?" She looked at him with utter contempt. "See? You didn't." Her insides quivered as she voiced how much that hurt. "The words *I love you* don't matter nearly so much when actions don't back up the sentiment."

"So you're not going to have a baby to, what—punish me?"

"Punish you? Have you heard nothing I've said?"

He grabbed his phone from the counter and moved for the door. "Oh, I hear you, Faith. Loud and clear."

In the distance, a dog barked.

She opened her mouth for a retort, then stopped. A flash of her parents screaming at one another formed in her mind. She turned and stared out the window into the harsh sunlight. Tears burned her eyes and her stomach knotted.

She wanted to be a good wife, hoped for a secure and intimate marriage. Perhaps there was no such thing.

There was only one fact she now knew for certain. She was not putting her career on hold to have a baby right now.

She was not.

24

Months went by, and her and Geary's relationship never really seemed to recover after the blowup on the morning following Dilly giving birth.

Geary traveled to more tournaments and stayed longer. His wins racked up critical points and his tournament standing climbed. Fishing enthusiasts and bloggers projected him to be next year's champion. His face appeared on the big spring cover of *Bass Fishing Today* magazine. He was interviewed on ESPN.

Faith buried herself at the station with more stories, which delighted Clark Ravino and earned her a full-time morning anchor spot. Then he dangled the big one in front of her, luring her even further into her career.

"Faith, I have good news," he said one day after she'd wrapped up the morning broadcast. "Come meet me in my office at five thirty. I want to take you to dinner."

There was a time she'd have worried about an impromptu dinner invite, wondering how to frame the fact she'd be home late so her husband wouldn't fuss. Now she simply sent him a text.

Home late tonight.

Of course, then she remembered he'd left for Arkansas that

morning and wasn't expected back until the weekend. So it didn't really matter anyway.

The momentary thaw in their relationship had been just that—momentary. Now the way they related to one another seemed to be colder than ever.

Clark took her to dinner at Brennan's, an upscale downtown restaurant known for its Creole cuisine. Despite her marital troubles, Faith found her stomach buzzing with excitement. His choice of restaurants signaled something big.

He waited until after their table waiter flamed the bananas foster and served up the sweet concoction over vanilla bean ice cream before he got down to why he'd invited her.

"Faith," he said, "over the past weeks I've been meeting with the boys upstairs. We all agree you are a talent we don't want to lose. We'd like to make you an offer."

"Oh?" She forced her reply to sound nonchalant. Word had been getting around about her, and rumor had it other stations were watching. He knew it and so did she. The key was to play this right, to extract every ounce of advantage and use this capital wisely.

His mouth drew into a slow grin. "Let's just cut to the chase. We explored moving you into the evening anchor spot."

Her heart skipped a frightened beat. "But . . ."

"But we have a better idea."

She held a spoonful of gooey banana mixture suspended in the air. "I'm listening."

Clark leaned forward. "We'd like to offer you your own morning program—something like a cross between Kathy Lee and Hoda and the Katie Couric show. You'd have your own studio and we'd tape daily in front of a live audience."

Her mind raced. Her own show?

She blinked and lowered the spoon to her plate. "That sounds wonderful. But what about my anchor spot?"

He tilted his head. "If you still want your morning slot and think you can juggle the workload, you can have it. In fact, the timing would work out well to wrap the news and pull your audience directly over to your hour-long show."

She finally let herself smile. "An hour, huh? Yeah, and what would we call it? The show, I mean."

Clark rubbed his hands together. "We've already commissioned a focus group. By far, the name with the best reception in the target audience was *Faith on Air*." He looked up at her like a pimply-faced kid who had just offered his girlfriend a promise ring. "So what do you think? Do you like it?"

Like it? She was thrilled.

"What about the evening anchor slot? I still want to be considered for any openings down the road. I'm not going to retract from my goal of making it onto *The Today Show* someday." She winked and gave him a wide smile.

He chuckled. "Well, this show fits beautifully into someday attaining your grandiose plans."

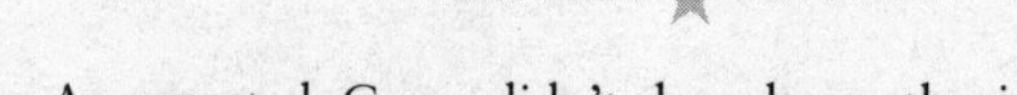

As expected, Geary didn't share her enthusiasm over her promotion, though to his credit he tried to hide the fact. "Oh? Well, that's good news. I mean, that's going to be a lot of work. But that's what you wanted, right?"

When she shared the news with Wendell and Veta, they expressed similar concern. "Oh, honey," Veta said while stirring up some brownies for their midweek Bible study group. "I hope they don't work you half to death. You're so busy now you barely have any time left over."

No doubt her in-laws had noticed the growing rift in her and Geary's marriage. They'd mentioned Wendell would be teaching a new series from the pulpit titled "Aisle Altar Hymn"—a not-so-subtle message to their daughter-in-law, she suspected.

She knew it would take far more than some Bible teaching to mend a relationship that was quickly coming apart.

After the announcement of the new show, Faith got caught up in a whirlwind of promotion activities. There were meetings, focus groups, logo designs, and head shots. She filmed promo clips and interviews to be aired during launch week.

After much consideration, the set designers went with cream-colored sofas against a pretty backdrop in shades of aqua—very feminine and inviting. The goal was to make Faith Marin a trusted friend on television, someone women across southern Texas could rely on to provide what they needed to know, when they needed to know it.

In particular, advertisers hoped to ride that idea all the way into her audience's bank accounts.

More and more often, as the weeks went by leading up to her big debut, Faith stayed in town at the condo she'd never let go. The idea to forego driving back and forth between the station and their place at Lake Conroe just made sense. Especially since Geary was so infrequently home anyway.

Excitement built as the big day neared for her debut program. The producers had a stellar lineup planned. The early minutes of the show would feature on-screen shots of city dignitaries wishing her and the new program much success.

That would be followed with an entertainment piece—a studio visit with an up-and-coming country vocalist named Jaslyn Ausmus. The chef would show viewers how to prepare bananas foster at home (hopefully without starting a fire), and then she'd offer their closing segment, a piece on aging gracefully.

She'd had to do a lot of talking but had finally convinced Clark and the others to let her bring Barbara Dover Nelson on for some "happy talk" about how she'd successfully transitioned after leaving the station and the keys to a happy retirement.

Faith waited until two days before the big show to call Geary.

"Hey, Faith—what's up?"

She held her breath while choosing her words carefully. "I see on the calendar that you get back to town tomorrow."

"Yeah, I'll be back for three days before I head out to Memphis. I'm doing a fund-raiser for at-risk youth."

"Oh, that sounds really great." She hated how timid her voice sounded. She wanted to ask him when their mode of conversation had become so measured and polite. When had they determined their differences were so insurmountable that they'd quit being lovers and decided to act like they were nothing but well-behaved acquaintances?

Faith couldn't even remember the last time they'd been the least bit physical with one another.

Did he miss her like she missed him?

"Geary," she ventured, "I have a favor to ask."

"Yeah, what's that?" She could tell he was eating while talking to her.

"*Faith on Air*'s premiere is in the morning. Tomorrow evening the station is throwing a party to celebrate. Will you come? To the party, I mean? With me?" Had she really just rambled? She held her breath and waited.

And waited.

"Uh, I suppose I can. Yeah, I can do that."

Relief flooded her. "You will? Thank you!" She rushed on to give him all the details he'd need to meet up with her at the party venue.

Knowing Geary would join her at the party buoyed her spirits.

For far too long, the distance between them had been growing, and frankly, she was frightened about how their relationship seemed to be disintegrating. She didn't know how to stop it. And she was lonely.

Sometimes at night, when everything quieted and she had only the sound of the clock on her bedside table and her conflicted thoughts to listen to, she would dare to wonder if she'd made the right decision. The cost of holding tight to her career dreams had been high. Maybe too high.

Throughout the dark nights she'd toss and turn while fighting to sleep, only to drift into a deep, fitful slumber hours before dawn. Then the alarm would go off and she'd wake to the sunlight of morning, when the life she'd wanted started all over again.

25

You wouldn't find a better party than one thrown by a television station trying to promote a new talk show in which they'd heavily invested. Photo ops alone from these types of events were worth gold. No doubt KIAM-TV planned this celebration to mine every bit of public relations currency.

The party would be held at the Houstonian, an upscale hotel in the heart of downtown with stunning wooded views and a price tag that signaled Clark had pulled out all the stops. The guest list read like a who's who in Houston. Invitations were extended to the mayor and his wife, several politicians, sports celebrities, and even some television stars living in the area.

Most importantly, two executives from NBC in New York were flying in.

And the spotlight would be on her.

Clark had graciously rented her a suite so she could get ready for the party and then stay over when the celebration concluded. She was definitely getting the star treatment.

Of everyone she intended to impress, her husband was at the top of the list. Perhaps now he'd see why she'd been so reluctant to place her career on hold. He'd see what was possible for her. She hadn't been selfish in wanting to wait to start a family. She didn't have her priorities mixed up. She only wanted to let her career have its due first. Once she'd climbed to the top, there'd be time to divert her attention to starting a family like Geary wanted.

Many women anchors had successfully balanced a media career and raising children, including Katie Couric. So could she.

Deep down she thrilled at the idea her own children would someday look at her with pride. It'd been a long way out of the pit. And who knew where she might go from here.

Faith looked at her reflection in the mirror. She'd chosen a safe black sheath dress—sleeveless. To make a statement, she'd discarded the standard notion of a strand of pearls and instead donned a bib necklace made of large tangerine stones accented with turquoise. Appearance mattered when in the public eye, and she couldn't wait for everyone to see this little eye-catching ensemble.

Especially Geary.

Admittedly, she hoped if everything went just right this evening, he'd stay over in her suite. Perhaps they could finally move a bit closer, even if by inches, and repair some of the damage their relationship had sustained.

Maybe he'd finally understand that the only way forward was to accept her career and know that their marriage may not look like Wendell and Veta's—or even Bobby Lee and Dilly's—but that they could still have a bright future ahead in their own way.

But he'd need to do some compromising.

For good measure, she spritzed on some of the Romance cologne he liked so much.

Downstairs, the room was packed with well-wishers and wannabes.

Clark immediately appeared by her side and moved her through the crowd, making sure she made contact with the VIPs.

The mayor's wife held out her hand. "Faith, congratulations on the new show. I am thrilled with the concept and will be watching."

Faith extended her hand. "I hope you'll be a guest sometime."

The woman's eyes brightened. "Oh, I'd love that!"

Clark maneuvered her through the crowd, stopping for necessary greetings, until they made their way to the other end of the crowded room where he guided her up onto a dais. At the back of the staged area, a massive banner displayed the show's logo and her image.

Faith checked her watch as she took her place by his side, worried Geary hadn't shown up yet.

Clark clinked his fork against his champagne glass. "Could I have everyone's attention?"

The room silenced and all eyes turned to watch.

"First, thank you all for being here. On behalf of KIAM-TV, let me welcome you." He turned to Faith. "We are more than excited to bring one of the most appealing and relevant shows for women to morning television—*Faith on Air*."

Applause broke out across the room. When the clapping quieted, he continued. "We are doubly excited to showcase one of broadcasting's newest and up-and-coming stars. Faith Marin's depth of experience, her intellectual curiosity, and her on-camera persona make her the perfect choice to anchor *Faith on Air*. Her unmatched energy, savvy, and versatility enable her to connect with audiences in Houston and across the southwestern United States," Clark said. "News is a definitive daily habit for our viewers—and Faith Marin will work with our talented editorial team to pioneer a new chapter of morning journalism."

This time the crowd went wild. In the midst of a noisy ovation, whistles rang out and confetti dumped from the ceiling, dusting the room with tiny bits of gold paper. Taking her cue, she moved to the microphone.

That was when she saw Geary standing near one of the hors d'oeuvres tables watching her, his arms casually folded. The sight instantly helped settle her jitters.

"Thank you," she began. "It goes without saying, I suppose,

that I am thrilled with the opportunity to host this new program. I hope you all will join me each weekday morning, first on the news desk and then on *Faith on Air*, where we'll be covering news and topics that people care most about—a lifestyle show with news components that reflect Houston and the people who live here."

Clark slid his arm around her waist. "Now let's have a good time!"

As soon as Faith could extricate herself from the onstage activities, she hurried to where she'd seen Geary.

He wasn't there.

She changed course and continued her search, quickly maneuvering past pockets of well-wishers gathered around servers with trays of bacon-wrapped shrimp and crab-filled mushrooms. Faith's eyes darted left and right.

Still no Geary.

She'd just about given up when she felt a hand on her shoulder.

"Hey," he said when she turned.

"There you are. I was afraid you left."

He looked confused. "Why would I leave when I hadn't even seen you yet?"

She shrugged, her uncertainty making her feel foolish. A sidelong glance at what he was wearing made her cringe. She should have told him this was a more formal affair.

Her husband shifted his feet. "I'm not really dressed right, I guess."

Trying to cover, she quickly shook her head. "No, you're fine." She pointed to one of the servers. "Are you hungry?"

"Nah, I ate at Mom's."

Of course he had. "Well, how about something to drink? Champagne?" The minute she said it she remembered he almost never drank alcohol. But this was a special occasion.

She glanced at the floor, then back at him.

Geary, maybe guessing at how she was feeling, mustered a smile. "Look, you did really good up there. This is a big deal."

She cleared her throat, thinking it was generous of him to say so. She touched his arm. "Thank you for coming, Geary."

He drew a deep breath. "You smell good."

She laughed. She couldn't help it.

He laughed too.

The lighthearted exchange made her want to lean in and whisper the suggestion he stay over with her in the room the station had rented for her.

"Faith—over here." Clark waved her over. "I want to introduce you to the guys from New York."

She paused, gnawing at her lower lip. "Come with me."

"Nah, you go," Geary said. "I'll wait right here."

She nodded. "Don't go. I'm serious, don't leave."

His eyes followed her as she made her way to Clark. Her producer's arm slipped around her waist and he guided her forward.

A quick glance back let her know Geary didn't care for the gesture. While she knew Clark meant nothing inappropriate, she casually sidestepped, letting her boss's arm slip from her back.

They neared a group of three men.

"Faith, I want you to meet the brass." Clark waved over a server and took glasses of champagne and passed them around.

She held up her hand. "No, none for me."

"Ha, I'll take hers." One of the men laughed and downed one glass. His pudgy fingers set it on the tray and reached for another.

Clark's face broke into an uneasy grin. "This is Randolph Hessing. He's the network's publicity director."

The gray-haired fossil looked at her from over top his champagne glass and nodded. She noticed his body slightly weave.

Likely so did Clark because he whispered to the server before turning his attention to the other two gentlemen. "This is Darin Frost and Alexander McElroy. Programming."

She extended her hand and both men told her how excited they were about her new show. "Thank you," she said. "I'm delighted with the opportunity and what we have planned ahead."

Mr. Frost nodded. "Houston demographics are strong for a program of this sort. All projections I've seen look promising." He smiled. "Makes me wish KIAM-TV was still an affiliate."

"Even so," Mr. McElroy added, "New York is watching."

His comment dangled like a shiny ornament on a Christmas tree with wrapped packages underneath waiting to be opened.

Clark's eyes twinkled. "You watch all you want, boys, but I've got her under contract. At least for several more years."

The men exchanged knowing looks and smiled. She smiled too, understanding contracts could be bought out.

Geary surprised her then by approaching. "Hey, I hate to break into the conversation, but I just got word I have to leave for a tournament early in the morning and I wanted to tell my wife goodbye before I head out."

"Already?" Faith asked. There was no mistaking the disappointment in her voice. Reluctantly, she turned back to the men. "Uh, this is my husband, Geary Marin."

Mr. McElroy eagerly stepped forward and extended his hand. "The bass champ?"

Her husband pulled his hand from his jeans pocket and shook the guy's hand. "You follow the circuit?"

"My son does. Trevor is an avid fisherman. We spend a lot of vacations on the water."

"Yeah? How old's your kid?"

"Fifteen."

Mr. Hessing scanned the room. He leaned forward on his toes, then rocked back. "Do you see a server?" He held up his plump hand, his glass already empty.

"Ah, great age." Geary placed his hand on Faith's back.

"So, you're her husband?" Mr. Hessing's words were slurring

slightly now, making everyone a bit uncomfortable. She never understood why people overindulged, let alone at business functions.

Geary scowled and lifted his ring finger as proof. "Yes, sir. I sure am."

"Well, she's pretty as Cleopatra." The older man's gaze drifted to Faith, his double chin folding over the stiff collar of his white shirt. "And she has some great pyramids."

Her husband's hand dropped from her back. "I beg your pardon?"

She grabbed his hand and squeezed, a silent message imploring him not to make a scene. Clark quickly apologized and the other two gave Mr. Hessing a harsh look.

Geary's jaw turned rigid. "Uh, like I said, I need to get going." He quickly shook hands and turned to leave.

Faith raised an eyebrow at Clark, who looked mortified at what had just happened. "I'll be right back," she said.

As she walked away, she heard Mr. Hessing in the background. "A joke. I meant it as a joke."

Geary was already several paces ahead of her. She had to scramble to catch up. "Geary, wait."

He kept walking.

Out of breath, she finally reached his side at the door and followed him out to the parking garage. Her husband could be supportive, charming, even funny. Right now he was none of those things. "Geary, talk to me."

He whirled on her, his face and neck now red. "What was that in there?" he nearly shouted.

"Shhh—keep your voice down." She reached for his arm but he pulled away.

"I guess I just clued in that you and your pyramids are eventually planning to move to New York." He flung his arm in the direction of the party. "I mean, isn't that what all this means? You anchor the weekends, then the morning show. Now you have your own talk show with plans to take on the evening broadcasts as soon as Ravino consents. Then on to New York?" He turned and marched toward his pickup. "Where does that leave me? Leave us?"

"Geary, stop. That isn't—I mean, you've misunderstood."

"Have I?" he challenged. "In this grand scheme, just when were you planning to quit pleasing creeps like that guy inside and instead focus on *our* life?"

"And you aren't off fishing your way onto the big stage? Isn't that the pot calling the kettle—or whatever the term?"

"I have to work. I'm the provider."

Was he kidding? "News flash. This isn't the seventies."

"Yeah, well, maybe it should be. Maybe there wouldn't be so many messed-up kids if—"

"You think I can't be a good mother and work?" The reality of how her husband really felt about the matter was sobering, to say the least. She'd never have suspected the full extent of his archaic attitude.

He folded his arms like a petulant child. "And you want to park our children in day care with me playing drop-off/pick-up dad?"

"That's not fair. Lots of mothers have careers and use day care."

He clenched his fists. "Not my wife!"

Angry tears formed, wrecking her makeup. "I will not be bullied into doing things your way, Geary. I won't be manipulated by some giant pout."

He rubbed angrily at his chin. "No—I don't suppose you will." He took a deep breath to temper the moment. "And I refuse to put family on hold while you buff your rising star."

His words didn't frighten her as much as the look in his eyes. "What—what do you mean?"

Geary opened his pickup door. "There's a fine line between fishing and just standing on the shore looking like an idiot."

"What—" She could hear her own voice grow shaky. "What are you saying?"

He climbed inside his truck. Before he closed the door he looked back at her. "I'm not sure what I'm saying—only that when it comes to us, it seems you've already decided to cut bait."

26

Faith sat stiff in her new wheelchair feeling a little lightheaded—literally, in that her head was no longer encased in the protective helmet that had covered her vulnerable skull since the shooting.

A middle-aged woman with blonde hair pulled back in a French knot and tortoise-shell reading glasses parked on top of her head came from around her desk to greet her. "Faith, you may not remember meeting me earlier. I'm Dr. Vivian Henbest—Dr. Viv is what most of my patients call me." She extended her hand and pointed to a seating area meant to replicate a cozy living room in the corner of her large office. "Let's talk over here, shall we?"

The attendant who had escorted Faith from her room upstairs guided the wheelchair and positioned her facing a traditional-styled sofa covered in ivory material. The sofa was accented with pillows in shades of blue, one in brown leather. A large rattan trunk served as a coffee table.

"Thank you," the doctor said, dismissing the guy who had wheeled Faith down. She placed a file on top of a stack of magazines on the table and sat.

The attendant locked her wheels in place. "No problem, Dr. Viv."

"I'm afraid I didn't get lunch, so please indulge me for a few minutes." The doctor pulled an energy bar from her flowing jacket pocket and unwrapped it. "I'm so delighted you are at this point in such a relatively short period of time, given your injuries." She took a bite and chewed.

"Relative to what?" Faith replied, wondering how anyone could characterize the amount of time she'd laid in that hospital bed as anything but what it was—lengthy. As far as she could tell, the horizon that stretched in front of her would be filled with nothing but the same.

The thought depressed her.

"Good point," Dr. Viv said as she finished up the snack bar and wiped her hands on a used napkin she'd fished from the same pocket. "Like I mentioned, my face is likely not one you recognize, although I've been immersed in your care since your arrival. Along with Dr. Wimberly, your surgeon, and Dr. Craig Adamson, who is managing your rehabilitation, I am the third leg of your managing team. I'm a neuropsychologist, which is a fancy word for someone who specializes in the relationship of the nervous system and the cognitive function of the brain. My role will be to help you journey back to emotional health."

"I need a quack?" Immediately, she wished she'd tempered her choice of words. It seemed that since her TBI—traumatic brain injury—certain thoughts could pop inside her brain and out of her mouth. No filters.

Dr. Viv didn't seem offended. "Well, some of my colleagues might challenge the term *quack*, but if it walks like a duck and talks like a duck . . ." She smiled and shrugged.

Well, at least this woman didn't take herself too seriously. Dr. Viv had a friendly face despite her severe jawline and thin lips. She wasn't exactly pretty—more studious. Faith wasn't a huge fan of the whole Soho look, but the doctor pulled it off pretty well. And clearly, she'd done something right to attain a position of this impressive level.

Dr. Viv pulled Faith's file from off the table and opened it. She slid her glasses onto her nose and read through the contents briefly before looking up. "So, Dr. Wimberly and the team just recently replaced your skull flap. Must seem nice to go without that helmet, huh?"

Faith nodded.

"And you've been put through a battery of tests this week to assess your cognitive and motor skills."

Again, Faith nodded. She had in fact spent the week trapped in lengthy sessions with bright-eyed people in white coats.

"Okay, Faith, listen carefully to this list: *Kentucky*, *Idaho*, *China*, *Wyoming*. Which term in this list doesn't belong? Or this one: *chair*, *book*, *fork*, *people*."

She answered the first correctly on her initial try. Admittedly the second stumped her for several moments. Finally, her brain kicked in and the answer became apparent. "People," she responded.

"Can you tell me why?"

"Unlike the rest in the list, *people* is plural."

From the sofa, Dr. Viv gave her an encouraging smile. "Based on the test results, you are very fortunate. Your level of cognitive impairment is minimal." She glanced at Faith's limp hand. "You've suffered some obvious physical consequences, but the team believes proper rehabilitation, coupled with simple reduction of swelling and brain tissue healing, will eventually restore a good level of function on that left side."

Dr. Viv pressed her glasses back on top of her head. "The main thing to remember is that your recovery is a process and requires a lot of patience on your part. Sometimes the unseen injuries end up being the most impactful. There are very real physical components to the psychological elements of the trauma you suffered—some the medical community understands fully, and frankly, some we do not. Brain chemicals play a huge role in our moods, our ability to cope and feel joy. Electrical activity is also a major component that the scientific community is still seeking to explain. That's where I come in. I will be the one who will assess how your TBI has injured your emotions and ability to feel."

Faith tried to adjust herself in the chair. "Yeah, I get that. But it seems to me I don't have any choice but to cope with what happened. There isn't much way to change things, now is there?"

"No," Dr. Viv admitted. "But we can help you maneuver how you think about all the changes imposed on your life. This room will be a safe place to voice what's happening on that critical emotional level."

Good gravy, Faith thought. That was all she needed on top of everything else thrust upon her. She couldn't even go to the bathroom by herself, couldn't bathe or brush her teeth without assistance. Now she had to satisfy this woman's need to get inside her head (no pun intended) and try to unscramble how all that made her feel? How did she think a woman who had been anchor of *Faith on Air* would feel about sitting here in a wheelchair with her head wrapped in a thick white bandage? Clearly, it was unadulterated and immense joy to know her limbs on the left side dangled like cooked spaghetti noodles.

"Oh, okay—yeah, that's great," she lied. The way she figured, the more she pretended to cooperate, the sooner the highly intelligent mind doctor might move on to someone else.

If she played this game right, Dr. Viv with her little half glasses would soon bore and turn to some poor kid who'd gotten in a severe motorcycle accident without a helmet, or a wife whose husband sought to control her with a Smith & Wesson 39 held to her head.

Dr. Viv studied her for several moments. "Faith, we're going to be spending a lot of time together over the coming weeks.

I always like to start the process with a very baseline question." She leaned forward slightly. "Are you glad you survived the shooting?"

Faith scowled. What kind of question was that? "Yes, of course. Why wouldn't I be?"

Dr. Viv leaned back and casually placed her arm on the sofa back. "That's a good question. Why would someone in your exact situation be prone to answer that question differently?"

Faith lifted her chin, knowing where the doctor was going with this. "Well, let's see. Yeah, I can see where someone could be in a dark place, mentally speaking, after having their entire life ripped out from under them."

"What's been the hardest thing—for you?"

"It's all hard." Faith's unstable emotions failed her again. She wanted to appear stoic. Instead her eyes filled. "Look at me. I'm broken."

"Faith? What's the hardest thing?"

This was where she needed to say being separated from the people she loved. Or maybe the doctor would buy it if she claimed being the news instead of reporting it.

She opened her mouth, ready to spout her pretense, but something inside her caught.

Time now had a new meaning—before and after.

Her life was now filled with antiseptic and medical odors. Stiff hospital mattresses and scratchy pillowcases. Plastic chairs and chipped Formica tables filled with stupid little puzzles meant to stimulate her arm recovery.

She hated the way tears would form at the drop of a hat. How she was reduced to bathing when someone told her she could, eating when someone delivered a tray, and worse, using the toilet with someone standing outside the door in case she fell.

Her legs—she wanted to shave her legs. Tweeze her brows. Paint her nails.

She longed to make it through one night without lying awake listening to distant footsteps and beeping and crackly voices over the intercom.

She hated feeling helpless.

Her jaw set. She took a deep breath and ventured a look in the doctor's direction. "I—I guess it's the fact that I'm not even me anymore."

27

TIRR Memorial Hermann, the highly acclaimed rehabilitation and research center located on the Texas Medical Center campus in downtown Houston, was known for being the leading traumatic brain injury recovery center in the United States.

Faith had done a feature on the remarkable success stories, never anticipating that one day she'd be needing the same expert help in learning to function again.

Geary slid on her bed slippers and patted her leg. "Are you all ready for the big move?"

As if on cue a nurse appeared, clipboard in hand. "Well, looks like the big day has finally arrived. Are you all packed up?"

Geary moved the few bags against the wall and gathered them up. "Yes, she's ready," he answered for her.

After a short transport, Geary helped her settle into what would be her new home for the next month or so. Here she'd learn to walk again and to use her left arm—at least to the extent possible as her brain continued to heal.

Dr. Wimberly had come in the night before to bid her well on the next leg of her journey. "We have every reason to believe you will have substantial improvement to mobility over the course of the next weeks. Especially under the capable care of Dr. Adamson and the rehabilitation team."

She couldn't help but tear up. "Thank you, Dr. Wimberly. For everything."

He patted her good arm. "Oh, I'm still on your team. Your new home is only across the complex. I'll be dropping in to check on you on occasion."

Unlike acute care where everything was designed to stabilize the trauma her body had experienced, the focus now would turn to helping her live with her new normal. While her injuries were not near what so many other patients suffered, she was nowhere close to being able to live successfully on her own—at least not yet.

She would continue to meet with Dr. Viv, of course. Her new rehab team would be under the direction of Dr. Craig Adamson, a brilliant man who had spearheaded cutting-edge research in traumatic brain injuries and strokes.

The room at the rehab hospital looked quite different than where Faith had spent the past weeks. While it was still very much a medical facility, much care had been given to making her surroundings as home-like as possible.

First, there were several floral bouquets covering nearly every table surface in her new room. One from the station, a bright mix of pink peonies and coral roses accented with stems of blue delphinium. Another, a massive bunch of red roses in a crystal vase, was from Oliver Hildebrand. The card read, *Best wishes for a full and speedy recovery. You are one of the strongest women I know.*

She wished she felt the same.

Her bed was covered with a light comforter in a melon-colored print that matched the draperies. Artwork hung on the walls and lamps with pretty shades starkly contrasted with the harsh overhead lighting in acute care. The biggest thing to catch Faith's attention was the television mounted on the wall. She finally had access to the news.

As soon as possible, she begged off with Geary. "Thank you for everything you did to help me get settled."

He placed the final nightgown in the wooden chest against the wall and slipped the drawer closed. "Happy to help, babe."

She leaned back against her pillows and closed her eyes.

"You look tired."

"Yes, I think my body is reminding me not to take things too fast. I'm pretty tuckered."

He smiled at her. "You want to get some rest? I can come back in the morning if you want."

She nodded. "Do you mind? I just need to rest up. I have my round of assessment testing this afternoon."

"Wow, these folks don't let any grass grow under your feet." He leaned and gave her a hug. "I like that. Sooner we get you fixed up, the faster you're back home with me." He kissed her then, an impetuous kiss straight on the mouth. A kiss that made her heart stutter. A kiss that made her insides stir.

She pulled back, caught the fire in her husband's eyes.

Obviously, the matter was settled in Geary's mind. They were a couple again. In her own, she couldn't help but feel like a puppy rescued after being hit by a car. Anyone with half a heart would feel compelled to take her in.

Quite by accident, earlier Geary had let it slip he planned to take another leave from the circuit, even though he was currently in the lead and likely to be a real contender for the championship.

"You can't do that!" she'd protested. "Geary, promise me you won't stop now. You mustn't. Not when you are this close. Please—"

"Look, the matter is settled," he said. "Career aspirations can wait. You need me—here with you."

It was at that moment Faith realized that life was often written in the simple language of need—her need to feel secure and that her life had purpose, his to be needed.

While the actions of a madman had robbed her of her steady places, Geary was flailing about, still trying to hold on to his.

"Geary," she began. She waited for his blue eyes to focus on her own. "Please hear me. I desperately need you, I do. But not in the way you might think." She took a deep breath and jumped off the edge of what was now their marriage, hoping her words would land on firm ground and not shatter their fragile renewed relationship.

"The shooter's bullets struck me down. Please don't make me carry the weight of believing he ended your career dreams too." She reached for his arm. "I need you to go on—to win if possible. In some way, that will be like spitting back. I need you to do this for both of us—and especially for me."

Geary ran his fingers through his dark hair. "But I—"

"No buts. I need this."

She wasn't sure he totally embraced the idea she conveyed. Still, his shoulders sagged with resignation.

"Fine. Have it your way, Faith. For now," he said. "But the minute I believe you'd be better off with me here by your side, all bets are off."

In the early aftermath of the shooting, Geary had followed the medical team's advice and allowed no visitors, not even his parents. Thankfully, he'd guarded her privacy like a bulldog—especially aware how easily photographs might find their way into the wrong hands. Extra caution had been in place, even to the point of transporting her over to the TIRR Memorial without any prior announcement in the media.

Personal tragedies, especially if connected to a celebrity, could be exploited for pure monetary purposes. This she knew well.

No doubt every station in Houston, including her own, had scoured her social media pages for photos beyond the standard airbrushed head shots. They'd look for vacation photos, snapshots of her family—anything that would personalize the situation and build empathy for the poor woman who had been shot.

She knew that was how things were done, yet she'd never been on this side of a story. While Geary and the medical personnel couldn't create a fortress between her and the media, with careful planning, they'd made things a bit more difficult—at least in the early weeks. But Faith wasn't naïve. She couldn't stay in a protective bubble forever. Calls and emails had been flooding the hospital's public information office.

Family, friends, and co-workers were pressuring Geary for an opportunity to see her now that she'd been released from intensive care. Like it or not—it was time. She didn't feel right putting it off much longer.

With little discussion needed, she and Geary agreed Wendell and Veta would be her first visitors.

As always, they were right on time.

There was a rap on the door and Geary peeked inside. "You up for some company?"

She straightened her bedcovers. "Sure, come on in."

It's so easy to presume that while your own world has ground to an absolute halt, so has everyone else's. But outside the walls of the hospital, grass still grew and got mown, freeways still clogged with drivers battling to get to work on time, and women still had their hair cut and styled—even her mother-in-law.

She liked Veta's new look.

Geary leaned across the bed and gave Faith a gentle kiss on the forehead. Wendell and Veta stood close behind him, appearing tenuous. Upon seeing her, Veta teared up and Wendell placed his hand on his wife's shoulder.

Instinctively, Faith's hands went to her bandaged head. "I—I must look a fright."

"No, you look—well, like an angel sitting in that bed." Veta moved closer. "Faith, sweetheart. We were so afraid we'd lose you, honey." Her voice choked and she turned to Wendell. "Weren't we?"

Wendell grew a little misty-eyed as well. "You have no idea how many prayers went up on your behalf."

Veta nodded. "Oh yes. There were prayer vigils from that first night. Our church family was devastated by the news." Her mother-in law patted Faith's arm, the one she couldn't move. "As were we."

The sentiments expressed were authentic. Despite her in-laws' overzealous nature, they had been good to her from day one. Annoying, but good.

The Marins were the kind of people who hung on to joy in any circumstance and never seemed to have to rummage for it. But no doubt that fateful day out at the Johnson Space Center had shaken them both.

She'd missed them, and wanted them to know. She reached out her good hand, inviting them closer.

Veta didn't need further invitation. She quickly bent and scooped Faith into her ample arms. Faith rested her cheek against her mother-in-law, taking in the way she smelled of vanilla, while Wendell grasped her good hand and squeezed.

Their affection took Faith a bit off guard. She felt a lump building in her throat.

No doubt they'd been pained to learn of the troubles in her and Geary's marriage. That a pair of laidback Columbia sports loafers simply couldn't dance with Cole Haan power pumps, and that their son and daughter-in-law had considered turning off the music.

Veta especially would believe these differences could be worked out—especially if they turned to God for help.

Then the shooting and the terrible aftermath. When everything changed.

She patted Veta's hand. "I've missed you," she managed, not sure what to say beyond that. Veta nodded and stepped back as if she'd used up her time.

Neither was Wendell reticent when it came his turn to hug her. He folded her in his arms. "I'm so glad you came back to us. In those early hours we just didn't know—" His voice tangled with emotion and he drew back. "We're so thankful God brought you back to us."

She couldn't help it. Her own throat constricted with the realization Geary's parents indeed loved her. Somehow she'd believed they would blame her for everything and might even be glad if she exited their family picture. She should have known better.

Suddenly, she felt exhausted. It was as if the weeks of being hooked to all those tubes had siphoned all her strength and her body now often betrayed her with fatigue. Leaning back against the pillows, she momentarily closed her eyes.

She felt them watching her.

In the past, she and Geary hadn't been able to find the magic recipe—or the will—to work things out. And now . . . well, now she was broken. Sadly, Geary deserved a wife who was whole and able to give him that family he so wanted.

Thanks to her stubborn nature and a stray bullet, she'd wasted the opportunity to give him children. Like Wendell, he would've made such a good father.

"Faith, are you okay?"

She opened her eyes to Geary. "I'm sorry. I'm just so tired tonight." She turned to her in-laws. "They had me up today and in a wheelchair for several hours."

Veta immediately grinned at that good news and picked up her pom-poms. "Oh, Faith. Honey, that's wonderful. You're making such significant progress."

Wendell joined the cheerleading squad. "Geary tells us the doctors say it's likely you'll walk and have complete movement again—once your brain has had time to fully heal." He gave her arm a reassuring pat.

Geary brushed her cheek. "Look, I guess we'd better go. Let you get rested."

Her fingers clutched his. "No, please don't. I'm tired, but it's truly good to see all of you." She was talking too fast but didn't care. Hours ticked slowly inside these walls. "I wanted to ask a huge favor."

He nodded. "Anything. What do you need?"

"I want to go outside."

Geary stepped back. "Oh, I'm not sure, Faith. That might not be such a great idea."

"I asked Dr. Adamson this morning," she assured him. "He said getting out briefly would do no harm."

Geary's face was shadowed with concern. "You just got the helmet off."

"Dr. Adamson says the earlier I get started navigating back into some semblance of normal life, the better. In fact, the chance for full recovery is increased."

Wendell rubbed his chin. "Well then, let's get after it."

Veta placed her hand on her son's arm. "I understand your concern, son, but I agree. If her doctors gave consent, let's move Faith outside, get her some fresh air. It'll probably do her a lot of good."

Geary reluctantly pushed the call button. "All right, if you all think so, I suppose it'd be okay. But let's not have her out there long."

Minutes later two nurses showed up. Faith's in-laws stepped outside the room to let her have some privacy, and the nurses helped her into her wheelchair and strapped her in. Geary tucked a lap blanket around Faith's legs and wheeled her into the hallway and to the bank of elevators where Wendell and Veta waited.

Wendell smiled and clapped his palms together with the same enthusiasm he'd exhibited in the bowling alley all those months ago. "What y'all say? Let's get after this little field trip, shall we?"

On the first floor of the hospital, the elevator doors slid open to the lobby, revealing the first slice of regular life Faith had experienced since that horrible day at the Johnson Space Center.

Strangely, the first thing she noticed was natural light streaming in from massive windows. On the other side of the glass, carefully manicured bedding areas were planted with sego palms, variegated green hostas, and yellow lantana. Beyond that, a parking lot filled with cars.

Such a normal scene.

"You doing okay?" Geary asked.

"Uh-huh. I'm fine," she lied, now feeling herself slip into a bit of anxiety as strangers milled around the floor heading to various destinations.

As Geary wheeled her along, people turned to look—an elderly couple, a businessman with a briefcase, a man and wife and their teenaged son. Across the room more people watched them from behind the main desk.

They'd ventured about halfway through the main lobby when a little girl pointed. "Hey, Mommy. What happened to that lady's head?"

Her heart raced wildly and sweat broke out under her bandages. The air thickened and she couldn't quite fill her lungs. She felt shaky, unsure, and she hated it.

Suddenly, the doors opened to outside. She smelled green grass. Heard a distant plane engine.

Then she saw the back side of a little boy standing next to his mother.

Next, a shadowy figure out of the corner of her eye.

"Back. Back. Back!" She rocked in a frenzied motion.

Alarmed, Geary leaned over her. "What's the matter, babe?"

Adrenaline swept through her entire being. "Get me out of here," she pleaded, wanting nothing more than to use both hands to free herself from the wheelchair so she could run. Hide.

No matter what her mind conveyed to her body parts, nothing would respond—especially her left side, which leaned heavily against the chair.

She was trapped. Inside the chair and inside the nightmare building in her mind.

She had to get out!

Please—let her out!

Wendell and Veta exchanged worried glances. Her mother-in-law grabbed her hand and squeezed. "Sweetheart, it's okay. We'll go back upstairs." She nodded at her son. "C'mon, let's go."

Back in her room, Faith cried uncontrollably, and she kept crying for about half an hour. Her neuropsychologist was summoned.

Dr. Viv arrived within minutes, clipboard in hand.

Geary rubbed the back of his neck. "I don't know what happened. She wanted to go outside and enjoy some fresh air, and then as we approached the doors of the lobby, she seemed to lose it."

"Will she be all right?" her worried mother-in-law asked.

Dr. Viv explained that TBI patients often experienced out-of-control emotions and moments of severe panic in uncomfortable surroundings. "She'll be just fine, I assure you."

Faith wiped at her eyes, aware they were all speaking of her like she was not in the room—a fact that annoyed her.

Still looking very concerned, Geary and his parents followed Dr. Viv's recommendation and left for the evening. Before departing, Geary took Faith's face in his hands. "I'm sorry, sweetheart. I'm so sorry." He knelt by her bed. "I'll be back tomorrow, okay?"

She couldn't look at him. Instead she pulled her face away.

Alone with her now, Dr. Viv turned. "Faith, talk to me. Tell me what you're feeling."

She looked at the doctor, still feeling shaky. "I saw him."

"Who?"

"The shooter—I saw the shooter."

28

Faith stared at the large piece of hand-thrown pottery filled with real sunflowers on the sofa table in her doctor's office.

"You like that?" Dr. Viv pushed her glasses up into her hair. A pretty gold earring in the shape of a feather dangled at her ear.

"It's nice." She looked around her office, at the earth-tone walls painted to look like suede. Above the sofa was a large framed painting of an adobe house in the desert.

"Thanks, I made it. And I bought that print in Sedona. It was painted by a young woman born without legs. I couldn't help but marvel at the extraordinary talent she showed despite her physical limitations."

"Looks lonely." Faith picked at the blanket tucked around her lap.

The doctor looked at the painting again. "Now that I really study the piece, I can see where you might say that. There are no people." She turned and pulled her glasses from her head and shifted them into place. "Maybe that's what attracted me. I enjoy solitude."

"Not me."

Dr. Viv nodded slowly. "Yet when you were moved into a setting with people last evening, it caused you great anxiety. That's what I'd like to talk about today."

Oh, here it comes, she thought.

"Does that make you uncomfortable? Talking about last night, I mean?"

Faith folded her hands neatly in her lap. "No, not really. Frankly, I'd like to understand why I freaked out like that."

"Tell me. You said you saw the shooter. Do you remember what he looked like?" Dr. Viv paused while Faith considered her words.

She looked the doctor in the eyes. "I said that. But I couldn't have seen the shooter. The shooter is dead."

"Yes, he's dead," Dr. Viv confirmed.

Despite the reassurance, questions plagued her. Questions she'd wrestled with since her mind had been aware enough to wonder about that day. "I want to know what happened."

"Okay. What do you want to know?"

"Everything."

After a long pause, Dr. Viv's eyes softened. "Let's start by you telling me what you remember."

Faith nodded. Since waking from the coma, she'd tried to assemble the fragments of images floating through her mind, tried to piece it all together.

"Don't try too hard. Just tell me what comes to mind and I'll help you fill in the rest."

She closed her eyes and concentrated. "It was a sunny day," she began. "The station was busy, really busy. They sent me out to Johnson Space Center for a field interview with—with Senator Rohny. I can remember Clark sending me out. I remember the entrance to JSC and the man at the security gate. I—I recall standing. No, wait. I remember seeing the senator step from her car." Faith opened her eyes and looked at Dr. Viv. "Her staff miked her up. Everything is muddled after that. I vaguely recall setting up.

Doing a sound check." She furrowed her brow, trying to remember. Frustrated, she shook her head. "That's about all."

"Okay, that's fine."

Faith hurried to add, "I guess I don't remember the shooter then—so what I said earlier doesn't really make sense, does it?"

Dr. Viv picked up Faith's file. She opened it and pulled a news clipping out and slid it across the coffee table that looked like a big antique trunk. She watched closely as Faith picked up the article. With the photo.

She flinched. "Is that him? The shooter?"

Dr. Viv nodded.

Faith studied the face carefully, noted the haunted eyes, the shallow grin. "But he's not much older than a teenager."

"His name was Lawrence Matthews. He was twenty-five and his father had been forced to retire early during the last round of budget cuts, which caused extreme financial stress."

"So he just shot people?" The idea made her want to hit something. "He shot more than me. Who else?"

"The senator."

"Yes, okay—that makes sense." She squeezed her eyes closed as if the motion could protect her from the scary parts, the images that now formed in her mind. "I remember now. He shot the senator and some of her staff. There was chaos. Lots of people running."

She looked back at the article, studying the details provided—information that slammed against her heart. She glanced over at the doctor, stunned. "He shot thirty-seven people?" The idea sickened her. The magnitude of hurt and pain created by this monster—even at his young age—scraped at her emotions and left them raw.

Her eyes widened. "Wait—I wasn't alone that day."

Dr. Viv shook her head cautiously. "No, you weren't."

Faith rubbed at her limp left arm where feeling was beginning to return. She concentrated, trying to turn the fragments of recollection into something solid she could hang on to.

She didn't have to. Dr. Viv had another article. And another photo.

The girl was young and pretty. Cute haircut. She worked as a media consultant out of Los Angeles.

An image suddenly flashed in Faith's mind—a mental picture of lifeless eyes and blood. Faith's entire body screamed in protest as she remembered the media consultant and how she had been shot in front of her.

Her breathing grew labored, and inside she felt her resolve to learn everything about that day crumple. "Her name was Lynna Scowcroft." Her heart pounding, she let the article drop to her lap. "I—I didn't want her to cover the shoot with me that day." A hole opened in her heart, and a wave of sadness rolled in and crashed against it. Tears welled.

The unchecked evil that had spread rampant that morning repulsed her, made her feel sick inside. "What about my cameraman? What about Scott Bingham?"

Dr. Viv shook her head. "I'm sorry."

Faith's hand went to her throat. She struggled to breathe. "Dead?"

"Yes."

A moan escaped Faith's lips. She bent and wrapped her right arm around her gut, then winced when she accidently hit the tender spot where a bullet fragment had torn into her flesh. She slowly shook her head. "I can't—I can't do this."

Dr. Viv stood and placed her arm around Faith. "I'm here. And we'll only go as fast—or as slow—as you desire."

Faith wiped at her eyes and tried to ignore the heaviness in her stomach. "Just give me a minute," she finally said, trying to catch her breath.

"We're not running a race here. Take as long as you need."

Scott Bingham had a wife and twin girls. He'd taken his family to Estes Park in Colorado for Christmas last year where his parents met up with them. His daughters spent hours making snow angels in snow they'd never before seen. She'd seen photos on his Instagram account. That sweet family's loss could never be fully imagined. A senseless and cruel loss. As was Lynna's.

Even though she'd had professional reservations about Lynna Scowcroft, the bright young woman did not deserve to be mowed down and have her life ripped away. Faith's mind could see her yet again. Her eyes empty of life, her head resting in a garnet-red puddle.

Faith snatched the photo of the shooter from her lap. What kind of evil beast would disregard humanity and snuff these precious lives?

She shuddered.

The same monster who had aimed his gun at her.

29

There was an uncanny resemblance between a school cafeteria and the rehab lab at TIRR Memorial, down to the long tables lined with hard plastic chairs and the physical therapists who wandered the room like teachers monitoring students during a test.

From her wheelchair, Faith looked down at her left leg, willing the limb to move. Since she'd started rehab, some feeling had returned, thanks in part to the excruciating abduction exercises where physical therapists stretched and maneuvered her muscles in a fashion that alleviated atrophy and fostered brain-to-limb communication.

As painful as that early motion became, the therapy failed to compare to what was being asked of her now.

Debby Sparks, or Sparky as she was known on the PT floor, gave her an encouraging smile. "I know it hurts. But you won't always be broken. Try to remember that every tiny bit of success moves you that much closer to going home and back to your life."

Could she really go back? Might there be some magic wand that could be waved, causing her long auburn hair to reappear, the skin across her abdomen to return smooth and without the hellish scar, her limbs to be healthy and whole again? Would she really run to her car to get out of the rain? Or shop for a shirt that didn't button up the front?

Sparky lifted Faith's leg and flexed her knee again. "C'mon, Faith. You're not trying."

She looked away, not bothering to respond. Instead she stared blankly at a large plaque on the wall that read, *Mile by mile, it's a trial; yard by yard, it's hard; but inch by inch, it's a cinch*.

Sparky frowned and let out a sigh. "Okay, maybe that's enough leg work for today."

Faith was then moved to another station where they expected her to do some hand exercises.

She knew her treatment plan, which included repetitive routines—long and often boring hours spent inching between parallel bars, rocking her weight on balance boards, and squeezing little rubber balls to gain flexibility—were all necessary to her physical recovery. But when a cute little PT intern gave her a dimpled smile and set three cans of Play-Doh in front of her, Faith had had enough.

"No," she protested. "I'm done."

Becky—at least that was what her name tag said—tilted her sweet little blonde head and urged her to reconsider. "C'mon, it'll be fun. You'll see."

With her good hand, Faith shoved back from the table. "I'm not a child!"

The girl's smile slid from her face, replaced with wide-eyed horror. "I—I didn't claim you were."

Faith rolled her eyes. "No?" She pointed to the little cans on the table with their brightly colored lids. "Look, I'm just done for today." She turned and waved at Tom, the attendant who had wheeled her down to the first-floor therapy center earlier.

Thanks to recurring panic attacks, she was one of the patients with a yellow armband, designating she must be attended to for her safety when outside her room. She felt labeled, just like all her personal belongings were labeled with her name and patient number.

She hated it. All of it.

What she detested most, besides the fact that she no longer owned her own life, was the way all the professionals—the physicians and case manager, the occupational and physical therapists, even Dr. Viv kept reassuring her all this was temporary, that she would return to normal.

What a bunch of bunk!

There was no more normal. And she resented them playing that manipulation card.

She knew she was being cranky, that she should be grateful for all the superb medical help and facilities that were at her disposal to assist in her arduous recovery.

Back in her room, she closed her eyes and for a splinter of a second saw the woman she used to be—smart and hardworking, a researcher who could ferret out the most elusive facts of import to a story. A woman who also had the ability to connect with her guests and viewers on a personal level, someone witty and interesting.

And beautiful. She'd been beautiful.

She wiped a tear trickling down her cheek.

What the highly trained medical experts could never confirm is that she'd ever return to the anchor desk, to her job and duties at the station. Her recovery would take months, possibly even years. Her career was finished. Everything she'd worked so hard to attain, now a vapor whisked away by circumstances outside her control—circumstances her poor damaged brain couldn't even fully recall.

"You okay, Miss Faith?" Tom's big brown hands parked her chair next to her bed.

"Yeah, I'm fine."

Tom nodded, knowing she was lying. "Well, you sit tight. One of the nursing staff will be right in to help you back in bed."

She reached for the remote control on the bedside table and found the power button to the television. The clock showed it was nearly time for the noon broadcast, and she was glad she hadn't missed it.

She pressed the button and the monitor on the wall immediately lit, showing a commercial for financial services, followed by another showcasing the new line of Chevrolets. That sparked a new thought. Would she ever drive again?

Before an answer could form in her mind, the opening credits for the KIAM-TV news program flashed on the screen. The logo in the shape of an eye appeared with the slogan *Your Eye to the World* scrolling underneath. As the familiar tune played in the background, a sharp pain hit Faith's chest. Not the physical kind, but an emotional stab as sharp as a knife.

Her body's visceral reaction caught her off guard, and she struggled to catch her breath.

Given her severe injury and the hospital policy regarding limited visitors in acute care, she'd not connected with any of her coworkers since that horrible day. Of course, everyone at the station likely attended memorial services for Lynna Scowcroft and Scott Bingham, worried they'd have to don their black dresses and suits again for hers.

In some ways she wished they had. As ungrateful as that sounded, how could she face a future knowing her broadcasting dream was gone?

Worse, how could she live so dependent upon others? On Geary?

While she'd been told her brain would heal and that the medical team expected remarkable recovery ahead, currently she couldn't even dress or go to the toilet by herself. It was as if she'd blinked and someone had snuck in and robbed her of everything that really mattered.

For the first time, she understood her brother's plight.

There were some things in life you'd do anything to reverse.

The inability to change your circumstances only highlighted the cold reality that moving forward might even make things worse.

Her former coanchor, Mike Jarrett, was on the news desk. So was DeeAnne Roberts. Giving late-night favors to the boss had apparently paid off. That, and a shooter's bullet.

"And now for a story everyone here at KIAM-TV is delighted to report. Our friend and former anchor Faith Marin, who was shot several weeks ago by the same man who shot Senator Libby Heekin Rohny as well as thirty-six others that fateful day at the Johnson Space Center, was successfully transferred to TIRR Memorial Hermann this week. Her physicians describe the brain-injured anchor as 'doing great.'"

The screen flashed to Dr. Wimberly. "I'm very pleased to bring the news that Faith Marin's transfer from the acute care to our rehab facility here at Memorial Hermann went flawlessly. While the assassin's bullet did damage some portions of Ms. Marin's brain, she is recuperating remarkably well."

The cameras returned to Mike and DeeAnne at the desk.

"We're told Faith's injuries could have been a lot worse," Mike said. "As reported earlier, this was a tangential gunshot wound. Fortunately, the bullet's path did not travel crosswise through her brain."

DeeAnne looked into the camera. "We're told Faith's physical therapy and rehabilitation will be a four- to six-month process. Her medical team projects a high level of recovery and then she'll be released home. Everyone here at the KIAM-TV station sends our love and prayers, and if our friend is watching we hope she knows we're all cheering her on."

Faith pressed the button on the remote and the television faded to black.

She leaned back against the wheelchair and squeezed her eyes shut against tears. In so many ways, life within the hospital walls had become so insular. The broadcast reminded her of a life beyond antiseptic smells, needles, and a head heavily wrapped in bandages. Of a life where she'd been a rising star, where she felt confident and beautiful and capable of anything.

She wanted her old life back, and if what Mike and DeeAnne reported was accurate, she'd be trapped inside this room for another four to six months. Nearly half a year.

While that thought nearly took her under, another idea pounded at her wounded and bloody soul.

In reality, she was no longer the woman Geary married.

How long before Geary tired of playing nursemaid?

30

No doubt Faith's cranky disposition had been reported to Dr. Viv, because as soon as the dieticians picked up her lunch tray of uneaten meat loaf and steamed carrots, another nurse showed up at her door.

"Let's get you freshened up for your appointment with Dr. Viv."

Faith turned up the volume on the television. "That's not until tomorrow."

The nurse moved to the bed and pulled back her covers. "Your session has been moved up."

Within an hour she was sitting in Dr. Viv's office, staring at tweed draperies and the world outside the window.

"Faith, talk to me." Dr. Viv's glasses were pushed up on her head and she had a pencil wedged above one ear. "I'm going to be honest. I don't like what I'm hearing from your therapy team."

Faith looked back at her. "Am I being scolded?"

Dr. Viv raised her eyebrows and thought a minute. "Well, yes. I guess you are."

"Don't you have some children you can direct all that at?"

"You're angry." Dr. Viv stared at her and waited.

She was tempted to just sit there and see how long she could make this game play out. But even the thought of that tired her.

She let her chin drop to her chest and picked at her pants with her fingers. "Yeah, you got that one right." Sometimes it was amazing how highly educated PhDs could be so simpleminded in their assessments. Of course she was angry. Who wouldn't be?

"Anger is understandable, given your situation. But holding that emotion inside and not dealing with it is counterproductive and harmful to your progress."

"Is that so?"

"Yes, and it looks like we've got some work to do—emotionally speaking."

Faith knotted her good fist and did her best to curl the fingers on her bad hand. "Please don't patronize me with psychospeak."

That made Dr. Viv break out in a grin. "Indulge me." She pulled her glasses onto her nose and glanced through her file. "It says here you have no family."

"That's right."

"Tell me about them—your family."

She stared at a rustic blue vase filled with bare twigs. "There's nothing to tell, really. Both my parents are dead."

"And your brother?"

Faith's head shot up. She scowled. "What does my brother have to do with any of this?"

Dr. Viv pressed, "Does he live close? Your brother?"

She took a deep, steadying breath. "I haven't talked to him in a long while," she said, mentally willing Dr. Viv to move on.

After making a note in her file, the doctor did just that. "Tell me about Geary's family. Are they a support system you can rely on?" She looked up. "My notes say that your father-in-law pastors a church?"

Taking care not to mention the pending divorce, Faith grasped at a subject that was a bit safer. "Yes, the Marins are very supportive. Geary's dad leads a church congregation out in Lake Conroe—that's where they live. His mom reminds me of that matriarch on

Duck Dynasty. She cooks and does crafts. She teaches Bible study and runs the local food bank."

Dr. Viv smiled. "Wow. Makes me tired just listening."

Faith smiled. "You don't know the half of it."

"Your husband has a sister?"

"Yeah—Dilly. I suspect she's kind of mad at me."

Dr. Viv leaned forward. "Oh? How so?"

Faith cringed. How could she have been so stupid? She'd never meant to open any can of worms and invite questions that might lead to the fractured state her marriage had been in when the shooting occurred.

It was bad enough knowing the entire Marin family had likely blamed her for the marital rift. In her weakened emotional state, she'd been lured into believing all was well when they'd visited.

Given their faith, they had no choice but to forgive and come alongside her and love her like Jesus. That was just their way.

"Faith?" Dr. Viv prompted.

She avoided making eye contact. "I misspoke. I didn't mean mad, really. My brain gets confused still. More like busy. She's raising four children all under the age of six."

"Wow, she must have her hands full." Not to be deterred, Dr. Viv posed more questions Faith would prefer not to answer. "What is your relationship with her? Are you close?"

She had to give her answer some thought. Her fingers rubbed lightly at the edge of her bandaged head. "We get along. We're just, uh, very different."

"How so?"

"Dilly is very domestic. She's entirely comfortable in chaos. And her choice in men—well, let's just say Bobby Lee is a nice guy in a lot of ways, but he's definitely not my type."

Dr. Viv listened carefully. "And what is your type?"

Faith glanced in her direction, letting her confusion show. "Well, Geary—of course."

"Yeah? How'd you meet?"

Faith told her about that day at the tournament, how she'd wanted to get the perfect shot and climbed out on that bass boat, only to fall overboard when the wake hit the side. "He rescued me. Pulled me right up out of the murky water and settled me on the deck of that boat. I looked pretty goofy, I suppose. I mean, I was sopping wet and had slimy green plant stuff all in my hair." She smiled at the memory. "I can't believe he was attracted to that."

She told Dr. Viv about standing him up when the big story on the bridge broke, and how instead of reacting badly, he'd invited her to a crawfish feed at his folks' house. She described how it felt to overhear him tell his niece he intended to be her Prince Charming.

"He sounds like a keeper, like someone you can trust to remain by your side no matter what comes." Dr. Viv looked at her with those probing eyes.

What did she want her to say? That she'd nearly thrown their marriage overboard? The lawyer's business card on her desk back at the station was proof of that.

"Faith, what's the matter?"

"Huh?" She shook her head. "Nothing's the matter."

Dr. Viv's expression intensified. "You're crying."

Faith was as surprised as her doctor to find that true. She lifted her hand and wiped the tears running down her cheeks, hating that her emotions were so vulnerable and left nothing to the imagination. She wasn't used to being so transparent. Managing her image had been a very effective tool she'd clutched tightly in the past, and she wasn't at all willing to loosen her grip on something that had always worked so well. Now she didn't seem to have any choice. She'd lost control of her limbs and her ability to hide.

Dr. Viv gave her a minute to collect herself before forcing Faith to pry yet another finger from her safe shell. "I'd like to know about your mother. What was she like?"

She shifted uncomfortably in her wheelchair. "Mary Ellen Bierman is not an easy woman to describe."

"Try," Dr. Viv urged.

"I don't see how talking about my mother has anything to do with getting me out of this wheelchair and back to my life."

Dr. Viv leaned forward and patted her good knee. "Trust me, Faith. I'm here to help you. Tell me about your mom."

"Well, it's complicated. I'm not really good at complicated."

"Don't worry about all that."

They were quiet for a few moments, and Faith thought of a dozen things she would like to say.

She'd like to tell Dr. Viv about how her mother used to kneel with her on the living room floor and cut out paper dolls from the dozens of magazines she often collected—*Ladies' Home Journal*, *McCall's*, *People*, and her favorite, *Modern Screen*.

Or she could tell about the time she came home from school to find her mother splattered in lavender paint, how her mom had covered Faith's bedroom walls with the pretty shade and made a matching bedspread every bit as nice as Marcia Brady's on television.

The accounts would certainly portray her mother in a good light, and the stories were true. Somehow, though, when she opened her mouth, a different set of words came out.

"I was nine years old and on my way home from school. That was back before stranger danger—when it was safe to walk in your neighborhood without adult supervision. Normally, I walked home with Cherie Reay, but on that particular day her mother picked her up at school for a dentist appointment and I was left to head home alone.

"About halfway to my house, I heard a noise in the bushes by old Mr. Tyson's house. Some whimpering. I went to check it out and to my delight discovered a little puppy, one of those little mixed breeds with lots of fluffy brown hair and a face that looked like a teddy bear.

"It took me nearly a half hour to coax that little dog into my arms, but once I held him he nestled against my neck and made himself right at home. He had no tag, and when we asked around no one had lost a dog matching that description. At the time I was convinced God had given him to me as a surprise gift. I begged my mom to let me keep him, and finally she consented. Teddy Jr., who was four at the time, came up with his name—Cocoa Puff, after his favorite cereal."

Dr. Viv smiled. "Cute."

Faith's throat tightened as she continued. "Yeah, Teddy loved that dog as much as I did. Which is why he was devastated when he forgot to fully close the front door and Cocoa got out."

A pained look crossed the doctor's face. "Oh dear."

"Yeah, my mother slammed on the brakes as she pulled into the driveway that day, but it was too late. The impact didn't kill Cocoa and there wasn't any visible blood, but both his back legs were clearly broken."

Faith stared out the window at a formation of stark white clouds floating in the vast blue sky. "Both Teddy and I were frantic, of course. I tried to console my little brother while Mom gently placed our injured puppy in a pillowcase—a lavender one from off my bed. She told us to stay while she took Cocoa to the vet."

Dr. Viv lifted her chin. "What happened next?"

Faith turned to her. "She came home without Cocoa. Told us there was nothing the vet could do."

"So the injuries to the dog were much more serious than it first appeared? That must have been very hard for you and Teddy. And your mother. I'm sure she felt awful."

"I thought so too—until a week later when I learned she'd never taken Cocoa to the vet."

Dr. Viv frowned. "What do you mean? What did she do with the dog?"

Faith shrugged helplessly. “I found my lavender pillowcase washed up on the shoreline behind our house.”

“What? Your dog?”

Faith nodded and focused back on Dr. Viv. “Mother didn’t believe broken things could be fixed.”

“Wow. That’s quite a—a remarkable story.” Dr. Viv swallowed. Her solemn expression softened. “Tell me more about your brother.”

Sorrow tightened Faith’s resolve. “I guess you’d say he’s pretty damaged as well.” She rubbed at her limp hand. Her heart pounded as she considered the risk of giving voice to her darkest secret, unable to stay silent even one more second. “We’re all broken. Or at least we were,” she corrected. “My mother bailed on us—she killed herself. Teddy was with her when it happened.”

Dr. Viv’s hand went to her chest. “I’m sorry that happened to you, Faith. That must have been very difficult to overcome.”

Unshed tears burned in Faith’s eyes. “Devastating—especially for Teddy. He was always a mama’s boy. He survived by self-medicating. Meth primarily. And heroin.”

Dr. Viv paused, seeming to try to take that in. She stared at Faith with an unfamiliar intensity, narrowing her eyes as she studied her face. “And you?” she finally asked.

Faith blinked away the dull, empty ache. “Me?” She forced a smile she hoped would hide her bitterness. “I became a celebrated news anchor.”

31

Faith spent a restless night mulling over why she'd been so free to disclose information she'd kept buried for years. She stared into the darkness of her hospital room, wondering what had gotten into her. Why had she chosen to uncover all that now? She'd known a long time ago that revealing her family junk would do her no good.

The look in Dr. Viv's eyes, while sympathetic, was exactly as she would imagine. She didn't need anyone's pity. Never had.

The discussion held no merit whatsoever. Self-help books would say her inner child had never healed and that was the source of her anger. To buy into that theory meant she'd have to discount a man dressed in army fatigues who had pointed a gun at her head and blown her career—her life—to smithereens.

Now she felt naked—too out there—like she'd let information out of the bottle that could never be stuffed back in.

Clearly, her emotions were out of control. While that was a typical symptom of traumatic brain injury, she couldn't just let uncaged feelings rule over her mouth.

By the time the nurses showed up to help her to the restroom and aid her in getting dressed, she was exhausted and certainly in no mood for the clumpy steamed oatmeal waiting for her on that dining tray.

She didn't need to step on the scales to know this diet filled with carbs and preservatives was killing her weight control. While she may never again sit behind a news desk, she didn't care to let her figure go.

In fact, she'd given her appearance particular consideration lately. Even started wearing a little makeup again. So when members of her medical team showed up later in the morning announcing it was time for the head bandages to come off, she was thrilled.

At least part of her was thrilled. She was also very nervous. No doubt there was good reason no one had offered to help her to a mirror.

"Good morning, Faith. Are you ready to get those bandages off?" A perky nurse Faith guessed to be in her late fifties bounded in the room with a huge smile plastered on her face. The gazelle of a woman left her feeling even more tired.

"I'm Lawana Maxwell and I'm a huge fan. Watched you every morning, darlin'. When I was on shift, I taped *Faith on Air*. Loved that show." She brandished a package of sterilized bandage scissors and a bright attitude that was in stark contrast to Faith's own. She glanced at the untouched dining tray. "You're not hungry?"

Faith shrugged her good shoulder. "Not a fan of oatmeal, I guess."

Lawana grinned as she swooped the tray out of the way. "Well, when I'm finished here I'll make a personal trip down to food service and make sure the dieticians get something edible up here. Bad enough you don't get to sleep in your own bed at night. The least we can do is provide palatable food."

Faith smiled, liking her already. And she smelled fresh and clean—like the laundry aisle of a grocery store.

"Okay, let's get this done, shall we?" Lawana tore open the

sterile packaging and removed the scissors and a smaller tool with her gloved hands. "This will only take a minute," she promised.

The scissor blade was chilly against her skin. The nurse clipped carefully, then unwrapped the gauze around Faith's skull. Lawana bent over and took a closer look. "You're healing nicely," she reported.

Next she took the other tool in her hand. "This won't hurt, but you're going to feel some pressure when I remove the staples."

She nodded and held her breath.

It was then she noticed Geary standing in the doorway. "Hey, do you guys need me to come back later?" he asked.

"Not on my account," Lawana said, plopping the first metal staple into a waiting metal bowl. She dabbed at the place on Faith's head with a bit of clean gauze.

Faith waved him in. "This nice lady tells me this is only going to take a few minutes."

He nodded, came into the room, and planted himself in a chair by the window. "People at the news station have been calling. Clark and some of the others would like to visit. Are you ready for that?" he asked, looking like he believed it might be too early yet.

While she wasn't entirely assured of the fact, she confirmed she was ready. "Why don't you tell them they can come tomorrow?" she suggested.

Lawana pulled the final staple and stripped the thin rubber gloves from her hands. The effort made a snapping sound. "Well, we're all finished here." She looked at Faith. "Do you want a mirror before I tie your scarf on?"

Faith saw a flash of something on Geary's face that she'd never seen before. Just the ghost of an expression, and in another state of mind she might not even have noticed the hint of alarm cross his features.

Geary was the steadiest man she'd ever known, and when she saw the look on her husband's face, her heart grew cold.

"The mirror." She pointed. "Could I have the mirror, please."

Faith drew a deep breath and looked at her reflection.

The sallow color of her skin was still evident, as were the dark circles under her eyes she'd tried to hide with concealer earlier. But as she lifted her hand, her breath instantly caught.

Approximately four inches above her right eye, a large and rather deep divot dented her skull. The skin along the hook-shaped scar running from the front of her ear to the back of her neck was mottled purple and angry pink. The harsh overhead light spotlighted patches of tiny black bristles poking through scabs and flaking skin.

She looked scarily broken—like a monster.

She dropped the mirror to the bedcovers, unable to cry—to react.

Lawana patted her. "Honey, give it time. Your appearance will improve. I promise."

"Just cover my head, please." She swallowed and closed her eyes, feeling another layer of despair blanket her soul.

Lawana failed to notice. She wrapped the scarf and secured the pretty fabric in place by tying a bow at the base of Faith's neck, then stepped back to examine her work. "Lovely. Red is your color." She gathered the bandage pieces and the bowl of staples. "Okay, you take care."

Faith forced a weak thank-you. The nurse left the room, promising to follow up on the meal concern.

Then the two of them were alone.

She let herself picture her and Geary intertwined with sheets in a bed on a tropical island, their bodies sleek from the muggy outdoor temperature and the heat of their honeymoon.

A snapshot of time never to be repeated. Not when she looked like this.

"Geary, come over here and sit." She patted her covers with resolve.

Her husband complied and sat on the wedge of space at the end of her bed. He placed his hand over her blanketed foot, the one she still couldn't completely feel. "Everything okay? Did that hurt—removing the staples, I mean?"

"Fine. I feel fine. But that's not what I want to talk to you about."

"Okay," he said slowly, looking slightly puzzled. "What's on your mind?"

She swallowed against the fear of being misunderstood. "Geary, why are you here?"

He frowned. "What do you mean? What kind of question is that?"

For a split second, she considered ending the conversation. It would be so much easier to default to the comfortable, the secure—but that would only stave off the inevitable. Eventually they would be forced into a much more difficult situation. And if she let more time pass, she might never survive what would no doubt come.

No, it was better just to face up to the fact that eventually he'd tire of her broken state. How could he find someone like her desirable? And most certainly he'd start to feel burdened with the role of caretaker.

"I want you to listen carefully to what I have to say. You are a wonderful man, Geary Marin. With a whole life ahead that should be spent with someone who can cook you breakfast, stand by the lakeside, and cheer you on, someone who can—"

His pleasant expression rolled up like a window shade. "What—you're breaking up with me?"

"This isn't junior high. This is real life." She lifted her chin. "Look at me. My head is dented and mangled, my hair in patches. Have you noticed I'm in a wheelchair, that my limbs are broken? I'm broken." Her voice grew more intense with every word, more emotional. "No matter how much you want to ride in on a white horse and be my Prince Charming, you can't fix this. You can't fix me."

He stood then, his fists curled in tight knots. He took a deep breath, seeming to weigh his words carefully, finding them too heavy to carry. "I don't understand why you keep pushing me away. I am not a perfect man—far from it. At times I'm thoughtless and demanding." He combed his fingers through the top of his hair in frustration. "I made plenty of mistakes." He looked at her with those blue eyes, intense and passionate. His voice darkened with jagged emotion. "But you don't just throw us out. You don't just go to an attorney the first time your relationship hits a hard patch."

"But—"

"But nothing!" He was raising his voice now. "Life is messy, Faith. People disappoint. Our hopes and dreams sometimes get dashed. At times we're all guilty of selfishly putting ourselves first and we don't consider the feelings of the people we love. Myself included. But that does not give you permission to give up on us. That does not allow you to just toss me aside like I mean nothing to you."

She realized then how deeply she'd hurt him. She hated herself for that. Even so, how did that change anything?

She was a mess. And she had no idea how to change that.

Geary deserved far better.

He deserved to be able to have children—to marry and create a family like his own. If she let him stay, all that would be lost. She wasn't even sure she could have babies now.

She loved him deeply—always had. She'd still felt a deep connection to him, even when she'd met with the divorce attorney.

Sometimes love required sacrifice. There were too many reasons they couldn't be together—it was true then and it was especially true now. Some reasons she couldn't even begin to explain.

Faith wasn't sure she was capable of being the wife he deserved, and she didn't want to find out. He needed some nice gal who wasn't broken and damaged. She owed it to him to let him go.

The night he'd placed the lock on the fence at the pier in Galveston, they'd been naïve at best, never knowing the difficulties that they'd face ahead. It was time to give back that key and unlock his obligation to stay.

He studied her until she had to look away. There was only one way to do that.

Staring down at the bed, she let the bitter words roll out of her mouth. "The bullets—it's likely I can't have children. With me, you'll never have that family you crave. I won't do that to you."

A hard lump grew in her throat. She looked up at him. "You need to go."

He stepped back a bit, as if her words had hit hard and knocked him off-kilter. "I know what the doctors said. Do you think that matters to me? You're what matters—only you." He shook his head in frustration. "Despite what you think, Faith, you are in the process of healing. In all likelihood you will walk again. Even if that weren't the case, I'd want to be by your side. Don't you get that?"

She tried not to let her voice shake. "You need to go," she repeated, a little more sternly this time. "Please go."

His hands dropped to his side. Geary looked at her with deep sadness. "Fine, have it your way. I'll leave—for now. But I'm not giving up on us."

She watched as he slowly turned and walked out the door.

32

The following morning, Lawana Maxwell showed up in her room with a dining tray in hand. "I thought I'd personally see to it you had a good breakfast—just like I promised." She slid the tray onto the bedside table and rolled it into place, then with fanfare lifted the metal cover off the plate. "Voilà! What do you think?"

The plate held an English muffin split open and toasted with hollandaise sauce drizzled over poached eggs and ham. Faith rewarded the nurse with a wide grin. "You're an angel in disguise. How did you know eggs Benedict is my favorite?"

"Anything to brighten that pretty face. You looked so glum when I walked in." She removed the plastic wrap from on top of a stemmed glass of grapefruit juice. "All this will get better, you know."

Faith nodded. Yes, with hard work she'd train her brain to communicate with her limbs. Even now, feeling was returning exponentially. Someday she might even learn to run, but that didn't change the fact she lived in a broken world where shooters could mow down people with bullets. She couldn't change that fathers weren't there for their daughters when they most needed them. No rehabs or churches could change the effect crazy mothers had on their children's lives—leaving some to use meth to ease the pain and some to be too broken to love.

Lawana patted her arm. "I know that's hard to imagine now, but you just wait and see. Now eat up." She glanced at her watch. "I'll be back in a bit to help you get cleaned up. I hear you're going to have some company this morning."

Faith nodded. "Yeah, the news crew is coming by."

Lawana leaned close. "Tell me, what's Mike Jarrett really like? He's so cute."

She raised her eyebrows at her nurse.

"Oh, don't give me that look. Married women can still look at the menu. They just can't order anything to eat." She winked and left the room, chuckling to herself.

Alone again, Faith filled her stomach. But no amount of gourmet breakfast could begin to fill the emptiness left in her gut after Geary had walked out the door.

Over a thousand times since that moment, she'd fought not to pick up the phone and call him—tell him she'd made a mistake and invite him back into her life. But each time she closed her eyes, her life spanned ahead, empty and all alone.

Her heart ached for how hurt he must feel right now, not completely understanding why she'd pushed him to move on—why she had to let him go.

What she secretly feared most had come true. Even so, she'd face the dark years ahead multiple times over before she'd allow him to fish in a bottomless lake with no fish swimming in it.

With the help of another nurse, she showered, taking care not to look at her head when she passed the mirror. She'd slept in her scarf, but in the middle of the night it slipped, and when her hand reached to straighten the fabric she dared to run her fingers over the top of her bare skin, across the rough places and the scabby indentation where the bullet had grazed her head.

She let herself recall what it was like to run her fingers through her long auburn hair, the prickly stubble that currently grew in patches evidence she was different now.

Everything was different now.

That was especially so when Clark Ravino and the others showed up for their scheduled visit.

"Faith, it's so good to see you," Clark said, giving her a hug. Mike Jarrett, Cathy Buster, and Cammie Watson echoed a similar chorus, a little too brightly. They were all there.

Chuck Howell cleared his throat, obviously emotional. "You look as pretty as you did that day out on that bass boat," he said, clearly trying to buoy her up with happy talk.

Her hand went to her scarf. "Well, not exactly. But I'm blessed to be here."

Glances were exchanged, all a silent tribute to Scott Bingham. And to Lynna Scowcroft.

After a thick silence, she tried to lighten the moment. "So if you are all here cheering me up, who's back at the station running things?"

Clark rubbed at his chin. "We left Mark Grubie behind. Not sure how wise a decision it was to leave the station manager in charge, but, well . . ."

Everyone chuckled.

Cathy moved closer. "We are so happy to see you. You don't know what it means to all of us to see you here, to know you're making such great progress and everything."

"Yeah, that was one scary day," Lucas Cunningham, the technical operations manager, added.

Clark threw him a look. "Well, we're as anxious as anyone for you to get out of here." He grew earnest then and his eyes misted. "Faith, you'll always have a place at the station. I hope you know that."

"Thank you. I'll take you up on that," she lied, putting on her best game face. "You know me. Nothing can keep me down for long."

They all chatted for several more minutes before Clark handed her a small box wrapped and decorated with a fancy bow.

She raised her eyebrows. "What's this?" She smiled and tried to unwrap the package. Immediately she was faced with her disability. While it was temporary, the fact was she'd get caught up in some semblance of normal and then reality would sneak up on her and snatch away the illusion.

"Here, let me help," Mike offered.

Inside the package were an iPad and a card that read, *We have faith in our Faith*.

The moment bowled her over and she fought to maintain her wild emotions. "What—what is this?" she choked out.

Clark's lips turned up in a slight smile. "Footage of the early days—of the outpouring of love and concern. We loaded the files onto this tablet and included images of some of the emails and letters that came pouring into the station in those early weeks." He looked at the others. "We're still getting viewers writing the station wondering how you are and when you'll be back."

Mike grinned. "It's been great for ratings."

Cammie Watson elbowed him. "Goodness, Mike. Spoil the moment, why don't you?"

Mike winked. "Faith can take it."

Faith leaned back against the pillows, relishing these people and the world they represented. Perhaps if she worked hard enough to regain her physical abilities, she might be able to rejoin them. Not in front of the camera, but perhaps in some capacity. She could still research. She could still write.

Clark glanced around the room. "Well, look. I think we've stayed long enough. We don't want to wear you out."

She reached for him. "No—don't go yet."

Before he had a chance to change his mind, her PT therapist showed up, ready to take her downstairs. Her co-workers were forced into saying their goodbyes.

"Take care, Faith," Mike said.

"We're all keeping you in our thoughts and prayers," Cathy assured her.

When they were gone, she turned to the therapist. "What do I have to do to get out of here as quickly as possible?"

★

That night after dinner, Faith settled in and took the iPad from her bedside table, clicked it on. First she googled Geary and checked his tournament standings. While remaining steady, his rank had taken a hit when he'd skipped tournaments in the early weeks while remaining by her bedside, confirming her decision had been the right one.

He needed to focus, to get back to his life without being dragged down by an invalid wife.

Next, she googled her brother—just to make sure there was no report of an arrest, or worse, his death.

Finding nothing, she let herself move on to the files Clark had loaded. The first was Mike Jarrett on camera.

"Breaking news: We're getting word that a shooting has taken place at the Johnson Space Center. The spokesman for the Harris County Sheriff's Department has reported several victims, including Senator Libby Heekin Rohny and several of her staff members. Senator Rohny had called a news conference and was announcing budget cuts. A dozen or more individuals have been injured, many critically. In addition to Senator Rohny, it's reported that there are multiple fatalities."

Mike's face paled and his voice cracked as he pushed through his obvious emotion.

"KIAM-TV crew members were on-site covering the story, and we've learned in just the past few minutes that at least one, and possibly more, of our news staff has been shot."

Faith's own eyes filled as she listened and thought about the terror of that morning, of Scott Bingham and Lynna Scowcroft, the senator and her staff.

She took a deep breath to steady herself in an attempt to block an onset of mental flashbacks that might take her under again. In the end, her thirst to understand all that had happened that day overrode her stilted ability to cope, and she elected to keep watching.

One clip showed photos of the victims, including her own. A voice-over report informed the listening audience that the critically injured were being transported to local hospitals, including Memorial Hermann Trauma Center.

Another clip showed makeshift memorials at the entrance to JSC and crowds gathered with candles outside the hospital. One woman held a big sign that read *God Bless You, Faith Marin*.

Churches across the metro area gathered in special prayer services. The mayor and the governor both gave statements assuring constituents that there had been a lone shooter and he was now dead, taken out by a sniper shot to stop his terrorizing rampage. The very shot that had saved her own life.

In another film clip, a list of the victims' names scrolled with their ages. Her gut wrenched as she noted the age of the youngest—four years old.

An image formed in her mind. One of a little blond-haired boy in a Thomas the Train T-shirt with a KIAM-TV Junior Anchor sticker secured in place.

As if in real time, Faith's mind played back the boy's mother smiling, then seconds later the young woman folded over top of her son, pleading with the shooter.

Trembling, she squeezed her eyes shut against the horrific memory and buried her face in her good hand, letting the iPad rest in her lap with that list still on the screen.

She sat like that for several minutes, shaking, tears flowing down her cheeks. She shook her head, trying to cleanse the evil acts of that madman from her conscious.

By morning, despite an extraordinary effort to the contrary, she was still struggling to maintain composure and not fall to tears when she met with Dr. Viv for her session.

"You've taken a step back, it seems." Dr. Viv pushed her glasses up into her hair and poured two cups of coffee from a table on the other side of her desk. "I'd hoped seeing your friends from the news station would lift your spirits."

Faith stared off through the window where the sun was still shining brightly despite the darkness of her mood. "Another memory returned."

Dr. Viv handed her a mug filled with the steaming coffee. "Oh? Let's talk about that."

Numbness flowed through her veins. "Talk? What good does all this talking do? No amount of discussion will change anything. That little boy will still be dead."

Dr. Viv sat on the sofa. "What little boy, Faith?"

She tried to focus on the warmth of the steaming mug instead of the coldness she felt inside. She would eventually learn to walk and use her arm again as her brain healed. At least that was what all the medical professionals predicted. But the scars would remain—both on the outside and on the inside. And the world would still be broken.

Did she even want to remain in a world where everything was so terribly, horribly broken? What was the purpose?

"Faith? Let's talk about what you remember about the little boy."

"Huh?" She looked back at Dr. Viv. "Oh yeah. The boy." She took a sip of the coffee. "Well, the station left me some film footage of the early hours after the shooting."

Dr. Viv frowned. "I see. I wish they would have cleared that with me first." She set her mug on a nearby table and leaned over her knees. "Faith, it's really important that you recognize that in addition to the physical limitations you currently are working through, your brain mechanism itself has also suffered an injury that needs healing. That is why you meet with me. That is why we talk through some of these things. Otherwise, your mind may cause erratic thinking—thoughts that could be harmful. Do you understand?"

She nodded slowly. "Yes, I do." Somehow she'd been spared in the shooting. Yet here she was considering that she wished she wasn't here. That reasoning seemed so disrespectful of those who'd lost their lives that day—a callous dismissal of that little boy's life.

Determined to do better, she focused on Dr. Viv—on her kindness and offer of help. "There was a little boy there that morning. The victim list said he was four. I saw him that morning. He was wearing a Thomas the Train T-shirt and I bent and placed a sticker on his chest." Faith's eyes welled with tears. "He was so cute. Blond and had chubby little cheeks. He didn't deserve to die," she choked out. "His frantic mother tried to save him. She couldn't."

Dr. Viv took the mug from her hand and set it next to her own on the table. She took Faith's hands. "That little boy's name is Conner Anderson," she said, her voice quiet. "He survived the shooting and is in our pediatric rehab ward."

She openly stared at the doctor. "He—he's alive?"

Dr. Viv nodded. "Yes. He's very much alive. Unfortunately, he did suffer a spinal cord injury that has impaired his ability to walk—perhaps permanently."

She tried to let the news sink in. "But I saw the shooter point. Saw him shoot."

Dr. Viv's face turned solemn. She leaned back into the sofa. "Yes. Sadly, Conner's mother was killed that day. Even more tragic is that she was a widow. Her husband, Conner's father, was killed in Iraq two years earlier."

The news took Faith's breath. She found herself struggling to inhale. "That little boy is an orphan? Who's taking care of him?"

Dr. Viv shook her head. "I'm afraid he has no one. Without

family, he's a ward of the state. Before long, he'll be ready for release. It's weighing heavy on his medical team, myself included."

Faith's muscles tightened. "So, what—he goes into foster care?"

"I'm afraid so."

"Will you take me to visit him?"

Dr. Viv raised her eyebrows. "Who? Conner?"

"Yes," she said, not willing to take no for an answer. "I want to see him."

"Faith, I'm not sure that's a good idea. It may cause flashbacks that wouldn't be healthy for him at this stage. He's having nightmares as it is."

"Maybe my visit would be a good thing. Healing in the aftermath of something so evil is difficult, but perhaps having someone to journey with—someone who was there too—will make the process easier for him," Faith urged, not willing to consider that the connection they'd made that day, however brief, wouldn't be vital to both of their healing journeys. "Maybe he could use a friend. I know I could."

"A four-year-old?" Dr. Viv paused, appearing to reconsider the possibility that the visit might benefit both patients. At last she nodded. "Let me see what I can arrange. I guess there's no harm in letting you visit. I'll be there as well, and if I see any signs of distress—"

"I understand," Faith assured her.

Finally, she had something to look forward to.

33

The pediatric floor was a short ride up in the elevator. Faith found herself both excited and a little nervous. Perhaps she'd oversold the benefit of connecting. This kind of trauma and the aftermath challenged even the strongest adults, let alone a child who had his father taken from him, and now his mother—literally in a fashion that would scar his little mind forever.

It was also that thought that propelled her—no, *compelled* her—to want to come alongside this little fella, to provide whatever comfort she could. She knew what it was like to face a harsh world through the eyes of a young person, not able to completely make sense of pain inflicted by others.

In some ways, since she'd heard he was alive and all alone, it was as if some unknown force had taken up residence inside her and had fueled an instant obsession—one to love a little boy who needed to be cherished.

So much of her own future life had been robbed. She now faced so many limitations. But this one thing—without even having seen him again—Faith sensed deep inside herself.

She was going to make a difference in his life.

When the doors slid open, Dr. Viv wheeled her out of the elevator. "Are you ready for this?"

Faith nodded. "I've never been more ready."

"Well, be warned. He's been through a lot of trauma. He may not respond well to a stranger. So be prepared to take it slow."

"Okay," she said, glancing around the floor. Here everything was smaller. The whirlpool against the wall, the parallel bars, and even the stacking stairs were miniature sized. Watching children working to gain mobility after suffering physical trauma made her heart ache.

"There he is." Dr. Viv pointed to a wheelchair parked by a window. She pushed Faith's wheelchair in that direction. "Conner? I have someone here who wants to see you."

Faith leaned forward and took in the little guy—his blond hair, the little train engines he held in his dimpled hands. The sadness in his eyes.

"Hey, buddy. Do you remember me?"

He gave her a quiet look, followed by a generous offer to look at one of his trains. "This is James."

"Oh?" she said, taking the little red engine and examining it. She handed it back. "That's a good one. What's this one's name?"

"It's Thomas."

Her heart became weighted inside her chest, overwhelmed by the emotions pooling inside of her. "You like trains?"

He nodded. "My mommy's in heaven."

Her heart thudded. "Yes, I know. I bet you miss her a lot."

His little blond head bobbed. "She's with my daddy."

Sensitive to his pain, she leaned forward and touched his arm. "My mommy and daddy are in heaven too." She made herself smile and added, "My name is Faith. Dr. Viv tells me your name is Conner."

Dr. Viv knelt by his wheelchair. "Faith wants to be your friend. Is that okay, Conner?"

Without hesitation a grin sprouted on his face. "Yeah. That's oh-tay."

Faith and Dr. Viv exchanged glances. Dr. Viv stood. "Well, I'm going to leave you two alone for a few minutes. I'll be right back." She positioned Faith's wheelchair so that she and Conner faced one another, then patted Faith's shoulder and turned to go.

Once they were alone, Conner frowned. "Your wegs are bwoken too?"

She nodded. "Yes, one of my legs isn't working. I have to do exercises to strengthen the muscles so I can walk again. Do you do exercises?"

He pointed to the whirlpool. "Sometimes I go swimming in the water. The wadies let me take Thomas and James with me—'cuz sometimes I get scared."

"I get scared too sometimes," she admitted.

He patted her knee. "I'll pway for you—that you'll be bwave."

"That's unacceptable." Faith shook her head. "No, I won't allow that."

She'd lain awake all night, making herself even more vulnerable to her emotions. No matter. This situation demanded intensity.

She wanted this like she wanted air.

"I'm afraid there aren't any viable options." Dr. Viv's voice turned patient. She leaned back on her office sofa, her glasses folded in her hands. "These things have a way of working out. Really, they do. We've already contacted several churches who have agreed to help get the word out to anyone looking to adopt."

"And?" she asked.

Dr. Viv opened her glasses and slipped them onto her face. "Well, Conner's spinal injury is permanent. It's a lot to take on. But I'm sure a family will be found. Like I said earlier, we'll keep him here as long as possible."

"I don't want that little boy in foster care."

"None of us do, but sometimes these things are out of our

hands. I'll continue to see him even after he's officially released. Emotionally, he's very fragile, and the next months are critical to his future emotional health." She grabbed her file and opened it. "But enough about Conner. Right now it's time to focus on you. Tell me why Geary hasn't been to visit lately. Did something happen?"

Her head jerked up. "That's private."

"I'm here to help you, Faith. What you're thinking, feeling—it's all relevant to your own emotional health. Do you want to tell me about it?"

"Not really," she replied, hearing her own petulant tone, one that sounded like she was the four-year-old. She quickly corralled her attitude. She was an adult and shouldn't cower from telling Dr. Viv the truth. "Look, I never really disclosed the fact that we were having issues prior to the shooting. I'm simply continuing on the same course as before, which shouldn't cause alarm."

Dr. Viv nodded slowly. "Let's talk about that. Your marriage, I mean."

Faith took a deep breath. "I don't think we're so different from a lot of couples who wake up and realize they have very diverse personalities and approaches to life."

Dr. Viv looked unconvinced. "Earlier you told me you thought he was a keeper."

"I believe those were your words," Faith reminded her. "I'll grant you that I fell in love with Geary—probably still love him in a lot of ways. But a little less than a year into the marriage we encountered some fairly severe difficulties. Difficulties that highlighted the fact that internally we were two very different people. In order to go forward, one of us was going to have to morph into someone we were not cut out to be. That wasn't acceptable. I wasn't going to change, and I never would expect Geary to either." She looked at the doctor. "Some things are just too broken to fix."

"Like you?" Dr. Viv suggested.

"What? I don't understand what you mean." Why did she feel

like she was under a microscope every time she had a session with Dr. Viv?

"Often what we see in TBI patients is an effort to isolate. For a number of reasons, really. One being the feeling that no one could ever really understand what you've been through—what you face. Another is the misunderstanding that you are now damaged and unworthy of a relationship."

There were those microscope eyes again, looking at her in a way that made her squirm. She hid behind a chuckle. "Well, sounds like you're on to me. What can I say? I'm broken. A real Humpty Dumpty."

"A good man loves you. Why are you pushing him away?"

Clearly, Dr. Viv wasn't going to let her slide past this one. She had an agenda. Still, Faith's marriage was her private business. Any motivation for leaving Geary was not up for interpretation or discussion. Especially not with some stranger who only sat across from her because it was her job.

"I guess you're the one to answer that, aren't you? I mean, you're the neuropsychologist, the one charged with picking up the pieces and putting them all back together again." She couldn't believe how mean she sounded, or that she didn't really care.

Dr. Viv smiled. "Okay, I'll play Mother Goose. Here's what I think—I believe you had a very extraordinary and immensely difficult childhood. Your father wasn't there for you. He was far too busy skirting around. Your mother was half crazy and her antics were emotionally dangerous for both you and your little brother. Like you said, Teddy Jr. self-medicated. You became the family hero—the one bent on surpassing the shame of your family."

The doctor glanced over the contents of her file. "You were class president, on the debate team, in the Spanish club, a school ambassador—and that was just high school. It says here you were awarded a full-ride scholarship to several prestigious schools, turning them all down to study here in Houston—likely so you'd be near your brother. His life was spiraling after the damage of your mother's behavior.

"You graduated summa cum laude with a degree in journalism and then landed your first job at one of the largest stations in Houston—KIAM television—beating out several other qualified candidates. You worked night and day, and in almost no time you were not only the morning anchor but the host of your own television show, *Faith on Air*." She looked up. "Have I missed anything yet?"

Faith sulked and shook her head.

"Good, then I'll continue."

The determined doctor seemed to believe she alone held the glue gun that could paste her shattered pieces together. Strangely, Faith found herself appreciating that someone got it. Life had not been a bed of roses, so to speak. But she'd been determined and had not played the victim. She'd raised herself up and above it. All on her own.

"On the surface, you've spent nearly all your adult years desperately trying to show the world you are valuable, while beneath it all you push anyone away who tries to get close because you're afraid they'll discover what you fear most is indeed true."

Okay, now the doctor was getting in her business. And she didn't like it. Despite her resolve, her erratic emotions betrayed her and she teared up. "Yeah, and what's that?"

"You are desperately afraid that once anyone gets to know the real you—the authentic person you are deep inside—they'll discover you're broken. You long to be cherished, but you push everyone away. You won't let anyone love you to that extent. Not even your husband."

Dr. Viv leaned forward and placed her hand on Faith's knee. Her touch felt like an electric shock. "You hide behind achievement, but that will never fill you up. Add the emotional trauma of having your life threatened by a madman, and you can't argue the fact all this has left you crippled. And I'm not talking about that wheelchair."

The doctor's words swept her up and knocked her foundation loose. Made her angry. Faith's tears became real now, flowing hot down her cheeks. "You think I don't know all that?" she challenged. "I've read all the self-help books, Dr. Viv. And I'm the one who had a gun pointed at her head. I'm well aware of how all that affected my life."

"Maybe so, but you've never considered the possibility that someone who is broken doesn't have to be fixed before she can be loved." Dr. Viv's gaze grew more intense. "Your treatment is at a critical junction. As the physician in charge of your emotional well-being, I believe it's important for you to acknowledge where you are on this journey to health, so we can link arm in arm and get you farther down the path to stable health."

Dr. Viv gave her knee a pat and leaned back. "You have a lot of strikes against you—a bad childhood, a wounded spirit as a result, and then you found yourself the victim of a horrendous crime. Allow yourself to heal—both physically and emotionally. Don't just go through the motions like none of your therapy matters. Let others love you and help you. You do that and I can promise you'll quickly find yourself on the path to recovery."

Faith looked back at her miserably. "You mean Geary?"

"For starters." Dr. Viv pointed to her arm and leg. "You're already getting back the use of your limbs as your brain heals. After appropriate rehabilitation, you'll eventually walk out of here. My job is to make sure you walk out with your anger and emotions healed as well."

Faith considered Dr. Viv's assertions. To a great extent, she had to admit the doctor had done her homework, had accurately assessed the situation, and was correctly reporting exactly how she felt inside.

Yes, she'd tried to be the best she could be—the most accomplished. All in an attempt to overshadow the shame she'd lived with all those years, the hurt and sadness.

Yes, she was angry.

A thousand times she'd pondered why God would allow her to be at the Johnson Space Center that day, why she had to suffer all that followed.

Why her entire life had to be ripped apart.

But in her brief time with little Conner Anderson, life took an unexpected turn. One that for now she intended to keep to herself.

Normally she'd never sit and listen to this psychoanalysis. She was far too practical to give much credence to how she was shaped by her early life experiences, even if it made a lot of sense when spelled out the way Dr. Viv had just meticulously done.

But that was before she'd sat with that sweet little boy who was now alone in the world—a little guy who was as physically broken as she.

He needed her. Frankly, they needed each other.

Faith was going do everything in her power to get well. Yes, she'd learn to walk again—both physically and emotionally. If Dr. Viv thought she was recklessly dealing with her marriage, with Geary, she'd fix that. She'd do whatever it took to be well, because now everything wasn't just about her. Now she had other considerations.

Dr. Viv had pulled back the curtain and exposed her carefully staged life—a life that would no longer be viable going forward. Not if she was going to live with true purpose.

What if Dr. Viv and Geary were right? Could she really learn to walk again?

She took a deep breath and looked Dr. Viv in the eyes. "I love my husband."

Dr. Viv nodded. "I know you do. Now, what do you say we get to work?"

A gentle smile nipped at the corners of Faith's mouth. For the first time in years, she felt her load lighten. She was going to change—she was going to heal her marriage.

And together, she and Geary were going to adopt Conner Anderson.

34

Back in her hospital room, Faith stared out the window. After weeks of storms rolling in off the Gulf, clear blue sky finally hung above the Houston skyline.

She wheeled herself closer to the bedside table. She wanted to be different. Here was the starting point.

With trembling hands she grabbed her cell phone. Holding her breath, she dialed.

Faith's chest pounded. The ringtone sounded three times with no pickup. Not wanting to leave a message, she moved to end the call when he answered.

"Faith? Faith, are you okay?"

"I'm fine," she quickly assured him. "But I need to talk to you. I know you are likely getting ready to leave for the Guntersville tournament, but—"

"I'll be there," he promised, his elation palpable.

She hung up, thinking about all they'd been through these past months. With their marriage on the brink of coming completely apart, her and Geary's entire world had been ripped even further by an angry shooter's bullets.

She had to wonder now why any man would stay. Especially

when she'd so often walled herself off from the intimacy she craved by pushing Geary away.

Could a relationship so tattered ever really be made whole?

Dr. Viv had said she needed to let others love and help her, that if she wanted to get emotionally well, she'd have to learn to trust Geary and let him be her hero.

At first she'd argued. Foolishly she'd allowed herself to believe she could somehow do this life without him. Even before the shooting, she'd tried to convince herself her marriage was disposable. But the truth was, Dr. Viv was right.

Mending her relationship with Geary was the only way to heal and move forward.

Less than an hour later, Geary made good on his pledge. She heard a slight rap on her door, and her skin flushed. "Come in."

He peeked through the door. "Hey."

Geary timidly entered the room, holding his fishing cap in his hands and bearing a look of hope that caused her heart to cave. She'd caused him so much pain. But she couldn't let those thoughts derail her now. She needed to focus on what Dr. Viv said—broken people like her were still worth loving.

It was in that frame of mind that she beckoned her husband into the room. She had nothing much to offer, only an authentic version of herself.

She'd pushed him away at every turn. Didn't deserve his forgiveness.

Still, she'd made a decision to come to him just as she was. Scarred and broken and in need of reconciliation.

She motioned him to the bed, patting the place beside her. Swallowing against the tightness in her throat, she pushed out the words that needed said. "Geary, I'm so sorry."

His hand covered her own. His deep blue eyes gazed into hers. "You don't have to—"

"I—I never wanted to hurt you, Geary. Pushing you away was—

well, it was my way of self-protecting. At least that's what Dr. Viv tells me."

He looked confused. "You don't have to protect yourself from me. I'm here—I always will be. If you're mad, say so. We can fight about it. We can search for solutions. What I can't deal with is being shut out." His eyes softened. "I love you."

"Deep down, I know that. But I—" She paused, not quite sure how to convey what she needed him to understand.

She lifted a shaking hand to her scarf, laid her fingers on the fabric, and pulled it down.

"Geary, this is the ugliest part of me—my scars. And you should know there are ones you can't see, deep wounds on the inside."

She looked at him then, daring him to respond.

Those deep blue eyes filled with tears. He reached out and touched the places where the staples had pierced her skin. She felt him slowly run his fingers along the ridges and patches of sprouting hair, tenderly taking in the bumps that marred her once perfect skull.

"You're beautiful," he choked out. "To me, you are beautiful."

His fingers went to her chin and he lifted her face to his own. His lips joined hers, first softly, then with far more urgency.

Suddenly, he stopped.

A flash of something Faith couldn't name crossed his face. Geary jumped up and looked around the room. With purpose, he marched over to the bureau that held her clothes. He leaned his shoulder against the side and shoved the heavy chest of drawers across the tiled floor until he'd wedged it in front of the door. "There, that should do it."

She frowned in confusion. "What are you doing?"

Her husband pressed his finger against his lips. "Shhh . . ." Grinning, he moved to the bed, unbuttoning his shirt.

"Geary?" Suddenly, his intention dawned. "What are you thinking? We can't—"

"No more talking," he said, sinking beside her on the bed. He scrambled to unbutton her top and then they were skin to skin.

A bolt of desire shot through her.

And over the course of the next several minutes, Faith learned there were parts of her body that still worked just fine.

35

The next weeks were grueling. She was up at dawn, then spent hours on the PT floor with a team of therapists, all working to strengthen her brain's ability to communicate with her muscles.

Geary was back out on the circuit, and while he was away, she had a lot of work to do. And good reason to do it.

"I know you are still feeling some loss of sensation in your left arm and leg, but it's important to remember these limbs have not been injured," the therapist explained. "The only reason they are not working is that the signals coming from your brain are misfiring. We're going to do some exercises that force your brain to remember how to tell your leg to walk, your arm to pick up items. Then we'll have you getting in and out of bed on your own, walking and being able to go to the toilet unattended. You'll return to the household activities you enjoyed prior to the injury."

Faith smiled widely. "Okay, let's do it."

A variety of exercises were employed to accomplish regaining her function and mobility, starting with a regimen of standing from a sitting position. No matter the promises made that her therapist would hold and support her body until her legs learned to function again, slipping from the chair and shifting weight onto her legs felt a bit like jumping off a cliff with no bottom in sight.

She had music therapy, singing along with her favorite CD while the therapist held Faith's limp fingers in her own and helped her strum the strings of a guitar. Art therapy included holding a paintbrush and carefully dipping it in a small container of paint, then swathing the brush across a large piece of paper using wide strokes and then smaller circular motions, guided again by a therapist.

She walked the parallel bars and kicked a soccer ball, even if clumsily. And she stood in place and carefully shifted weight from her right leg to her left, over and over until her brain started to fire up and communicate—slowly at first, then gradually increasing.

Often Faith went to bed aching inside and out from all the effort.

But she remained steadfast. She had a goal and she toiled to attain success. Failure was not an option.

Geary left for his final round of tournaments this season. The reasonable thing to do was to wait until he was home to drop her news and tell him about her plans regarding little Conner. But something inside her wouldn't let her suspend her excitement, so she finally mustered her courage and told him over the phone.

As expected, upon hearing the entire story, her husband shared the ache she felt over all the little guy had faced and his unknown future. But the new information, her desire to adopt Conner, gave him reservation.

"Oh, Faith. I don't know," he said when she opened up about her intentions. "I desperately want a family too. You know that. But adopting right now is a lot to take on so early in your recovery. I mean, we need to get you home first, don't you think?"

"Of course. I'm not talking about rushing out and doing something foolish. I need to be physically ready before we can take this on," she quickly assured him. "But I've never wanted anything more. Geary, just wait until you meet him. You'll soon understand why I feel so strongly about moving forward. There's a lot at stake."

Silence.

"Geary?" She swallowed hard, knowing this was yet another chance to be different. She didn't push. Instead, she held her arguments and waited.

"I'll tell you what. Let's take this a step at a time. When I get home, I'll meet him. We'll talk to Dr. Viv and I'll pray about it. If it's God's will, little Conner will end up in our home. But we need to take this slow. Make sure it's the right thing for everyone involved. Agreed?"

"Really, Geary? Thank you! You'll love him too. I promise."

"I don't doubt that. If he's stolen your heart, he must be a very special little boy."

Her heart soared. "When will you be home?"

She could almost see him smile at the other end of the phone. "Won't be long. I'm on the road outside of Broken Arrow, Oklahoma, and I'm heading out to a tournament in Florida. It's the big one."

"You qualified? Geary, that's wonderful."

"Yeah, say a prayer."

He sounded excited yet a little weary. She wanted to assure him everything was going to be all right. "Geary?"

"Uh-huh."

"I'm so proud of you."

They agreed he'd come to the hospital the minute he got back to Houston. She promised to watch the tournament on television and told him she was anxious to see him.

In the meantime, she'd focus on getting well and keep her attention on that adorable little boy two floors above.

With the help of Lawana Maxwell, the nurse who had lifted her spirits with eggs Benedict, she got her hands on a set of Thomas the Train coloring books and a large package of crayons. She presented them to Conner when she visited after lunch.

"Hey, buddy. I brought you something."

He looked up at her. "For me? What is it?"

She handed him the gift. "Do you want to color together?"

He nodded. "But I'm not very good at it. My mommy used to help me stay in the lines." His face turned sad. Faith's heart squeezed at the thought he would never again see the woman he'd loved.

"I can help you stay in the lines," Faith offered.

He shrugged. "Oh-tay."

Over the next hour, they sat side by side coloring a scene featuring Thomas, Gordon, and Percy—engines she'd learned all about using the same vigor utilized in prepping for a celebrity interview.

Finally, Faith got up the nerve to say what was foremost on her mind.

"Conner, if you ever feel lonely, I'll be your friend. All you have to do is have a nurse come get me and I'll come be with you."

Little Conner clutched the red crayon and pushed it back and forth across the paper with purpose. "Fanks, but I'll be oh-tay."

His response took Faith a bit off guard. She tried again. "I mean, you know—if you ever feel scared or sad, or just need someone to hold your hand."

He looked up at her then. "Oh-tay. But I'm not awone. Jesus is wif me."

Her breath stalled. "Jesus?"

"Yeah. Mommy said no matter whatever happens, Jesus is my fwiend."

She swallowed—hard. "Your mommy was very wise. Maybe—maybe I could be your friend too."

He finished coloring and laid the crayon down, then turned to her. "You can be my fwiend." Without skipping a beat he picked up the box of crayons and held them out to her. "Wanna color another picture?"

She pulled the blue crayon out of the pack. "Sure. Which one?"

Back in her room, Faith pondered her time with Conner Anderson. While his deep grief over the loss of his mother was apparent, the child had an underpinning of faith she envied.

His mother had been incredibly wise to instill that understanding within her son so that he knew without any shadow of a doubt that Jesus loved him personally and would never leave his side.

If she had known that kind of faith as a child, perhaps she wouldn't be so broken now, so reluctant to give up control and let God guide her path.

Certainly the Marins had that level of faith. She'd seen it time and again—especially when they loved her even when she was bristly. Given the chance, she intended to show them she was grateful and she loved them back.

Even Bobby Lee.

And if God permitted, she'd be Conner Anderson's mother—not a replacement for the woman who had birthed him and provided such a sweet foundation, but she'd build on that and be by his side, loving him and providing for him.

Funny thing—she'd so wanted to be a widely recognized news celebrity. That goal didn't hold a candle to the desire now smoldering in her gut, her longing to be Conner's mother.

In a twist of fate, or perhaps by God's hand, her life had been spared that day while his mother had died. No longer would she live a life spent trying to find value after having lived with such shame. She now realized that was no life at all.

Conner had lived. So had she—and together they would become the family she'd always longed for. And he'd have an extended family—the Marins—people of faith who would help to foster what no doubt had been important to his mother.

How better to have her own faith strengthened than by giving her life away to a little boy in a wheelchair who needed a mother?

Her hand went to her stomach, to the place where the shooter's bullet had scarred her flesh . . . had maybe even kept her from giving birth in the future. She'd heard Wendell say from the pulpit—in God's design, even things meant for evil could turn to good.

The notion reminded her that the very thing that had torn her and Geary apart—his persistence to start a family—would now be the glue that would give them one purpose. She was learning she needed to hold plans loosely. Not be so stubborn. Sometimes God had other ideas.

Lawana helped her from her chair into bed. After physical therapy, she could now assist the effort by standing, as long as she had someone near to support her. "Well, look at you!" Lawana said, her hand at Faith's back. "I can't believe the progress you've made in such a short time. Especially once you put your mind to it."

Faith could tell her she'd spent years accomplishing much through sheer determination, but this time that would not be entirely true. Sure, she'd given 100 percent effort, but she'd also sent up a couple of prayers, asking for help.

A rare approach in the life of Faith Marin.

When she was settled and alone, she reached for the television remote. The bass tournament weigh-in was being broadcast on one of the cable sports channels. Earlier, she'd texted Geary to wish him luck and tell him she'd be watching. He hadn't answered, but that was understandable. He'd been on the lake all day. Hopefully snagging a lunker that would tip those scales in his favor, landing him the trophy and a wad of cash and prizes.

The monitor flashed on the main stage with lights, music, and a brightly colored backdrop. The leaderboard showed Geary as a finalist, a fact that thrilled her.

Despite adversity, her husband had worked hard, remained focused. With everything in her, she hoped he'd be rewarded for the effort.

Within minutes, the announcer took viewers through prepared video rundowns showcasing the bass fishermen and their journeys to this spot. Geary's showcased his prior win of nearly four years ago, then turned to a poignant story of how he'd temporarily quit the circuit to care for his cancer-ridden grandfather, followed by the tragic shooting where his wife had been gunned down and left physically impaired.

The story had a definite emotive factor she knew had been carefully designed to connect with the viewing audience. Even those who normally did not follow the championship circuit would hope for her husband to come out on top. In her profession—or former profession—she knew this was the kind of thing that garnered attention and ratings.

She also knew Geary would hate that the sympathy card had been played on his behalf.

Up on the big stage, several of the finalists weighed in, followed by projections that the weight totals might not be enough to garner the big prize win.

Finally, it was Geary's turn. He was next to last to go on stage with his bag of fish.

A pickup truck eased his boat up in front of the stage. With much fanfare, Geary waved to the cheering crowd and made his way to the live well at the back of the deck. He opened the latch and retrieved a bright yellow bag—the official weigh-in sack for the tournament. Inside were the bass Geary had pulled in that day.

Faith bit at her fingernails. He had forty-six pounds, six ounces coming into this final day. He only needed a total weight of over eighteen pounds, two ounces for the five fish in the bag to land in the lead.

The emcee's voice rang out, announcing what was at stake—one hundred thousand dollars and a pickup and boat.

The music's frenzied beat increased and the spotlights shone over the crowd like a dance club. The camera quickly panned to Wendell and Veta sitting out in the audience.

Back on stage, the yellow bag was dumped onto the scales by

the official, the tension palpable as everyone collectively held their breath until the results were announced.

"Twenty pounds, four ounces!" the emcee screamed. "We have a new lead. Geary Marin is in the lead!"

Faith willed her left arm to lift, and it did slightly. She clapped her hands together, thrilled for her husband. Truly she was over-the-top ecstatic he had such a good chance of walking away with the top award and champion designation.

The camera followed him off the stage where a woman with tight jeans and shoulder-length dark cocoa-brown hair stepped to his side and gave him a hug. They said something indiscernible, then the woman smiled as cameras flashed.

Stacy Brien.

That vixen looked as smug and dangerous as she had that day on the Marins' lawn during the crawfish feed. What was she doing at the tournament sidled up to her husband? And why was she smiling so big?

Faith grabbed her phone. She pounded out a text with her thumbs, willing her brain to send the proper signals to her left hand.

Congratulations! Looks like you've found someone to celebrate with.

She moved to press send—and stopped.

Almost immediately she regretted what she'd about done. Her hand went to her head all stubbled with hair trying to regrow. She fingered the divots in her skull, the marks where the thick metal staples had been.

Dozens of times in the last days, she'd stared at her image in the mirror and wondered who was looking back at her. She remembered Geary telling her she was beautiful.

Perhaps so—but she certainly didn't look like Stacy Brien.

Hot tears ran down her cheeks as she looked back at the television monitor. Geary was holding his championship trophy above his head now. He was beaming.

This was where she had a choice to make—believe the lie she wasn't worth loving, or believe her husband, that he loved her completely and without reservation.

True, she couldn't compete with Stacy in the looks department. Not anymore. No matter what pep talk came out of her husband's mouth, Faith needed to come to terms with that.

She had no choice but to recalibrate the way she thought about her worth.

Conner Anderson needed a mother. An emotionally healthy woman who did not falter at every opposition was essential to his well-being.

She'd be there for him. And she wouldn't do it alone. Geary would be by her side.

36

The therapist placed two tennis balls on the table. "Okay, Faith. I need you to pick one up with your right hand and the other with your left."

Faith firmly grasped the ball in her right hand. Her grip on the ball in her left hand was weak, but she was able to wrap her fingers around it.

"Okay," her therapist said. "As you slowly lift your right hand, I want you to try to make the exact same movements with your left hand." Faith's brain was able to give clear signals to her right hand. The hope was that if she could move both hands simultaneously, the right guiding the left, the movement might further retrain her brain.

Faith concentrated, lifting her right and left hands in tandem. She actually willed her left hand to lift that tennis ball. One inch. Two inches. Three inches. She lifted the ball four inches into the air. It was a triumph.

"Good. Excellent!" The therapist beamed. "Okay, that's enough for today."

Faith thanked her. She concentrated and moved herself slowly along the table and toward her wheelchair. In just the last week, she'd made remarkable progress. She had nearly her entire arm movement back, and exercises like those today were quickly restoring her dexterity. While still somewhat clumsy, she was walking on her own.

The team warned she might never return to exactly the same physical abilities she had prior to the shooting, but in six months or so, few looking at her would notice.

Back in her room, she pulled her phone from the pocket of her yoga pants. As she went to place it on her bedside table, it rang, giving her a start. She glanced at the face, which read *Unidentified Caller*.

"Hello?" she answered. She fingered the soft petals of a tulip in another bouquet that had been sent over by the station with a card that read, *Hearing you might be going home soon. You'll always have a place back at the station.* The card had been signed by Clark and all the others. She smiled at the heartwarming gesture.

"Hello?" she repeated when no one responded. Suddenly, her heart pounded. "Teddy, is that you?"

"It's me," a voice said, a voice that barely sounded like her brother's. "I called to, uh, to tell you I'm sorry."

"Don't be. I survived. The shooter's bullet didn't take me down completely."

"No, I know that. I'm . . ." His words slurred terribly.

"Teddy? Teddy, are you all right?" Alarm rose inside her. Clearly, her brother was anything but all right. "Where are you? I mean, I want to see you. Teddy, I need to see you. Please, please tell me where you are."

"Please don't hate me. I—I needed the money," Teddy nearly whimpered. "I'm sorry."

The phone went dead.

Panic rose in Faith's chest. She knew better than to try to call her brother back. The past had taught her he wouldn't answer.

Why had he called? Why now? And why did he keep saying he was sorry?

Unless he was going to . . .

She'd heard that desperation one other time. Her mother.

Could it be possible Teddy Jr. had finally reached the end of his tolerance for life lived at the bottom of the pit? Was he considering taking a similar path?

That possible notion chilled her to the bone. She clasped the phone and did the only thing she knew to do.

She called Geary.

Faith sat on the edge of a straight-backed chair in her room, picking at her pants and willing Geary to return her call. When he hadn't picked up, she'd left a message. Without giving a lot of details, she'd tried to plainly let him know the situation was urgent with these words: "Geary, I need you. Please come."

She watched the clock on the wall ticking off the minutes—twenty-six, to be exact—since Teddy had called. *Please, Lord, let Geary call back.*

As if on cue, the phone trilled. She picked up. "Geary?"

"Faith, I'm on my way. What is it? Are you okay?"

His voice was like cool water dousing the raging worry magnifying in her mind with every second. "I'm fine. But I need you, please hurry."

Geary arrived in record time, given the distance and five o'clock traffic. As he rushed into her room, she met him standing. He lifted his eyebrows at the sight. "You—you're on your feet. Both of them," he said, grinning.

She nodded and grasped his wrist. "Sit, I need your help. And we don't have much time."

Giving her husband the condensed version, she told him about her brother and the call, confiding for the first time the entire story and how bad off her little brother really was—how his addiction had pulled him under, drowning his ability to function properly and extinguishing any sort of normal sibling relationship between the two of them. "This time it's different. I know his voice. He's in real trouble. I'm scared of what he might be planning to do, and we have to find him."

Geary nodded. "I'll do whatever I can," he said, rubbing his chin. "But, babe. We don't even know where he is."

Someone rapped on her door. "Faith?"

Geary jumped up and swung the door open.

Lawana Maxwell stood there in her white nurse uniform. "Faith, you'd better turn on the television. I'm afraid there's something you'll want to see."

37

On the television, DeeAnne Roberts, whom Faith had learned was now with another station, sat across from Teddy Jr. "Let me start off by saying how grateful I am that you agreed to this interview." She was dressed in a fuchsia-pink suit jacket and cream-colored slacks. Gold chains were stacked on her wrists and hung from her neckline.

Teddy noticeably squirmed in his worn jeans and button-down, the sleeves rolled up, exposing sharp bony angles at his wrists. "Yeah, uh—no problem." His eyes were wide and deep, glossy.

Faith's hand went to her throat. "Oh no! No." She looked over at Geary, frantic, a dull thud inside her chest. "He's high."

They both watched in horror when DeeAnne smiled slowly, as if she wanted to take something that wasn't hers and didn't want anyone to notice. "Well, as you know, your sister is a much-loved television personality, someone the entire viewing community admires. When she was gunned down by a shooter at the Johnson Space Center on that fateful day, we all watched in horror." Her face drew into the appropriate emotion before she continued. "Houstonians have hoped and prayed and cheered her on as we've followed her surprising recovery."

Photos of Faith on various field reports and then images of the aftermath of the shooting appeared on-screen.

Faith's blood flowed in slow motion, slugging into her heart's ventricles like searing molten lava.

"They've paid him," she said absently. "They broke the golden rule and paid for this interview. And it's not going to be good."

Now she understood her brother's cryptic message. So did Geary and he leapt into action.

He pulled his cell phone from his jeans pocket. "I'll handle this." After a couple of clicks he said under his breath, "Got it." He dialed and held the phone to his ear, waiting.

On the television, DeeAnne glanced at her notes briefly. "Let's talk about your sister a little, provide our viewers with a little background."

Teddy's eyes darted between the camera and the anchor. He ran his hand through his sandy-blond hair. "Yeah, what do you want to know?"

"My notes say your sister grew up right here in Houston."

"Yeah. We lived over in Baytown. She used to walk me to school every morning." His mouth drew into a slight grin. "Kept the bullies away, know what I mean?"

Faith stared at the image on the screen, both horrified and fascinated. She hadn't seen her little brother in over three years. He looked just as she remembered, except he was much thinner. His hollow cheeks and severe jawline told her eating might not be one of his daily habits. Sadly, he looked shriveled and all used up—like vegetables when they'd been in the crisper far too long.

DeeAnne cocked her head to the right. "Yes, let's talk about your time in Baytown. Your father was"—she checked her notes—"an RV salesman?"

Teddy nodded. The dark circles under his eyes made him appear haunted.

"And he died very early? Is that right?"

Again he nodded.

Geary's voice grew louder from across the room. Faith held up her palm, trying to quiet him so she could listen.

"And your mother." DeeAnne said this as a statement. Faith chewed on her nail. The woman in the anchor chair was the sort of person who would try to discover as much as she could to use the information to her benefit. Obviously, she believed she'd hit the jackpot. She was after ratings and was a master manipulator who would compliment herself, while disguising the fact she was holding someone else underwater to do it.

Teddy frowned. "I thought you wanted me to talk about Faith."

DeeAnne leaned back. "Yes, of course. I just think viewers would like to know a little background about your sister." She gave him a flattering smile. "Let's talk a minute about that day at the Johnson Space Center," she said, switching gears. "How did you learn of the shooting?"

Teddy rubbed at his eyebrow. "That's when I had a job. I was working laundry over at the Omni—nights. Some dude came in pushing another load of sheets and he was talking about this shooting out at JSC that happened earlier in the day, some senator being dead and all. And then he said my sister's name." He cleared his throat and straightened in the chair. "I had to check it out so I sweet-talked a maid into letting me into one of the empty rooms, and I turned on the television and all." He shook his head. "Worst day of my life."

DeeAnne's eyes narrowed. "Worse than finding your mother dead?"

Faith could see the sweat on Teddy's brow. "I—my sister. I ain't talking about that."

"How old was your sister when your mother killed herself?"

Teddy turned angry. He stood and yanked the microphone from his chest. "I'm outta here."

DeeAnne reached for him. "No, wait. I have just a few more—"

"I'm done," he said and tossed the wire to the floor and walked off the set.

The antics were not that unexpected. DeeAnne took a deep, satisfied breath and smiled at the camera. "I apologize to our viewers. The story here is that the woman who launched her career by saving a young man from throwing himself off the Fred Hartman Bridge, did so while hiding the pain of her own mother's suicide." DeeAnne lifted her chin slightly. "And now Faith Marin sits in a hospital here in Houston, fighting to learn to walk again after being shot by a madman."

Faith could barely breathe. "How dare she?" She balled her hands into fists and gritted her teeth in anger.

But she knew the drill. Networks were willing to run even the most egregious nonsense, all for the sake of increasing viewer buzz. Her personal life had been thrown as bait in hopes of luring the watching public from other stations—from her own KIAM-TV.

It was a low move.

One she'd never done, but had come dangerously close to at times.

Geary slammed his phone into his shirt pocket. "I know where your brother is—or at least where he was about an hour ago."

Faith mustered every neurotransmitter inside her brain, willing each to cooperate. Only faltering slightly, she stood. "Let's go."

Geary shook his head. "You're not going anywhere. I'll go find your brother."

Faith grabbed his arm. "Teddy Jr. will never let you approach him. I've got to be there."

Her husband looked at her as if weighing his options.

She teared up. "Geary, please. I couldn't take it if something happened. Please take me to him."

He slowly nodded. "Okay, if your medical team agrees it's safe, I'll take you."

Within the hour, calls had been made and she'd been helped to Geary's pickup. As he lifted her inside, his familiar scent filled her nostrils and made her feel less anxious.

In her mind too much time had passed since her brother's phone call. Clearly he'd felt low and was under the influence—a dangerous combination.

"Please hurry," she urged Geary, who had called the station while the interview was airing, demanding to speak to their station manager. He learned her brother had walked out of the interview without getting his payment—another dangerous sign.

Luckily, the station folks caught up with him on the sidewalk and offered to pay for a cab. Geary now had the information where Teddy Jr. had been taken and dropped off—Baytown.

She knew there could only be one place he'd go in the town where'd they'd grown up. She gave Geary the address.

On the way there it started to rain, first a steady drumbeat of drops on the windshield, then turning to a torrent that made it difficult to see the road ahead.

Geary's hands gripped the wheel a bit tighter. "Are you okay?" he asked without taking his eyes from the road.

"Yeah. I just never imagined my first trip out of the hospital would be—this."

"Faith, I don't understand. Why didn't you tell me?"

She watched the wipers doing their best to sweep the glass free of the water that blurred her vision. "Geary, all of my life I've felt broken. I know that's difficult for you to understand coming from your background, with a mother and father who love one another, who are committed to their children, and who love God. You have no idea what it feels like to compare your own situation and wonder what you did to deserve so much less."

He glanced at her then. "Less?"

"Yes. My career offered a respite, a place where my own accomplishments overshadowed my defective genesis. At KIAM-TV, all that mattered was how I looked on camera, what story I scooped, the ratings."

A semitruck passed in the adjacent lane, spraying water and making visibility even more treacherous. Geary leaned forward and concentrated, but she knew he was listening.

"Imagine what it was like to come into a family like the Marins. I should have felt fortunate. Because of God's providence I now had what I had lacked all those years—stable, healthy people who wanted to love on me. Albeit too much sometimes and in ways I was unaccustomed to, but your family and even the church members were nothing but gracious."

"But it all seemed to just rub you wrong."

"It did. Your family was simply a reflection of what my own lacked. Think of it, Geary. In every situation the people who were supposed to love me the most simply bailed on me. First, my father. His physical needs and desires took precedence over me and Teddy. My mother, even. She was always eccentric, but his unfaithfulness broke her. She was never the same after he died in that car and she learned he'd had a younger woman with him. That event seemed to just be more than she could wrap her fragile self around."

"You never told me what happened to her."

"It was a night in November, much like this one. Despite the storms rolling in off the Gulf, she donned a swimsuit and walked across our backyard with a bottle of vodka in her hands."

"I'm so sorry," Geary nearly whispered.

"I came home from a movie to a dark house. I finally found Teddy outside, sitting in the reeds by the edge of the water with Mama draped over his lap. He was soaked to the bone. When I knelt beside him he simply said, 'Mom went swimming.'"

The exit to Baytown loomed up ahead. Geary turned on his blinker. "But that sounds like an accident. She drank too much and just made a foolish choice."

She nodded and wiped at her eyes. "We thought so too, until

we found her goodbye note a day later. She even wrote out her own obituary, leaving out all the bad parts and making it sound like we were the Brady Bunch or something."

Geary reached across the seat and grabbed her hand. "I'm so sorry I expected you to mold into my family without considering there might be reasons why you were pulling away."

"How could you possibly have figured any of this out? I was far too broken to reveal what was really going on inside of me."

Minutes later he pulled up in front of the address she'd provided. The house was empty now, boarded up. The sidewalk in front was crumbling and the front lawn nothing but weeds.

She hadn't been back in years.

She hadn't liked living here then, and she hated it now. She only hoped she wasn't too late.

Geary helped her from the truck. He removed his shirt and tried to shelter her from the rain, to no avail.

"Stay here, Geary. This is something I need to do alone."

"But—"

"Alone," she repeated, not leaving room for argument.

She could sense his reservation, understood it even, but to his credit Geary stayed back and let her continue, despite her faltering steps.

She willed her legs to carry her.

The bluster nearly drowned out her husband's voice. "Please be careful."

She rounded the corner of the house, stepping carefully and concentrating on every move—lifting one leg then the other, just as she had while on the balance bar in physical therapy.

Lightning flashed, illuminating the scene before her.

She saw him then, Teddy Jr., huddled by the water's edge.

Her heart flooded with relief. Faith hurried forward as best she could until she was close enough to place her hand on his shoulder. "Teddy?"

He turned, sobbing.

She knelt on the muddy ground and embraced him. “Teddy, I’m so glad I found you.”

He looked at her, misery dimming his eyes. “I thought she loved us.”

“She did, Teddy. She was just broken and didn’t know how to show us.”

Epilogue

Faith sat under the hot lights, waiting while the production assistant attached the microphone to her lapel. Mike Jarrett leaned over. "You ready for this?"

Despite a bit of nerves, she nodded enthusiastically. "Yes, I'm ready." She took a deep breath and looked to the camera monitor where Lucas Cunningham silently held up his fingers.

Five—four—three—two. He pointed.

Mike leaned forward. "Welcome, everyone. Today here at KIAM-TV we have a special treat for our viewers. Many of you recognize this lovely lady sitting beside me—our own Faith Marin. She's back with us today after a lengthy absence following the day she was tragically shot by a lone gunman out at the Johnson Space Center."

Music cued the leader that flashed on all the monitors on the wall. Her image appeared from behind the anchor desk. More pictures rotated through the short segment of her reporting from the Fred Hartman Bridge, of the piece she'd done on River Oaks, and of her on the set of *Faith on Air*.

The images caused her throat to constrict with emotion. She

was struck by how confident she appeared in all those shots—like nothing could knock her off-kilter.

As the segment faded along with the music, Mike picked back up. “Many of you have followed Faith’s remarkable recovery, as have all of us here at the station. We’re all so very pleased to welcome her back to the anchor desk this morning.”

She smiled widely. “Hello, everyone. It’s good to be back. Thank you for all of your prayers, good wishes, all the cards and letters. You don’t know what those sweet gestures meant to me, and how knowing you were all rooting for me helped in my recovery.

“I’m not going to lie—the road was long. I’m no longer the same—not on the outside certainly, and not on the inside. I still have a ways to go. But starting on Monday, I’ll be back here with you hosting *Faith on Air* three days a week. We’ve got a lot to explore together, journeys to take and stories to sift.” She fought to maintain her emotions. “While some did not survive that tragic day at the JSC, I was given a second chance. I promise I intend to make the most of it. And I hope you’ll come along.”

She smiled at the blinking red light. “It’s good to be back.”

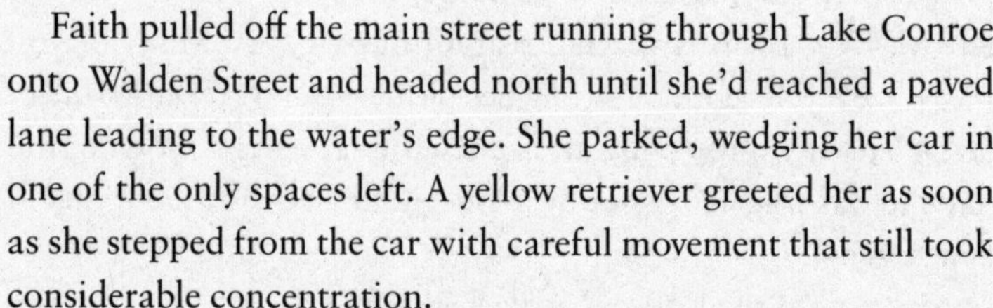

Faith pulled off the main street running through Lake Conroe onto Walden Street and headed north until she’d reached a paved lane leading to the water’s edge. She parked, wedging her car in one of the only spaces left. A yellow retriever greeted her as soon as she stepped from the car with careful movement that still took considerable concentration.

She ruffled the dog’s furry head with her left hand. “Hey, girl—where’s the party?” In response, her four-legged friend circled with excitement and barked, her tail wagging.

Faith smiled and moved down the sidewalk toward a newly built house wedged on a sprawling lawn leading to a cove—her and Geary's home. She took a breath, and instead of climbing the two steps up to their inviting front porch scattered with rocking chairs and pots of red geraniums, she walked around, past the far end of the porch and Conner's wheelchair ramp.

Summer had arrived, as it always did, to Lake Conroe. With it came long, hot days that baked the pebbled shores along the water's edge.

Music and laughter floated on the heavy air as Faith joined a noisy crowd gathered in her backyard.

Veta was the first to notice her arrival. She stepped away from Gina Rudd and Alma Cheesey and waved her arm. "There you are!"

Wendell, in his apron, greeted her as well. "Just in time. The pots are ready for the crawfish to go in."

Faith moved forward and gave them both a big hug. "I appreciate you both helping with everything." She looked past them, to the water. "Where's my guys?"

Veta pointed to where Geary eased his boat up to the dock and tied it off to a post. After shutting off the engine, he stood and lifted out a small wheelchair.

Faith waved her arm and her husband waved back. So did a little blond-haired boy who held a fishing pole in his hand.

A commotion drew all their attention back to the house. Bobby Lee lugged a cooler, with Dilly following close behind with a little girl on her hip. Little Violet Grace had a big pink bow in her soft brown curls and her thumb in her mouth.

Dilly's stomach bulged with number five—due in a couple of months. There was a time Faith would have faulted the Sitterles for that decision, but no longer. In her mother-in-law's wise words—it was their family to raise.

From behind their parents, Gabby and Gunner tore across the lawn. Together they held their younger brother's hand, pulling him along at a pace where he could barely keep up. "C'mon, Sam, hurry up."

Dilly shouted across the lawn, "Now, you kids, don't play too rough with him."

Gunner yelled back, "We won't. We'll play smooth," making them all laugh.

Dilly turned to her mom. "You know what Gabby asked us last night? She asked where babies come from."

Wendell lifted a huge bag of crawfish from the cooler. "Yeah? What did you tell her?"

Bobby Lee lifted a second bag. "Ha, I told her when two poodles dance on a woman's stomach, it makes a baby."

Faith's eyebrows lifted. "You did not!"

"Yes, he did," Dilly confirmed, bumping her elbow into her husband's side. "But I quickly corrected the misinformation and told her children were a sweet gift from God."

With her whole being, Faith knew that to be true. From the moment she'd laid eyes on Conner, her heart had opened wide and she'd claimed him as her own, allowing the orphaned child entrance to a place deep inside her that had once been so broken. There was a time when she'd not been able to love with that kind of wild abandon.

Now nothing could tear her away from the family God had given her—nothing physical or emotional.

Geary wheeled Conner up next to her. "Hi, Mommy Faith! Did you go to the telebision?"

"Hey, sweet one. I did. How's my Conner today?" She looked at Geary, who winked in her direction.

"I'm so good and happy. We got three basses."

"Bass," Geary corrected.

"We caught three bass. Big ones." He stretched out his little arms to show her as Geary brushed a kiss across her cheek.

"So you had fun?" Wendell asked him.

Conner nodded with enthusiasm. "Yes—yes, I did."

Geary patted his son on the shoulder. "And now we're back to help you finish getting ready for the party."

Conner took Faith's hand and pulled her down toward his face. "Yeah, when's Uncle Teddy going to be here?"

As if on cue, her brother sauntered across the lawn in their direction. "Hey, anybody home?" he hollered.

Joy bubbled inside as she waved at him. "Down here. You ready for your big party?"

He joined them and shook hands with Bobby Lee and Wendell. Then he turned to hug her. "Truth? I'm not sure. But my sponsor tells me it's important to celebrate your victories."

Veta patted him on the back. "A year sober is a huge victory, Teddy. I'm glad we could celebrate with you."

"One day at a time, Veta. One day at a time."

Geary handed him a cold bottle of Dr Pepper. "Hey, Teddy. Glad you could make it."

Teddy nodded, hesitated. Then he stepped forward and gave his brother-in-law a quick hug. "Thanks, man. I couldn't have done it without you. And your family."

"Speaking of . . ." Veta pointed back toward the house. "I need some help bringing down all those cupcakes, and the rolls. Oh, and the butter. There's some in Faith's fridge next to her chocolate pie."

She and Geary exchanged a private smile. She elbowed her husband. "I know what you're thinking, and yes, I took the plastic wrap off this time."

Gunner raced up and grabbed the handles of Conner's wheelchair. "C'mon, Conner. Let's go play."

Immediate alarm rose inside Faith's chest. "Uh, I'm not sure that's such a good idea." She looked to Geary.

Before her husband could intercept the situation, Teddy stepped forward and took hold of the handles himself. "What do you say I come along with?" He bent down. "That okay with you, buddy?"

Conner's face broke into an enthusiastic smile. "You betcha, Uncle Teddy!"

Relief spilled as Geary's arm went around Faith's waist. She leaned against his shoulder and chuckled at the sight of her brother running across the grass surrounded by children.

Together she and Teddy Jr. had endured a family situation she'd never wish on anyone. Her parents had been broken people—unable to love each other and their children properly. And they'd passed it on, crippling her as sure as the shooter's bullet had left her injured and unable to walk.

She liked to imagine her parents would have done better, had they known God and embraced the healing he offered.

Yes, sometimes evil came—but God was always bigger than evil. He'd turned the worst day of her life—the day she'd been mowed down by a shooter's bullet and left for dead—into a catalyst for huge blessing.

She was grateful to finally be healing. And doing so in ways only God could orchestrate.

Faith lifted her left hand and wiped at her cheeks as she took in the scene before her—the people gathered who all supported her and cared about her.

She turned and kissed her husband's cheek. "I love you," she whispered, tucking her auburn hair behind her ear.

Geary gave her a squeeze. "I love you too, babe."

Faith looked out over the quiet water in the cove and smiled. There was one more important thing she would never forget.

Sometimes broken things got fixed.

Author Note

If you've read my earlier books, you know I often pull ideas from courtroom cases I've worked on or reports in the news into my stories. *A Reason to Stay* is no different.

In early 2011, I watched with the rest of the country as news media reported on the terrible shooting that left Congresswoman Gabrielle Giffords fighting for her life. Like so many, I followed her painful journey to healing and prayed for her recovery.

Ms. Giffords's story hit very close to home.

While I was not a victim of a shooting, years back I suffered a stroke, the result of a brain bleed that required multiple cranial surgeries and a protracted hospital recovery. I was intimately acquainted with some of what Gabby faced, and my heart was broken for her.

A Reason to Stay is a very personal story. Not only does Faith Marin face a brain injury and the subsequent struggles to recover, but she must also deal with keeping her marriage intact—her real fight.

This summer, my husband and I will celebrate thirty-five years of marriage, a landmark in a journey marked with opposition. Looking back, I know that we only made it by the grace of God.

Over the course of our years together, both of us had to make a decision.

I'm grateful we chose to stay.

Acknowledgments

Creating a book is a joint effort, and I'm so very grateful for the entire team at Revell Books: Jen Leep, Lindsay Davis, Jessica English, Twila Bennett, and the outstanding sales, marketing, and publicity professionals. I'll let you in on a secret—O. J. Simpson isn't the only one with a dream team.

I especially want to express my gratitude to Editorial Director Jen Leep. Her vision to offer contemporary stories that explore deep heart matters wrapped in emotional complexity is extraordinary. Her support of what I write is so appreciated not only by me but also by my readers. May God pay you back, Jen.

Lindsay Davis, partnering with you to market these Texas Gold books has been such a pleasure. You are bright and innovative and dedicated. Mostly, I appreciate how you never hold your breath when you pick up the phone and hear me say, "I have an idea."

Speaking of ideas, one of my best was to partner with my agent, Natasha Kern. No one works harder to represent her clients with excellence. I am blessed to have you by my side.

This book featured a few worlds that required some expert help.

The men in my family are avid bass fishermen and often compete in tournaments, including the big Bass Champs tournament run by Chad Potts. I was talking to his wife when the idea for this book formed.

I needed a lot of help in understanding how the tournament circuit works. Thank you to Steve Patnode and the Toyota Texas Bass Classic for providing this wide-eyed novelist with media credentials, allowing me backstage access, and arranging interviews with the contestants. I enjoyed talking with bass pros Mike Iaconelli, Cody Meyer, Gary Yamamoto, and their wives.

I am especially grateful to Craig Meyers of our local NBC-5 station here in Dallas. The tour and time I spent with you meeting the anchors, producers, and technical professionals were invaluable. I hope I did the newsroom justice in this story. You all deserve a *Dateline* package of gratitude. (Oh, and sitting in the anchor chair was a thrill!)

Big hugs go to bestselling romance author Deeanne Gist. Thank you for helping me plot the way Faith and Geary would meet. Your idea to have her topple from the boat was brilliant!

A good friend from childhood, who is now a physical therapist, helped me with Faith's rehabilitation in the hospital. Thanks, Debby Sparks Dixon!

Some of you in Memphis might recognize a character name in my book. I named one of the rehab nurses Lawana Maxwell to thank her and her team at Highland Church of Christ for hosting me and several other authors at their fall women's ministry event. We were all so honored to be invited to talk about the importance of inspirational fiction and the way stories change lives. It's the reason Jesus told stories.

I could not do this without the support of my family. Allen, Jordan, Eric and Brandy, and my little Preston and Lydia—you are forever embedded in my heart.

Last, but certainly not least, thank you to my readers. I love the emails you send, the notes of encouragement, and the messages telling me how these stories have affected you. Connecting with you on Facebook, Twitter, Pinterest, and Goodreads is such a pleasure. Please know this—you are in my mind every minute I sit with my fingertips on the keyboard.

Keep reading for a
sneak peek of
the next book in the

1

I'm sorry. We really need someone a bit more qualified. All of the positions we currently have available require a college degree—at a minimum."

Leta Breckenridge fixed her eyes on the woman standing behind the table lined with job application forms. "Oh—okay. Well, thank you for your time anyway." She placed the glossy brochure back in its spot on the table, taking special care to line up the edges with the dozens just like it. Her fingers lingered for just a moment before she gave the lady in the suit a weak smile and moved on.

With a sigh, Leta pulled a pen and a notebook from her bag and marked off another company name from the list.

Taking time off work to attend the job fair this afternoon was turning out to be a waste of time. She couldn't even get her foot in the door at most of the companies she was interested in, even at an entry-level position. Not without having finished her degree.

Same story as always.

Determined not to let the situation get her down, Leta quickly glanced down at her watch. She'd stay another half hour before getting ready to head back to the store. Maybe she could talk Mike into letting her make up the hours—and the lost earnings.

"Leta?"

She turned in the direction of a vaguely familiar voice just as Cassie Manning broke through the crowd, a wide smile planted on her face. "Leta, I thought that was you. Long time no see."

She quickly tucked the notebook back in her bag before letting herself get drawn into an embrace. "Hey, how are you?" Her friend smelled . . . expensive. Like the little samples she'd collected from the Macy's counter last week while in the mall with Katie.

Her former classmate gave her a puzzled look. "What are you doing at the job fair?"

"I'm—uh—I'm here with a friend." She couldn't believe how easily the lie slipped from her tongue.

"Oh? What is your friend looking for? Maybe I can help." Cassie pulled a small gold case engraved with her initials from the pocket of her suit jacket. "I'm the human resources director for Greater Austin Enterprises. Have your friend stop by our booth. We're looking for candidates for our new division in Dallas, if she's willing to relocate."

Leta took the business card without bothering to look at it. "Uh, thanks. I'll let her know."

Her stylish former classmate, dressed in an impeccable plum-colored suit with matching heels, slipped the case back in her pocket. "What about you? Where did you land after graduating?"

Leta rubbed her sweaty palms against the fabric of her own skirt, one she'd been lucky to find in her generous roommate's closet. How was she supposed to explain she'd relinquished her dream of becoming a landscape architect and instead settled for working in the floral department at Central Market? Or that she'd taken on a second job at a dive bar just to make ends meet? *Yeah, let's tell her that.*

In a stroke of pure luck, her friend's phone rang, giving Leta a reprieve. "Sorry, I have to get this." Cassie turned and buried herself in a conversation, leaving Leta to ponder the best way to extricate herself before being put on the spot again.

In a quick move, Leta pulled her own phone up and pointed to the screen as if she'd just received a text. She whispered, "Gotta go. Catch you later."

Cassie nodded. "Hold on," she said into her phone. Looking at Leta, she said, "You've got my card. Call me for lunch sometime, okay?"

Leta nodded a little too enthusiastically. "Sure thing." She blew a kiss and scurried off down the aisle, past all the well-dressed job seekers pitching their hard-won credentials to waiting personnel directors like Cassie.

Outside, Leta slipped on her sunglasses and scurried to the other end of the parking lot where her car was parked. Despite the late fall day, the temperature lingered in the eighties. She couldn't wait to get out of this skirt and back into crop pants and flip-flops, and to enjoy the nice weather while it lasted.

An Austin winter didn't exactly replicate a Currier and Ives photograph, but despite the lack of snow, it had been known to turn cold and freeze on occasion. Sometimes without much warning. Given that, these temperatures were a treat.

She pushed the key into the ignition and started the engine with a relieved sigh, never knowing when her fourteen-year-old Chevy Blazer would give up the ghost. Her mother had bought the used vehicle nearly ten years ago, bragging that it had been a one-owner car with low miles. Now, with the odometer close to 150,000, one never knew when the ole gal would take her final breath.

Leta headed north and twenty minutes later pulled onto Burnet just south of 45th, then slowed in front of a small ranch-style house. Like many of the homes in the modest Brentwood neighborhood, the house she lived in had been built in the sixties. Her mother had rented it from Ben Kimey, a gray-haired widower who lived two doors away, when Leta was still in grade school.

She used to know everyone up and down the street, often delivering her mother's infamous chocolate meringue pies to their neighbors on birthdays and holidays. Now, most of the residents were strangers and the houses had fallen into various stages of disrepair.

Recently, Mr. Kimey agreed to pay for the paint and Leta had done her best to remodel and upgrade the outside of the house a bit, painting the front door a brick red, which offset the tiny covered porch nicely. She'd also splurged and lined the steps with ceramic pots filled with white azaleas. She longed to do more but simply couldn't afford the expense.

She parked in the narrow driveway alongside the house, gathered her rather large file of leftover résumés, and headed for the front door. She climbed the steps and went for her keys. Suddenly, the door swung open.

"It's about time you got home." Her roommate pulled her inside. "Where have you been, anyway? Come in and sit. I met this new guy and—" Katie stopped midsentence. "Hey, why are you home so early?" She slapped her forehead. "Oh—the job fair. I nearly forgot. How'd it go?"

Leta tossed her bag on the sofa and slumped down beside it. "Oh, just dandy."

Katie sank to the floor and sat crossed-legged. "What happened?"

She let out a heavy sigh. "Nothing happened. That's the problem. Once these companies learn I don't have my degree, they won't even look at my résumé."

"It's not like you never attended college. You finished three years. Doesn't that count for something?"

Leta shook her head. "Not much. I mean, even the credits I do have don't exactly have broad application in the current job market."

Katie gave her a sympathetic look. "C'mon, it can't be that bad."

"It's like a merry-go-round. I can't afford to quit working so I can return to school, and I can't get a better job until I finish school. At this juncture, I'm just going in circles and getting nowhere."

Her friend leaned forward and patted her knee. "Leta, I know you. You're smart and innovative. There's little doubt you'll figure all this out. I promise."

"Maybe—if I can get a lucky break somewhere along the line." She knotted her long brown hair at the back of her neck. "Enough about all that. Now tell me about the new guy. Let me live vicariously through you."

"You're twenty-six. You might want to make time to date."

Leta held up her palms. "I know, I know. Now spill."

Katie's eyes brightened, the way they always did when a new guy came onto the scene. Leta tried not to feel jealous. Her roommate was blonde and cute and had a personality that drew everyone to her, especially men.

Not like her. Leta tended to stand back and evaluate a social setting before engaging, a trait that didn't necessarily translate into a bounty of dating opportunities.

That and her schedule pretty much squelched any kind of social life.

Katie drew a big breath. "Well, his name is Bart. That's his nickname. His real name is Rubart Nelson. Who names their kid Rubart?" She popped up and darted for the kitchen. "Want some sweet tea?"

Leta shook her head and watched as her roommate withdrew a glass from the cupboard and moved for the refrigerator. "He said his grandmother used to call him Ruby." Katie visibly shuddered. "How lame is that? Anyway, I met him at Halcyon over in the Warehouse District. He was behind me in line to get coffee and we just started talking. He was so easy to talk to. We ended up sharing a table and sat there for nearly three hours."

"What does he do? For a living, I mean?" Katie had a tendency to date men in dead-end situations, and who often lacked the monogamy needle in their moral compass.

Her friend stopped mid-pour. "That's the best part. He's in

commercial real estate. Leases retail space in shopping centers." Her voice raised several octaves. "And—get this part—he locates building sites for Walgreens and Office Depot. He drives a BMW and wears khakis, polo shirts, and leather loafers."

Leta lifted her eyebrows. "Well, that is an improvement." The last one had a wardrobe of holey jeans and Hooters T-shirts and was a drummer in a band that played on weekdays out at the Broken Spoke on South Lamar. The loser had broken her best friend's heart and nearly drained her bank account dry.

Katie returned to the living room and Leta stood and hugged her. "I'm glad. Really, I am." She slipped the glass from her friend's hand and took a deep swig.

"Hey, I asked if you wanted some."

She handed the glass back, now half empty. "Sorry," she said, grinning. "Sorry to cut this short too, but I've got to get going. I have to be at the store in less than an hour and I want to shower first."

"Someday *your* great guy will show up. You just wait and see," her roommate called after her as she made her way down the hall.

Leta laughed and hollered over her shoulder, "Ha—I guess my mom isn't the only one who lives in a fairy tale."

A former legal investigator and trial paralegal, **Kellie Coates Gilbert** writes with a sympathetic, intimate knowledge of how people react under pressure. She tells emotionally poignant stories about messy lives and eternal hope.

Find out more about Kellie and her books at www.kelliecoatesgilbert.com. While you're there, don't forget to join Kellie's Reader's Club. As one of Kellie's VIP readers, you'll receive exclusive news about her books, exciting giveaways, and (shh!) maybe some special and exciting opportunities made available only to Kellie's Reader's Club members.

Meet

KELLIE COATES GILBERT

KellieCoatesGilbert.com

Sign Up for Updates

Read Kellie's Blog

Learn about Upcoming Events

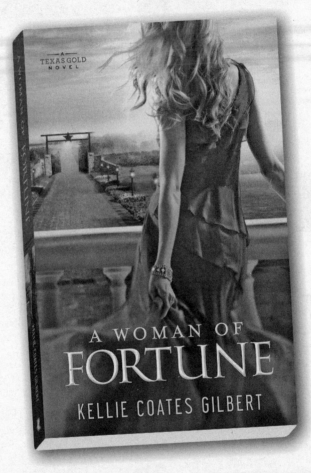